——— Book one in the Furious Fannies series ———

THE FURIOUS FANNIES

A humorous, raunchy novel about a
sexually diverse group of sassy women
known locally as The Furious Fannies,
learning to play rugby.

**Created and written by
Quinton Rumford**

**Grosvenor House
Publishing Limited**

This book is published by
Grosvenor House Publishing Ltd
Link House
140 The Broadway, Tolworth, Surrey, KT6 7HT.
www.grosvenorhousepublishing.co.uk

This book is a work of fiction. Any resemblance to
people or events, past or present, is purely coincidental.

A CIP record for this book
is available from the British Library

ISBN 978-1-83615-337-5

Three Books in the Furious Fannies Series

1. *The Furious Fannies*
2. *The Furious Fannies – Season One*
3. *The Furious Fannies – Foreign Fields*

Dedication

This is the first humorous novel of a series of three and is dedicated to all those who play, bond, strive, and watch womens team sports, particularly rugby union.

Liz
With best wishes and thanks

Quinton Rumford

AKA
Chris Page.

About the Author

Quinton Rumford is the pen-name of a former rugby union player, coach, and avid supporter of Bristol Bears men and womens rugby union sides. He is also a full-time writer with twenty-five completed and sardonically humorous and unpublished novels that are being published now as a legacy project. He lives in Wiltshire with his wife and they have two adult children and a dog called Freddie.

Website: qrumfordauthor.com

The Furious Fannies

'A real *Bohica* moment, what does that mean...?'
'It's army slang for *Bend Over Here It Comes Again...*'
Both girls burst out laughing, they knew what that
meant from all ends up....

'Machismo without panache is a dead stallion...'

The rugby forwards were nick-named the Howie's,
short for Howitzers and the backs called the Petticoats.
The two youngest Petticoats – Romany and Gita – were
also virgins and in a squad of multiform sexual diversity
and raucous banter were christened by Heidi – the chief
wag and enforcer of the side – as the Petticoats with a
cherry on top...

'You are an incubus of great mediocrity not to say a
useless dollop.'
'Who you calling a useless dollop?'
'Whats the matter, incubus got too many sylabbles in
it?... USELESS DOLLOP?'

'The rugby authorities place a bung up the chuff of
female referees when they are trained. This means that
they are in a position of permanent incontinence that
accounts for their bad temper, sour face, and non-stop
blowing of the whistle to relieve the pressure...'

Prologue

It was two days to go before her diverse group of women – nicknamed the Furious Fannies –assembled for the first training session. Two days before the mixture of congenital oddballs, social misfits and relatively normal young women that held a mirror up to the Wiltshire sisterhood she had recruited, got together to see if there was a ladies rugby team in there scratching and clawing to get out. Then there was Ginnie herself, a twenty-seven-year-old sexually frustrated disaster area who had never managed to hold down a relationship with a man for more than three months. Was she good enough to play the game, captain and control this team and make the category life change she envisaged, or sleepwalking into a toxic shit storm of spitting cat-house proportions?

The Furious Fannies Squad – names, position, and occupation

Forwards (Nick-named the Howie's for Howitzers)
Sarah 'Rocky' Cook – Loose-head Prop/Pack Leader. Hospital procurement manager.
Gina 'Bohica' McKinnon – The Happy Hooker. Tattooed and married Army private.
Mary-Jane 'Biggie' Bagnall – Tight-head Prop. Dairy farmer and very solid citizen.
Ellie Cooper – Elegant black lock. Hotel Receptionist/ Masters archaeology student.
Heidi Prager – Second-row. A posh, unemployed Goth. Loves a fight & louche team joker.
Mandy 'Judo' Sawyer – Blind-side flanker, Judo black belt & martial arts teacher.
Sonja 'J.J' van Leer – Open-side flanker. South African care assistant & former player,
Billie 'Put the Fire Out' Hayden – Number Eight and fire-fighter.
Backs (called the Petticoats)
Tanya 'Flipper' Bryan – Scrum-half, housewife, former gymnast, and mother of twin boys.
Mollie 'Magical' Cook – Fly-half and kicker. Van driver.
Romany 'Blue Streak' Cutler – Left-wing. Traveller and scrap metal collector.
Ginnie 'The Skipper' Joy – Founder, captain, inside-centre, and office manager.
Iona 'Tea Tray' Pierce – Outside-centre. Former Pro. Athlete and now personal trainer

Gita Rodrigues – Right-wing, Anglo-Indian, waitress and squash player.

Avril 'Love-Bites' Gordon – Full-back and left-footed kicker. Married Army PTI

Replacements (Howie's and Petticoats)

Jenny Hynes – Centre/Wing. Software developer, stepmother of two girls

Kayla Taylor – Prop/Front-row. Construction student and former hockey player.

Stella Winters – Full-back/wing. Construction student and future wife of Kayla above.

Cassie Betts – Prop/front-row replacement. Welsh and black former champion body builder.

Agnes 'Aggy' Dillon – Centre/wing. Former varsity rugby blue. Management trainee.

Silvie Greatorex – Lock/Back-row, petrol station employee, former hockey player.

Sheila Bates – Wing – Council cashier and former hockey player.

Alfreda 'Alfie' Cushing. Hooker/front-row, unemployed/former rugby player.

Sian Robartes – Athletic black cousin of Ellie Cooper's boyfriend, utility back.

Coach – Lindsey Chene – warehouse worker and former alcoholic sacked lady's rugby coach.

Assistant Coach – Sherry Moyes – lorry driver and former man now in transition

Groundsmen – Jimmy Corbett & Gavin Morris.

Others – lovers, rugby officials, supporters, rivals, family, and friends.

And – Claude Dillon, CEO of the second largest mutual building society in the UK.

Chapter One

If sex with men – looking back from the lofty position of her twenty-seven years on this scarlet earth, the last eleven of which she had been an ardent and enthusiastic devotee and keen tryer – had proven to be a more satisfying pastime; Virginia (Ginnie) Joy—now there's a name for a subject like this—would not have given it up as a lost cause. When it *had* worked it was marvellous and broke the daily case-hardening inflicted upon her by a safe but ultimately repetitive supervisor's job at the head office of a large building society, a mortgage on a miniscule singles apartment in a noisy Swindon block, ownership of a small unreliable eight-year old car and, not when driving if she could help it, too much alcohol – and was still, despite the claims of some of her pill-popping, line-snorting clubbing friends, the nearest she ever got to the inner peace and sublime elasticity that comes with moosh-drenched fulfilment.

When it bloody worked, in her case this didn't seem to be very often.

And with this occasional burst of spun-gold orgasmic sunshine came all the indulgent male bullshitting, slobbering, oedipally fixated, ego-boosting, fantasy-acting mess, and prematurely frustrating hoops she had to jump through to get to one of those rare moosh-tingling occasions that she should be so favoured. She wouldn't give it up, just the toxic, clingy mummy's boy messy relationships that for her always seemed to come with it. From here on in permanent men – unless *extra special* and how rare were they? – would be banished to the nether regions of her life, peripheral occasional's brought in when *she* needed an erect, twenty-minute staying rock-hard pork bayonet to salve *her* need and keep *her* sane, *without* if such a thing was possible, the white noise and childish attention that lasting proximity to its tumescence demanded. The whole male ego-stroking business had become, quite simply, just too much bloody trouble for the minimal gains that accompanied its required machismo pampering.

It was time for Ginnie to move on.

From here on in she would make her own rules, do her own thing, instead of hiding her common sense and natural practical ability to get things right and done behind the fake shining eyes of adoration she had formerly used to gain those precious and rare pulsing droplets of fulfilment from a self-serving male and anyone else who stood in her way.

Her older brother Robert – now a teacher and married to the very pregnant Emily, also a teacher – had a nick-name for her when they were younger and it had been 'Peppery.' He'd given it to her because she was independent and tempestuous and couldn't be told *anything* by him or their long-suffering parents. Since then, her attitude had changed as she had boldly taken her embryonic teenage independence out to an uncaring world and gradually learned that for her to lead a more harmonious life and get the occasional boyfriend and the sexual release that supposedly accompanied these ambrosial relationships, she had to acquiesce and flatter, pretend, and act the grateful companion. Well, that hadn't worked either and so now she would go back to being 'Peppery' again. Acquiescence or nodding agreement with opinions she even mildly disagreed with was out. No shit would be taken and the sass would be hard and to the point and dished with a brutal honesty. Her de facto face to the mundane and uninteresting – other than work which was necessary tedium to be tolerated to pay her bills – would now come with the curl in her generous lips of bored disdain. *When* it suited her mood, she would spit and swear like a cornered hermit addressing the heavens on a thunderous night, and when it didn't, she would turn on her heel and sashay away without a backward glance leaving a raised single digit. It was time to move her still young life onto a more fulfilling and honest place, all she needed was something to hone it all into a focussed and committed gaol.

And now, after two months of watching and thinking and discussing it with Aggy, her friend from the office where she worked and whose idea it was, *she bloody-well had it.*

*

At first the local evening newspaper was rather reluctant to take her advertisement. It was the first test of the new 'Peppery' Ginnie and she rose to the challenge magnificently. Eyes blazing, she demanded to see the manager immediately the young girl behind the tall counter with the sign saying 'Classifieds' had read, curled her glossy lip and then refused to accept her copy for an advertisement. The otherwise cocky girl was somewhat taken aback by the fierceness of the new Ginnies insistence and despite, or perhaps because of, the small, neck-craning interest from the watching queue forming behind her, dashed off into an inner sanctum to comply bearing this tiresome pain-in-the-arse woman's intended advertising copy at arm's length as if it would poison her elaborate nails.

'I must say it's an unusual request,' said the smarmy, balding Advertising Manager with a small smile waving her into his closet-sized glass domain behind the counter. 'And not one I can recall that we've had in our classifieds before…'

'Then it's about time you broke that particular old out-of-date duck then, isn't it?' Ginnie said marching in to his busy-looking little business hole with her jaw stuck out pugnaciously.

The manager, who wore a badge naming him as Derek, shrugged and looked again at the piece of paper the receptionist had given him with Ginnies advertisement copy in bold capitals. 'Perhaps we could tone it down a little bit…?'

'Why? There's no swear words, no overt sexual references or innuendo, nothing that going to upset the old gals and giff's who read your moribund rag…'

'Moribund' she thought. Where did that come from, an Aggy word probably? I must get mad more often, it increases my word power.

'Giff's?' he said ignoring her star turn and pompously picking another word.

'Men,' she replied sharply. 'Giffer's being middle aged and upwards. Old farts if you must, crumbly males who smell of tobacco and fried onions and have dandruff on their collars and dog hairs on their trousers and crackpot opinions…giff's to me and my friends… unless you'd prefer fogies.'

She was enjoying the new her but resisted the urge to add 'like you're gonna be in a few years' time.'

'Okay…' he said hesitantly looking back down at the bold type. 'But this advertisement *does* have specific sexual references besides referring to females *only* between the ages of eighteen and thirty-five to get together for group fun and playing activities.'

'Where are the specific sexual references?'

'Here,' he said tapping the section that she and her friend and confident Aggy Dillon at the head office complex where they both worked, had sweated over for ages to get the right feel and knew exactly what he was referring to. Aggy had wanted it to be even more risqué which would have never got passed this dickhead of a job's worth.

He again tapped the copy.

'This word you have spelled out with an asterisked beginning sounds pretty much like a well-known epithet to me m' dear starting with 'f'.' He curled his thin lips around the 'm'dear' and couldn't bring his sparsely ringed mouth to even whisper the 'f' letter.

She leaned over and made a point of reading the name tag on his lapel that she already knew.

'That's not a well-known *epithet*, she said disdainfully. 'It's a little subtle innuendo and something that I suspect is way beyond your ability to understand… *Derek.*'

Her sneered insults were getting to him and deep red flush began to crawl up his neck.

'Now that' he said racking up the pomposity and getting to his feet, 'is way beyond what I and this newspaper will stand for…'

'Do you have a sports section?' Ginnie said softening her approach a little before he threw her out.

He came down from the high horse he'd climbed on, sat down, and stroked his thinning scalp with a shrug.

'Of course, we do. Our Saturday sport's reporting is renowned for its factuality and professionalism and we carry all the local sporting leagues in our midweek roundup.'

'Well then, you should have understood that the subtle innuendo of the word in question – which would have started with an 'r' if I hadn't used the asterisk – refers to *rucking,* because, you see *Derek,* I 'm looking to start a ladies rugby team not an orgiastic gathering of lesbians for sexual activities...'

The broad grin that followed left the poor obviously hen-pecked man whose only defence against the world of strong women he'd married into and from which his only relief was to be found here in this little closet of an office from which he could occasionally rule a small part of an inconsequential world...left him floundering, speechless and stuttering in embarrassment.

'Okay, you'd better have a seat and we'll start again,' he said eventually slumping back into his own chair and from which, until this aggressive but good-looking harpy had crossed the threshold, he'd ruled this irrelevant mini-world of small ads and classified requirements.

It took them five minutes to compromise on an advertisement that satisfied them both and he agreed to run it for three nights starting on the following Thursday. The *...u...c...k...i...n...g just had to go otherwise he wouldn't have accepted it. Her parting shot was a cheeky invitation to the newspaper to sponsor them.

'Well, if you start to get some winning results we might run a few lines on the games,' he said. 'Have you chosen a name for the team yet?' He opened the closet door to let her out as he asked the question.

'I have' Ginnie replied purposefully stepping on his toe as she stepped through the door.

'It's the Fantail Furies and you're gonna want us in every week of the two thousand and eighteen playing season before the nationals get onto us because we're going places and will sell more newspapers than all your other local whist drives, cribbage, darts, and domino leagues have ever done. Goodbye....' She hesitated and then again disdainfully looked down at his pathetic name tag as if she'd forgotten it.

'Derek.'

The advertisement was a great success with thirty-two replies. Who knew that the former railway town of Swindon and its downland surroundings harboured so many young ladies looking to relieve tension with some down-to-earth grovelling in the Wiltshire mud learning to ruck, maul, and scrummage and generally knock seven barrels of shite out of each other in the interest of getting an oblong shaped ball from one end of a pitch to the other?

Ginnie had missed the pre-Christmas start of the lady's rugby season at the end of 2017/18 but hoped to use the second half of the season to prepare the team with perhaps a couple of matches towards the end before the summer break.

But first, the interviews.

Chapter Two

'Me names Gina McKinnon, I'm in the army stationed at Tiddy barracks...'

'Ginnie Joy, how do you do...Tiddy?' Ginnie questioned as they shook hands outside the small interview room in the foyer of the Swindon hotel Ginnie had booked for the two weekends plus an extra Saturday of the interviews.

'Tidworth, part of Salisbury Plain and home of the brave and workshy, khaki land for the army ground fighting forces and those of us who couldn't hold down a proper job anywhere else...'

The fit looking young lady with the vague mixed Irish and cockney accent grinned and then followed Ginnie into the interview room and sat down on the single chair alongside the table opposite Ginnies laptop and mobile phone. She had heavily tattooed muscular arms revealed by neatly rolled up army fatigues to the elbows and matching camo pants. Her boots were army burnished; hair cut neat and short and she wore a little eyeliner and lipstick as if to soften the hard military image. She added a chuckle to the smile then leaned forward over the table and looked Ginnie in the eye.

'I hear you're looking for a few fit gals to start a rugby team...?'

'I most certainly am and you're the first one I've seen. Ginnie and Gina eh, could be fun when we're doing lineout calls or whatever...'

They smiled at the proximity of their names little knowing that it would get even more complicated when a Gita joined the squad.

Until that point Ginnie had been feeling a little apprehensive about the interviews but in the face of this smiling and obviously fit and open young lady it all disappeared.

'How long have you been in the army Gina?'

'Six years. I joined when I wuz eighteen. Married Dave last year, another squaddie whose a tankie – mad little sod charges around Salisbury Plain in a CR2 all day – before coming back to our quarters and chasing me around the place...' she grinned.

'CR2?'

'Challenger 2 tank, a fire-breathing metal dragon with a big gun sticking out the front...bit like Dave really...' the grin turned into an infectious giggle.

Ginnie giggled with her, hoping this girl would join up. She was fun, fit, and irreverent.

'Have you ever played rugby Gina?' Ginnie asked getting back to the reason they were there.

'Nope, but I've watched any number of games cos Dave plays for the army an' I kinda like the idea of smashing into other girls on the way to scoring a try...'

'Do you know the rules and any of the positions?'

Gina grinned. 'Some of the rules go right over me 'ead but if I 'ad a choice I'd be a hooker' she said without hesitation accompanied by a wink to cover the overt reference to the double meaning. She crossed one shiny boot over her thigh and continued.

'A happy hooker, Dave tells me it's a position, the rugby one that is, for feisty type's an' I'm certainly one of those – it's the Irish in me which is the reason why I joined the Army in the first place. I've passed all me physics wif flying colours but ain't so good on the written stuff.'

'Your physics?'

'Martial arts, assault courses, swimming in full combat gear, climbing, shooting at moving targets, unarmed combat and running, forever bloody running. I'm crazy about all that sort of stuff, even ran a half marathon a couple of weeks ago and beat most of the blokes...cept Dave. 'E was miles in front of everybody. The skinny buggers built like a butcher's dog, fit as a flea and twice as randy...'

This girl was heaven sent, Ginnie thought trying to remain objective.

'What position does Dave play?'

'Winger, told me to tell you he would help wif the training if you like but I'm not sure about that. He's a horny little sod at the best of times and being around a bunch of girls rolling in the mud might get 'im all juiced up...as it were.'

'Then *you'd* have to sort *him* out,' Ginnie said with a raised eyebrow.

'Yeah, a real *Bohica* moment, probably in the bloody car park as the horny little sod would never wait til' we got 'ome...'

'A real *Bohica* moment...?'

'Army slang, means Bend over Here It Comes again...'

They both burst out laughing. They knew that one from all ends up.

'I've also got a mate, Avril. She's an Army P.T.I. Built like a whippet and just as fast, played in goal for a local

Tiddy ladies football team 'til they were disbanded a few weeks ago. She asked me to put in a word for her, got hands like a midwife an' a kick like a sex-starved stallion. Dave reckons she'd make a good full-back. Couldn't be 'ere cos she's getting married today... to another tankie called Mike. That's me next stop when we've finished 'ere, down the Tiddy church with Dave for the ceremony and in the pub getting pissed wif them an' a bunch of other army mates for the rest of the day to celebrate...'

Built like a whippet, hands like a midwife and a kick like a sexed-starved stallion. Ginnie doubted if it was possible for a potential female rugby player to come with a higher and more aptly phrased rating.

After some more general chat about where and when they would start training and play, spiced with lots of girly giggling and more sexual innuendo about tankie Dave the horny husband, the effervescent Gina left with both knowing they had bonded well and it was a done deal. It might even be two ultra-fit women for the price of one because Gina promised to bring Avril along to the first training session in two weeks' time – if she could still walk after her honeymoon in Blackpool. Having checked that she had Gina's correct email Ginnie said goodbye to her first and undoubtedly the best she could expect in her recruitment campaign and turned to face her next interviewee still laughing inwardly at the *Bohica* reference.

And then, in what would become the time-honoured fashion of highs followed by lows, the next one to walk through the door was a hesitant middle-aged man wearing a two-piece business suit over an M & S floral blouse, ladies sling backs with medium heels and heavy face make-up. Ginnie knew it was M & S because her mum had one just like it.

'Hello…um, I'm Terry Moyes but you'll have me down as…um… Sherry…'

'Take a seat,' Ginnie said waving to the chair recently evacuated by Gina and glancing at her interview sheet to hide her surprise and buy a little time.

'Yes, I have a *Miss* Sherry Moyes down for ten-thirty.'

What exactly are you she felt like saying meeting his/her eyes for the first time? The answer came immediately.

'I'm sorry for the deception but I'm a fifty-five-year-old divorced lorry driver trying to make the transition from being a man to a woman. I'm not there yet and have only just started, matter of fact this is my first outing without being *fully* dressed as a man…'

It all came out in a bit of a rush and for emphasis he nodded down at his medium heeled sling-back's and fingered the collar of the floral blouse.

'Do you prefer Terry or Sherry?'

'Sherry – every time if you don't mind.'

So be it, he was a she and Ginnie would use the female form of address.

'You do know I'm recruiting for a *women's* rugby team?'

'Yes, yes. I've got the advertisement here,' she fished out Ginnies ad from the suit trouser pocket and waved it at her.

Ginnie raised her eyebrows at her by way of enquiry as to what she was doing here.

'Well…um…it's like this. I thought this ad was an opportunity to finally take the plunge and become what

I've wanted to be for many years which is a woman. As such I need to mix with other women and discuss womanly things like clothes and make-up. Pretty impossible with my work as a lorry driver with little or no social contact with females. I could help you with the team, drive the team bus for away games – I've got a full HGV license although I'd have to change the gender and photo, – pump up the balls and hand out the tackle bags. I'm too old to play but know my way around a rugby field from my school playing days and could be useful in many different and helpful ways...I...um...' She swallowed hard and looked out the window for a few beats before getting up the courage to continue.

'I haven't had any of my bits done yet surgically but intend to have the first operation just as soon as I've got the confidence to book it. It's all about confidence really...I sat in my bedroom for a long time this morning trying to decide what to wear here – the full drag with a wig, dress, heels, and make-up...for the first time other than around my own house...and finally decided on a sort of halfway house...at least it's a start...' She patted the wig and lifted both sling backs off the floor in emphasis.

Although in the weeks leading up to today Ginnie had thought through most situations that were likely to occur, this was not one of them. She sympathised with Sherry's plight and might well have a useful general factotum spot for her but at this early stage in her recruitment campaign that was something all the other girls would have to buy into first. Whatever Sherry was, until she had the operation she was, as far as Ginnie knew, still officially a man. And this wasn't a transgender orientation exercise either, there were specialist places for that.

Ginnie made small talk for a few minutes before exercising her get-out clause by promising to check out the women's section of the Rugby Football Union's rules on such matters using changing room access as her reasoning, and would then let her know. If, that was, she thought, as Sherry tottered off out the door, the RFU *had* any such rules. She had spent a fair bit of time before these interviews reading up at the helpful RFU women's section online and found nothing about men in transition.

The eleven o'clock interviewee, albeit fifteen minutes late, stood the normal world completely on its head. She was a tall and thin, black-studded leather-jacketed Goth with a face and ears full of metal, a head of wild, untamed but stiff black dyed and gelled hair that stuck upwards as if she was plugged into the mains, unlaced black Doc Martens and, as if to maintain the sombre colour, grazed and bruised knuckles and an enormous black eye. Add a sullen pout to the rest of the ensemble that slouched through the door with a wary look in her heavily kohled other eye making her face very Panda-like, and Ginnies immediate impression wouldn't have got this one in a remand home let alone a ladies rugby team.

Although, on closer inspection she could see that there was a good-looking girl beneath the heavy Goth make-up and angst, not to mention the black eye.

'Heidi Prager?' Ginnie said referring to her interview laptop list before waving the creaking leather Goth into a chair into which she slumped with a painful groan.

'That's correct. Please excuse me but I was involved in a nightclub fracas last night and took a bony fist in the eye as well as a couple of kicks in the complexities...'

She spoke with public school pronunciation in clear-voiced English that took Ginnie completely by surprise as she was expecting sloppy guttural reply delivered with a broad local accent and the rolled 'Rs of lazy Wiltshire pronunciation.

'The complexities...?' She asked having paused for a few beats once again to get her bearings.

'The nether regions of my lower anatomy that were not made for the steel toe caps of Doc Martens at terminal velocity impact. In short, having been ejected by the ugly and shaven-headed bouncers from the nightclub, one was involved in a catfight with a pair of dissonant skanks from that place beneath the earth where Lucifer lives in perpetual fire and brimstone. One took a rather brutal kick in the burrow culvert...my sublime gash if you will...or, to put it agriculturally, a toe-cap in the twat...'

The burrow covert and sublime gash – wonderful and opposite ways to describe her fanny.

At least she's recognised the local hayseed in me, Ginnie thought, and lowered...eventually...the fanny words to where she could interpret it easily as a *twat*, although using *'sublime'* was a bit OTT...

Or was it? Perhaps to us women they should always be just that.

Heidi groaned as she placed one unlaced black-booted foot over the other.

Suddenly she grinned revealing a silver-coloured metal tongue staple.

'You were fighting with a couple of girls?' Ginnie brought the louche but beautifully rounded phraseology down to her own level.

'Rolling around in the gutter like Gloucester Old Spot's in a pool of watery shite.'

'May I ask why?'

Another grin accompanied by a nod of the stiffly gelled head.

'You may. It's the same reason I'm here. Simply put I just love to fight... Boys or girls, I'm not gender partisan when it comes to my opponent's. When I get a few tequila slammers inside me I want to punch people. It got me expelled from boarding school and kicked out of uni. According to my shrink, if I don't start to re-channel the aggression very soon it will land me in prison. That's why I'm here; your advertisement may be one of the answers, the violence of rugby maybe my salvation as also could be boxing or cage-fighting. Therapies to keep me out of choky...'

'You have a shrink?' Ginnie asked surprised. She had never met anyone who really *had* one of those. Some of her friends had been proscribed a few pills from the doctor for depression, yes, but a bona fide, laying on the leather-bound confessional couch of a live psychiatrist while he or she probed the mind and made notes in a leather-bound book? That was for rich people and Americans, wasn't it?

'Yeah, so do most of my focked-up well-orf friends... but then, they don't get a smack in the eye and kicked in the twat for *their* phobias.'

The other world righted itself a little with Ginnies spontaneous giggle.

'Have you got a job?'

'Nope, I live with my dear Mama who is rather comfortably well orf herself, but even she's getting near the end of a long and well-meaning tether and threatening to throw me out, so it's time to look at alternatives…'

'It's really none of my business but do you use drugs?'

'Occasionally, doesn't everyone?'

'Drugs, fighting, booze and rugby are a toxic combination and don't mix,' Ginnie said in her holier-than-thou voice cringing inwardly at the hyperbole because, apart from the fighting and rugby bits, she had tried the other two – especially alcohol – in some measure herself.

'Tell me about it' replied Prager dismissively. 'What I need is something, preferably violent in nature, to replace them…and rugby, although I know nothing about it, seems like a potential solution.'

Ginnie considered the black Panda-eyed and sullen apparition lounging in the seat opposite her.

Like the man/woman Terry/Sherry, Heidi Prager wanted an association with her embryonic team for therapeutic reasons to take her away from an unsavoury and potentially disastrous mess of her life. However, when the team had their backs to the wall, someone who had fighting qualities like this girl and who wouldn't back down, could be useful if those qualities could be correctly channelled. The only problem was her getting red-carded for punching the opposition when it suited her and therefore denying the team her services for the rest of the game…or games if she was suspended, or worse, dragging the other girls in to the fight with her. Sure, the fighting talk could well be a pose for the interview and Ginnies sake but the black eye looked like a real fist-driven shiner and knuckles don't graze themselves. And as for the sore twat, she'd take that as a given!

Seeing Ginnie weighing her up, Heidi offered a little reasoning behind her punchy rebelliousness.

'When I was eight my beloved Daddy was killed in a helicopter crash, his own helicopter and he was flying it back from a business meeting in Scotland with his sexy, over-bosomed little secretary. Daddy always had a bitch on the go cos Mama didn't put out sexually. The coroners report said that when he was found in the wreckage his trousers were around his ankles. They didn't tell us what state *she* was in but the implication was that they were *moistening* each other in some sexual way as they were flying along. Although Daddy was a bastard for the women, he was an inventive, ambidextrous sort and shagging and flying a helicopter at the same time was well within his compass.' She hesitated for a few beats and then grimaced. 'Unless, as Mama said at the time, the *actual* helicopter's compass or altimeter was obscured by her unshod knickers or something and he couldn't see how low they were and where they were going when his world exploded... figuratively, of course...'

Heidi Prager smiled quietly at the sick but poignant joke and then gazed out of the window for a while in contemplation before adding:

'Daddy was full of machismo and panache, he always said that machismo without panache is a dead stallion...

which is what he became. The world seemed to turn to utter shite from that moment on but I am told I inherited some of my…attitude from him.'

Moistening each other! That was another new one on Ginnie and beautifully explicit – and while flying a helicopter! And as for *'machismo without panache is a dead stallion…'* She recognised that from most of the men she had known. This girl, despite her weird looks and louche manner, had a wonderful way with words and was undoubtably up for a fight. If she could transfer that droll delivery to the changing room and the rugby pitch the team would be all the better for her presence. And another thing any team requires is someone to make them laugh when the going gets tough and if Ginnies own reaction was typical, then here she was.

She took Heidi's email and mobile details and told her to report for the first training session in two weeks' time.

'Before you come to training try and dry out, clean up and mend the bruises,' she said showing her the door. 'And shed the metal, it's not allowed on a rugby pitch. As for drugs, if I see any in the changing room or near the team…' She let the rest of the sentence speak for itself.

'Then there were *three* wise therapists',' drawled Heidi over her shoulder. 'Mama, the shrinky and now the rugby coach. How could a skank-fighting tequila slamming girl fail? Chou, Chou baby…'

Ginnie sat down again to collect her thoughts before the next oddball came through the door. Heidi had described her as a rugby coach which she wasn't. Team founder and player and maybe even captain, yes, coach no because she didn't know a thing about training and the way to go about it, which reminded her that it was a position that had to be filled and was probably the most difficult recruitment of all. She did however, have someone coming soon that could address this position.

She checked her mobile for messages, there was nothing that couldn't wait, before looking up as in walked the fifty-year-old tracksuit wearing Lindsey Chene who turned out to be the perfect answer to the very problem on Ginnies mind.

Having introduced herself – Chene was pronounced Chenee – she sat down and looked at Ginnie with a composed face and waited for the first question.

'Not here as a player, I take it,' Ginnie said with a reassuring smile.

'Correct. I could manage maybe five minutes or so in a game but even then, I'd have to be stretchered off…'

'So…?' Ginnie said.

Lindsey took a deep breath.

'I think…hope…that I 'm just what you're looking for. Until ten months ago and for pretty much of the 2012 -17 seasons I was the coach, changing room cleaner, touchline encourager, shoulder to cry on and general factotum of the Bellfield Road Ladies Rugby Union Team in Reading. Then, after a successful season – we were in third place of twelve in the league and won a couple of player trophy's – they fired me. *They* said it was for bullying the girls, a suitable excuse covering all manner of iniquities nowadays. *I* said it was because they wanted someone younger and there was no shortage of candidates, including my male assistant who got the job…'

How long were you, their coach?' Ginnie asked hardly daring to believe her luck.

'Eight years, four times winners of the Berkshire and Hampshire ladies' championship trophy with three of my girls going on to join Tyrell's premiership ladies' clubs and two of *them* subsequently selected for the England Red Roses squad and where they still are.'

'*Did* you bully them?'

Lindsey smiled. 'You will soon learn that the only way to get a diverse group of women to physically follow through with practised training drills *on the pitch and in a match* is to bawl at them from time-to-time from the side-lines. If that's bullying then I am as guilty as the next coach because we all do it. That's not bullying nor is it a slick answer but the truth. It takes quite a while to get a squad of twenty-five or so women to work cohesively and efficiently together on a rugby pitch, let alone turn up for training or the actual match with everything they need including sports bra, boots with the correct studs in for the conditions and, where required, tampons, just to get through the session.'

'What have you been doing for the last ten months?'

Lindsey shrugged and looked out the window for a few beats before answering.

'Moping around my council flat mainly. I'm divorced, my kids have long since flown the coup and my former husband has remarried. My dismissal from Reading, although it was made to look voluntary, hit me hard. I built that team over eight hard-working years; it was my life and there were times when I lost it so badly that I almost gave up...' Her voice trailed away.

'Can you still do it?'

'Bloody right I can.' She perked up and her lips settled into a determined line.

Ginnie looked down at the address on Lindsey's email.

'Reading to Swindon is quite a trek for twice a week training and Saturday home games.'

'I'll move down here. My flats on a month's notice and I'm pissed off with Reading...' She turned away and muttered. 'Where I live is a bloody shithole anyway.'

'Do you have a job?'

'Temporary only in a warehouse and easy to replace...'

'Do you still drink?'

Lindsey Chene went quiet and looked away before taking a deep breath and answering.

'I have had a bit of a problem with alcohol since losing the coaching job. If you take me on, I'll have a good reason to give the bloody stuff up...'

Ginnie leaned forward and looked without guile into Lindsey's face. She didn't want to lose this ultra-valuable lady but some things needed to be established right at the outset.

'Okay Lindsey, you have all the skills required for this job and to be honest you are perfect for it and will be very useful...you answer to *me* as the team founder and however hard it is to get these girls motivated, its gentle encouragement only. If there's any screaming and hollering to do, I'll be the one to do it as the captain and founder. And although I'd be the last person to condemn anyone for having a glass or two after training or a game...it's an occasional glass only when you're on parade with *my* team...rocking up for training or a game as pissed as a cross-eyed owl in a sand-storm is not an option…understood?'

This, Ginnie thought as the words came out of her mouth, was the Peppery of her youth that she had been looking for. It was also the first time she had used the term *my team* and it felt good. And she gave an inner nod to her friend Malorie for the owl quote which had been one of her staples on their Saturday nights out clubbing.

Lindsey Chene nodded and heaved a big sigh of relief.

'Understood and I'll give it one hundred percent. When do we start training?'

'Two weeks' time on a Tuesday and Thursday here in Swindon. I'll email you the details and you'd better let me know when you can get away to come down and look around the place before we start.'

'I'll hand in my notice with the job and flat on Monday and start replacing them down here right away. I've got a little car so will be able to come down for training even if I haven't got anywhere local to work or live.'

She got up to leave and then stopped at the door.

'Thanks, Ginnie, this is a lifeline for me and I won't let you down.'

As she walked away across the foyer of the hotel Ginnie couldn't help but think that, although she wasn't religious, someone up there was smiling down on her today. Sure, some of these women brought problems with their valued contribution, not the least being the gender-fluid Terry/Sherry, the aggressive but hilarious Heidi Prager and the possible drink problem that had just left with Lindsey, but if they, and she and the team, could get over those issues, the Fantail Furies would soon become a force to be reckoned with in West Country women's rugby. She checked her mobile phone; the one o'clock had cancelled and would come along at around four to see if Ginnie could fit her in.

Chapter Three

'Why have you called the team The Fantail Furies?'

The cheeky grin that accompanied the question came from a twenty-two-year-old mother of twin three-year old boys called Tanya Bryan. Before she had the twins – whose projected arrival had been a complete surprise – and then married their father in a rush, Tanya had been a budding gymnast who had competed at national level. The arrival of a baby, let alone twin boys, had taken a bit of getting used to and of course, put a stop to her career as a gymnast and, now, encouraged by her husband to get out and away from the twins to whom she'd been welded for their three years on this earth, she'd been looking for something physically to do while he took his turn looking after the very active boys.

Glancing down to check her notes because although it hadn't come up yet, she had been expecting this question on the chosen name, Ginnie took a deep breath.

'Fantail because it's a play on words that specifically relates to women as in fannies at the tail end so to speak – and Furies because, according to my older brother Robert whose an English teacher and understands Greek Mythology – The Furies, Tisiphone, Megaera, and Alecto, their names – were goddesses of vengeance and retribution who punished men for crimes against the natural order. Now, I don't have any grudge against men – she crossed her fingers under the desk when she said that because Tanya was very obviously happily married, 'other than the fact that most of the men I've met or been in some kind of relationship with have been a complete and utter disappointment.'

Robert had always been the brainy one of the pair and had rehearsed her for an hour on how to pronounce the Greek goddesses' names, but Ginnie was gradually catching him up in his quiet, dedicated teaching backwater of life as her experiences – mainly relationship disappointments and the reality of making her own way – hardened and equipped her to cope with an independent existence.

'That's a long-winded answer to your question but, in truth the Greek explanation is way over my head but I just liked the names and it somehow seemed to fit with a group of us girls taking on other teams from the sisterhood in a game of physical prowess...'

'The Furious Fannies or Fanny Furies, eh' Tanya giggled. '

Ginnie smiled and nodded. 'I like the first one and hadn't thought of it but the Furious Fannies has an appropriate ring to it. I can almost hear those on the side-lines shouting it out and it would also make good copy for the local newspapers as well.'

'Just until we hit the nationals' Tanya grinned, 'and get Facebook, Twitter and Snapchat on meltdown.'

'Do you know anything about the game and positions?'

'I used to watch it on the telly a lot and had a mad fancy for the cheeky Austin Healey who was an England scrum-half and now does commentating.' A wistful look came into her eyes at the mention of the former England and Leicester player.

'I think you're made for that position,' Ginnie said making a note. 'Not too tall and because of your gymnastics training I should imagine quick thinking, bendy and probably very nippy....and cheeky with it.'

'According to my husband I can bend and wriggle better and faster than a snake on speed...when the twins are finally asleep.' She grinned.

Ginnie grinned with her. It seemed that you couldn't keep sex out of these interviews. God knows what the sexual banter in the changing room and pitch training sessions would be like when they all got in the mood, especially Heidi.

And, why not?

'When do we start?' Tanya asked.

Pleased with her morning's work so far Ginnie had a half an hour before her next one and went out to the café off the foyer for a coffee. Stirring cream into her cup Ginnie couldn't help but think back on the morning. Most of the girls she'd met in her life thus far through her local comprehensive school, on-line college course, work and Swindon based socialising were normal. Sure, they, like her, had the usual hang-ups with money, booze, occasional drug use and errant boyfriends and such but that had been pretty much par for the growing-up course in her life thus far, but nothing like she was experiencing here. Her advertisement seems to have struck a chord and brought a couple of good potential players out of the woodwork as well as real oddball surprises.

Like Heidi Prager and Terry/Sherry Moyes.

'Miss Joy?'

The tall and beautiful full-lipped black girl wearing a mid-blue uniformed two piece, with long flowing dreadlocks and a badge with 'Ellie' on it who had been behind the hotel reception desk for the morning directing her interviewees towards the chairs outside her room, stood looking down at her.

'Yes?'

'Can I join you for a couple of minutes, it's my lunch break.'

'Off course, have a seat.' Ginnie moved her chair to make room.

'No interviews for a bit?' Ellie said sitting down placing her own coffee on the small, round table.

'Next one's at two,' Ginnie said. 'Had a one o'clock cancellation until four and for which I'm not sorry. Interviewing, although I've never done anything like this before, is hard work. Thanks for pointing them in the right direction.'

'They're here for an interview to join your lady's rugby team?'

'Thirty-three of them today, tomorrow and next Saturday morning if they all turn up in response to an advertisement in the Swindon Evening Advertiser.'

Ellie hesitated for a few beats looking down at her coffee before turning her big, dark brown eyes to Ginnie.

'What type of girls are you looking for?'

Why, are you interested?'

'Most definitely, if you think I have the necessary qualities to play.'

'Rugby can accommodate all sorts of shapes and sizes between eighteen and thirty-five, even older, providing they are fit or at least have the desire to be so. Tall girls are especially wanted...' she directed this comment and nodded directly at Ellie. This beautiful slim black girl must be at least six foot tall if she was an inch and had second-row written all over her according to the bare stats she had gleaned from watching a few games and the R.F.U. guidelines.

'It can be a rough game though,' Ginnie added. 'Grovelling around in the mud wrestling with other girls for a wet bar of soap called a rugby ball...'

'Oh, I know that, my archaeologist boyfriend plays for Wootton Bassett and I often go and watch the home games and then tend to his cuts and bruises afterwards.'

'What's Ellie short for?' Ginnie nodded at the badge.

'My full name is Elelendise Lucy Cooper.'

'Elelendise is a beautiful and unusual name.'

'Ellie is the nearest I can get to the full bit which does sometimes confuse people. Elelendise is ancient Saxon for 'misfit' or 'outsider.''

'Oh...and are you?'

'Not at all, my dear father is an ancient English languages curator at the British Museum in London and he and my mother, who both come from Grenada, gave me the name because they said – as you and many others have – that it was beautiful and unusual and far outweighs its old-fashioned origins.'

'How old are you?'

'Twenty-six and I've got a BA from Bournemouth and am currently doing a Master's Degree in Archaeology through the Open University with a view to digging up various parts of Wiltshire in search of Roman artefacts and clues to how they spent their time here. My boyfriend is already a qualified archaeologist and I hope to join him next year on various digs. This job in reception is to help me pay the bills.'

'Elelendise,' Ginnie said again rolling the word around her tongue.

'Stick to Ellie, it's easier,' the beautiful black girl flashed her perfect teeth in a smile.

Ginnie put Ellie's name and email address in her mobile and said she would be sending through the details of the first training session in a few days' time.

As Ellie glided sinuously out of the door and across the lobby to her reception desk, Ginnie had a thought. If this beautiful black girl could move and handle a rugby ball half as well as she looked when she walked it was another exceptional recruitment.

After a successful morning Ginnies first two afternoon interviews were disappointments. The two o'clock was far too big weighing in at around twenty-six stone and the one after who tried very hard to mask her severe illness by describing it as 'a central nervous system disorder that she had under full control with medication.'

'Are you referring to a form of Epilepsy?' asked Ginnie who knew a little about such matters as her Aunty Beryl had it and needed constant watch and medication. The interviewee gave Ginnie a shrug and a barely nodded affirmative. She put the pair down as gently as she could and stretched, checked her mobile for messages and went for a pee. On her way back across the lobby she glanced at Ellie behind the counter who gave her a big toothy smile and nodded towards the chairs outside her interviewing room and then gave her the thumbs up. Two women sat there waiting for her; one, a stocky, short-haired lady with glasses and a long plaited blond braid coming back over her shoulder to her waist at the front, and the other a rather delicate, pretty, blond with pink streaks in her blond bob and a demure way of sitting.

'Hello,' she said approaching them. 'I'm Ginnie Joy, are you here for the rugby interviews?'

'We sure are,' said the stocky one with the braid and glasses standing up. 'Sarah Cook and this is my younger sister Mollie.'

Sarah gave her a crushing handshake and Mollie settled for a shy smile. As sisters they were a long way apart in stature and looks and probably age.

Ushering them into her room Ginnie placed another chair alongside the visitor one in place and sat down behind her table.

'I only had you, Sarah, down but I'm happy to do you both of you're interested in joining us. Who wants to go first?'

Sarah cleared her throat indicating that it would be her and then began speaking in a crisp, no-nonsense way.

'I'm thirty-two and work as an Assistant Procurement Manager in the catering section of the Great Western Hospital. I'm in a Civil Partnership with a nurse called Lucinda and – here's the important and specific bit – have been playing as a tight-head prop and pack leader for the Supermarine Ladies R.F.U. team for the last six years where I'm known as 'Rocky.''

Ginnie kept her face neutral but inside she was churning with excitement. Supermarine had won the Dorset and Wilts league for the last two years and it was watching them play in a couple of local matches – and the England ladies' team on the television – that had first made up Ginnies mind to start her own team, and although she didn't remember seeing this lady play for

Supermarine, the very fact that she had been pack leader was a tremendous accolade to her skill and dedication.

'Why are you interested in joining us, a new start-up team, when you're already in the very best local side and well underway in this season?'

'Rocky' didn't hesitate.

'I injured my knee towards the end of last season and missed a lot of games. And when I went back to a training session last week there was over forty girls signed up for this year, at least eight of whom were props, and four of whom were already in the first fifteen squad. Also, like the men's sides, they were running a first and second women's fifteen this season and although the seconds are only just starting to get going there wasn't much left for me in the first team. Your advertisement then came along and I thought it was time for a change. And with only another two or three years left to play, if I'm going to play rugby it might as well be for the first or the only team.'

'How is your knee now?

'One hundred percent healed and now I'm fit and raring to go. Another thing, our older sister Vera was the Supermarine ladies coach and is the Ladies Director this season. It sometimes causes friction if Mollie and I are picked over others who may think they're more deserving of a place because of Vera's position...'

Now, Ginnie did remember Vera charging up and down the touchline when she went to watch Supermarine ladies play. She had been, as Lindsey Chene had said coaches must, very vocal, especially in the half-time circle.

'A case of too many Cook's' the demure Mollie muttered and then smiled. 'But Vera's not a Cook anymore, she married a Godwin.'

Ginnie turned to her.

'And you also played for Supermarine Ladies alongside your sister?'

'I have, for the last two seasons and only missed two games.'

'The two-league winning year's' Ginnie said mainly to herself. 'What position?'

'Fly half,' Mollie said quietly without emphasis. Not that she needed any, this demure, attractive little woman was the current holder of what is normally considered to be the most important position on the field regarding strategy and control.

'You wouldn't think it to look at her but my sister here has a side-step to dream of,' Sarah chimed in again. 'She can weave her way through a thunderstorm without getting hit by a single raindrop. She can also line kick from hand with uncanny accuracy. The only trouble is that the opposition soon pick up on these brilliant qualities and begin to try and smash her out of the game…'

Mollie smiled at her big sister and then confirmed the facts.

'So, I need the protection of my big sister so I can play and exhibit my skills. If she comes to you then I will as well…' she paused then added. 'I'm a better player with my sister and minder here on the pitch.'

'What will the reaction of the other big sister and the coach-director at Supermarine if you both leave?'

Mollie shrugged.

'Nothing, I think Vera's half expecting it because she knows we're here today. The others won't particularly like it but we haven't registered for this season yet so can go where we want. Besides, they have a lot more than they need and can pick and choose. Being the champion's carries a lot of kudos, there are a lot of girls who want to be a part of their success.'

Ginnie remembered her own RFU registration forms, none of which she had even mentioned thus far and certainly not had any signed.

They carried on chatting with Ginnie trying hard not to be over-enthusiastic about these two more heaven-sent players. Sarah had even heard of Lindsey Chene and her troubles at Reading and thought she would be a good coach. Mollie, who was twenty-six and a van driver for a car parts firm, had always been under the protective wing of her much harder older sister because there was a gap of fifteen years between her and Vera the Supermarine coach and first-born of the Cook girls.

When they had gone Ginnie sat there for a few minutes in a daze until Ellie came in with a coffee for her and sat down in the interview chair.

'Good?' she said bestowing her full-lipped smile on the dazed interviewer.

'Bloody unbelievable,' Ginnie said and then gave her a précis of the two Cook sister's skill sets and record with Supermarine.

'My only worry is whether the rest of us can live up to *their* abilities.'

'Course we can,' Ellie replied. 'We all need role models and they'll drag the rest of us up to the required standards. Anyway, your last and delayed interview from lunchtime's here.'

'And...?'

'She looks fine to me, a bit rugged perhaps but looks have nothing to do with it, do they. A battered visage could even be better on a rugby pitch in the heat of battle, nothing to worry about when you smash into somebody, eh?' Ellie picked up Ginnies empty cup and glided out through the door.

Look's, thought Ginnie getting up and following Elelendise Lucy Cocper's long, sinuous glide out to the foyer, have everything to do with it in your case. There might even be a few men come along to watch them play just to see this beauty flow around the pitch and their wishful thoughts would probably be of the 'Bohica' kind.

The solid and rather wet looking 'battered visage' lady holding a motorcycle crash helmet that stood as Ginnie approached was certainly no beauty. Ellie's 'a bit rugged' if anything did her a favour and the rain and mud spots that had splattered through the open face of her crash helmet and down her waterproofs didn't help.

She did, however, have solidity written all over her chunkily constructed figure. Ginnie silently reproached herself. I must stop looking at everyone in terms of the perfect build for a certain rugby position.

'Mary-Jane Bagnall,' said a broad Wiltshire accent thrusting out a calloused wet hand and crushing Ginnies in its meaty but damp embrace. 'I had to cancel the morning appointment 'cos one of our Friesian's was calving down and having a bit of difficulty.'

'You work on a farm?' Ginnie said waving her into the little interview room.

'I'm part owner, with me older brother, of six hundred acres of combined arable and dairy land just outside Shrivenham with a dairy herd of ninety-six; up at four-thirty every morning for the milking.' Mary-Jane plonked her crash helmet on the floor then dropped her wet gloves in it and dripping all over the floor slumped into the chair. She looked wet and weary. Ginnie looked at Mary-Jane's emailed reply to the advertisement.

'Twenty-one and a part owner of a large dairy farm, good for you,' Ginnie said smiling.

Mary-Jane shrugged. 'It wasn't supposed to be that way really, our dad died suddenly a couple of years ago at fifty-one years of age, just after I started at the Cirencester Agricultural College. 'I had to leave the course and come back to help my brother with the farm because our mum buggered off when dad died. Last we heard she was living in Canada somewhere with a Chinese bloke...'

'Okay,' Ginnie said at a bit of a loss as to what to say at this sudden rush of private information, along with the sexual innuendo it was another constant with these interviews. 'And you were up at four-thirty this morning...'

'Every morning seven days a week, feeding the bugger's, milking the sods and then shovelling their shit, then sleeping a bit and then getting on with the farm chores and doing it all over again.'

Mary-Jane's pudgy face suddenly cracked into a smile changing her entire persona.

'Ah, it's not so bad really, plenty of fresh air and exercise and nobody to boss me about.'

'Sounds like bloody hard work to me,' Ginnie said feebly, throwing in her own swear word to enjoin with this solid, strong-looking young farming lady.

Mary-Jane crossed her substantial thighs over with a crackle from the over trousers she wore tucked into her wet green wellies.

'Me brother thinks I need another interest besides the farm to cheer me up. He used to play a bit of rugby locally before dad died. He saw the ad and thought I was built for it…'

He was right there, thought Ginnie, this girl was built like the proverbial brick outhouse and a prop in the making if ever she'd seen one.

There she went again, judging on size in relation to a rugby position, which, of course, until today she had never judged another human being by in her life.

'Will you be able to get into Swindon Tuesdays and Thursday nights for a couple of hours training each evening week and Saturday afternoons for the matches when we start playing them?'

'Yep, I'll come in on the bloody tractor if my bike won't start and those times won't interfere with the herd management and milking.'

Herd management, thought Ginnie. That's what I'll be doing in a way but best not to mention it in those terms, the girls wouldn't like it.

Watching Mary-Jane leave, Ginnie couldn't help but think she had the front row sorted, the three positions of hooker and two props that the instructions on positional stuff she had downloaded from the RFU Women's section said was among the hardest to find. If the two tall girls Heidi Prager and Ellie Lucy Cooper passed muster that was the front five engine room sorted. Add in Lindsey Chene as coach and the other good recruits and all this was going very well.

A bit too well perhaps and beyond anything she had thought possible. Still, don't jinx it with negative thoughts, just keep going and try and repeat it again tomorrow when she had another full day of interviews lined up.

Chapter Four

The nine-thirty and first interview the next morning, a Sunday, and passed over by Ellie who was on the reception again, was Iona Pierce, an attractive looking thirty-year-old wearing fashionable skinny jeans with holes in the knees, nearly new Nike trainers and a purple tee shirt with 'The World's a Blob' written on a squashed face of the globe in green on the front under a smart red Thai silk jacket with each sleeve rolled to the elbows. She carried a mobile phone which she switched off and placed in a brown leather shoulder bag when she sat down and Ginnie couldn't help but compare this gorgeous, unmade up but attractive girl with the slim, fit looking figure, with that of the rugged Mary-Jane Bagnall, the 'solid citizen' that had been her last interview yesterday. That bodily diversity, according to the RFU website, was one of the great draws for the players, it was a game with something for all shapes and sizes...and looks thought Ginnie, although it didn't specifically say *that*.

'*Iona,* a very attractive name,' Ginnie said by way of opening.

'My mother had a thing about the Scottish Islands. I have an older sister called Skye and we often joke about what we *could* have been called...like Muck or Ulva for instance. Imagine what the kids at school would have done with those two!'

Ginnie returned her grin and then joined in.

'What, like put a 'V' in the front of Ulva?'

'Exactly, Skye and I used to fall about with that one and you can guess what we substituted the 'm' in Muck for.'

Ginnie then told her what the team was to be called… officially and unofficially, getting a giggle out of Iona.

'Someone called Vulva would just *have* to play for the Furious Fannies.'

'Have you played rugby before?' Ginnie asked.

'No, but I am currently a personal fitness trainer and trained hard for a few years until…'

'Until…?'

Iona composed herself and thought for a few seconds on how to broach the next subject.

'I trained as an alpine skeleton racer along with two other girls alongside Lizzie Yarnold, the British Champion, at Bath University Sports Centre. I got there by being a good county level sprinter at sixteen and then going on to train to be a heptathlete. I didn't make the grade in the heptathlon but changed and was then selected to join Bath in their skeleton programme. It was a specific elite athlete's programme for the Winter Olympics and I got lottery funding for three years. I had two great female role models and champions during this period, Jessica Ennis for heptathlon and then, with two other girls I trained alongside, Lizzie Yarnold in skeleton. Lizzie had already won gold in the Sochi Winter Olympics in 2014 and was odds on favourite again for the gold in the 2018 Korean Winter Olympics at Pyeongchang. This was the one I had targeted and the team would take two skeleton racers. My boyfriend at the time was a Bath rugby player and we were a bit of a celebrity couple around the Georgian splendour of that lovely city. Then the shit hit the fan...'

She stopped and wiped a tear from her cheek and then took a deep breath.

'I wasn't selected for Pyeongchang last year – the team was put together at least a year out from the games – and as if that wasn't hard enough after two years of dedicated training and trying to be the fastest down a steep ice-covered slope on a tea tray, I lost my lottery funding. Then my boyfriend began to get rough with me after he was dropped from the rugby team...' She touched her cheek again with the tips of her fingers indicating a blow of some sort. The proof wasn't long in coming.

'The last straw with him was a fractured cheekbone from where he hit me and so I left threatening him with the police if I saw him again. Another short but wasted relationship with the wrong man followed and then six months with an older woman before that also went tits up... as it were....' She grinned at her own joke before continuing 'So, with my tail between my legs I came home to Mum and Dad in Swindon six months ago to recuperate and reconsider just where I was going with my life...'

She paused again while Ginnie thought that her simple add in the local paper for a women's rugby team had, besides touching some long-lost ambition opened up a can of relationship worms and issues. All life was walking through her door here. If a newly qualified psychiatrist wanted to branch out on their own all he or she had to do was advertise for women rugby players and sit back and watch the conflicted roll through the door.

Ginnie could see more tears in Iona's eyes so gave her a little time to compose herself by suggesting that she go and get them both a cup of tea. When she got back to the room with two cups on the tray, Iona was her smiling, reassured self again.

'Sorry about that,' the former professional athlete said cheerfully. 'After all the training and effort, not being selected – although the gold was nailed on for Lizzie – still, after twelve hard months, bloody-well hurts. Losing lottery funding was also a big deal and as for that shit of a boyfriend and the other useless items that followed, I've given up sex in all forms for the foreseeable future.'

'I completely understand,' said Ginnie placing the tray on the table and only really understanding the boyfriend troubles. This girl had lived and breathed the rarefied air of a financially supported athlete for some time whereas Ginnie was a girl who hadn't even made the netball team at her comprehensive and would cross the street if there was a game of hopscotch going on the pavement her side when she was younger. As if reading her mind Iona ventured a question.

'Who did *you* play rugby for?'

'No one, I've never played rugby or any other sport in my life, which bodes the obvious question, what makes me think I can captain, handle an oblong shaped ball and play, for this rugby team?'

Iona nodded.

Since Iona had bared her soul Ginnie decided to do the same.

'Like you all my relationships with men failed, no matter how hard I tried to please them and act as sex bitch, mother, lover, ego booster, and fantasy actor.

Unlike you I was never physically abused, but I certainly had the propensity to pick the wrong one's every time. So, I decided to make a category difference to my life by doing something completely new and different. And, after some thought and discussion with my friend at the office where I work, that turned out to be starting and playing in a lady's rugby team. The idea just came to me one afternoon while I was watching a local ladies team playing. Strangely, although I have never played rugby, I have since studied it and watched any number of women's and men's games and am convinced I can do it with the right support. That's what these interviews are all about and I have to say, the calibre of the ladies I have seen so far, including you, has been outstanding.'

'I recognise all those male pleasing categories although they all came in one package for me' Iona said sipping her tea raising another obvious question in Ginnies mind. What is the matter with the world when men *and* women lovers can treat such a beautiful and athletically talented girl as Iona so badly?

'Have you given up on men?' Iona asked with a sly grin.

Unsure if there was a double meaning to the question bearing in mind Iona had mentioned a six-month period with a woman, Ginnie returned the grin and then answered truthfully.

'I've given up trying with them. Non-caring toxic masculinity that takes and does not reply in kind is a no-no from here on in. If one comes along that I fancy I'll bleed him dry then throw him out. In the meantime, they and *any* other relationship can wait, I've got a rugby team to form and training and games to organise, besides working a thirty-five-hour week to pay my mortgage on a small local flat. Are you still living with your mum and dad?'

If there was a potential sexual door, she hadn't slammed it completely shut. As for the 'bleed him dry and then throw him out bit' if bloody only.

'No. They were brill for a few months while I sorted myself out but now, I rent an apartment in Old Town on my own and have begun to establish myself locally as a personal trainer. And I'm gym fit again, although I'll never get back to being the elite athlete, I was…'

She paused and took a deep breath.

'Ginnie, I want very much to join your team, whatever it takes…'

'Iona, you are a definite and we'll work out a position later.'

The strong hug she got from Iona with just a hint of lemons in her perfume-dabbed neck when she left made Ginnie think afterwards that perhaps she shouldn't limit her own future sexual hook-ups to just men. She had, briefly, considered trying it with another woman several times when her male love life was at its usual low ebb but an opportunity never seemed to present itself so had gone back to men when the next disappointing slob came along on the basis that this time it might work. Thus far it hadn't but this attractive and outwardly athletic girl could change all that and her wide-eyed vulnerability and attractive face and figure was appealing. Throughout their chat Ginnie had been growing steadily more attracted to her and after all, she would be spending a lot of time with these girls.

Nah, stop it ya daft cow, an affair with a fellow team member was a sure-fire way to cause problems with the rest of them… wasn't it?

In a contrarian pattern that was becoming acceptably normal in these interviews, the next one through the door was a walking disaster and the first one Ginnie had truly taken an instant dislike to. Her name was Adele, and, as if she was the famous singer and expected instant recognition, no surname was offered on her emailed response to Ginnies advertisement or in her high-pitched no handshake introduction. With a back-combed, hair-sprayed stiff mass of brown hair piled on top of her head and then brought forward over her forehead as if eaves on a thatched cottage roof, over a pair of huge, glued-on black eyelashes that she batted up and down like a pair of crows on a chalk wall, garish red lipstick applied over and around a pair of too thin lips and individually painted long nails, all topped off with a silk pashmina down to her waist over thigh length black boots, she was an apparition of such poor taste and choices that Ginnie was glad no-one else could see who she was talking with. She briefly wondered what Ellie on reception had made of her.

'I've come for the quarterback's position,' Adele announced in her high-pitched nasal whine wafting in on a jet trail of cheap perfume and helping herself to the seat where Ginnie had so far sat on the far side of the table. 'Nothing else will do as I understand that the quarterback is the kingpin of the side and if nothing else, I am a kingpin, or queen bee if you'd rather have it that way...'

For first time in her interviews Ginnie understood why Heidi Prager, with or without an infusion of vodka and or amphetamines or whatever other stimulant she favoured, wanted to punch another woman. This overbearing, arrogant, cheaply dressed, and made-up apparitional stinking skank – an appropriate Heidi description that fitted perfectly – was too good for punching and was so far up her fat arse a punch would get lost in the shit storm. Ginnie decided to show her the door a.s.a.p. before she lost it. It was time to live up to her brother's former nick-name again.

'Quarterbacks don't play rugby,' she said through gritted teeth leaning in over the desk from the interviewee's side and fixing her with what she hoped was a menacing icy glare.

'Oh, don't they,' Adele said taken aback by Ginnies obviously confrontational stance but not enough to keep quiet. 'Never mind, whatever your queen bee position is I'm the girl for it...' She batted the eye crows up and down at Ginnie for a few beats.

Ginnie went on the offensive; there would be nothing gentle about letting this one down.

'I don't think that you're the one for my team at all and suggest you leave now!' She marched to the door and flung it open.

Ginnie found her Peppery anger uplifting and appropriate.

After more nervous batting eyelashes and rearranging her cheap pashmina as she slowly realised that she was being summarily dismissed, Adele finally got to her feet and flounced towards the door where Ginnie stood with the glare fixed on the waste of cosmetics that this skank – note to self; she must stop using that derogatory word of Heidi's but it certainly applied here– walked slowly towards her. She also realised as she came abreast of her that Adele's eyes, under the heavily applied black liner and batted lashes, had a certain reptilian quality to them that right now was eschewing all the initial bluster she had marched in with and showing a certain amount of fear. Good, she wanted to say and quarterbacks play in American football not rugby so you can fuck right off, but she resisted it and merely growled and glared at the trail of cheap perfume that squeezed warily passed her and then flounced across the lobby towards the front door. As the single-named apparition tried *pushing* the outside *pull* door and then hurled herself at it in frustration until it opened, Ginnie ventured a glance across at where she just knew Ellie would be watching her and the performance.

And sure enough, there she was sporting the biggest grin it was possible for a mouth full of perfect white teeth in a lovely black face to show that, without falling on the floor and curling up in a paroxysm of unrestrained mirth, she found this performance hilarious.

Ginnie looked around and seeing there was no-one else looking gave Ellie a prominent middle finger and then grinning herself went back into her little interview room and sat in her own chair. Ten minutes later she had forgotten about arrogant Adele as she listened happily to Billie Hayden. Billie – short for Willomena – was a twenty-eight-year-old, big, open-faced smiling girl with a brown ponytail who worked as a fire-fighter. She followed women's rugby and had recently been to a couple of England's games. The Red Roses of England were the current Grand Slam Six Nations champions and Billie had been to specifically watch her heroine, a potential international prop and replacement, also a fire-fighter called Shauna Brown. Shauna had recently publically said that she would not give up her job with the fire-service even if she was offered a central rugby contract with the RFU.

'This is my view as well,' grinned Billie. 'Regardless of how much money you offer me to play for the Furious Fannies, I can't be bought...!'

Ginnie had mentioned the nick-name that was already bedding itself in as the standard team referral. It got instant recognition such that she was already thinking that she might change the official name *from* the Fantail Furies *to* the Tanya Bryan suggestion of the Furious Fannies?

Perhaps not but as a nickname it had lasting appeal.

'Okay, we'll just have to take you on for nothing then, like all the other girls,' Ginnie had replied with a broad smile very much wanting this happy and bravely employed girl for the team.

They talked about positions and Billie's difficulty in getting away sometimes because of the shifts she worked, especially for training on Tuesdays and Thursdays. Saturday afternoons would be OK for the actual games because she could always swop the weekend shift with someone else because such shifts were worth double the money and sought after. Ginnie put her down as a potential number eight, which would mean that if they all turned out, the central spine of the team – the straight line running back from hooker (Gina McKinnon) through No 8 (Billie Hayden) to fly half (Mollie Cook) to full back Avril Gordon, Gina's army mate if she came and passed muster, was complete.

The next one to arrive was, arguably, the most important potential player on the team. Her name was Agnes Dillon and her father was the founder and current Chief Executive of the Wessex Mutual Building Society, an organisation he put together when resigning from The Nationwide Building Society, also Swindon based, where he had been the Finance Director twenty years ago. In that time Wessex Mutual had risen to become the second largest mutual society in Great Britain with three thousand employees, two-hundred and eighty retail outlets and seven million members, and had established its head office in Swindon where Ginnie worked, just three miles from the Nationwide, still the largest in the business with seventeen thousand employees and fifteen million members.

The fact that made Aggy so important to Ginnie was the potential use of the Wessex Mutual Building Society's Sports Ground. A modern and expensive building and grounds complex constructed just five years ago, it offered several sporting facilities including outdoor tennis courts, indoor badminton courts and a gym with basketball nets and floor markings, with changing rooms and showers, together with an outside all-weather running track with two football pitches and, the most important of all to Ginnie, a rugby pitch. Wessex ran two football teams, both made up of male employees and the gym, basketball and badminton courts were always popular with both sexes and needed to be booked well in advance all the year round. The all-weather running track and two outdoor tennis courts were also popular but tended to be fine weather usage only. There was a separate barn-like building where the office of the head grounds-man and his two assistants was situated with warehousing for mowing machines and assorted other equipment – including an almost unused rhino scrimmaging machine – but the rugby pitch, which separated the two football pitches, hadn't been used to play the noble game for two years since an embryonic attempt to form a male team had faltered and finally closed due to poor results.

When Ginnie had first begun to seriously think about forming her rugby team and discussing it with Aggy a couple of months ago, she had gone down to the sports ground to see the head groundsman. His name was Tony Newman and the pig had put his feet up on his tin desk and laughed at her.

'Women,' he had then sneered with a wink at one of his groundsman colleagues the other side of the room, 'don't play rugby dearie. It's a man's game and I'm gonna resurrect the men's team myself next season and run it properly. Not like that bunch of wankers we had here before.'

A fucking shithead and asswipe, Ginnie had thought looking at the sneering face and trying not to show any emotion.

'We'll soon see about that' she had said quietly and left knowing she had Aggy Dillon as her secret weapon up her sleeve, and when you had Aggy you also had her doting father, the majority shareholder, Chief Executive of the combined Wessex Mutual and God of all he surveyed around these parts.

Following three formative years at Marlborough, Agnes Dillon had then taken a degree in History at St Catherine's, Oxford, followed by an MBA at the Said Business School, also in Oxford. It had been a specific educational process worked out by Aggy and her father so that his only and much adored daughter could join his business and begin to groom her skills as his replacement in fifteen years or so when he retired. Somewhere along the line while at St Catherine's, probably through a boyfriend although Ginnie had never asked, Aggy had had become a rugby fan, then trainee and then a rugby blue and played on the winning team in the annual Varsity match between Oxford and Cambridge at Twickenham. She was a second-half replacement and played at outside centre and had become a devotee of the game.

Her management training at Wessex which began some months ago at the end of November, and would feature four-month periods or so in each department while she learned the ropes and Customer Services, where Ginnie was one of two Supervisors, was her first stop. They immediately bonded and became firm friends and it was with Aggy that Ginnie had first planted the seed of the formation of a female rugby team over a social glass of wine over the Christmas holiday. Immediately Aggy had added her enthusiasm to Ginnies drive and although they often lunched together in the staff canteen, no – one else at Wessex knew what Ginnie and Aggy were plotting...yet. But one thing they would make sure of was the come-uppance of that sneering chauvinist pig and sports ground caretaker, Tony Newton. Aggy had also said that to make the selection process fair she would attend an interview with Ginnie at the hotel the same as everyone else, and although they both knew her position, as Ginnies own, was nailed-on from both a rugby playing and daddy-as-boss point, they would keep it to themselves until the team was formed and in training.

'How's it all going?' Aggy said swinging through the door and giving Ginnie a big hug.

'I feel good about how it's going so far. Got a few really good players and will have a pretty good team by the time I've finished next Saturday.'

'Then, according to Hannah Arendt, you can become a Conservative.' Aggy said obliquely.

'Whose she when she's at home?'

'Arendt was an American political commentator in the sixties who said that the most radical revolutionary will become a conservative the day *after* the revolution.'

'Meaning…?'

'Meaning, that once you have put the team together your zeal will drop away and you will become just one of them rather than the leader who got them there.'

'My zeal, as you call it,' another word that Ginnie didn't ever recall using, 'will hopefully grow into that of a good player and captain who is pivotal to the teams function. If that's going from a radical revolutionary to a conservative, then so be it…'

Aggy was always throwing learned quotations about and it only served to make Ginnie feel just how inferior her own education had been because she had never heard of any of her quoted subjects or their pithy comments – as this one and, ditto – hardly ever made any sense of. But she was determined not to be undermined by her friend's erudition and vastly superior education to her comprehensive and online diploma course run by the local college.

Erudition, another Aggy word she understood but didn't ever remember using before her friend dropped into a casual conversation about her time at St Catherine's.

They spent the next fifteen minutes poring over Ginnies list of players so far and as Aggy got up to leave she added another interesting tid-bit.

'By the way, dad's going down to the Sports Club tomorrow morning to have a word with Tony Newton. He'll be lucky to still be employed at eleven o'clock. I'll let you know how it goes at lunch.'

'I'd love to be there to see the sneering pig's face,' Ginnie said with relish.

Within a minute of Aggy leaving Ellie was in with a coffee.

'Elegant, slim figure, well-mannered, good coiffeur and clothes and a dazzling smile,' she said placing the coffee down in front of Ginnie. 'Tell me more.'

'An Oxford blue at rugby and the best-connected woman I know,' Ginnie replied withholding any further information. 'That's on a need-to-know basis for the time being but I promise you'll be the first to know...or second...no, make that the third, just so long as you never mention again that hideous apparition of a single cell woman who called herself Adele a couple of interviews ago.'

She resisted the urge to say 'skank' and gave herself a mental pat on the back.

'Hideous apparition was right,' said Ellie flashing the big white-toothed smile again. 'You gave her what must have been the shortest interview ever...less than a minute by my calculation.'

'It was long enough to make me want to punch her very hard in the face.' Ginnie said sipping her coffee and bunching the other one of her bony fists.

'Now' Ellie said with her now trademark huge white toothed grin. 'you're beginning to think like an aggressive rugby player,' She reached the door and turned around. 'There are two more lambs out here waiting to come to the slaughter so try and remember that GBH is a crime, even on hideous women...' She turned around to address whoever was sitting there waiting to come in and who had obviously heard her.

'It's alright dear's, she's a poppet really ...when she's not getting ready to punch potential rugby girls...'

It took Ginnie five minutes to sooth the two local college students in their late teens that had come along as moral support to each other and crept timidly through the door expecting to see a fire-breathing dragon with bunched fists awaiting them.

The taller and best looking of the pair whose name was Stella Winters, finally began to open-up by haltingly explaining that she was a year into an HND course in Management Administration at Swindon College.

'Well good for you,' Ginnie said. 'I was nineteen when I started a two-year online modular HND course in the same subject run by Swindon College. I was working at my first job in accounts in Honda in Swindon at the time and studying online in my spare time and managed to get a level five accreditation. That course cost me two thousand pounds but it was worth every penny because then I transferred to Customer Services in The Wessex Mutual Building Society Head Office and haven't looked back since.'

There followed some general chat about the relevant courses the girls were doing at the college which settled them down; Kayla Taylor, the slightly smaller and plainer one, was doing Construction Engineering and wanted to build bridges.

'Are you playing any sport?' Ginnie aimed the question at them both vaguely thinking that they too might be a love pairing.

They looked at each other for a few beats until Kayla nodded at Stella and the pretty one cleared her throat.

'We're both fit and play hockey for a local team but the coach, a married man with two children, is a perve, groper, and sex pest. He's always coming up behind me and putting his arms around me saying it's only a matter of time before he meddles inside my knickers. I'm not the only one but it's making us both very uncomfortable.'

'Both?' Ginnie asked.

'Well,' said Kayla a little more assertively raising her jaw in determination. 'If there's any meddling to be done inside Stella's knickers, *I'm* the one who'll do it. When we have both qualified, we intend to marry.'

'Good for you both' said Ginnie keeping her face studiedly neutral. 'Leave the dirty hockey coach and his pawing hands and lewd suggestions and come and play rugby with me and my team of girls. You have my word that no-one will bother you here.'

Hopefully, she thought, but you could never guarantee such things because even though they are all women – apart from Sherry Moyes who she hadn't made up her mind about yet, they were a pretty diverse bunch covering most of the complex angles of normal heterosexual, lesbian and bi-sexual relationships – those bits that she understood anyway.

'We're not the only ones fed up with the dirty little sex pest,' said Kayla vehemently. 'There are a couple of other girls who he bothers as well and we've found a sort of collective strength in the #Me Too movement.'

'Bring 'em along to training,' said Ginnie, 'and we'll see where we go from there. If you get any trouble about leaving from the groping coach, tell him you'll go to the police about him. Creeps like him have been cropping up in court cases regularly lately.'

Another thing Ginnie was learning at these interviews was just how diversified women were in their sexual preferences. She had considered herself a somewhat loose libertine before these interviews but was a naïve nobody who'd lived a sheltered life compared to some of these girls. What was the current collective acronym... LGBT for Lesbian, Gay, Bisexual and Transgender? And who would have thought that a sex pest coach for a hockey team could be so helpful for *her* rugby team recruitment programme?

Bring 'em on, Ginnie thought, the Furious Fannies will take them all and turn them into rugby players...or something.

Then in walked Romany Cutler and her 'all of life is walking through her interview doors' thought took another decidedly oblique turn for the better.

She was on the small side of medium height, slim with long curly black hair and a slightly feral look to her gamine face. Her clothes were almost rags and on her feet were a pair of old and much scuffed trainers. She was also breathing quite heavily.

Before she sat down Ginnie glanced at her introductory email. Ah yes, she remembered it now. In three short lines a lady called Louise George who introduced herself as a local authority Community Travellers Liaison Officer, introduced Romany Cutler from a local settled Travellers Site at Hay Lane, near junction 16 of the M4. It said, simply, that Romany was a troubled but athletically gifted young lady with outstanding ability who would benefit greatly from working with Ginnies ladies' rugby team. Ginnie had emailed Louise back with this time and date for an interview and which she had obviously passed on to Romany.

'Romany, what a lovely name, how did you get here?'

'I run. Run everywhere cos no one can catch I that way.'

'You ran here all the way from the Hay Lane Travellers site?'

The feral, gamine and sharply pointed face scowled. 'Specially the boys and truancy men who wuz always arter me. Me granddad Cutler said 'ed brung me in the scrap van but I run.'

Ginnie was beginning to see what Louise George meant by 'troubled.'

'The boys on the site at Hay Lane?'

Romany dropped the scowl this time and replaced it with a shrug.

'Louise George said in her email introducing you that you have outstanding athletic ability…?'

The shrug again was followed by a near repeat answer.

'The truancy blokes could never catch I, the blokes on the site could never catch I, nuffin could catch I. Me granddad Cutler says I run like the wind.'

One who could dodge raindrops in a thunderstorm and another who could run like the wind; this team could be natures very own super-sisters.

'You live with your granddad at Hays Lane?'

'Jus me an im, me da was killed when 'is 'orse kicked 'im in the 'ead and me ma fucked off wif a bloke up norf.'

'How old were you when your dad was killed?'

She rolled back her tattered sleeve and looked at her watch. It was a cheap yellow plastic model with a standard dial. With her lips shaping every numeral Romany slowly counted from one using her fingers to touch each numeral.

'Five...' She said it very deliberately holding up her outstretched hand with five fingers splayed.

'How old are you now?'

Back to the watch and the exercise was repeated twice as slowly with much pursing of the lips and finger counting. Finally, she held up ten fingers, then seven more and a small crooked little finger.

'Seventeen 'and tairty.' This was said triumphantly with a white-toothed smile.

Ginnie was beginning to understand, she was seventeen and a half. The smile wasn't an Ellie standard beam of perfect ivories but then it didn't have the contrast of a black background, but it was surprisingly white for all that. This girl probably couldn't read or write which was why the truancy officers were always 'arter' her and Louise George had emailed on her behalf. Remarkably, she had worked out a way, or been shown how by her granddad or someone, to use the watch dial as an aid to working out numbers and therefore the time.

She saw Ginnie glance at the watch and provided an answer.

'Granddad Cutler says if you can tell the time, you got the time.' Because she was repeating an oft used quote by someone else it was grammatically good.

Romany didn't mention a grandma Cutler so Ginnie didn't ask.

Then Romany offered a little information without being asked.

'Granddad Cutler won't let I sign the dole. Gives I a fiver when we 'av a good day on the scrap. Say true Traveller make own way in life and sport like Tyson Fury and Billy Joe Saunders. S'why 'e let me cum 'ere.'

Ginnie Googled both names after Romany had left to run back to Hay Lane and was most surprised to see that both were current world champion boxers who espoused the Gypsy/Travellers cause. Tyson Fury even styled himself as the Gypsy King. She then emailed Louise George to thank her for arranging for Romany to come along and that she would like to see the athletic, elfin-faced runner at the first training session. She would also keep Louise onside this way; there might well be other young athletic Traveller ladies in her bailiwick. Ten minutes after she had sent the email her mobile rang while she was waiting for the next interview and it was Louise.

'Hi Ginnie, its Louise George working on a Sunday as you are. Thanks for the email about Romany and it's good to know she impressed you sufficiently to make the ladies initial training squad.'

They talked for a few minutes while Louise filled her in on the Traveller communities, she was responsible for and Romany in particular.

'Did she mention her granddad Cutler? 'Louise asked.

'Frequently, she obviously thinks a great deal of him and mentioned his little homily about time and using her watch for numbers.'

'If you can tell the time, you got the time.' Louise repeated with a chuckle. 'It's Romany's way of working out numbers as taught by her granddad and since neither of them can read or write he's taught her how to use the watch to be sharp about money and dates. It works, it might take her a while to get there but you would never short change either of them. She lives with him in a static caravan on the Hay Lane permanent site and he's very strict with her. Makes her brush her teeth twice a day and go out with him on his scrap van collecting old bits of metal and plays hell if she so much as even glances at a boy or the young lads on the site try and chat her up.'

'Good for him,' Ginnies replied. 'Won't let her sign on the rock 'n roll either and I noticed the very white teeth. Is she really seventeen and a half?'

Louise chuckled. 'I don't know. There doesn't seem to be a birth certificate which isn't unusual for the travelling community. They're an independent lot and can be very crafty about such things as age, especially with the girls who can easily be married and have a couple of kids by Romany's age. I would say a year younger at most but no more. I did notice that your ad said eighteen to thirty-five, is that a problem for you?'

'Not if she can run like the wind,'

'Oh, that she can. Rumour around Hay Lane says that none of the boys can get near her and plenty have tried, mainly because of her running ability and granddads careful watch over her. Old Tink Cutler has an old-fashioned gypsy pride and honour in his family and Romany is all that's left and he wants to do the right thing for her.'

'Got any more like her?' Ginnie asked holding her breath.

'I'll keep my eyes open. I look after three permanent traveller sites and anything passing through so there might be someone else like Romany. Incidently, do you know what one of their pet collective names is for us non romany types is?'

'Is it pikey's?'

'That's the common one. They have a better and more apt term – its 'gorgers.'

'I shall never eat again,' said Ginnie thanking her and signing off.

Ginnie's last interview for the weekend was a no-show so she packed her laptop in its case and checked her list. Fifteen squad members including some standout experienced players and a pack leader, an experienced coach, a happy hooker who could run for ever and her friend and the former army goalkeeper with hands like a midwife and a kick like a sex-starved stallion, a Winter Olympics trained athlete, an Oxford Rugby Blue, a girl who could side-step raindrops and line-kick with uncanny accuracy, and a traveller who could run like the wind. Then there was the fighting joker Heidi and transgender general factotum Sherry with an HGV licence, if required. She had another eight booked in for next Saturday at the hotel and so should be somewhere near her total of twenty-two or three squad members when they got together for their first training session which she would now try and squeeze in on the last Tuesday in the month at the end of February 2018.

Her first big glass of Sainsbury's Merlot went down without touching the sides when she got home that night before relaxing into a warm soapy bath. There was a more than even money chance now that this project was going to work out and be a lot of effort, sexual banter, and fun at the same time…wasn't there?

Chapter Five

Sitting in front of her computer at twelve-thirty on the Monday in her office fiddling with the positions of those girls who she wanted in the team, Ginnie felt someone watching over her shoulder.

'You're supposed to be working not playing with team selections,' Aggy said tapping her on the head. 'C'mon, it's lunchtime.'

Knowing that her friend had news for her about her father's visit to the sports ground earlier, Ginnie forced herself not to ask until they were settled with a couple of salads and Diet Cokes in the staff canteen. Equally, knowing that Ginnie was aching to know, Aggy chewed slowly and kept on smiling at her knowingly without saying anything. Finally, Ginnie couldn't wait any longer.

'Have you been upstairs to see your father?'

It was hallowed ground up there. Only other directors and high-ranking personnel – and his beloved daughter – were allowed in Claude Dillon's office on the top floor, his gatekeeper, the grey haired and stern Madeleine Mooney saw to that.

'I have' Aggy replied obliquely still toying with Ginnie and carrying on eating slowly without any further comment.

After a while Ginnie couldn't wait any longer and exploded.

'Aggy, stop it! What was the outcome of his visit to the sports ground this morning?'

'Oh, nothing much, really, he just fired that pig Tony Newton on the spot…'

Ginnie slumped back in her chair with relief.

Aggy leaned forward and motioned for Ginnie to do the same. Most people around here knew she was the daughter of the CEO and although Aggy had no airs and graces, she was careful with who heard what she said about conversations with her father and now, the rugby project.

'When daddy got there, he walked into the office and Newton was sat with his feet up on his desk reading a porno mag. His two fellow groundsmen were out cutting the grass on the pitches. He either didn't recognise daddy or was too busy looking at the photo's because he bellowed across the shed at him with a 'Who the fuck are you!'

Aggy guffawed and then lapsed into silent laughter before, wiping away the tears with a small white hanky, and resuming. 'Imagine that, feet up on the desk and head in a load of performing nudes and the CEO walks in and he doesn't even know who he is. Mind you, daddy did say that he hadn't been to the sports ground for about three years, probably Newton came after that. Anyway, unlike many people when he's mad, daddy doesn't shout or rant and rave, his voice just drops a couple of octaves and his annunciation gets very precise. The upshot was that five minutes later Newton had cleared his desk with daddy standing over him, more …er… porno erotica evidently – and was then escorted off the premises.'

Throughout the explanation Ginnies eyes had gone round with wonder and her mouth was agape.

'Close your mouth, you look like a fish. Daddies also asked me to tell you to get up there to his office for a chat about the rugby team as soon as you can.'

'What me, up to the top floor to see the boss! I've never been up there before,'

Ginnie wailed then clapped her hand over her mouth as others were turning to look.

'Then it's time you did. Daddy's a poppet and there's nothing to worry about so finish your salad and get up those stairs, he's got a one-thirty so you've got three quarters of an hour.'

After a quick once over of the hair and face in the ladies, Ginnie climbed the three flights of stair and presented herself at Madeleine Moody's paper strewn desk. She was famous throughout the building as the CEO's stern gatekeeper and P.A. No-one got near him without her say so. The butterflies were still swirling around Ginnies stomach which the slow climbing of the three flights of stairs hadn't subdued. There was a lift but she needed the time to compose herself. This was hallowed ground in the Wessex organisation, it was one thing to play at being the boss of an embryonic lady's rugby team at interviews in a local hotel or newspaper, but an entirely other to blindly enter the inner sanctum of the man who paid for her mortgage, kept her small eight-year-old Fiesta on the road, bought her clothes and every other bill she had accumulated in the six years she'd been employed here.

'Ah, you must be Ginnie. Go straight in, he's expecting you.' The grey-haired Madeleine, belying her fearsome reputation, smiled encouragingly, and waved towards the open door that was Claude Dillon's domain. Ginnie tapped timidly on the open door and stepped into the deeply carpeted inner office of he who must be obeyed. At least, unlike the delinquent groundsman Tony Newton, she knew who he was from his infrequent walks around the offices and the quietly and carefully enunciated speech he made into a microphone at every year's vast Christmas party.

*

When she emerged after a half an hour in Claude Dillon's office Ginnie thought her feet were way off the ground. She walked slowly back down the three flights to her large open plan office shared with two dozen others in Customer Services in a daze. Aggy was waiting for her by her desk with a coffee at the ready. The radiant look on Ginnies face told Aggy that it had gone well.

'See, I told you he was a poppet and there was nothing to be worried about' her friend and daughter of the mighty executive she had just spent one of the most enjoyable conversations she had ever had with a man said.

'Now tell me all about it.'

'Oh, this and that you know how it is?' Ginnie adopted a casually straight face and looked at her friend who knew she was being repaid for holding out on her earlier.

'I'm waiting,' Aggy said after a long silence trying hard to adopt the stoic stare of forbearance of the woman with four items in the supermarket pay queue stuck behind a fussy wife of at least five children with two over-loaded trolleys who can't find her debit card.

After another lengthy lull Ginnie finally grinned at her friend.

'Don't *you* know what we've been talking about?'

'Nope, it was for your ears only as the founder and instigator of the lady's rugby team. I might live in the same house as my mother and father but was only told about Newton's dismissal when I snuck in to see him in his eyrie in the clouds earlier.'

Eyrie, Ginnie thought. That's a lovely word to describe the plush office she'd just left; she'd look it up later for an explanation.

She sat down and blew out her cheeks before reaching for the coffee. Having taken a good swallow, she took a deep breath.

'It was all pretty unbelievable really. First off, he said I was to call him Claude and not Sir, as I started with...'

Aggy nodded. 'He always does that; it puts people at ease. Don't tell me, after that he said did you mind him calling you Ginnie...right? And before you know it, you're chatting away like old friends.'

'That's exactly right, you certainly know your father.'

Aggy grinned. 'No more than you know yours I suspect.'

'Hah!' Ginnie exclaimed. 'My old man's a carpenter for a joinery firm making windows and doors all day and is a pretty miserable old sod most of the time unless he's got a serious glass of something or other in his hand of an evening...however.'She went on to explain that they were to have the rugby pitch at the company sports complex – which was having its white lines repainted as they spoke – solely to themselves for practice every Tuesday and Thursday evening and for all home games when they started playing. The pitch had practice lights around it for the dark winter nights of training such as now and which would be switched off automatically at ten o'clock in the evening on practice days. She was to liaise with the two remaining groundsmen when she needed the pitch's grass cut, flags and goal post protectors put out for games and lines repainted and the rhino dragged outside for scrummage practice. The tall upright posts were being replaced and repainted today and would stay in place for the season, and there was a mini-bus holding around twenty-five people in the shed which we could share equitably for away games with the two football teams and the same with the basketball and badminton teams in the gym when the weather was too bad to practice outside. Ginnie waved a piece of paper at Aggy.

'These are the names, emails, and departmental telephones of the two remaining grounds-men, football, basketball, and Badminton coaches for liaison on sharing the mini-bus and facilities. The two footballs teams are all male, as is the basketball, and the badminton is a mixed team. We're the first Wessex all female sports team.'

'Perhaps we'll start a trend. This office has as many females in it as males so why not have female football and basketball teams?' Aggy said.

'Why not' said Ginnie. 'But I suspect those male football basketball and mixed badminton teams are like my rugby mob and don't necessarily all work for Wessex. I asked your father – Claude – about that and he asked Madeleine to find out but wasn't worried if they were peopled by non-Wessex staff. His take was that so long as the facility is being used to the maximum in all possible sports, it's being of value to the company and use to the business and the local community.'

'Just you wait until the Furious Fannies are making winning headlines,' said Aggy now also accustomed to using the nick-name and waving her arms to encompass the wider offices around them. 'There will be a slutglut of eager ladies flocking to your desk from all over this building pleading to become a part of it.'

'Slutglut' was another typical Aggy ingratiating word that Ginnie had never heard before.

She had confided to Ginnie over a few vodkas at the office Christmas lunch that she sometimes felt a little out of things with the other girls at Wessex because of her father's position. As a result, she sometimes used what she called the 'low vernacular' to get down and dirty with everyone and be accepted.

'Slutglut,' although completely unnecessary, was an Aggy word purposefully designed for her to blend; instead, it had the opposite effect of making her standout as an educated prat who couldn't even swear properly. Genuine friends like Ginnie would prefer her to be normal – whatever *that* was – while the fawning sycophants would laugh and encourage such idiotic language ingratiatingly as she rose up towards the senior jobs.

While Ginnie was cogitating on this Aggy had another question.

'What did daddy say about the team nick-name because he can be a bit of a prude at times?'

'Had a good chuckle about it, especially when I told him that the official one is the Fantail Furies and how it got turned around by one of the girls at the interviews.'

She stopped and looked at Aggy again.

'And....?' Her friend asked picking upon on something important that had so far remained unsaid.

'What he then did was simply unbelievable. He called his secretary in and Madeleine came in with some papers for me to sign. The first one was a bank account mandate for my copy signature. The account at the local branch of Barclays, under the heading of the Fantail Furies, would have *five thousand pounds* deposited in it within a few days for sundry expenditure such as shirts and petrol for the mini-bus and stuff, and I was the *only* one eligible to sign for it! Then he said a cheque book would be issued within days for me to use on rugby business only. His Finance Director would expect a monthly breakdown of costs and would show me how to fill in the expenses sheet…'

Ginnie just shook her head in wonder before taking a drink of her coffee.

'Aggy,' she said after a suitable period had passed when her friend had just nodded at her in shiny-eyed approval. 'Did you *know* any of this was coming?'

'No, not at all but I'm not surprised. He did ask me last night at home all about you and the proposed team but I thought it was just polite conversation over dinner because he knew I was your friend and was keen to play for the team myself.'

Ginnie stirred the dregs in her cup while she glanced at her notes.

'There's more?' Aggy asked leaning forward.

Ginnie moved her head from side to side as if she couldn't believe what she was about to say.

'He asked me how much I'd spent so far on the advertisement and interview room at the hotel. I told him it was sixty pounds plus VAT for the ad and two-hundred and forty for the room for three days including next Saturday. Within a couple of minutes Madeleine was back with three-hundred and fifty pounds in cash and a petty cash voucher for me to sign when she handed it over. Aggy! Can you believe this, I've got back every penny I have spent so far and a further five grand in a bank account for future team expenditure…!'

Aggy nodded sagely. As the recipient of her father's love and generosity for her entire life, none of this surprised her.

'I told him that it was never my intension to get back anything. I was happy to spend a few quid getting the thing off the ground and then see how it went by charging each of the girls a couple of quid each week to cover expenses. One thing's for certain,' said Ginnie. 'This wouldn't have happened without your help. Thank you.'

'Don't thank me, just get on and do what you have to with the team so we can all roll in the mud with impunity and too hell with the consequences.'

There was one small matter that Ginnie didn't mention to her friend. Claude had been insistent that his daughter's place in the team was earned purely on merit. How could Ginnie *ever* replace her unless it was injury driven?

Chapter Six

'Just a small-town girl livin' in a lonely world
She took a midnight train goin' anywhere...'

Ginnie had poured herself a generous glass of Sainsburys
Merlot as soon as she got home that Monday evening
and whirled around her small kitchen as she belted out
the old Journey standard which was number one on her
Spotify list.

'A singer in a smoky room
A smell of wine and cheap perfume.'

She stuck her nose in the glass with the tune then took a
gulp before spinning round and striking a pose using the
half empty glass as a microphone. That miserable old
couple upstairs would be banging on the floor again at
the noise but sod 'em, it had been a very good day and
she was celebrating.

'For a smile they can share the night
It goes on and on, and on, and on...
'Don't stop believin' hold on to the feelin'
Streetlights, people, don't stop believin'
Hold on streetlights people...'

Her mobile was humming away on the small table. She
stopped twirling and switched off her laptop through

which her tune was playing and glanced at the caller number; it was a new one to her. Another good gulp emptied the glass and she picked up the mobile.

'Is that Ginnie?' said an unfamiliar but friendly female voice.

'Speaking'

'This is Vera Godwin, Director of ladies rugby at Supermarine. I've just had my younger sisters Sarah and Mollie round for a cup of tea singing your praises, so thought I call and wish you luck and see if there's anything I can help you with?'

This day just keeps on getting better Ginnie thought.

'Hi Vera; its good of you to call, I hope it's okay that your sisters are joining my squad?'

'No problem at all. Matter of fact it helps me out because, as they may have mentioned, there can be bad feeling about the coach always picking her sisters to play – despite the salient fact that they are both automatic selections due to how good they are. The problem this year is that we have so many girls, right now there are forty-four signings for the coming season. So many that I am going to run two teams this year, a first and second fifteen, which was another reason for my call…'

'Oh?'

'Well, my second fifteen will be like your team, a mixture of experience and complete novices so, after say 4 or five weeks of initial training we'll both need to test them against similar opposition. What say we have a friendly game or two when you're ready?'

'Brilliant idea,' Ginnie said as this day just kept on improving. 'Lets make it a home and away fixture to see just how well we're both doing.'

They chatted on for a few minutes with Vera promising to email the contact details of the firm who supplied the Supermarine shirts and other kit such as gum shields and sports bras. She also reminded Ginnie to get two different colours of training vests for when the squad is put into two groups for practice or touch games. Ginnie also asked her about girls playing during their menstrual cycle.

'It's a minefield.' Vera replied. 'The big women's soccer teams and England's Red Roses are doing a lot of work on it but nothing much has come down to our level yet. What I always do is make a note of when each girl is due and the effect it has on each one. Some can play through it; some find it a minor inconvenience and some are completely debilitated. That's why you'll always need at least a half a dozen extra's as each game approaches just in case. Lindsey Chene will have a good grasp on how to cope with it...'

'You know Lindsey?' Ginnie said surprised...

'I know *of* her and how badly treated she was at Reading Bellfield Road Ladies. As you'll soon realise, there are no secrets in this still rather small local world of women's rugby and Lindsey's dismissal was a case in point.'

'She said it was due to her age?'

'She's right, it undoubtedly was, but their loss is your gain, she's a good catch and will be a great help to you...'

After Vera had rung off Ginnie poured herself another Merlot. The bottle was now half empty and by the time she had eaten something and watched a little television, would be drained of every drop. Note to self, don't get into a habit of drinking too much, especially with Lindsey, she had a problem with booze and needed to get over it, but, in the meantime, great days like this don't come along that often so needed celebrating. Feeling exhilarated by events and a little inebriated by the Merlot as she got into bed, she suddenly had a thought about a remark of Heidi Prager's when Ginnie had asked her about having a shrink.

'Yeah, so do most of my focked-up well-orf friends... but then, they don't get a smack in the eye and kicked in the twat for their phobias.'

When Ginnies fit of giggling finally subsided she raised her glass of bedtime wine and silently toasted the future of the Furious Fannies and its standout players and personalities.

This was going to be a hell of a lot of fun, wasn't it?

*

The week crawled by. Ginnie emailed the sports supply company Vera sent her and got back a detailed online catalogue. Her and Aggy had decided on the team colours of pink and black weeks ago. Women's match shirt sizes came in small, medium, large, extra-large and 'special measurement' with art work for logos etc. to be supplied. Next season when they started playing in a league where shirt colours might clash with the away side needing to change, another set of differently coloured playing shirts would be required but that could wait. As per Vera's reminder she also ordered for immediate delivery thirty training bibs, fifteen in blue and fifteen in red. That way they would have plenty of spares. Thanks to the bank account now set up in their names she could pay for everything immediately without touching her own limited cash. Sports bras required bust sizes and gum shields in general sizes that needed moulding individually in hot water. Before ordering the actual playing shirts in their distinctive black and pink quarters with 'The Fantail Furies' over the left pink breast and 'Sponsored by Wessex Mutual Building Society' in light blue around the top of an oblong rugby ball over a fantail design on the right black side, Ginnie had a think. Undoubtedly, they would be become known as the Furious Fannies or even the Fannies but decorum of a sorts required the correct name on the shirts, especially as now they were linked to the mighty Wessex company sponsorship. Perhaps she should keep the 'Fannies' off the shirts and let it just become the popular nickname that was already taking on a life of its own. The shorts were black and the socks pink and black hoops and innitially each girl would be providing their own playing boots, trainers, and tracksuits for training. This, according to Vera, was normal. If anyone – like perhaps Romany – found these purchases difficult Ginnie would pay for them out of the fund. On second thoughts she would buy these for the speedy little traveller anyway, perhaps through Louise.

On the Thursday morning Aggy brought a nerdy looking young man in rimless spectacles and a number one trim on his tightly shorn head to her desk and introduced him as Julien, a designer from the Wessex in-house Graphic Design Studio. Her father had agreed over dinner with her the previous evening that the artwork for the shirt logos should be professionally done in-house and Julien went away with some sketches and idea's and promised to have the designs mocked up within a day or two.

As she left Ginnie's desk Aggy gave her a wink. 'There's nothing ephemeral about this rugby side, we're here to stay and it's working engine is you and I...a partnership,' she said. 'You keep getting and wooing the recruits and I'll work the parental internal requirements...'

Which was all very well Ginnie thought watching Aggy's distinctive hip sashay as she walked away; until you don't make the team sheet for one reason or another? Let's hope that's a freighted clash that never happens and Ginnie can keep a lid on her 'Peppery' temper with her friend and new work rugby confident. Aggy's contribution was vital because of her father's position and her playing ability but every day now Ginnie was growing into the founder and player role she had determined for herself right from the off. It may have begun as a partnership but Ginnie was determined not to lose control and continue to be pivotal to the processes.

As for that other new Aggy word, *ephemeral*, she would look it up when she got home.

After lunch Ginnie emailed Lindsey Chene with a map and arranged to meet her at the training facility on the following Sunday morning to show her around and discuss the then team members, and given that at her current rate of progress she should get another four or five at the Saturday interviews they should have a near full complement, ovulation, partners, husbands, parents, grandpa and all the other problems that came with them.

'It's Sonja with a 'j' and van with a small 'v' and Leer as in a suggestive look,' Sonja van Leer said introducing herself in a familiar way that she had obviously done before. Her accent was very clearly South African and she was the first interview on the second Saturday.

'Okay Sonja with a 'j'' Ginnie said smiling at the bright, breezy, and willowy lady with long dark hair and faded denim jeans and jacket who walked into her room and gave her a strong handshake. 'Putting the leer to one side for now, sit down and tell me how you're going to make my rugby team unbeatable...'

Sonja sat and thought for a moment then took a deep breath and began.

'First off I've been in this country for three English winter months now and have never been so bloody cold in my life...' Bloody came out as bleddy. 'So, I've got to keep moving just to stay warm and that makes me a girl of non-stop action. Secondly, I am a full-time live-in carer for a ninety-six-year-old lady in Marlborough who keeps me on the go from morning to night – and sometimes through the night – and since the house she lives in has four flights of stairs and she hardly ever leaves the top floor and the kitchen is on the ground floor, I've got the fitness of a hungry cheetah running down a wounded springbok. And thirdly and most importantly...'she paused to catch her breath and flick the long coil of dark hair from over her right eye where it had fallen.

'Thirdly, I'm thirty-two years old now and played for a South African ladies rugby team called the Durban Belles for six years as a back-row forward. It was a good team in a competitive league and I'd still be there playing for them now but for an abusive husband followed by a messy divorce and a year's harassment from the slimy bastard who, even after the legal separation, still wouldn't leave me alone, so I came over here to get away from him. Luckily, we didn't have any kids. There it all is in a nutshell. So, that's my story Ginnie, what's yours?'

'You,' Ginnie said quietly hoping for emphasis, 'simply have to join my team because you're perfect for it in every respect…and here's why.'

When Sonja with a 'j' left both had done a brilliant job convincing the other, and on Ginnie's provisional positional list she had Sonja with a 'j' down as an open side flanker, another important position filled. The care of the old lady wasn't a problem for training because Sonja had her in bed by six thirty every evening and for games on a Saturday afternoon she was entitled to a day off each week when another girl would relieve her.

The next one, in what was almost expectantly becoming the incipient trough that followed the glorious peak, was a shy, timorous little girl of sixteen called Pamela Goncharov who had studied ballet and was taking her 'O' Levels. In truth Ginnie couldn't see the grit, stature and drive she was looking for in this shy little thing that had crept through the door like a timid mouse, and used age as her reasoning for not accepting her.

'Drop me an email this time next year and we'll get together again and re-evaluate,' she said seeing the crestfallen Pamela to the main door like a mother hen.

It was Ellie's day off and there was another thirtyish lady in the blue two-piece uniform on the reception desk called Maggie. 'I don't suppose you fancy playing ladies rugby, do you, Maggie?' Ginnie said to her by way of introduction as she walked back to her room.

The instant look of distaste that flicked across Maggie's face told Ginnie she'd made a wrong call.

'No thanks love, can't stand the game to be honest. Too aggressive what with all that charging around screaming, cursing, and shouting, I like my pastimes simple and quiet, dog walking and a bit of embroidery in me spare time and an occasional glass of sherry and that's about it...'

Embroidery, dog-walking, and sherry – old fashioned and perfectly acceptable bucolic past-times that were okay– unless you had suddenly become an aggressive rugby union recruiter looking for female warriors. Still, you can't win 'em all, Ginnie shrugged and went back to her room and her 'screaming, cursing and shouting' recruitment campaign.

Cassandra (Cassie) Betts was next and if ever a woman and her 'sport' was custom made to lighten Ginnies mood this was her. Olive skinned with a perfect short-cut afro halo of blond dyed hair and dressed in a purple track suit with matching gleaming and new white trainers she walked confidently into the room wafting baby oil and good health and gently shook Ginnies hand.

'I'm told that when I shake hands with ladies, I have to be gentle,' she said in a quiet Welsh-accented voice sitting down, 'otherwise I can break fingers.'

Ginnie couldn't help the arches of surprise her eyebrows made.

Cassie responded immediately. 'I'm a body builder. Under this tracksuit is probably one of the most perfectly formed female bodies, according to my husband Les who always baby oils me from tip to toe prior to a competition – and any other time he can – you will ever see.'

She reached inside the tracksuit and produced two A4 sized photos and passed them over Ginnies table. The first one was a glossy black and white shot of a glisteningly oiled, olive bodied and serious-faced Cassie in the briefest white bikini top and minute diamond pieced thong on a stringed bottom. The pose was the traditional body builder one of both beautifully muscled arms stretched straight out from the shoulders with elbows and wrists bent to almost touch the shoulders with one leg forward of the other forming a side-on pose at the bottom dominated by enormously knotted muscles everywhere, especially her thigh muscles. Her breast-less, narrow-waisted entire body was ribbed and honed to perfection that glowed with the oil Les had rubbed in before the shot. Under this photo was another A4 black and white photo showing Cassie in the same pose but this time with a broad smile, wearing a neckless of medals around her neck and around her on the floor a forest of silver cups and certificates in picture frames.

'Wow,' exclaimed Ginnie tapping the photos. 'All this and you want to play local ladies *rugby*?'

Cassie shrugged. 'I started off at fiftteen by becoming a weightlifter in Cardiff. My Dad was a Welsh Champion and so my brother and I followed him into the sport. By the time I was nineteen I knew I didn't have the necessary dedication it took. Les had come along by then and we wanted to get married and the hours required in the gym each day were difficult, especially as I had to work in a petrol station as well. We got married and settled in Tredegar where Les worked as a Sales Rep for an animal feed company calling on farms and wholesalers. Then he got promoted to Manager for Wales and the South West of England and we moved to Swindon. So now Cassie girl is straight outta Swindon…'

Ginnie grinned along with her; it was difficult not to.

'Not Compton?' She said showing she understood.

'Nah, a yokel from Swindinium now. Anyway, I missed the working out with the weights and it was something I could do at home in my own time…'

She paused for a moment.

'Does Les do it with you?' Ginnie asked looking down at the two photos again…

Cassie laughed. 'Nah, he's built like a pipe cleaner and can't stand physical exercise. Sticks to rubbing me down with the baby oil…' Her face went studiedly serious. 'See, we can't have kids so body building became a bit of a substitute for me. Then I got good at it and started to win competitions until we moved up here.'

'I can see that,' Ginnie said tapping the photo with the medals, cups, and certificates. 'So, getting back to my question, why rugby?'

Cassie was silent for a while as she thought about her answer.

'Body builders,' she said suddenly, 'are, in the main, a conceited bunch only interested in their own muscle definition. We'll spend hours working on a particular group of muscles then spend the rest of the week looking at that section of the body in the mirror. Glorification of one's own body is all and, quite frankly now I've won pretty much everything I could…' She nodded down at the photos, 'It also gets harder as you get older and body building contests have become a back-biting turdfest of snide remarks, steroids and other muscle enhancing drugs if you want to win, or maybe it always has been like that, although I always managed to avoid that stuff *and* remain competitive. Anyway, I've just had enough. I'm thirty-four now and I'm bored with it and the whole business of mirror body vanity. I'm fit and can still work out, we have a gym at home, but it's time to move on. Anyway, rugby, as was dinned into us at school, is the national sport of Wales, Gareth Edwards, Millennium Stadium, Bread of Heaven and all that patriotic Welsh stuff.'

'What does Les say about this?'

'He's cool about it so long as he can still slather on the baby oil...'

'You can't slather oil on for a rugby game' Ginnie said.

'Good' said Cassie with a grimace. 'I'm sick of the smell and greasy feel of the bloody stuff. Anyway, he can still get his oily kicks in the privacy of our own home.'

'Can you run and catch a rugby ball?'

Cassie thought for a moment.

'I can learn,' she said flexing her beautifully muscled shoulders.

That's two of us then, thought Ginnie putting a 'yes' alongside Cassie's name and a question mark under the position she might play but with muscles like hers propping up a front row of the scrum was the most likely.

There was then a no-show followed by a couple more of whom one, a fit twenty – five-year-old medium height and slim Anglo-Indian girl called Gita Rodrigues who played squash, was of interest and Ginnie put her down to attend training. That gave the team a Gina, Gita, and Ginnie – more fun with the play calls there when they get going.

The other and final booked interview, a forty-four-year-old woman who claimed she was as fit as a fiddle and good with a rugby ball in her hands, was a no-no and although Ginnie let her down as gently she could thinking guiltily as she did so that she was being ageist the same as Lindsey Chine's Directors had been at Reading, the pronounced limp that this lady walked in and out with was proof that it was the correct decision. At the very least two functioning legs were a necessity.

And that was it; the interviews from the ad were over. Ginnie had eighteen potential players plus Lindsey Chene as coach and Sherry Moyes, the gender fluid factotum who she still hadn't made up her mind about. It was a couple short of her target but the calibre was way above what she had envisaged. There may well be a couple more to come from the hockey team with the pervy sex pest coach and she still had a couple more ideas where others could come from. Add in the generosity of Claude Dillon with her allocation of funds and usage of the training ground, vehicle, and facilities, and it had been a very successful start.

Now all she had to do was learn to become a rugby player and captain herself, and since the captain was expected to be one of the standout players, her next task – to learn how to play the game well herself in a few short weeks – was arguably twice as difficult.

Chapter Seven

Monday morning found Ginnie sitting at her new work desk trying hard to concentrate on the job that paid for everything but, as usual since the interviews failing to get her mind away from rugby and the excellent recruits she had found so far. Madeleine Moody, CEO Dillon's secretary, didn't help by ringing and asking her to pop up and see her and when she had time, which was, of course, immediately, and where Ginnie was presented with a folder containing two cheque books, a debit card, a statement to the effect that five big ones sat in the freshly opened account named as The Fantail Furies, and a bank mandate showing her copy signature and stating that she was the only one authorised to use it.

Now it was real. Real money in the shape of £5,000 in an account accredited to The Fantail Furies that only she could spend and would immediately do so by paying out for the kit she had ordered. To celebrate, she sat at her desk and started to make a list of training neseccities and had no sooner written down 'six Gilbert rugby balls and four kicking tees' when Aggy, who had her own small office off the large open plan Customer Services section, appeared alongside.

'You have an inbuilt sense of when I'm not actually doing what I'm employed to do,' Ginnies said with a smile. 'When you're the boss of this lot it will be impossible to sneak off for a pee without getting docked for it.'

Aggy grinned back at her and waggled her index finger.

'Qualis pater, talis filia.'

'Meaning...?'

'It's Latin for 'like father like daughter.'

'What are you doing lunchtime?' Ginnie asked getting away from the high-brow stuff.

'Nothing, what do you have in mind?'

'I thought we might go down to the Sports shop in town and purchase a few needy items.' Ginnie flashed the cheque book and debit card at her and used the one word of Latin that she *had* understood. '*Pater* has made good on his promise and I have funds to burn.'

At twelve – thirty they roared off down into Swindon in Aggy's blue BMW M3. She was an impatient driver and swore mightily if anyone got in her way and then tailgated them until they turned off in disgust. Once inside the Sports Emporium as it was called, Ginnie asked the young male assistant if she could see the manager.

'I am he.' Replied the grinning youth pointing to his badge that bore the legend of Allan Dix– Manager 'What can I do for you?'

Ginnie explained that she was forming a ladies rugby team and would like to open an account.

'Ummm...we're cash only really unless the account is a well-known local employer who is likely to use it a lot.'

Placing her hand on Aggy's arm to keep her quiet because she had sensed her bridled start at his statement, Ginnie leaned in close to the doubtful face of Allan Dix.

'How does the Wessex Mutual Building Society grab you *Mister Dix*? She snarled adding a curled lip of disdain to his unfortunate obvious name. 'Three thousand *local* employees, seven and a half million *account* customers, two football teams plus badminton and basketball, two tennis courts, and an all-weather athletics track...*plus* she put up her hand to stifle his pathetic reply because he had attempted to open his mouth...'my twenty-strong ladies rugby team who also have *their own pitch...*'

He knew when he was beaten and so shut up and just looked at Ginnie like a beaten puppy awaiting the next slap.

'Big enough for you or do we go to the other sports shop in town with our business?'

With both girls glaring at him with daggers drawn, Allan Dix folded and began to mumble and stammer.

'I'm...s...sorry. I've only b...been here t...two... weeks and don't know m...my way round...'

From that point on he was putty in their hands and they left a half an hour later with six Gilbert rugby balls – pumped up and ready to go, a waterproof marker pen for writing on them, a rugby ball pump and four kicking tees. Just for good measure Ginnie told him to prepare a fully documented receipt including the overall ten percent discount and she would pay in cash with her new debit card.

'And you can stick your account where it hurts' Ginnie said marching purposefully out of the door. 'And if any of my girls come in here to buy *any* rugby or other sports gear make sure you give them maximum discount and proper service, *if* they ever come in here after this bloody mess.'

With Aggy carrying the balls in a net they managed to suppress their laughter until they got outside and in Abby's car where they collapsed with tears rolling down their cheeks.

'Poor old Dixie,' said Aggy starting the car when they had retained a little equilibrium. 'Probably hand in his notice after that on the basis that the town is full of screaming rugby harpies all coming in to hassle him.'

'Bloody idiot,' Ginnie scowled. 'Dix is a name that suits him'…. the plural anyway.' She raised her voice to a falsetto and paraphrased the young shop manager's opening statement.

'We're cash only really unless the account is a well-known local employer who is likely to use it a lot.'

Which started them both off again and Aggy missed a turning off Swindon's only well-known feature, the islands within an island known locally as the Magic Roundabout.

Having transferred the balls, marker, and pump and kicking tees to Ginnies car they grabbed a quick sandwich from the canteen and went their separate ways. When Ginnie got to her desk there was a folder of full-colour artwork awaiting her with a compliment slip attached from Julien in the Graphics Design Section. A quick glimpse left Ginnie breathless, it was beautiful and made the whole project somehow even more real. She quickly put the folder down the side of her desk as one of her Customer Service Assistants approached her. She would study the artwork at home tonight; in the meantime, there was real work to be done.

Before she left the office that evening Ginnie placed a carefully worded A4 sheet that she had prepared on her computer on the main notice board outside the canteen.

Underneath a rough picture of a rugby ball with wings and wearing a small frilly tutu and a big lip-sticked smile across its length sailing high between two uprights and paraphrasing her original ad in the Swindon Evening Advertiser – without the asterisks and raunchy references it simply said that a ladies rugby team was being formed to play and train at the company's sports complex and would any interested ladies between the ages of sixteen – lower than the eighteen of the original – and thirty five, contact Ginnie on her internal extension or mobile.

At home that evening she ignored the last bottle of Merlot winking enticingly at her from the kitchen worktop, and put on her tracksuit and trainers and went for a run. It was time to begin her personal quest for fitness. She didn't want to turn up for the first training session scheduled for next Tuesday huffing and puffing like an old steam engine after the first few minutes. The tracksuit and trainers were a throwback to the boyfriend before the last whose name was Mark, and who'd started off as they all seemed to by flexing a slim, well-muscled body in a bar where Ginnie was enjoying a drink with friends late on Friday evening. Having lifted his shirt and twisted a perfectly formed six pack in her direction he casually asked her if she'd like a drink. Three weeks later he had somehow manoeuvred his presence out of his mates flat and into hers where he'd pretty much taken over, or at least his messy way of life had. He was a regular runner and a one hundred sit-ups a day type to maintain the six-pack and went jogging with a group every Saturday and Sunday morning, He persuaded Ginnie to run with him a couple of evenings every week as well, hence the nearly new tracksuit and trainers she'd bought. In truth she rather liked the regular jogging and was beginning to gain a certain level of fitness before Mark, complaining about an old football injury to his knee, began to stop running. Soon afterwards the sit-ups stopped and he began to put on weight. He was unemployed 'just for a while to get his bearings' and was often to still be found in bed when she got home of an evening. Add to this the mess he made everywhere around what had been her neat and tidy little flat, and the fact that he never seemed to stop eating and he didn't contribute a penny to their food, alcohol, and occasional nights out, and it soon became apparent to Ginnie that, once again, she'd picked another loser. All of which she might have put up with if he'd been any good in bed, but despite her usual slave-like adherence to his sexual fantasies, the idle bastard had the staying power of a retired gnat.

So, one Sunday while he was out having a lunchtime pint with his mates with the twenty quid he'd bummed from her, he came back to find all his smelly clothes and other bits and pieces in his bags outside the flat door. His persistent ringing on the door bell brought a determined Ginnie with her arms folded purposefully across her chest to the chained gap through which she told him in no uncertain terms they were done and to fuck off out of her life and stay fucked off.

Although Ginnie didn't realise it at the time, his summary rejection was another sign that the 'Peppery' Ginnie of her youth was making a determined comeback. There would be others.

And now the almost unused tracksuit and trainers would be put to good use.

The next useless male item to enter her bed was an older divorcee called Adam and although she didn't make the mistake of allowing him to spend the few nights they were together at her flat, she had mistakenly thought that as he had been married, he would at least be able to handle her sexual needs.

Wrong again. All he did was sob his heart out about how he missed his former wife and wanted to get back together with her. Then, after the break-up with Ginnie he threatened to post online some nude and suggestive tongue-lolling pictures she had foolishly let him take in an unguarded and tender moment. Although he then relented over a drink, she still didn't trust him and closed her Snapchat, Tinder, and Facebook accounts. Being seen suggestively naked by people didn't bother her much, perhaps some slight embarrassment would be faced at work, but it was her mum, dad and brother and his wife eyeballing them in their quiet lives causing a family sexual upset that was a concern, because some vindictive sod, probably a friend or the dickhead divorcee in question, was sure to let them know where to look.

Thus far she had not tried any of the online dating sites that seemed to be springing up all over the place, with her abysmal track record she could pick a loser for free and fuck up a relationship without it being with a total stranger that cost her money to meet.

After a couple of gentle miles jogging around the darkened streets and surprised at just how comfortable it had felt, she showered, opened the Merlot and with a towel round her wet hair settled down with a glass and the six rugby balls and the waterproof marker pen. Carefully writing 'Property of the Fantail Furies' on each she admired her handiwork, it was another proud milestone. Opening the artwork, she then studied the clean and expert lines and black and pink colours with which Julien had produced the shirt, socks, and short designs.

As the quick glance she'd afforded them in her office had shown, the designs were beautiful. Having studied the perfection of the shirt logo's carefully she propped them up against her far wall and raised her glass to them. They were hers to keep as Julien would provide finished artwork and sizes for the kit maker and she might even get the designs framed, they would look good on her walls.

Her dreams that night had the loud background of *'Sing Low Sweet Chariot'* by the many tens of thousands of the Twickenham faithful as she glided down the centre of the pitch sidestepping murderous tackles by beefy, snarling women with huge hands until…as she was about to dot the ball down under the posts for the try of the century to a screaming crescendo of noise, she suddenly woke up.

If only, she thought getting up for a pee.

*

The following morning in the office she rang Stan Mackay and asked if he could help her. Stan was the Manager of Building Services at Wessex which included cleaning, laundry, toilets, decorating and grounds maintenance. Affectionately known as Stan the Wink and a Pint Man, he occupied a large cavernous warehouse at the back of the main offices where he and his staff shuffled about taking delivery and racking pallets of toilet rolls, cleaning fluids, office furniture of all types, carpets, mats waste paper bins, light bulbs various and office abrasive and smooth floor pads for the giant cleaning machines, soaps and spare dispensers, emulsion paint and rollers and the thousands of other bits and pieces required to keep a huge building like theirs clean, germ free and functional. Ginnie had met the urbane and ever smiling portly Sam four months ago when her Customer Services department had moved into the larger open plan office they now occupied. With a friendly wink the near retirement Stan the Wink and a Pint Man had arranged for Ginnie to have a small round meeting table next to her desk with four chairs.

'Managers only' he'd said tapping the table with an exaggerated wink as one of his assistants put it in place. 'You owe me a pint.'

'You say that to all the girls, Stan, but many thanks anyway,' Ginnie had replied.

She had never seen him in a pub or at any one of the firms parties or get-togethers so had been unable to repay him. Internal rumour had it that he was teetotal and it was all a pose. Now she wanted more.

'Ah' Sam had said with a warm chuckle when she introduced herself on the internal phone system. 'You've called to buy me that pint you owe me for the table and chairs.'

'Memory like an elephant' Ginnie had said. 'How about we make that two pint's and a packet of crisps?'

Five minutes later she had the promise next day of two new sanitary towel dispensers in each of the home and away changing rooms at the sports complex with the requisite disposal bins underneath and a promise to keep them stocked and tidy.

'They'll be emptied and restocked each week the same as all the others in this building' Sam had said. 'The changing rooms are already on the weekly cleaning roster for every Monday because of the weekend football so they'll be spick and span regardless of who uses them when you need them on a Tuesday, Thursday, and match days. Just you make sure that I get an invite to the first home game. I like a bit of rugby and a load of women rolling around in the mud would get me all excited for the rest of the weekend.'

'Only if you're gonna give me a wink as well?' she said.

'I've got both eyes closed as we speak,' he said with a chuckle.

Ginnie thanked the old boy profusely – Stan was sixty-four if he was a day – and promised she'd let him know everytime they had a game. It would be a sad day for Wessex when Stan the Wink and a Pint Man Mackay retired, regardless of how good his replacement was.

Having put the phone down Ginnie began gazing into space. It wasn't the first time she had come across a comment relating to the potential sexual allure to men of watching a group of women rolling around in the mud playing rugby. Gina McKinnon had mentioned it as a juicy turn-on for Dave, her ultra randy tankie husband when Ginnie had asked if he would be interested in helping with the training, and she herself had thought that the sinuously-bodied Ellie would attract men to the side-lines by just gliding around the pitch with or without the ball. And while providing a turn-on for men had not been any part of her reasoning for getting the project going, it had come up in passing a couple of times so she should keep the sexual attraction in mind when looking for people to come and watch their games and when trying to attract other sponsors.

Little did she know at this stage that her own personal relationship with her chief benefactor and the main alpha male sponsor, and who she worked for, would follow this route, and become a major fixation for him and her...

Chapter Eight

The week flew by as Ginnies real work-load, the important one that paid the bills and had nothing to do with rugby, increased hugely due to a customer service mailer her department had to organise to every account holder. The second one in six months, it advised of another 0.25% reduction in their savings account interest. Although it didn't say so an internal staff email from the Finance Director said it was due to the impact of Brexit and the new low rate of borrowing interest offered Wessex by the Bank of England.

The reasons didn't bother Ginnie that much. The logistics and costs of systematically getting out the hundreds of thousands of mailers she did understand and it took a lot of organising with six of her ten team members permanently occupied getting them all out the door.

Tuesday and Thursday evenings she went for a run again. She needed it to clear her mind after the frantic days of work and had, mistakenly, thought it would get easier after the first one went so well. Not a bit of it. On the Friday morning when all the company mailers had been safely despatched and with aching calf muscles from her run, she once again turned her thoughts to rugby and composed an email for each of her selected players thus far in respect of the first training session the followingTuesday. It gave each of them the address and postal code of the sports complex and mentioned copious car parking space, the suggested kit they bring along including boots if they had them, otherwise trainers, and a towel as hot showers would be provided. A tracksuit with a woolly top would also be useful as the early March evenings could get chilly, and beanies and or scrum caps, although not provided, were by personal choice. Sports bras however, would be provided with the shirts, shorts, and socks when the actual games started but if individuals wanted to wear one for training, they should bring it along. Sessions would start every Tuesday and Thursdays until the end of the season and begin every evening at six – thirty p.m. and aim to finish at nine p.m. Ginnie would also be bringing along their completed RFU playing ladies registration forms for signature and they would be introduced to Lindsey Chene, their coach and who would be taking the training sessions and, of course, meet their proposed teammates. She sent Romany Cutler's email to Louise George with an added PS that if the running Traveller couldn't get there Ginnie would pick her up at six-fifteen at the Hay Lane site. By return Louise replied that her granddad, Tink Cutler, would be bringing her in the scrap van and that *he* had also purchased a new pair of boots for her. On Lindsey's email Ginnie put a smiley Emoji and said she had bought six new rugby balls, a pump and kicking tees and would bring them along when they met at the sports complex on Sunday. As far as she knew tackle bags and a rhino scrimmaging machine were already there for their use and the pitch had been marked out and had lights. That jogged her memory to send an email to Jimmy Corbett, the new head groundsman who had replaced his former boss and total prat, Tony

Newton. Could he kindly ensure that the pitch and changing room lights were on every Tuesday and Thursday night from next Tuesday until the nights were light enough to train, and the hot water on because they were starting training that night? Within an hour she had also heard back from Lindsey saying she had found a flat in Swindon and would be moving in after they're visit to the sports complex on Sunday. Almost immediately a rather grovelling reply had come back from Jimmy to the effect that everything would be ready for her and not to hesitate if she needed anything else.

Power, she muttered to herself, such as that enjoyed by Claude Dillon, was reputed to be an aphrodisiac and with this sort of immediate acquiescence from his employee's she could see why.

She agonised for fifteen minutes over an email to Terry/Sherry Moyes, her gender-fluid factotum and in the end invited her along on the Tuesday. If the girls objected to her transitional presence, she would just have to tell her it was a no-go. Afterall, they would need him to drive the minibus as he was a qualified lorry driver and anyway, she'd binned any number of inadequate boyfriends so one more misfit wouldn't make much difference, notwithstanding his wig, potential penis tucking away operation or medium heeled sling-backs.

Receiving an eating-with-knives-and-forks-lunch sign from across the office from Aggy, she was just about to get up and join her when her internal phone rang.

'Is that Ginnie Joy?' A friendly female voice enquired. Ten minutes later she was sitting in the canteen with Aggy eating tuna and mayo sandwiches, when they were joined by the internal caller, a software development lady from Wessex Technical Services called Jenny Hynes. Jenny had seen Ginnies sheet on the notice board and was interested in joining up. Although it was hardly the slutglut Aggy had prophesised, every decently fit-looking girl was a plus; especially now that Ginnie almost had a full complement of the twenty she had originally started out looking for.

'You look pretty fit Jenny, d'you play any sports?'

'I used to be a mad keen gym bunny until my husband complained about the muscles and said I was getting stronger in the arms and shoulders than him and losing my femininity. So, then I resorted to spinning every second night to keep fit and lost the muscles...'

A quick flash of Cassie Betts body-building photo's crossed Ginnie's mind.

'Spinning...you mean like making wool and yarn and stuff on a wheel?'

Jenny chuckled. 'It's a term for riding a static bicycle at home to a set programme, you know like spinning the pedals. Keeps me fit and stops any unladylike bulges developing except in the leg's which is alright with the old man. He's twelve years older than me and much happier now that he doesn't have to worry about me throwing him out of an upstairs window.'

Jenny chuckled again and Ginnie and Aggy found themselves smiling with her.

'Know anything about rugby?' Aggy asked.

'Not a lot, my dad and three brothers were all about football at home and I didn't play any sports at school or uni. Too busy making cow eyes at the boys.'

'What university did you attend?' Aggy said sensing an educational sister.

'Essex, Computer Science degree and then straight here as a Technical Trainee; I've been at Wessex nine years now.'

'Do you have any children?' Ginnie asked getting away from the educational inferiority complex she always felt when universities were mentioned.

'Two girl's, fifteen and thirteen. Paul – my husband – was married before and lost his wife to cancer and came with the two girls when we got married. Suited me as I never wanted any kids so being a step-mum with a ready-made family was fine.'

'How do you feel about the aggression of rugby?'

'That's why I'm here today. Spending the entire working day immersed in the complexity of software coding and then having a couple of hormonal girls to contend with when I get home…phew.' She blew out her cheeks and shook her head negatively. 'Smashing around a rugby pitch with a like-minded group of girls seems the perfect way of letting off steam to me.'

'What are you doing next Tuesday night?' Ginnie said nodding at Aggy.

On the Saturday morning Ginnie went back into the Sports Emporium in Swindon, this time without Aggy. Mention by Louise George that Tink Cutler had bought a pair of rugby boots for Romany reminded her that she also needed some. When he heard the doorbell ring as she opened it, Allan Dix's face fell as he turned to see who it was and for a moment Ginnie thought he was going to run out the back of the shop and disappear. Instead, he gulped and forced an obsequious smile to his lips as he edged warily towards her.

'I need a pair of ladies rugby boots, size six,' she said evenly, proving that she'd come in peace this time.

'Ah,' he said heaving a visible sigh of relief that he wasn't going to get an instant mouthful this time of abuse. 'There are no rugby boots specifically made for ladies. For a size six I suggest we look at the kid's selection.'

Twenty minutes later she had a pair of Adidas Malice boots in bright scarlet with orange diagonal stripes at forty-five pounds, including two different lengths of studs, a stud key and spare laces. Dix had been particularly attentive even calling out from the back of the shop for his assistant to come and serve another couple of customers who had arrived when he was showing Ginnie the boots.

'Malice' she had muttered to him coyly reading from the box when trying them on. 'Suits me down to the ground, don't you think?'

Wisely he held his tongue.

Having paid for the boots in cash with money left over from the bundle Madeleine Moody had reimbursed her, Ginnie was about to leave when Dix asked her a question.

'Are you still recruiting for lady team members?'

'Possibly, do you know someone who is interested then?'

'I mentioned it to my girlfriend and she said it sounded like something she'd be interested in...she likes martial arts and has a black belt in judo.'

'Does she beat you up and throw you around?'

'All the time,' he said ruefully, 'seems to make her happy.'

No wonder Dixie had quelled when she walked into the shop, Ginnie mused. He was another man like Derek at the Advertiser when she went to place her advertisement. Work was the only place they could indulge in a little male posturing until they got home or the Peppery Ginnie and her mate Aggy happened along. She almost felt sorry for him, but only almost.

'Sounds like a girl after my own heart. What's her name?'

'Amanda Sawyer.'

'Email address?'

He told Ginnie and she copied the Tuesday night email to her that everyone else had received from her mobile with an addition welcome to the squad intro.

'Tell her I'll have a registration form with me on Tuesday. She doesn't have to join but can't play any games unless she does. It's to cover the insurance in case she gets injured.'

'Thank you…er…Ginnie.'

She turned to him by the door.

'There's just one other thing *Allan,*' she said sealing their newly forged accord with a glance at his name tag. 'Don't you dare sell any more scarlet Adidas *Malice* boots to any other lady in my group, they're for me only, call it the captains prerogative, okay?'

'From now on they're out of stock,' he said. 'You're the only lady with Malice.' His smirking face had given away his quiet pleasure at the retort.

'Careful now,' she said over her shoulder keeping the Peppery personality going 'Don't get *too* bloody flippant.'

When she got back to her car, she had a call from her mother asking her if she was too busy to call in at the weekend and said she would get back to her. Then back at the flat she had an email from Malorie, one of her Saturday night friends. There were four of them plus

Ginnie, Malorie, Sheila, Marie, and Bella and at least one Saturday a month, usually after payday they met for a few drinks in an Old Town pub before going on to a club or two. All were working girls in their mid to late twenties and single except Bella, who was engaged and planning marriage to an accountant called Tim in the summer. None of them knew or would be in the slightest bit interested in her rugby project, especially Malorie, who had had a rather over-large boob job done last year that might have helped with her pulling a man from time-to-time but was a couple of bouncy silicone-filled impediments when it came to charging around a rugby field.

In response to Malorie's email enquiring if Ginnie was 'up for it tonight' she paused over a cup of coffee in her little kitchen. Malorie would have also sent the same message to the other three and usually any three or four of the five would get dolled up and be at the pub at nine o'clock.

But tonight Ginnie, a stalwart attendee in the past, wouldn't be among them. She emailed Malorie that she had a family gathering tonight and wouldn't be able to make it. It was a white lie but senseless socialising was out until she got her rugby project up and running. Then she rang her mum back and said she would pop in for a cup of tea Sunday afternoon, so that diminished the porky she'd told Malorie...a little.

Their Saturday night girl's piss-ups had become a little futile and sad and nowadays always turned into lonely heart man-hunts as the alcohol went down – other than the faithfully engaged Bella who still joined in wholeheartedly with the drinking. The other four of them would invariably get legless on vodka shots or tequila slammers and taxi home in the early hours with an unsuitable but available man, before falling into bed with him for some overly quick drunken sex. Only to wake mid-morning having spent an uncomfortable night in one quarter of their own bed next to a snoring, muttering and smelly male who now had a hangover erection that was demanding further attention. He would then again squirt too quickly and go back to sleep while she crept around her own apartment trying not to disturb him. It had become a vacuous, frustrating process, with guilt seeming to factor in when she had finally got rid of him and showered away his stale odours and dried semen. Even then she had invariably still, as with her last two of Mark and Adam, entered a relationship with them. It was the triumph of hope over experience, an apt phrase she had read somewhere. In her case it was rarely a triumph and the experience had become a futile waste of effort and time. So, no more senseless socializing on Saturday nights but just in case she would remain on the pill because somewhere out there in the big wide world was a man who just might…a big, big might at that…have the answer and let's face it, a girl should hedge her bets when it comes to getting her rocks off without pregnancy, shouldn't she?

She then drove down to Sainsbury's and stocked up with some essentials including her now stable pasta and Merlot to accompany her quiet night in, then locked her apartment door, poured a serious glass of the red stimulation and added a bowl of pasta and some black pepper crackers to the tray, put her ancient but clean Paddington Bear jim jam's on and settled down in bed with her laptop to watch a rugby game online she had long promised herself.

One hour and forty-one minutes later she had watched the build-up and the entire 2016 Thirtieth Women's Varsity match at Twickenham. Her bottle of red stimulation juice was empty and there were cracker crumbs everywhere on her duvet...but she had the answer she was looking for. In the lowest scoring Oxford versus Cambridge female match ever in its history and after a tense finish close to the Oxford line, the dark blues had finally won by three points to nil. And Aggy, her friend and rugby confident, had come on as a substitute ten minutes into the second half at outside centre and played very well with three good line-breaking carries and any number of important tackles. Twice painfully staggering to her feet after multi-person mauls, Aggy finished the game covered in the famous Twickenham mud with her hands held triumphantly in the air, before having a big celebratory hug with the other girls in the Oxford team.

So, the oft references to 'her Varsity Twickenham blue' made by her friend were true, she was exactly what she had always said she was.

Not that Ginnie had ever *really* doubted her.

Had she?

The following morning, she got up early with a vacant head from the bottle of wine she had finished and went for a run. It wasn't raining and being a Sunday there were several other joggers about, all of whom seemed to be in a cheery and wavy mood. As the running was getting easier, she did a mile longer than before then got home and showered before eating a leisurely breakfast of muesli and kiwi fruit.

Running, muesli and kiwi fruit on a Sunday morning. Who was this saintly lady?

Then she printed out the team names with her notes and set off to meet Lindsey Chene at the sports complex.

Lindsey was waiting for her in the car park when she got there and after a friendly hug they walked towards the pitch. The lights around the edge were on an automatic timer switch Ginnie explained and would come on before dark and off at nine-thirty every night. If it was a dull afternoon, they could be over-ridden. As they walked along the crisp white lines towards the gleaming white tall uprights, two male football teams came streaming out of the changing rooms and made for the far pitch with its football posts at either end.

'That's good,' said Ginnie. 'It means the changing rooms are empty and we can have a look round without a load of testosterone-fuelled-banter from half-naked blokes.'

As they walked into the changing room they were joined by the younger one of the two remaining groundsmen, a vaguely familiar young man called Gavin who Ginnie had emailed on Friday asking if he would be there. Although she hadn't spoken to him at the time, Ginnie had first encountered Gavin and his new boss Jimmy Corbett when she had first come down here to be insulted by Tony Newton. Now he couldn't do enough to help her and walked them through the complex pointing out the storage cupboards where the tackle bags, cones and other training aids were kept, then bounced on the shiny blue Rhino scrimmaging machine.

'I'll make sure this and all the other stuff is out on the field every Tuesday and Thursday evening,' Gavin said. 'The lines will be repainted every two weeks unless heavy rain washes away the whitewash and let me know when you have a game on and me and Jim, the other and now chief groundsman, will put the flags out and goal post protectors on well before the game starts.'

'Looks as if it's hardly been used' Lindsey said patting the Rhino.

'It hasn't. The other lot didn't bother with it.'

He showed them the newly installed tampon machines and their bins – *two* to each changing room – and said there had been a fair bit of banter earlier when the men's football teams had seen them.

'I'll bet,' snarled Ginnie. 'Just make sure they get used to them and keep their grubby hands off or I'll make sure that *you* get the bloody blame.'

'Yes ma'am,' he replied quietly turning away, aware of who was behind the sacking of Tony Newton his former boss and just how much power this young lady had access to.

'Can we see the showers?' Lindsey asked.

They walked through the changing rooms which were festooned with clothing on pegs and shoes and sports bags on the floor, and into the clean and dry showers. Each changing room had ten individual showers in one long, white, and blue tiled wet room.

'Individual temperature controls here,' Gavin said pointing to the nob under the shower head.

'Have the hair dryers arrived yet?'

He opened a cupboard in the toilets section and pointed to a stack of new-looking boxes. 'One dozen in each changing room, each with a plug on ready to go, they came on Friday courtesy of Stan Mackay.'

'For the women's rugby squad use only.' Ginnie growled receiving a nod of acknowledgement.

Ginnie also made a mental note to thank Stan the Wink and a Pint Man Mackey on Monday.

'What do you think of the facilities?' Ginnie asked when they were sitting in her car.

'Bloody marvellous,' said Lindsey. 'As good, if not better than anything I've ever seen before and a proper groundsman on hand to do everything. When I first started, we used to change in the open in the freezing car park and shower when we got home. It's a long way from there to this. 'One thing's for certain, the girls won't be able to make any excuses about the facilities.'

'Talking of the girls,' Ginnie said getting out her list.

For the next hour they went through each player. Lindsey was particularly impressed with Sarah 'Rocky' Cook, the former pack leader with Supermarine and her sister Mollie. Aggy Dillon playing for Oxford in the Varsity match at Twickenham also got a thumb's-up as did Sonja van Leer's experience playing for the Durban Belles.

'She should also be good,' Lindsey said when Ginnie had been through Iona Pierce's notes, 'and these two' Lindsey tapped Gina McKinnon and her friend the PTI Avril Gordon. 'I've had army types before and they're always fit and respond to proper instruction and coaching.'

She was sceptical about Romany Cutler and the body builder Cassie Betts and the others all got a 'we'll just have to wait and see what we've got.'

Ginnie hesitated with Sherry/Terry before just shrugging and passing him by. She would see how he fitted in on Tuesday.

'What about you?' Lindsey said. 'Where do you see yourself in the team?'

'Captain and inside centre' replied Ginnie without hesitation. She had been expecting this question as she had with the interviews had decided to put a confident spin on it.

'And you haven't played any rugby before?'

Ginnie held Lindsey's gaze and then replied with more than a little defiance. 'No, but as you'll soon see I'm fit, aggressive and apart from needing some practise with ball handling skills, strategically aware of the role that needs playing.'

Lindsey held her hands up in a form of surrender.

'Okay, okay. I believe you. I've just seen your determination when dealing with Gavin the groundsman and if you can play rugby as well as you can organise and recruit these girls, we're both onto a winner.'

They went over a few more details then parted with a 'see you on Tuesday evening' and Ginnie drove over to see her mum.

Ginnie and her mum had never had an easy relationship. Unlike her quiet and studious older brother Robert, Ginnie had been rebellious from an early age and her mother, preferring the quiet life like her son, had simply let her daughter get on with it. As far as her father was concerned, he worked to keep a roof over their heads and that was the extent of his family involvement. The emotional side of parenthood seemed to pass him completely by and he looked on as these two babies grew rapidly into young adults with a mixture of perplexed indifference and occasional grumbles behind the highly held pages of the *Sun* newspaper. By the time she was fourteen Ginnie was making her own decisions on pretty much everything she ate, wore, studied or did. As Robert worked his way diligently through his GCSE's, Ginnie, two years his junior and way behind him in her educational application began to figure out where boys fitted into the scheme of things...especially older boys. The average fifteen-year-old boy at school didn't interest her; they had no money, little in the way of interesting conversation unless it was about last night's Premiership football match, and, something, she had begun to acknowledge increasingly as a need became apparent, knew little or nothing about sex despite a propensity to boast to each other of their nightly conquests. And since she put the barest effort into her own exams her results were, as she had guessed they would be, way down there at the bottom of the tables when they were posted on the school notice board. So, university or anything other than the lowest form of stopgap in further education was out.

When she was almost sixteen and fully aware that, as a budding nymphet she would probably have to take the initiative to lose her virginity, she shamelessly promising an apprenticed baker by the name of Maxwell Wallace the shag of a lifetime. The consequence of her boldness was that she lost her virginity in a Sunday afternoon summer field of buttercups to Maxie boy. He was nineteen, gentle in manner and deed, had a ropey old car and knew how to unhurriedly roll on a condom. Afterwards, although it hadn't lived up to the hype – a lesson there that seemed to have lasted her a lifetime – she felt a superior knowledge to the other girls at her comprehensive school and who, like many of the boys, were given to boastful references to how many times they'd 'had it' the night before when most of them would have run a mile if a raised penis had been waved anywhere near them, let alone to be taught how to gently roll a rubber on its pulsating length. It was five or six frustrating and quick relationships later that she finally appreciated the 'unhurried' manner that Maxie the baker boy had brought to her first and many other sexual encounters with him, but by then he was history. Her problem with him was the baking, powdery white flour he always had about him, in his car, clothes and body and even his hair. It even trickled out of his pockets from time to time and once, when he'd got his wallet out to remove a condom, he had to blow the flour from the packet.

Baking flour, boring old industrial quantities of low-grade bread-making powdery crushed wheat with, according to Maxie, a gluten content of between 9-11%, was important. His unhurried sexual mannerisms were entirely self-raising, he'd said with a leer stroking his stiffie before letting her roll on the condom as he taught her to, and entirely due to the many patient hours he spent each week kneading dough.

The sight and slight smell of flour still, after all these years, turned her stomach or, as Maxie had said at the time, perhaps it was the smell of burning rubber.

When she was seventeen and one month out of school, she used her Saturday supermarket job money to buy some clothes in a charity shop and attended a job interview at Honda. She got the job as a trainee accounts assistant, ditched Maxie boy and went on the pill determined to never look or roll on another slimy condom.

Strangely enough now, after something like twelve years of self-taught independence from her parents, including part-time college because, at eighteen she'd finally come to understand that without some educational qualifications she'd never get a better job, she had moved from Honda to Wessex, got her own car and a mortgage on her apartment with her employer – her mother had been ringing to ask her opinion about all manner of girly things lately such as clothes and make-up. The rapprochement – a French word that Aggy used and Ginnie quite liked and remembered, and had taught herself to say correctly – seemed a genuine attempt to make up for being so remote for so long. Elizabeth – her mother's name – had turned fifty just six months ago and that might well have been a contributing factor, plus the fact that her brother Robert and his equally nice and quiet wife Emily, also a school teacher, had just announced that they were expecting their first baby. Fifty and about to become a grandmother, two milestones that could possibly have caused – and here it comes again – the latest rapprochement with her daughter.

She got to the house where she had been brought up in Stratton, a peaceful suburb of Swindon chiefly notable by the site and smell of the Arkell's Brewery and, just down the road close to the Honda factory where she had worked, the main local Crematorium, about mid-afternoon. Her mother would have cooked a roast dinner and placed it on the table at one o'clock. They would now both have eaten and be anchored in front of the television with her father hidden behind the Sunday tabloid he read every word of every day.

'Look what the cat's dragged in' he said dropping the paper a fraction so he could see who had walked into the lounge.

'Ginnie!' her mum said getting to her feet and coming to give her a hug, 'cup of tea and something to eat?

There's a nice piece of pork with crackling in the kitchen that's still warm.'

'Tea will do fine, mum' she said stroking the ears of Chilly, their very old black and white cat who had come to say hello.

Later they retired to the kitchen so as not to disturb her father who had dozed off with the paper spread across his burgeoning stomach.

'It was our wedding anniversary yesterday,' Elizabeth said pouring the tea. 'Thirty years.'

'What's the symbol for thirty years?' Ginnie asked adding milk to their teas.

'Pearl' replied Elizabeth.

'Purgatory more like' a gruff voice came from the lounge showing that, as usual he wasn't asleep or reading the paper and was listening to every word they said.

'Shut up Henry,' Elizabeth said sharply towards the open door and then to Ginnie 'he forgot as usual.'

'I was busy' he said to the crackle of the newspaper as he picked it up again.

After a half an hour and some desultory chatter with her mum interspaced with barbed grumbles from her father, Ginnie left. Their bickering and constant disagreements on all and every subject always got on her nerves quickly and she breathed a long sigh of relief in the car.

Two days to go before her diverse group of women assembled for the first training session. Two days before the cross-section of players, oddballs, misfits, and relatively normal young ladies that held a mirror up to the Wiltshire sisterhood she had recruited, got together to see if there was a rugby team in there somewhere fighting to get out. Was she sleepwalking into a toxic shit storm or making the category life change she had envisaged?

She would soon have the answer; Tuesday night couldn't come soon enough.

Chapter Nine

When Ginnie pulled into the sports complex car park at six o'clock on Tuesday evening, she was surprised to see that she wasn't the first one there...or the second. Lindsey Chene was already sitting in her car with Romany Cutler in the passenger seat.

Getting out and giving Ginnie a hug Lynsey pointed at Romany still in the passenger seat.

'Her grandpa dropped her off twenty minutes ago so rather than him hang around I sat her in with me. We've been catching up on her running everywhere...'

With a swish of fat tyres on the gravel surface a big red Jaguar F Pace driven by a handsome young man with a haughty looking middle-aged women looking straight ahead in the front passenger seat pulled up alongside them. The back doors had dark tinted glass so they couldn't see who else was in there...until the long, tracksuit covered legs with black trainers began to unwind from the back seat followed by Heidi Prager with a black leather sports bag in her arms.

It was very different looking Heidi Prager.

Gone was the black hair reaching heavenward held airborne stiff by gel, now replaced by a soft black pageboy bob. She didn't have any make-up on and no facial metal could be seen. The enormous black-eye she had sported at the interview was now just a shadow and her grazed knuckles had also cleared up. She was still a Goth in her dark colouring but had effected a sartorial effort and was ready to go.

'Hello Heidi' Ginnie said. 'This is Lindsey, our coach.'

'Hey Lindsey' Heidi said jumping quickly out of the way as the Jaguar shot backwards, spun on its back wheels and with the haughty woman still staring purposefully forward surged out of the car park covering their feet in sprayed gravel.

'Who's the handsome racing driver?' Ginnie said shaking the gravel out of her tracksuit bottoms as the Jag screeched out onto the main road and roared off down the dual carriageway.

'That focking dickhead is Mama's latest toy boy,' Heidi drawled. 'His name's Damian, gay as a hussar's helmet plume and twice as flaky. Mama prefers her companions that way because ever since she had me, a difficult birth by all accounts, she has renounced sex, so this way she has a handsome male escort – a gay toy boy if you will – but doesn't have to put out for him, as it were.'

As was now normal with Heidi it was far too much personal information.

She grinned at them both and then continued in her sardonic, off-hand way.

'Damian lives with us and is pissed off at me because all the way here I've been winding him up by calling him mini-dick and saying that if he was two millimetres shorter, he would be a woman and could join the team…'

Lindsey couldn't help it she erupted with a shriek of laughter.

Any nerves that Ginnie had that this first gathering would be anything but a hoot was immediately settled by Heidi's outrageous humour. God only knows what the tall Goth would say when the gender-fluid Sherry arrived. And in truth Ginnie didn't care just so long as this wonderful Heidi was around to spread her louche comments around and put everyone in a good mood.

'Gay as a hussar's helmet plume and twice as flaky...'
Delivered in Heidi's drawl of perfect English it was priceless.

Romany then got out of Lindsey's car and Ginnie had to struggle to stop giggling and greet her and introduce the two would-be players.

Others began to arrive. Next two stepping out of a small car was the Cook sisters, Sarah and Mollie, then Mary-Jane Bagnall pulled up on her motorbike with her kit bag tied on the back with bailer twine, followed by Gina McKinnon and her Army PTI friend Avril Gordon in an old but sound looking MGB with the top up. Tanya Bryan leapt out of her husband's car and blowing kisses to the twin boys strapped in the back seat, slung her kit bag over her shoulder and gave Ginnie a high five. She was followed by Ellie Cooper elegantly unfolding herself from the front seat of a grey and chrome Mini Cooper driven by her black boyfriend. Arriving at the same time both in Fiat 500's, Iona Pierce drove in followed by Billie Hayden with Iona's Fiat receiving admiring glances from more than one girl due to the bold florescent pink strip flanked by a thinner green one each side off centre. Behind them a magnificently muscled Cassie Betts in a skimpy tee shirt and trackie bottoms stretched and flexed having climbed out of the car driven by her oil-slathering husband Les. Gita Rodrigues arrived quietly by taxi and as she was paying the driver off was almost run down by the fast-peddling Jenny Hynes on a tricked-up mountain bike with knobbly tyres. Allan Dix from the Sports Emporium was next roaring in too fast on a red and black Honda Fireblade with his matching helmeted, judo-throwing girlfriend Mandy Sawyer clinging to him on the pillion seat.

Trust him to have a big dick-swinging Fireblade which was massively against type, thought Ginnie recognising the Honda two-wheeled projectile because she'd had a brief fling with a guy who'd also had one. More to type Sonja Van Leer was next up rattling to a stop in and old Vauxhall banger that had seen better days. Finally, as Dixie boy showed off with a tyre-burning weelie exit, they were joined by the two Swindon College students, Kayla Taylor and Stella Winters, who walked down the drive having caught the bus.

As each had arrived Ginnie introduced them to Coach Lindsey. So, there they all stood chattering away with sports bags by their feet with Ginnie somewhat anxiously glancing at the entrance awaiting the last two: Aggy and Sherry Moyes. After a couple more minutes hanging around and with her watch saying it was now six thirty, Ginnie and Lindsey pointed towards the changing rooms and suggested they go and get ready. As they began to walk towards the building in the fading early March gloom, the lights suddenly came on as the time switch kicked in bathing the rugby pitch in light with its flags at the halfway line and in the corners, white lines standing out and the tall gleaming posts with their protecting blue sleeves around the bottom. Without any prompting everyone stopped and looked at the scene in awe. Suddenly it was real, they were here to learn to play this game together.

'All we need now darlings' drawled the wry English and perfect pitch of Heidi's voice, 'is the Emporer with his thumb down and the hungry lions getting ready to munch the soft and battered female flesh.'

'And Russell Crowe with his leather whip and short stabber' sighed Tanya Bryan raising a giggle about her favourite movie, Gladiator.

'Personally, I'd rather have Connie Nielsen' said Rocky Cook referring to Crowes co-star.

'Ollie Reed for me' piped up another voice that sounded like Ellie.

'Let's have 'em all' said Heidi 'so that the Furious Fannies can get...well...furiously focked by whoever turns you on all ways up from the very start.'

Everyone laughed, even the quiet Gita Rodrigues. Led by the irrepressible Heidi and before they'd even got in the changing rooms, the sexual dye and central tenet of the team was cast in Heidi's louche image.

As they got changed, they prattled and giggled and began to bond. Iona showed Romany how to lace up her new, day-glo green boots which she was obviously very proud of, while Ginnie passed around the registration forms for them to sign. She signed Romany's herself by putting p.p. before her signature followed by Romany's full name. Then Lindsey started a monthly period list adding the date of each girls ovulation followed by a training or playing code of 'F' for fine to play, 'M' for maybe and 'S' for severe. When asked her dates Romany again produced the battered old watch and slowly, to everyone's wonder, worked out the dates.

In an aside to Ginnie, Lindsey tapped her list and pointed out a real problem in that four of the girls came on within a day of each other, with two 'Maybe' and two 'Severe' the squad could be reduced by four players once a month and with only twenty so far, they could be left with little or no replacements if someone was injured.

Ginnie acknowledged the fact and said that she was still at least three short of her total target of twenty-three and that others would be coming.

Sarah Cook carefully placed her glasses in their case in her bag and quickly and expertly placed a contact lens in each eye before handing a spare pair to Lindsey.

'Anyone else need contact lens?' Lindsey said loudly over the hubbub. Three of the girls wore specs for reading only but had good enough eyesight to train and play.

'So' said Heidi, 'that's the bloody and the blind fannies sorted,' what's next?'

The banter, as Ginnie had come to suspect throughout the hotel interviews and just walking from the car park, with Heidi at the helm, was risqué, sometimes filthy and charged with sexual innuendo. Just like a crowd of men really, she said in an aside to Iona. Perhaps, she thought as everyone got ready and stood up flexing and bending in the changing room, it was a good job Aggy and Sherry wasn't here.

And then suddenly one of them was as a hesitant and nervous looking Sherry Moyes edged in through the home changing room door and stood there looking at Ginnie with a silent cry of help on her heavily made-up face.

She was wearing new skinny jeans, dazzling white new trainers, a brown cashmere roll neck jumper and an ash blond wig to her shoulders. Her lined, fifty-five-year-old face was close to tears and she was twisting a hankie in her hands. Ginnie leapt to her feet and strode across the changing room floor and placed her arm around Sherry's shoulders.

'Hush everyone I want you to meet...Sherry, our kit person, driver and general factotum.'

There was quite a long pause as everyone weighed up this tranny newcomer.

Heidi, as was now becoming usual, was the first to respond and recognise the situation as she raised her hand to Sherry with a friendly smile and the DNA of this diverse team of lady rugby players clicked smoothly into place.

'Hey girl, welcome to day one of the final paradigm and mixed genomes of the greatest sporting team of congenital misfits of the sisterhood this side of Wonderland.'

The ice of surprise was instantly broken by the marvellous louche drawl of already the established group comedian and smiling broadly Iona Pierce and Cassie Betts walked over and both gave the hesitant Sherry a kiss on both cheeks. Immediately the rest of them got to their feet and followed suit. A voice, probably that of Gina McKinnon piped up plaintively from the group now clustered around Sherry.

'I thought this was rugby training not an English class. What's a bloody paradigm?'

The grinning pack leader and hospital procurement manager that was Rocky Cook answered.

'The interpretation of paradigm that *I* prefer is *antitype* and, before anyone asks, a genome is the full set of chromosomes that we all have...'

Although Ginnie was expecting it no one asked what a chromosome was.

Cassie Betts flexed her muscled arms in the classic body builders pose and replied in a loud, Welsh accented voice to the ceiling.

'So, we're all antitypes and that is *just* a beau…ti…ful thing to be my darlings.'

And suddenly everyone was laughing and cheering while Sherry, overwhelmed at the welcome, sobbed unashamedly making a mess of her carefully applied slap.

*

Having worked through twenty minutes of stretching exercises, a process Lindsey said must take place before each training session or game to warm up the muscles, the coach used the whistle around her neck and got them in a circle to discuss what she called the bread-and-butter basics of the game.

'This' said Lindsey holding up an oblong rugby ball, 'as some of our experienced players here already know, can be your best friend or worst enemy. To befriend the bugger, you never, *never*…let it bounce if you can help it, especially if it's coming towards you from high spiralling kick. If you *do* let it bounce the awkward sod will always go in the opposite direction you expect and make you look like a bloody stupid idiot and lost soul. Mollie' she said throwing the ball at the former fly half for Supermarine showing she had taken on board Ginnies notes on each player. 'Step back to the goal line and loft a few spirals towards the girls on the twenty-two-metre line and let them see what I mean.'

She lined the girls up twenty-five metres away behind the line and told each one to take a decision as to whether to run forward to catch the ball on the full or *try* and take it on the bounce. Sherry joined Mollie with the net of five other balls and to act as retriever and Mollie, casual as you like, began lofting balls at them. The chunky Mary-Jane Bagnall drew the short straw of being first and as the first kick flew arrow straight towards her from high out of the lights, she fell over and the spiralling ball bounced off her ample bum as she led in the grass. Nobody laughed; they had their turn to come. Next up was Ellie who glided forward towards the incoming ball and then dropped it.

'Show 'em Sonja' Lindsey said pushing the South African care assistant forward who caught the high ball perfectly, as did Rocky Cook, Mollies sister. Kayla didn't get under it and it proved Lindsey's point by chasing the bouncing ball almost all the way back to the kicker without laying a finger on it, Gina caught it after a bit of a fumble and then it was Ginnies turn. She got well into position under the high spiral kick and managed to keep a hold of the thing. It was her first ever kicked rugby ball catch and it was all she could do not to smirk as she handed the ball back to Sherry. Stella completely lost it in the lights and it bounced in front of her at right angles to her position and jumped away like a demented dervish, Iona ran smoothly into position and caught it as if she'd been doing it all her life, Cassie never got anywhere near the ball and it shot off to her left from the ground, whereupon she waddled after it like a mother hen chasing errant chicks and still couldn't grab the spinning bouncing thing. Avril – she with the hands like a midwife and kick like a sex-starved stallion and who admitted to Lindsey beforehand that her and Gina had been practising on the army rugby pitch for a couple of nights – managed to grab it out of the air first time, and then it was Heidi's turn.

'Stand aside team mates' the tall, somewhat jerky Goth said strolling into position. 'I have never dropped a rugby ball in my life, probably because no one has ever kicked one towards me before.'

With her long thin arms open wide to receive the extra high spiral Mollie delivered, Heidi got her uncoordinated and jerky body nicely into position underneath it and then somehow got her head in the way and it bounced off her forehead, knocking her to the ground.

Everyone fell about while a chastened Heidi ruefully climbed to her feet and walked back rubbing her head muttering that she'd lost the little focker in the lights. Luckily, Lindsey said, the spiral was beginning to unravel by the time it got to her so the ball hadn't hit her point first otherwise it could cause real damage. With varying, mainly pathetic results the others had a go and then Lindsey did some basic passing with the command of 'pass back or at least level, and run straight.' After more fun and games and dropped balls all over the place she brought everyone into a line on the goal post line and put her whistle up to her mouth.

'This is the last exercise because we were late starting due to all the admin stuff. When I blow this whistle sprint as fast as you can to the half-way line and then back here.'

As the whistle went Romany shot off like a scalded cat. She had a crablike sprinting style that saw her arms and legs working separately to each other rather like a swimmer doing the crawl. But it worked wonderfully as she spun round on the halfway line and got back before anyone else had got anywhere near her. Twenty-five metre's behind Romany, Gina, Tanya, and Iona dead heated for second place followed by Avril, Gita, Jenny, Mollie, and Ginnie. The next group included the two students, Kayla and Stella alongside Amanda and Billie, and then came Ellie, Sonja, Sarah, and Heidi and finally well behind everyone the heavily panting Mary-Jane and Cassie walked over the back half together. As the girls took a break sitting around on the grass, Lindsey sat next to Ginnie.

'If we can get a rugby ball into Romany's hands and teach her some basic side steps and swerves, she'll become a try-scoring machine because she so fast. I don't think I've ever seen a young girl with such speed and we'll have to be careful we don't lose her to athletics or another team like Supermarine. Some of the others are also good runners. Iona showed her background as a trained athlete with balance and pace, Gina will run all and day and make a devastating hooker and Tanya will make a brill scrum half with her wriggling ability…'

So, her husband says, thought Ginnie remembering the comments at her interview.

Right on queue Tanya Bryan, freed up from three years of housebound twin child care, bounced to her feet and showed her gymnastic pedigree and joy with a cartwheel and full 360-degree body air spin before alighting softly with both her hands held high as if finishing off a floor exercise. The others, still puffing and gasping for air after the run broke into spontaneous applause.

'There's some real talent here,' Lindsey said quietly in an aside to Ginnie. 'And some raw but strong pack player's as well. With the right work, increased fitness, and application to the basics we can mould this lot into a half decent rugby team. What happened to your friend Aggy?'

Ginnie, who had forgotten all about Aggy's no show gasped. 'I'll give her a ring on my mobile as soon as we get inside.'

When she called, Aggy picked up while sitting dejectedly in the Great Western Hospital's A & E Department waiting to have a surgical collar fitted from the whiplash effect of the car accident, she'd had on her way to the training session.

Chapter Ten

On the Wednesday morning a slightly stiff, achy Ginnie was sitting at her desk at nine-thirty when the normal hubbub of the open plan office suddenly went quiet and everyone put their head down and looked extra busy. Even the telephones, an eight-hour ringing constant, seemed to shut up as a smiling all around Claude Dillon strode purposefully through the room towards Ginnies desk.

'Good morning, Ginnie; May I?' He gestured at her single guest chair.

'Good morning…Claude, of course' she said waving at the chair. He was God around here and could sit where and how he liked, on her lap or perch on her head if he wanted.

He sat down, put the parcel on her desk and leaned forward.

'I thought a quick progress report on Aggy might be useful. She told me you rang her at the A & E last night?'

'Yeah, she didn't show at the first training session and I knew she was looking forward to it. How is she?'

'Fine, no major problem other than a nasty cut on her forehead along the hairline and the whiplash injury for which she is to wear a surgical collar. She is going to take a few days off from work and, of course, this means that she won't be able to train or play rugby for ages. Of all the inconvenience – I heard this morning that her car is a write-off as well – not being alongside you in the early stages of getting the rugby team going is already really annoying her.'

'Sounds like a pretty bad crash if her car is a write off.'

'It was and she was lucky. Her mother and I saw the car after having been at the hospital with her and it was a wreck. Probably driving too fast as usual and then had to brake suddenly and the car behind couldn't stop in time.'

'Anybody else hurt?'

'The driver of the car that hit her was pretty shaken up but nothing too serious. We should be thankful; it could have been far worse all round.'

'Can I come round and see her, bring her up to date with the first training session last night.'

'Off course, you know where we live in Lechlade?'

'I do.'

'Come whenever you like, Aggy's not going anywhere.'

'Would tonight at about seven thirty be okay?'

'I'll tell her.' He leaned forwardwell aware that most of the ears in the office were straining to catch his every word. 'Something for you from me' he said in a whisper tapping the parcel. 'I bought it a couple of days ago and was just waiting for the chance to deliver it.'

He stood up and with a cheery wave that took in everyone in the department strode off through the busy looking heads bent industriously over their screens. As he left the office as if by magic the phones all suddenly began to ring.

Gods can do that, mused Ginnie to herself, control the telephone exchange with their very presence.

She put the parcel in her desk and locked it. Within less than a minute, Minnie James, her most senior assistant and a nosey old spinster who'd been at Wessex forever and could sense gossip at a hundred paces, arrived next to her desk with a file in her hand as cover. She nodded at the locked desk.

'Love letters from the boss then?'

Every large office or company has a Minnie in it somewhere. A vindictive old spinster who lived alone with just a cat and who was overtaken constantly by younger people for promotion, spend most of their time dissing gossipy shite and moaning about those around them who do a good and proper job while she treads water, contributes as little as possible to the running of the company and is largely ignored.

'Minnie' said Ginnie sweetly in a low voice that didn't carry. 'The Chief Executive has given me a book on how to get rid of nosey parkers in the office so bugger right off and get on with some real work before I decide to implement some of its suggestions.'

As spinster James bristled away in a flounce, Ginnie knew the old cow would be spreading gossipy shite for the rest of the day that the CEO and Ginnie were having a tempestuous affair and he was giving her presents openly in the office. Fortunately, no-one in this office took any notice of the old cow.

She'd have a look, at the parcel in her car lunchtime.

At eleven o'clock she had a call on her mobile from a young lady who introduced herself as Sylvie Greatorex. Sylvie was, she explained, the lady who ran the Badminton game at the sports complex and although she didn't work for Wessex, had called to say thank you for getting the sanitary towel machines installed.

'I've been asking for them for two years and getting nowhere and this morning I went down the club to get some kit from my locker and lo and behold, there they are together with a whole bunch of new hairdryers. Gavin, the young assistant groundsman to Jimmy Corbett, told me that you got rid of that shite Tony Newton *and* arranged for the sanitary towel machines, bins, and dryers. He said that you're a girl to be reckoned with and then gave me this number so I thought I give you a ring and say thanks.'

They chatted away for a few minutes before Ginnie asked her if there were any of her female Badminton playing friends who would be interested in playing rugby...adding 'as well' so it didn't sound as if she was poaching.

'Well, me for a start. I've been getting bloody bored with slapping the old cock backwards and forwards over the net for some time now...'

'There's only one place for a slapping cock,' quipped Ginnie thinking as she said it that the worst of Heidi's mannerisms, without the splendid louche delivery, were rubbing off on her already. 'And that's buried in...a man's trousers with the zip locked firmly shut.' She finished the raunchy phrase off in true Heidi style.

Sylvie burst out laughing and then said 'Don't I know it.'

'Are you married?'

'Was, two small kids and very happily divorced.'

'Can you get away for training and to meet the other girl's tomorrow night at six-thirty?'

'Sure can. I live with my mum and dad and they love having the girls with me out of the way. That's one of the reasons I took up Badminton, well, that and a big swinging dick called Andy whose history now.'

'Slapping cocks and a swinging dick, a girl after my own heart,' Ginnie said. 'See you tomorrow.'

One door shut's, thought Ginnie shutting off the risqué call, and another one...

Placing the parcel in her shoulder bag at lunchtime she bought a Kit Kat and cardboard coffee from the machine in the entrance hall and went down to her car in the car park.

Tearing off the brown paper she found a glossy, new hard-back book titled *Mud, Maul, Mascara* the autobiography of the former England lady's rugby captain, Catherine Spencer and only just published the previous month of February. Inside the flyleaf was a brief handwritten inscription in a broad-nib green fountain pen scrawl: *From C with love.*

C for Claude, no kisses – with love.

Fuck me, thought Ginnie unable to stop the lurch in her stomach. Minnie James just might have something to gossip about and wouldn't that be something.

At seven-thirty on the dot she pulled up at the end of the long gravel drive leading up to the imposing Manor house on the outskirts of Lechlade, a small town at the beginning of the Thames a few miles from Swindon. She had been there once before for a coffee, brandy and thick towel cosseting when her and Aggy had been on a rowing boat trip down the mighty winter river when that sport was being considered alongside rugby, with Aggy having had some chances at Oxford of becoming a rowing as well as a rugby blue. Although she wasn't selected to join the elite group training for the ladies Oxford and Cambridge Boat Race, Aggy had maintained an interest in rowing, an interest quickly discounted when she slipped and fell in the shallows when they were disembarking on the landing stage by the old stone bridge in Lechlade. Knackered, cold, and wet they had made a mess in Ginnies car until, staggering into the vast and warm Manor house kitchen they were greeted with brandy, coffee, and thick towels by Frances, Aggy's mum. Quickly regaining their senses of humour having dried out and warmed up, it was decided that the mud of winter rugby was preferable to the freezing cold of the winter river Thames.

Skirting Claude Dillon's large grey Bentley parked in front of the massive oaken entrance door bathed in the lawn lights pointed back at the house, Ginnie tugged the large brass bell push. After two more tugs the heavy door began to open very slowly revealing a sad looking Aggy with a huge pink-coloured collar around her neck and a row of stitches disappearing above her left eye into the shaved hairline.

'Oh, you poor thing,' Ginnie said stepping inside and turning to close the heavy door before giving Aggy a careful hug.

'At least' her friend said fighting back tears and touching her forehead, 'The scar up here won't show when my hair grows back.'

Having said a cheery hello to Frances, Aggy's short grey haired and still attractively thin mum, Ginnie sat with her sad friend at the granite island in the vast and beautifully fitted olive coloured kitchen with a Wessex crested mug of brewed black Columbian coffee and brought Aggy up to date with the training session.

Heidi's raunchy quips brought a smile to Abby's face as did the immediate acceptance of Sherry into the fold.

When Ginnie mentioned the sprint to the halfway line at the end, Aggy was keen on who came where.

'That Romany is a lightning-fast potential try machine' Ginnie said before paraphrasing Lindsey's remarks about getting the ball into her hands and teaching her to side step and swerve. 'And you would be brill at helping her with that.'

'How do you know I would?' said the morose Aggy.

'Because I watched a video the other night of your Varsity game at Twickenham and you were bloody marvellous. Standout runs from mid-field with a body swerve to die for.'

Aggy smiled. 'You saw that, you sneaky thing. Anyway, I was only a second half replacement.'

'But you *bossed* the second half and without doubt won it for Oxford.'

'And' said a male voice behind them as Claude came into the room and carefully patted his daughters shoulder 'you will soon be doing the same things for the...Fannies.'

Both the girls giggled with Ginnies slightly nervous titter coming from a suddenly tight chest.

When Ginnie left an hour later Aggy had cheered up and was eagerly looking forward to getting along to training.

'Six weeks at least' she said giving Ginnie a hug. 'You'll be playing the first game around then.'

As the heavy door closed behind her Ginnie was fumbling in her bag for the car keys when Claude suddenly appeared alongside.

'Thanks for coming Ginnie. You've cheered her up no end.' He said opening her car door and standing aside so she could get in.

'I'm gonna miss her,' Ginnie said getting in her seat and putting the key in the ignition.

'Never mind, you've got the book to occupy yourself with now, eh?'

'Yeah, thanks for that. It was so very thoughtful of you.'

'Just remember' he said leaning down to her open side window which was broken and never closed properly. 'I'm always around, both upstairs at the office and here…. for a short while longer.'

For a slightly awkward moment Ginnie though he was going to put his head through the car side window and kiss her and had no idea how she would react. He didn't and stepped back. Praying that her old car would start at the first press of the starter – it sometimes took three or four tries depending on the state of the battery – she pressed the button and was relieved to hear the engine roar into life. As she crawled down the long gravel drive, she risked a glance in the rear mirror. Bathed in the glow of the front lawn lights he was still standing there looking after her.

'I'm always around, both upstairs at the office and here…for a short while longer,' she muttered to herself repeating his words and wondering what that meant as she accelerated onto the empty main road.

'Was he coming on to her, leaving the company or just being nice?'

Okay, so her stomach had lurched but that was probably because of who he was…wasn't it?

Chapter Eleven

For the Thursday night training session two new ladies arrived. One was Sylvie Greatorex, the Badminton playing lady who'd rung Ginnie to thank her for the sanitary facilities and hair dryers. Sylvie was thirty-one years old, tall, and willowy but by her own admission, not very fit. And, at around the same height as Ellie and Heidi, she was custom built for the position of lock.

The other girl came along with Kayla and Stella, the pair of student absconders from the hockey team and its pervy, groping coach. Her name was Sheila Bates and she was a fit twenty-year-old who had been a county swimmer before leaving to take up hockey. She also brought the news that the groping hockey coach had run off with one of the other girls and hadn't been seen or heard of – specifically by his wife and two children and the police who were looking for him – for a week. The girl he'd disappeared with was eighteen and her parents were frantically trying to find her and had reported her disappearance. Kayla said that she had also been one of the girls who were interested in joining them in the rugby team.

'She's an empty- headed dumbo who kidded all of us she wasn't interested in his pervy groping until the coast was clear and she reached her eighteenth birthday. Being old enough now to know better *and* legally able she's buggered off with the slimy rat.' said Kayla dismissively. 'I'll give them another week before he gets fed up with living on the run in cheap boarding houses and she sees through his bullshit.' Stella, Kayla's intended, nodded wisely at her lover's prescience and kept her thoughts to herself.

For their second training session they really got down to it. Earlier that day the post room at the office had telephoned Ginnie to say there was a large parcel for her. It was the thirty training bibs that she had ordered in two different colours – red and blue – and she had brought them along for the session. Now, whenever Lindsey wanted to break them up into two teams for touch or any other practice games, they would be able to recognise their own team. It was also gratifying for Ginnie to see that everyone now had a pair of rugby boots. Making that quite expensive purchase was proof that they were going to at least try and stick it out, plus, as none of the boots were branded as Adidas Malice's, Dixie boy had kept his promise.

Sitting around in the changing room after the second and far more strenuous session that mainly involved more of the basics, most of the girls were too muddy and worn out to do anything other than slump on their seat and gaze into space. Iona asked Sherry, who had brought four hairdryers into the room, if she had considered HRT.

'Most certainly' said the bewigged and track-suited faux male lorry driver sitting down next to her. 'From what I can gather, as a former man I'll need a lot of hormones as I get deeper into it, much like a post-menopausal woman would.'

'What's this certificate thing I've read about?' asked the newly married army PTI Avril taking her top off with complete calm abandon to reveal a perfectly ripped body and a pair of large purple love bites just above her right breast.

'Ah that' smiled Sherry. 'It's called the Gender Recognition Certificate and is supposed to be proof that the transformation either way is complete. It takes years to get and can include surgery to legally turn me into a woman. I'm a long way from that and although reassignment surgery isn't necessary to get the certificate, I have the money and will have most of the work done when I get up the courage.'

'Well, when you do have your bollocks chopped off and the other dangly bits tucked away, we'll be right there for you and with you...in more ways than one,' grinned a weary looking Heidi. 'Then when we play naked rugby you can join in with no differences to the rest of us...apart from boobs and getting them is a piece of cake nowadays...silicon cake."

Ginnie glanced at the two new girls to gauge their reactions. Both seemed very matter-of-fact about Sherry or it could be that they were too knackered to care but her acceptance seemed nailed on now and no one minded, or had said anything – about the former man in the changing room.

'I'd play naked rugby' said Gina showing off her multiple tattoos with her top off, 'especially if it's in the mud, there's something sexy about rolling around in the mud with no clothes on.'

'Better than baby oil' said Cassie with a grin.

'The rules, besides our tits and other sensitive areas, would be sure to get in the way' said Rocky, 'especially in the close quarter work like in the scrum.'

'Imagine that Ellie' said Heidi looking across at the other tall lock, 'in that case we'd have to stick our most noble swedes up a naked props bum.'

Grimacing the tall black girl held her counsel as the others giggled.

'You should be so lucky' Rocky said throwing a lump of mud at Heidi.

'My bum is a no-go area' muttered Mary-Jane 'Biggie' Bagnall, the solidly built farmer girl and an obvious prop causing all of them to burst out laughing.

'As is mine,' said Gina when the mirth had subsided. 'Everyone's head is banned from there, even my husbands.'

Ginnie just sat there and smiled as the ribaldry swirled around her. Although some of this banter was close to the knuckle it was a part of the necessary bonding process.

Unlacing her well-worn boots Lindsey got back to rugby matters and began to talk about the training targets for the two sessions next week and finished by adding,

'Our Thursday session will always be the harder one of the two because you will have four days to recover before the next Tuesday session.'

'Just so long as we're not playing on the Saturday' Gina said. 'When do you think we'll be playing our first actual game?'

'When we're ready, I guess but Ginnie has already arranged a couple of home and away pre-season friendly games…'

All eyes turned to the captain who was picking mud out of her long-studded Malice boot bottoms.

'Supermarine seconds in three or maybe four weeks time or when Lindsey thinks we can take them on without making complete prats of ourselves.' Ginnie said throwing a piece of mud at Iona who caught it and returned the favour.

'That' barked Rocky Cook with a competitive gleam in her eye looking at her younger sister across the room, 'will be a bloody game to look forward to, right Moll?'

'Piss all over 'em' replied the other ex-Supermarine wonder side-stepper quietly who never got wet in a thunderstorm. 'And knowing Vera, our older sister and their Director of Rugby, they'll be ready and up for the fight because we're the pair of upstart turncoats who left them.'

'This' said Heidi with relish 'is why I became a rugby player. If it is a war, I'll be leading the charge from the front…'

'No, you won't' said Ginnie softly but with a steely authority, 'we will *all* be in it together, right Cassie?'

Cassie Betts only had her knickers on as she leapt to her feet and struck the muscle rippling body builders pose that was becoming her trademark.

'Bring the lumpy bitches on, that's what I say, eh girls?'

Even the two new girls and Sherry joined in with the cheering.

The two Supermarine games became the focus at each training session as the girls began to identify with and grow into their positions. The experienced prop and pack leader Sarah 'Rocky' Cook began scrimmaging work with the forwards and, with the experience of Sonja and Lindsey the rhino became a standard bit of kit at their sessions. Sherry wrote 'Supermarine

Forward' and 'Supermarine Back' on two tackle bags and the girls ripped into those with extra gusto. Gina McKinnon, the happy hooker, a beautifully fit and perfect selection for the position according to Lindsey, also resurrected her interview introduction to Ginnie of BOHICA and it quickly became a squad staple when charging into a tackle and from there a rallying cry to the rest of the girls to join in. Heidi loved it and would scream her own version of 'Bend over Heidi is Coming Again' as she galvanised her jerky, slightly uncoordinated long body ferociously into a ruck, maul, or tackle.

Another Gina interview staple that her army friend Avril had a kick like a sex-starved stallion turned out to be true. The former goalie had a powerful left foot and when shown how to correctly place her non-kicking right foot alongside the teed-up rugby ball and swing her left foot through the line correctly by Mollie, the ball went a long way. Not with the accuracy, yet, of Mollie who would be first kicker and handle the line kicking from hand and short kicks of up to thirty metres out from the posts, but distances of forty-five metres were possible by Avril when the practice accuracy began to pay dividends. According to Lindsey her maximum kick distance at five metres inside the halfway line and over the bar – when she got it right – was an enormous length of kick for a girl and something very few men could achieve with accurancy.

When the training squads were split into two teams, no-one wanted to be in opposition to the deft, side-stepping Mollie. Rushing her when she had the ball in her hands was tantamount to being made to look like a clumsy fool as at the last possible moment she just wouldn't be there and the rusher was left grasping at thin air or face-planting mud as the fly half jinked to the left or right. Another revelation was Tanya, the scrum half as she began to develop a long and accurate spin pass. It was a position, Lindsey said, that like Gina at hooker was perfectly made for her acrobatic cheek and bendy, lithe body and the ability to spin out a long pass from the back of the scrum was a big plus. Her half-back combination with Mollie was set to become a partnership of wonder that would become another of the Fannies secret weapons.

Working with Iona as her outside centre, Ginnie was herself making giant strides. Always aware that as captain she had to hold down the position of inside centre by skill and the correct decision making, especially as Aggy would be coming back one day soon, Ginnie ran around her neighbourhood and practised every night her side-stepping and swerve, individual skills she hadn't had time to work on with Lindsey. She was a fast and balanced runner and developed an early swerve at speed to the left or right that was better than average. She also became adept at spinning out decent length passes to the belly buttons of Iona, Mollie or either of the wingers, and tackled like a back-row forward – according to Lindsey – and even worked on a ground-hugging grubber kick that was gradually bearing fruit.

Amanda Sawyer with her judo black belt also added something to what Lindsey described as the weakest part of the women's game, that of tackling. Big, strong women will score tries by happily running straight through a forest of opposing players using what the coach called the Māori sidestep – meaning no side step or swerve at all and simply staying straight and strong into the tackle but bending into the tackler and bumping them off or running right over them – because, the coach said, women usually tackle like waving powder puffs. To bring the opposition to the ground, study the men's game and hit the opposition low and hard around the legs when they had the ball in hand and were coming at you. No-one can run if someone has their arms wrapped around their knees or ankles, no matter how strong or fast they were. Amanda added another dimension to this credo by showing how to let an opponent with the ball get level with the tackler before using a one-armed hip throw to bring them down judo style. Timing was all and as several of the girls who'd received this treatment could testify, it bloody worked and hurt and usually left the tackled girl breathless and resulted in the ball coming loose in a knock-on.

With all these burgeoning skills and tough teamwork building towards something special, there was the ace in the hole that Lindsey had identified with their very first run, just one special and true cloud of absolute and golden stardust.

Romany and her dazzling speed over the ground.

When Ginnie asked Lindsey just why this rather awkward looking running style made her so quick, she said it could only be leg speed and cadence coupled with balance and excellent fitness – *all* the rarest requisite athletic attributes coming together in one probable and talented seventeen-year-old and quite small girl.

'Romany' said Lindsey quietly, 'is the fastest and most natural talent I have ever seen in a teenage girl and we're gonna lose her to one of the big teams in the Women's Tyrell's Premiership as soon as we go public,' Lindsey would mutter to Ginnie as Romany flew around everyone and dotted the ball down again at a training session. 'Saracens Women, Harlequins, Ealing, Loughborough Lightning, all the top lady's teams will be round waving cheque books in the air and she'll be off.'

Ginnie would shrug and say so be it and that no team should be defined by one player and good luck to Romany if that happened but in her heart she determined to hang on to the speedy little traveller girl at all costs.

Mollie, Iona, Avril, Tanya, and Ginnie, and Aggy, when and if she returned – the other main Petticoats, as Heidi had nicknamed the back's – had one single purpose during a game and that was to get the ball into Romany's hands in space and then just let the traveller go and score. A try was all but guaranteed because no-one could get near her, especially now she was learning with Lindsey's and Mollie's careful instruction, to feint and swerve. Gita, on the other wing was moderately fast and would score from time to time as would Iona and Ginnie and Avril, but theirs would be a team effort whereas the flying little traveller didn't need anyone else but the ball and a few yards of clear space and she was off.

After every training session Ginnie would give Aggy a call on her mobile and go through what they had been working on. By the sixth session and when Aggy still hadn't come back to the office or to a training session, Ginnie was running out of things to tell her. She had turned down a couple of invitations from her to come out to the Manor house again with the excuse that she was so tired after the sessions that she simply just had to collapse in bed. While it was partly true, Ginnie also wanted to keep away from the manor just in case

Claude was there. She wasn't sure what he wanted and, equally, wasn't sure how to handle it if he did come on to her.

Then one Friday morning he rang her on her office extension and invited her out to lunch. He apologised for not being in touch for a while but had been in Hong Kong and Singapore for a couple of weeks on business and then away for a week in some place called Davos in Switzerland where, he said, the global great and the good from politics, banking and business meet once a year in a great big jolly.

'Would you rather that we meet somewhere locally for a bite to eat or jump in my car downstairs?'

Ginnie thought quickly. If she got in his huge grey Bentley in his designated parking space downstairs half the office would be gawking at her. She answered quietly looking around just in case Minnie the Minx was hovering around but she was sitting at her desk over the other side of the office pretending to read a report.

'Why don't we meet somewhere?' There, the Rubicon had been crossed, she thought. Appropriately, 'Rubicon' was another Aggy word. I am using his daughters words on her father' Ginnie thought.

'Okay, let's say The Plough at Wanborough at one o'clock they do a super light lunch there.'

Then he put the phone down. With her heart fluttering Ginnie looked at the clock. A quarter past twelve – just time to put her face on before leaving, the clever bastard. He'd taken away the decision as to whether she would *accept* or *decline* lunch and replaced it with *how* and *where* did she want to go.

When she got to the Plough, Claude Dillon's large grey Bentley was nowhere to be seen in the sparse car park so she waited in her car and checked her mobile. Suddenly he appeared at her window. Opening the door, he apologised for not telling her but weekdays he drove into the office in a small Toyota Yaris unless he was off to somewhere important in London or elsewhere.

'Although I love to drive it people around here don't like big expensive looking cars swishing around the country roads and tend to try and cut me up or wave a couple of fingers at me, so I keep down and dirty with the proles by driving the Toyota.'

He smiled and waved to the next car along, a white perfectly ordinary little Japanese car in which he'd been waiting.

They sat in a corner table of the back bar and ordered some drinks and food. Ginnie stuck to Diet Coke and an avocado salad and he had a small beer and steak sandwich. He told her that Aggy would be back in the office on Monday and although she was still getting headaches, the surgical collar had been removed. The doctor had specifically forbidden her to play or practice at rugby or any other sports for the time being.

'How are you getting on with the book?'

'It's brilliant and perfect for me right now. The only trouble is that I keep it on my bedside table but keep falling asleep having read the same bit as the night before. What with work, training, and a couple of nights a week running around the neighbourhood in the evenings as well to get my fitness levels up, I'm usually knackered by ten o'clock.'

Perhaps 'knackered' wasn't a word you used to the Chief Executive and your ultimate boss but sod it, it was done now.

Their food and drinks arrived and they got stuck in. Ginnie had to admit that he was good company telling her amusing anecdotes about some of the people at Davos which as far as Ginnie could tell was a pretty big annual deal with attendance by some world-famous names that even she had heard of or read about in the gossip columns.

'Ginnie' he said wiping his lips with the napkin as he finished off the steak sandwich. 'There's something I'd like to discuss with you.'

Here it comes, she thought keeping a straight face, *the mistress proposition.*

It was nothing of the sort although, she thought afterwards, it could be a major part of the softening up process.

'How many people are there in your department?'

'Twenty-three,' she said masking her surprise at the question.

'And you're the supervisor of…?

'Ten customer service assistants with a couple of vacancies.'

'And you report to Steve Harrington, the Marketing Director, is it a busy role?'

'I'm flat out all the time, especially with the two vacancies although HR told me yesterday that they think they have filled one of them. But then, I would say that I'm always busy to the Chief Executive, wouldn't I?' She grinned cheekily.

He smiled and nodded. He wasn't what Ginnie would call a handsome man but then at around the mid-fifties, who was. He had a generally slim figure with a small pot belly – call it a thickening waist – beginning to show over his beltline, was always well-dressed, had an appealing firm jaw line and – something that Ginnie always found attractive in a man – firm yet full lips under a cool but level gaze. He was clean shaven and had brown eyes which were mirrored in Aggy's colour and direct stare, and a full head of his hair which was gradually turning grey but kept short.

'It's Claude, Ginnie. Forget that Chief Executive rubbish, especially when it's just the two of us and we're out of the office.' He leaned forward and muted his speech. There was another couple at the nearest table although as far as Ginnie knew they were not from their company.

'Okay Claude but you know what I mean.'

'I do but the reason I brought up the subject was that Steve Harrington wants to expand Customer Services by another twelve to fifteen staff, and that means with anything up to forty-four staff in the department, we will need a permanent manager for the supervisors to report to...'

'Oh...' Ginnie said surprised that he was telling *her* this.

'And as much as I might like you with your mouth open, I have obviously taken you completely by surprise.' It was one of the phrases that she remembered later. 'The facts are that *you* are a candidate for the manager's position because you are one of two departmental supervisors in situ and, I must confess, *my own personal favourite for the position*. It would mean going on a course for a couple of weeks but we could always arrange that in the off season, after all, we can't have you missing rugby training, can we?'

Ginnie took a deep breath. Her heart was beating like a trip hammer and she wasn't sure if it was the sexual innuendo in his words or the fact that she was a favourite for promotion. Probably a bit of both, she thought taking a swig of her Diet Coke to regain a little of her cool which was somewhere in the middle of the Sahara right now.

'Ultimately the decision is Steve's but a recommendation from me…' He ginned at her and let the sentence end. 'Interested?'

'Oh yes.' She closed her mouth and took a deep breath. Can't have Claude getting too excited. He leaned forward again.

'Because it's a manager's job we'll have to go through the motions of internal interviews for prospective candidates but if you want it the job's yours…'

She nodded dumbly.

'There's just one caveat,' he said rising and going over to the bar to pay the bill.

What, she thought watching him take out a black credit card and wave it over the proffered machine on the bar. I let you shag me from time to time?

He didn't say anything as they walked out and he opened her car door.

'The caveat?' she said unable to help herself getting in her seat.

He just smiled and put his finger to his lips in a 'shush' motion before closing her car door and then motioning her to wind down the window.

'The caveat Ginnie is that we…' he looked around to make sure no-one was listening…' take our time.'

Then he walked around to the driver's door of the little Toyota and got in.

All she could think about on the way back to the office was that she hadn't thanked him for lunch. Later as she sat moon gazing out of the window in the office, she reassessed every word including the difficulties she would have with Aggy if she found out Ginnie was shagging her father. *If* that was his intension, despite the clever sexual innuendo and the caveat that *we take our time,* she still wasn't sure. She'd been chatted up by men since Maxie the baker and flour bedecked condom roll-on boy but never so obliquely or cleverly. Perhaps that was how married Chief Execs do it when they want to shag a staff member, or was he being careful because of the whole Me-Too movement and the fact that she was his daughter's friend? One thing she was sure about and that was the extra ten to fifteen grand a year that departmental managers got. Her life would be a lot easier with that and she might even be able to get a new car. It also meant, she thought looking sideways at the furniture she was always stacking with rubbish to cover the second-hand scars of a hard life, that the meeting table and four chairs Stan the Wink and a Pint Mackay had given her as managers only favour, would soon be legal.

Take as much time as you need Claudie boy, I'll still be here with my mouth wide open, and I might even tart it up with some fetching lip gloss if that's your turn-on.

Chapter Twelve

Aggy did start back on the Monday morning and true to her father's word the surgical collar was missing. They had an excited rugby catch-up meeting in her office on her identical small managers meeting table and chairs to the set Ginnie had, following which her friend told Ginnie that since she was still getting headaches her doctor had told her that rugby was out for at least another six weeks.

'That means' said a mournful Aggy 'that I'll miss the two friendly games with Supermarine – if I'd have been fit enough anyway having missed all the training so far, and then the season will be over and I'll have to wait until August of next season training starts. It seems that I'm doomed to spend my rugby career on the replacements bench or watching from the side-lines.'

'Never mind' grinned Ginnie thinking that now she didn't have a problem about who to drop in Aggy's place – Iona had been showing up very well alongside Ginnie as one of her centre partners in training – or at least she could defer the decision until they started training for next season. 'You can slice up the half-time oranges.'

Aggy grinned slyly at Ginnie before speaking.

'There was one special advantage about the whole rotten episode though…'

She did one of her long pauses when holding back a juicy tid-bit.

Ginnie yawned and waited saying nothing. She was getting used to this stagnant with-holding pause and knew the answer would come in its own good time. And sure enough after a shorter than usual wait Aggy burst out with it.

'I have been receiving succour and comfort from my own personal physician...'

Ginnies eyebrows must have given away her surprise because Aggy giggled pleased at the reaction.

'You mean you got a man out of it somewhere along the line?'

Aggy nodded. 'His name is Alistair and he was the young doctor on A & E at the Great Western Hospital on the night I arrived there after the car hit me from behind. After sitting there for at least three hours with him fussing around me he fitted the collar and then asked me out.'

'And you of course played hard to get...?'

Aggy got all dreamy.

'Not a bit of it. He was so handsome and good with his fingers...massaging my neck muscles I mean...and I felt so wretched that I accepted the date right away. We've been out four or five times since although it wasn't much fun until the collar came off...'

'Bloody hell,' Ginnie said to the ceiling. 'The girls only gone and fallen in love with a doctor whose good with his fingers...'

When Ginnie got back to her desk there was a message from the post room that a couple of big boxes had arrived for her.

The shirts, shorts and black and pink hooped socks had arrived and within two minutes the pair of them were excitedly tearing open the boxes at the back of the post room.

*

'We'll start at the beginning' Ginnie said to the weary squad at the end of the next Tuesday night training session referring to the important ceremony about to take place in the changing room. Standing alongside her Lindsey reached across to the pile and handed Ginnie a neat bundle comprising a pink and black quartered folded shirt, black shorts, and a pair of pink and black hooped socks. 'These numbers on the back do not mean that the shirt is yours permanently because all positions are subject to change due to who is sick or on the replacement bench for any one game. They are also our best guess for the moment for positions but these too may change as other girls push for the place and therefore the shirt.'

She glanced down at the first bundle Lindsey gave her with the number facing and then at her list.

'Number one, loose head prop and pack leader Sarah 'Rocky' Cook.'

Lindsey's clapping was instantly taken up by everyone else as Sarah came forward and accepted the bundle from Ginnie with a kiss on both cheeks.

'Number two and the Happy Hooker Gina 'Bohica' McKinnon.'

'Number three, tight head prop Mary-Jane 'Biggie' Bagnall.'

'Biggie' had become Mary-Jane's nickname as bestowed by Heidi. The grin she gave everyone had just a hint of her fighting back the tears of pride behind it.

'Number four and lock 'Ellie Cooper.' The languid Ellie glided across the floor as if she owned it and gave her trademark white-toothed grin. Her very presence on the pitch was good enough; she didn't need a nick name.

As Ginnie was handled the number five bundle by Lindsey her voice was drowned out by the cheering. Heidi Prager had become a squad favourite with her endless wit and fierce exhortation for everyone to 'kick ass' harder, faster, and with more venom. What Heidi lacked in skill she made up for with her endless and laid-back quips and total commitment to the cause. With her grown-out pageboy hair flopping down over her eyes and none of the face metal showing because she had stopped using it for training, the black-eyed Goth had come a long way in the short weeks since joining. Heidi accepted the bundle and cheek kisses from Ginnie and then, for good measure, gave Lindsey a couple of pecks on the top of her head as well.

Most of these nick-names were down to Heidi and coined over the seven training sessions they'd had so far. It had become almost a badge of office to receive one from the gangly and lippy Goth, a mark of respect that the girl was making her presence felt in the right way by developing as a player and getting a 'moniker' in the process.

'We could swop that shirt for one of the Petticoats' Ginnie said to Heidi by way of a joke.

'I'd rather fellate a frantic ferret' replied the droll Heidi sitting down with her tightly held kit bundle on her knee.

'Wots a fellate Heidi?' Asked Romany who was beginning to adopt Heidi as her heroine.

'An eating disorder my little darling' came the instant reply. 'Like anorexia but with sausages...'

Cassie was bent over her knees helpless with silent laughter.

Unabashed and with the quip going right over her head Romany carried on. 'Me granddad gives me sausages sometimes. Wots anor...anor...?

'Never mind my love, just score five tries in your first game against Supermarine and I'll explain and even get you a real one to gnaw on...'

By now the entire changing room was rolling around with laughter. When they had settled down again Ginnie continued.

'Number six and blindside flanker Mandy 'Judo' Sawyer.' To cries of 'throw baby throw'Allan Dix's black-belted girlfriend accepted her bundle with a quiet grace.

'Number seven and open side flanker J. J. van Leer' This announcement was greeted with another roar as Sonja the South African spelt with a small j, and now known as a result as J.J. proudly accepted her bundle.

'Number eight, Billie 'Put the Fire Out' Hayden.' As Billie smilingly accepted her bundle the chants of 'Billie, Billie, Billie,' rang around the changing room.

'That concludes the 'Fannie Howies'' Ginnie said using the abbreviated Heidi expression for the forwards of Howitzers, a word she got from Gina when asked what was absolutely the biggest gun the army had.

'Now the Fannie Petticoats,' Ginnie said using Heidi's other expression for the backs. 'Number nine and scrum half Tanya 'Flipper' Bryan.' To whoops of 'flip it Tannie'' Tanya accepted her bundle. If there had been room everyone knew the former gymnast would have done a complete 360 without anything touching the ground.

Ginnie paused for a moment before accepting the bundle from Lindsey knowing that the next one was probably going to get the loudest cheer of the lot.

'Number ten and fly half Mollie 'Magical' Cook.' Sure, enough the changing room erupted led by her sister Rocky as the shy and retiring Mollie, who let her skill as a raindrop side-stepping and kicking little genius playmaker do the talking, accepted her bundle.

Another very loud cheer greeted 'number eleven and left winger Romany 'The Blue Streak' Cutler.' When her name was called at first Romany didn't move being a bit overwhelmed by the occasion until a shove from behind by Gina propelled her hesitantly towards Ginnie. The eyes in the elfin face shone with pride and delight as the fastest girl in the team and named accordingly by Heidi, clutched her bundle to her chest. It was a pity, Ginnie thought giving her a kiss on both cheeks that her granddad wasn't here to see it. He too would have been so very proud of the girl he was responsible for bringing up.

As the cheering died down Ginnie gestured to Lindsey to put the next one aside and move on but it was noticed by Heidi.

'Why have you missed out number twelve Ginnie?' she asked knowing full well the reason.

'Oh, I'll do it later.' Ginnie replied off-hand.

'You'll bloody well do it NOW!' A loud chorus came from everyone present.

This time it was Lindsey who stepped forward and held out the bundle and made the announcement.

'Number twelve, inside centre, Captain AND THE REASON WE'RE ALL BLOODY WELL HERE' she bellowed over the gathering hubbub, GINNIE THE SKIPPER JOY...'

It was undoubtedly the loudest and longest cheer of the night and Ginnie, despite being red-faced with embarrassment, couldn't help the tear that escaped to roll down her cheek as she accepted the bundle and cheek kisses from Lindsey.

Gradually the fuss died down and Ginnie placed her own bundle down and picked up her list.

'If this was a beauty contest our number thirteen would win it. But it's a rugby game and therefore our outside centre and former professional athlete is happy to get down and dirty with the rest of us. It's Iona 'Tea-tray' Pierce...'

This was a nick-name that didn't belong to Heidi but was given to Iona by Sarah 'Rocky' Cox after she watched a two-year old video of Iona sliding down a pure ice banked track to win the Austrian skeleton title at ninety miles an hour. The commentator had called the skeleton by the more commonly known 'tea-tray' name and the name had been bestowed. Iona had also become one of the stars of the side during practice with an uncanny knack of being where the ball would alight after a kick or fumble. Lindsey said this second sight was a gift from on high and couldn't be taught and if Aggy had been fit the contest for this place would have been very close. Iona's hug with Ginnie when she collected her bundle still carried the slight musk of lemons, even after her post training shower.

'Now it's the turn of our other winger with fast feet, number fourteen Gita Rodrigues.'

The quiet Gita although not as fast as Romany on the other wing had not been christened with a moniker yet, although it was only a matter of time before Heidi got one for her. The Anglo-Indian was somewhat reserved but had been gradually coming out of her shell as she became more confident with her surroundings, the constant rude banter, positioning and catching and handling the oval shaped ball.

Ginnie then looked at Gina McKinnon and winked. 'When I was interviewing a certain happy hooker, she said she had an army mate who, and I quote, 'had hands like a midwife and a kick like a sex-starved stallion. She's our wonderful full-back and number fifteen Avril 'Love Bites' Gordon...'

The former goalie and army PTI bounded up to Ginnie, took her bundle and kissed her and Lindsey. Recently married and obviously regularly enjoying the sexual side of the union, Avril always unashamedly jumped in the shower covered in purple bruising around her breasts caused by her new husband's lips, something Heidi just couldn't ignore with the nickname.

Next came the replacements with numbers 16 for Jenny Hynes, 17 Kayla Taylor, 18, Stella Winters, 19 Cassie Betts with an enormous cheer as the Welsh body builder was very popular and gave her trademark muscle pose, 20 for Aggy Dillon which Ginnie would keep for her because she wasn't there, 21 Silvie Greatorex and 22 Sheila Bates.

Ginnie held her hands up for quiet.

'I have two bundles left. They are both for very special people and neither of them has a number but a name and position instead. The first one is...' she picked up the shirt and turned it round so everyone could read it. It simply said 'Coach Lindsey' and the whooping and foot stamping went on for ages as the former sacked Bellfield Road Coach and recovering alcoholic from Reading held it up and wiped the tears from her cheeks and gave everyone a cuddle.

When everyone had calmed down Ginnie picked up the last shirt from its bundle. They all knew who it was for but didn't know what it would say.

'Last but by no means least an invaluable member of our sisterhood...'Ginnie held up the shirt back so everyone could read it. It said 'Sherry' and then underneath 'Assistant Coach...'

The tumult was riotous as a deeply moved Sherry Moyes collected the shirt while openly sobbing. When the noise and foot stamping finally died and with the tearful Sherry still holding the shirt aloft with the words facing, Heidi's louche drawl got everyone giggling again.

'There obviously wasn't enough room on the shirt back for the last word of 'Driver.''

Ten minutes later when they were filing out with bundles firmly clutched under their arms and kit bags in the other hand, Lindsey made another important announcement.

'Don't forget training at the usual time on Thursday. It will be vital because on Saturday at two-thirty we kick off our first friendly game here at home against Supermarine Ladies Second Fifteen...'

'At last, my warrior clan of Furious Fannies,' breathed an exultant Heidi, 'war has finally been declared and those of us gals who favour the male barbed penetrator can get back to watching out for the usual sideline of sausages with bald heads with all of them thinking of the prospect of congress with our sublime gashes rolling around in the mud at which they will bang away until the dogs howl...'

She held both her hands up to Romany as if to say *do not* ask any more questions about the sublime gashes or sausages...

'*We* are vegetarians' quipped Stella Winters, future wife of Kayla Tayor, the two former hockey players who had left because the coach was a sex pest.

'Well actually, we are...' Stella grinned and looked at Kayla...'PAPTU'S'...they said in unison.

Heidi looked at them both 'And they are...?' She asked but already suspecting the subject matter of their answer..

Together the giggling girls said 'Pricks are Poisonous to us. Its a Saffic acronym....'

There were some chuckles around the changing room.

A puzzled looking Romany tugged at Heidi's arm 'Wot are they on about Heidi?'

'Sausages again my little streaker. Gives them indigestion...'

Romany thought about this for a few beats before replying.

'Me granddad gets that from eating pickled onions...' she said innocently to the room at large.

By which time the entire squad was rolling around on the floor helpless with laughter.

Chapter Thirteen

On the Wednesday morning at ten minutes to twelve Ginnie received an internal phone call of just five words from Claude.

'Lunch today at twelve-thirty…?'

She answered with her own sparse four.

'That's fine by me.'

The phone went dead. It was two and a half weeks since their last lunch and she hadn't seen or heard from him in the office either. She had, however, had her interview with Steve Harrington for the Customer Services Managers job and although no mention was made of the Chief Executives recommendation, the interview had gone very well and three days later her conformation and congratulations from the Marketing Director had come through the internal mail. An official confirmation would be placed on the Wessex website 'in due course' with her taking up the post by the end of April. The salary would give her an increase of twelve thousand five hundred pounds per annum and Ginnie had been quietly looking at nearly new cars online.

'Don't waste any words of greeting do you?' Ginnie muttered into the dead phone before replacing it in the cradle and taking her shoulder bag to the ladies to check her face and hair and this time perhaps add a little lip gloss…

Sure enough when she pulled into the Plough pub carpark in Wanborough he was sitting there in the anonymous white Toyota.

A couple of minutes later they were sitting in the back room of the Plough nursing a couple of non-alcoholic drinks having ordered the same avocado salad and steak sandwich as before, when Claude, having checked that no one was within hearing distance, leaned forward over the table.

'I need to be open with you about a few things that may come as a bit of a surprise. The first one is that in three weeks' time my decree absolute will be through and then I'll be a single man again...'

Stunned Ginnie could only gape at him with her Diet Coke halfway to her once again open in surprise and this time heavily glossed lips.

'Close your mouth,' he grinned. 'You know what it does to me.'

She did as she was told but her mind was tumbling and whirring all over the place. In an even voice he continued.

'Frances and I agreed over a year ago that after twenty-eight years of marriage it was time to call it a day. Our marriage had simply run its course and since neither of us are dramatic about such matters we sat down and discussed the natural outcome of a sensible and quiet divorce. Unfortunately, my wife is also a director and shareholder of Wessex Mutual and its subsidiary companies of which there are at least fourteen. I say unfortunately because although her holdings are small, they amount to huge sums of money and the legal untying of Frances from the business – her wish – is a complex dynamic and far more complicated than us just getting a divorce. As a result, there has been a steady stream of lawyers through my office and home with the necessary papers bringing it about. Her disentanglement from the business was all finalised a couple of days before I went off on my Far Eastern trip recently, as was the decorum of our well-mannered and quiet divorce which was at the nisi stage then and has been running in parallel with the business split. As the CEO and Frances, a former share-holder in the company, now a huge and important mutual society, we both felt that there was a moral imperative to our professional conduct regarding the way our personal and business separation was conducted.'

He paused to give her time to absorb this information.

'That's why you said the last time we were here that we had to take our time?' It was the only response she could muster as her mind was in turmoil.

'Precisely, and the fact that Frances and I have had separate bedrooms for over three years at home now – and let's face it with nine bedrooms to choose from at the Manor, it was no hardship – it was important for both of us to keep within the law and spirit of our marriage until the divorce was finalised. That will be the case when it becomes absolute on April 1st...'

'April Fool's Day' Ginnie said for no sensible reason. 'Does Aggy know?'

'Aggy has known right from day one and was included in the break-up discussions with Frances and I from early on. She was disappointed at first but pleased that both her mother and I will remain good friends after the divorce. Frances will get the Manor house and its six acres of gardens and parkland – actually, she got it three months ago and I've just been a lodger. She is particularly keen on the garden there which has received a great deal of TLC from her over the years and is one of her great passions...'

'So, you'll be homeless in three weeks' time then?'

'Hardly, I've bought myself a rather grand bachelor's pad overlooking the Thames at Lechlade just a couple of miles from the Manor. It's being renovated and repainted now and having a few personal bits and pieces added.'

'Lucky old you,' Ginnie said still not quite sure what was happening and where this was all going. Right on cue Claude picked this up.

'So, all this personal stuff was proceeding along in the required non-dramatic and quiet way towards the conclusion when, a few weeks ago a girl walked into my office with her piece of paper and began to tell me all about her ladies rugby team plans...'

Ginnie grinned. 'A rather apprehensive girl with tummy wobbles who'd never been up to the top floor before.'

'If you were nervous it didn't show. I was impressed with your commitment to the cause and the way you had thought it through. Even more so when I asked Aggy a few hidden questions at home as to just who this Virginia Joy was and what was she made of.'

It was on the tip of her tongue to ask him if Aggy knew about the two of them meeting lunchtimes but she decided to keep quiet. Her mind was still whirring like a spin drier and she didn't trust herself to say anything sensible so she just stuck to the obvious.

She looked down and was surprised to see an avocado salad on the table in front of her that she didn't remember arriving. It was a very quiet lunchtime and

Claude went to the bar to get them a couple more drinks. Right then Ginnie would have given her car in exchange for triple vodka with a dash of tonic or a large tequila slammer. When he came back and said his next statement, she could have downed the whole bottle without breathing...

'Y'see Ginnie,' he said placing their drinks on the table and then taking a deep breath as he sat down, 'I fell in love with that feisty girl as she was presenting her rugby team to me and have been unable to think of anything else since, no matter how hard I tried, even when I was in the Far East and Switzerland.'

Christ Almighty! Did he just say he was in love... with *me?*

'Your delicious mouth is open again and I may not be able to ignore it for much longer.'

'You'll just have to...please excuse me.' She muttered at him in a complete fug as she stood up. She badly needed the ladies loo for a few equilibrium gaining minutes and a pee. When she got there on unsteady legs she just closed and locked the cubicle door, sat on the toilet, and took several deep breaths as she replayed what she could remember of his words. There was something about moral *imperatives*, whatever they were and Frances already had the Manor. He would be legally single *in three weeks,* had already bought a posh flat in Lechlade and he was *in love with her...*

Bloody hell...

When she got back to their table, he was on his mobile to someone so she sat down and pushed the salad around her plate until he'd finished. He then reached across the table and stroked her hand apparently unworried now that anyone would see them. Perhaps,

Ginnie thought, the declaration of love had freed him up, an idea that was immediately nipped in the bud as he looked around guiltily and then let go.

'As far as your promotion to Departmental Manager' he said softly. 'I want you to know that it was entirely on merit and would have been yours even if we hadn't met.'

'Thank you,' she replied thinking that he would say that wouldn't he.

'Ginnie, I'm fifty-six years old and you are…?'

'Twenty-seven…and never been kissed.' She replied getting a little flippancy into what was becoming some very heavy stuff.

He smiled. 'Well, as I've said several times, I very much want to put that right but the point is I'm twenty-nine years older than you. Is that a problem?'

'Not to me it isn't. I can always introduce you as my dad…' She giggled and took the initiative by standing up. 'C'mon, I've got to get back to work at my new position otherwise I'll get the sack.'

She did not get any meaningful or actual work done that afternoon. Any of the Customer Services staff keeping an eye on their new departmental manager would have assumed she was already putting on the airs and graces of a lazy boss. Several came by to congratulate her on the promotion which was now common knowledge, including Simon Courtney. He was one of her best assistants and had been interviewed for her supervisor's job when she moved onwards and upwards. Unbeknown to him Ginnie had recommended him for the role and been told by Steve Harrington that the job was his but to keep it to herself while H.R. worked out the package details and the fit with the other dozen or so new recruits and whom, as their manager, Ginnie would be expected to interview alongside one of the H.R. team. Like all large companies Wessex had a strict grading and salary system into which they all had to fit but as a thirty-year old with two young kids and a wife at home, Ginnie knew the increase would be most welcome to Simon as hers had been.

She gazed out of the window with occasional glances at her computer screen to feign some work while wool-gathering about Claude's declaration at lunchtime. Like, what had happened to the girl who only a matter of weeks ago had replied to Iona Pierce's question *had she given up on men with* 'If one comes along that I fancy I'll bleed him dry then throw him out. In the meantime, they and any other relationship can wait.'

Hah! That was before the mighty aphrodisiac that had the power and success of a CEO had declared his love for her. The waiting bit was also playing out as a small truth as there was only three weeks until he was legally single. Or was it all bullshit? An old-fashioned game of fancy word's and salve to his conscience in these #Me Too days for him to get inside her knickers?

Didn't he know that he didn't have to bother with all this love stuff or time limits? She would willingly take him to bed right now, tonight if necessary. Afterall, they'd had two lunchtime dates now which was plenty of time to get acquainted and he was the supreme boss of bosses at her workplace and where he'd already facilitated a manager's promotion and salary increase. In the past she'd let strangers take her home and shag her after just a couple of vodka shots and an hour of chat down the club, so why not Claude after two lunchtime dates, total support of her rugby project and a twelve and a half grand salary increase?

Then what? Bleed him dry in his posh new flat until he gets bored and she gets a broken heart?

Still, she'd still have the manager's job and extra salary.

Wouldn't she?

Or is that being mercenary to a basically good human being who was just made that way and had to declare his love before they *moistened* each other?

Heidi's so very apt phrase about her dad screwing his lover as the helicopter plunged into the ground would stay with her forever. One thing was for certain, from Maxie the bakers apprentice and his floury condoms through any number of useless and frustrating men, Ginnie had never met anyone like this one.

*

On the last training session on the Thursday night before the Saturday game, Lindsey split them up into Howies and Petticoats and had them go over and over their set piece plays and positions. Under Rocky's barked tutelage and J. J's encouragement the pack and Howies replacements practised scrums and lineout's until they were fit to drop, such that it was left to Lindsey, Sherry and some of the backs who hadn't expired physically, to wheel the heavy Rhino back to its place in the shed afterwards. Meanwhile, the Petticoats ran and passed their attacking and defensive lines with Magical Mollie Cook at the helm receiving the ball from Tanya Flipper Bryan before directing her spin passes left and right at full pace to Ginnie, the loudly exhorting skipper, Iona Tea-Tray Pierce, and an occasional missed pass to Avril Love-Bites Gordon when she came into the line. If you had been given a nickname by Heidi, that was your singular call-out and so 'Magical' having received the ball from 'Flipper' gave it to the 'Skipper' who moved it along the line to the speeding 'Tea-Tray' and then onto 'Love-Bites.' Most of the time the ball ended up in either of the two winger's hands and Romany did her Blue-Streak bit flying down the wing on one side and the thus far unnamed Gita the other before dotting the ball down over the line. Fifteen times they ran the attacking line with only two dropped balls and one knock-on. Good numbers, Lindsey said encouragingly and that if they could be repeated in the game it would give us an attacking chance. As for the defence, that relied on our ability to deny them the ball through our tackling. Or, in Heidi-speak, 'smash them to the focking ground until their dimpled bum globes quiver in fright like jelly fish in a tsunami.'

In the changing room afterwards, Lindsey checked the period list – named by Heidi in her inimitable style as the Clot Slot – and where only one automatic pick for the team, Stella Waters, and one of the bench replacements, would be at her 'severe' stage and unfit to play on the Saturday, with two 'medium' sufferers, Billie 'Put the Fire Out' Hayden and Mary-Jane 'Biggie' Bagnall marginal but probably fit enough to start. No one wanted to miss out on the first game, including the replacements who Lindsey said, regardless of how the game was going, would all get at least fifteen minutes in the second half barring injury. Stella was suitably crestfallen at her bad luck and given a sympathetic hug by all her team mates.

Before she had left the office that afternoon Ginnie had rang Vera Godwin at Supermarine and asked if she knew any referee's and line assistants who were going spare and like the well organised expert, she was Vera had already arranged them. It would be a recently qualified woman referee she said who was glad of the match experience. The line assistants would be whoever the ref brought along but Vera had requested an all – women set of officials. Ginnies next call was to Gavin the young groundsman and she told him to have the pitch, flags, and post protectors out by 1.30 P.M. on the Saturday. Did she want the crowd roped off around the outside of the pitch, it kept them a reasonable distance from the players, he said? A good idea Gavin, Ginnie had said. Well, done, you're a star although for the very few supporters she was expecting a rope would be overkill.

Just learning to be a manager and reward good work she said to herself replacing the receiver as his effusive thanks began to sound overdone.

As the tired squad left the changing room to go home on the Thursday night, she also told them all to make sure all their families and friends knew about the game and to invite them along. Ginnie had done that very thing to Malorie on the previous Saturday when her clubbing friend had again emailed her in to ask if she was up for the night out. About time Ginnie had levelled with her about the squad and her part in it and invited her, Sheila, Marie and the about-to-get-married Bella along to the game on Saturday afternoon. It was doubtful if they'd come, Saturday afternoon was their time for shopping and several times Ginnie had accompanied them to Bristol, Reading or Cheltenham on the train to buy clothes. Ginnie also sent an invite to Louise George, the Traveller Community Officer responsible for Romany being in the squad and then one to her brother Robert. She thought about inviting her parents but decided against it, her miserable father wouldn't come out from behind his newspaper for long enough and her timid mother wouldn't venture out without him. And if they did get there, they would probably embarrass her by bickering the whole time.

Several times when he dropped Romany off for training or picked her up in his old rattling scrap van, Ginnie had had a brief conversation with her granddad, Tink Cutler. He was a man of few words and had admitted to Ginnie that rugby was 'furren' to him, which she had interpreted as 'foreign.' He was however, at great pains to tell her that he was very happy for Romany who never stopped 'yammering' about it to him from morning to night and if she was happy, then so was he. Ginnie didn't like to tell him that three months ago the game had been 'furren' to her as well. Romany said he would be staying for the game instead of leaving and coming back 'arter' to get her.

As the weary squad stood around the car park waiting for their lifts the irrepressible Heidi shouted as the red Jaguar F Pace roared through the gate with the mini-dicked Damian in leather driving gloves at the wheel. The poor stunted little sod could be hung like a bull on heat but he would forever be known to the entire squad as 'Mini-Dick Damian.'

'Just what Mama needs on a soaking wet Saturday afternoon watching her darling butt- muddy daughter give a charm of visiting female chaffinches from across town a severe physical twatting with a funny shaped ball...'

It sent them all home with an expectant smile on their tired faces and when she got home Ginnie had looked up the collective noun for chaffinches...which was, inevitably, a charm.

Chapter Fourteen

When Ginnie awoke on Saturday morning it felt as if she hadn't slept at all. She had purposefully gone to bed early Friday night to get a good night's rest and then tossed and turned all night spooling in and out of surreal rugby dreams. She had been a part of a rugby game where she kept dropping the ball, got hammered every time she tried to catch it or bent down to pick it up, dislocated her shoulder tackling a brute of a Supermarine female forward with a big black beard and hands like a blacksmith's anvil, and, equally weirdly, broke her leg when she cannoned into her brother Robert's wife Emily when chasing the ball down the side-line and was stretchered away to hospital. Finally, bringing a few precious hours of relief, having exhausted all the possible and mainly disastrous scenarios for herself and beloved team, she had finally dropped off at somewhere around four a.m. and was relieved to find that when she awoke, although still tired she was in one piece. After a long shower and big breakfast at nine o'clock she had a phone call from Billie Hayden to say her period was a bad one and she wouldn't be able to play today. Two players on the Clot Slot bench but it could have been worse. Ginnie called Lindsey and they decided to put Silvie Greatorex in at number eight as a replacement for Billie. Her next call to Silvie was greeted with loud whoops and promises to play out of her skin.

With time to kill Sainsbury's was the next stop where she stocked up on some necessities, pausing to ponder for a while at the wine section. Finally, she selected two bottles of Merlot and put the other two back. Four being her usual weekly haul she felt smugly sanctimonious by reducing it by two. One of which would go tonight after they had won their first game, if she had the energy left to unscrew the bottle top.

The weather was fine and it wasn't raining. Lindsey had said that with our Blue Streak speedster and plenty of pace in the Petticoats, a dry pitch was to our advantage.

By the time she had been to the dry cleaners and B & Q to get some batteries and a plug it was still only eleven o'clock when she got back to the apartment so she made a coffee and sat down to put a few words down on paper. The matches she had watched both in person and on the telly, always had a player's huddle before kick-off at which a senior player, usually the captain, coach, or pack leader, said a few motivating words. She was intending to do the same. Having scrapped the first three attempts as being pretentious and overly wordy, it was only a friendly game of rugby between two new ladies' sides, not a Popes speech to the faithful, she memorised a few lines that would do. If she faltered Heidi would no doubt wow everyone with a few exquisitly chosen phrases that would send them into battle like heroines on speed. Then she pressed her shirt and shorts for the second time and packed her kit.

At twelve forty-five, an hour and forty-five minutes before kick-off, she pulled into the car park to find that at least half of the team were already there with three of them, including Heidi in full kit tossing a ball about. The pitch looked resplendent with the white lines crisp and true and the blue flags hung limp without any wind. Gavin and Jimmy, the grounds staff, were still putting the ropes one metre from the match lines around the outside to keep the spectators away from the players or, if Heidi takes umbrage at some remark or other, the other way around. Sherry already had the tackle bags out under the posts at the home end nearest the changing rooms and Lindsey was working on lineout throwing accuracy with Gina, against dots she had already marked onto the same goal posts at various heights representing the leaps of the two tall second rows of Heidi and Ellie. As Ginnie got out of her car others arrived. There was an air of palpable excitement and good cheer about the place. Tink Cutler came rattling through the gates and as soon as he'd pulled up Romany shot out of the passenger seat with her kit bag and raced towards the changing room as if she was late for kick-off. Ginnie let her go and just stood there soaking it all up. Ellie was next uncoiling her long, sinuous legs from her boyfriend's Mini Cooper, then reaching back in through the door to give him a peck on the cheek before bestowing the full beam of her smile on Ginnie.

'Here we are then,' she said languidly walking towards the side-line where Ginnie stood.

'The big day has arrived.'

Rocky Cook and her younger sister Magical Mollie arrived next in Rockys car. Pleased to see them, Ginnie and Ellie rushed over to greet them.

By one-thirty the entire team were out on the pitch warming up. Lindsey was trying to ensure that no one was expending too much energy, with still an hour to go before kick-off there was a danger that some of them would expire before they started.

Then Vera Godwin, the Supermarine Director of Ladies Rugby arrived in the front passenger seat of a packed mini-bus and the opposition began to stream out of their transport with some of them already wearing their distinctive red and navy hooped shirts. Having introduced herself to Vera because they hadn't met only talked on the telephone, Ginnie escorted her and the team to their changing room and left them to it.

When she got back outside Sherry was trying to get everyone together for a team photo and Ginnie took her place with a rugby ball between her legs as captain in the middle of the front row where the smaller guys all knelt. Then Gavin the groundsman had to take another photo as Sherry took her place on the edge of the standing line up. As they began to go through their warm-up drills the Supermarine team trotted out to the pitch towards the far end for their drills. Four or five of them stopped to say hello to Rocky and Magical, whom they knew as former Supermarine players. As one big, wide-shouldered girl with grey blonde short hair trotted past Heidi, she gave her a scowl. The tall Fannies Goth, who was doing some gentle shoulder bashing with Ginnie, spat on the ground and nodded at the receding Supermarine player.

'A skank's head has just appeared from the snaky Hydra of my past enemies,' she said. 'Remember my Gothic shiner, black eye and sore twat from the interview?'

'How could I ever forget' Ginnie replied.

'Well, she's one of the pair of shite hawks who placed the metal toecap of her Doc's in the tender part of my burrow covert, what I called my *complexities* at the time…' Heidi scanned the rest of the Supermarine team who were also warming up. 'Those shite hawks usually hunt in pairs but I don't see the other bird brain. It's a good chance to even up the score a bit, eh?'

Ginnie rounded on her. 'Oh no you bloody don't Heidi, if you so much as glare at her during the game I'll have you off that pitch so fast your arse will break the sound barrier. This is our first game and it's a friendly so I suggest you try and show a little restraint. A little, er… rapprochement.'

That Aggy word again. Aggy words, Heidi words and now she was using one to the other, one day she would find some of her own.

Heidi grinned widely and raised her hands. 'Ah mon ami, c'est toujours la meme chose avec les Anglais, wiz rapprochement, wiz rendre.'

Serves me right Ginnie thought. I had French at school as well, should have bloody listened then I'd know what she was saying.

Just then before she dug an even deeper hole to bury herself in a young lady in black covered in badges came up to her.

'Are you the captain of the Fantail Furies?'

The Fantail Furies, it sounded so old fashioned now that everyone referred to them as the Furious Fannies or Fannies for short, but it was probably right that the referee should use their registered name.

'I am.'

'Would you like to join myself and the captain of Supermarine on the centre spot for the toss…to choose ends and who kicks off?'

'It would be a pleasure' said Ginnie following the black-clad young lady who couldn't be older than twenty-one.

The Supermarine Captain and number ten was a good-looking girl of about Ginnies height with auburn dreadlocks piled high on her head and a nose full of freckles. Her mass of hair was held with matching Supermarine colours of red and navy ribbons keeping it altogether. That, thought Ginnie, is a stupid way to have your hair for a rugby game and it will soon be all over the place as soon as you begin to run. Catching a blaze of colour at ground level Ginnie looked down to see that she was also wearing a pair of scarlet Malice boots with an orange diagonal strip, the exact same pair that Ginnie had on although hers was obviously new. Okay, Dix hadn't sold a pair to anyone in the Fannies squad so he'd kept to his word there but nevertheless, Ginnie figured it was a bad omen. The Supermarine captain introduced herself as Shannon, smiled and nodded downwards.

'Love the boots' she said without any apparent... malice.

She didn't try any strong handshakes either otherwise Ginnie – keeping her face neutral but still pissed off about the boots – would have got Cassie from the bench to squash her fingers. Ginnie lost the toss and Shannon said they'd stay as they were and receive the kick off. They shook again and with the referee and went back to their respective squads with Ginnie muttering down to her boots that they were to kick some opposing captain's arse.

It was all very well Ginnie telling Heidi to behave but she was getting pumped up as well and she still had the team talk in the pre-match huddle to come.

Two minutes later Ginnie was going through a gentle running and passing routine with Iona and Magical Mollie when she suddenly looked up and found that there were at least fifty spectators standing around the ropes...including Aggy and Claude and three of her four Saturday night boozing mates of Malorie, Sheila, and Marie. The almost married Bella wasn't there but it was still a surprise to find the other three of them had rocked up. With a slight feeling of guilt Ginnie was glad that they were on the opposite side of the pitch from Claude, their language and screeching could become a bit well, fucking agricultural at times. Not that she was ashamed of them...well, alright, maybe she would be just a teeny weenie bit anxious had they been stood next to Claude and Aggy yelling about how pissed Ginnie got on Saturday nights and how she often ended up in bed with a strange man. And there was her brother Robert and his wife the very pregnant Emily, both waving at her standing next to Flipper Bryans husband and anotherTim, who had the gorgeous twin three-year-old boys clinging onto his legs in identical dungaree outfits. Next to Tim was the nurse Lucinda who was in a civil partnership with Rocky Cook and had arrived in her own car and then came Stan the Wink and a Pint Mackay alongside a young man she didn't recognise. The portly Stan, who she had emailed as promised that the game was on, gave her a coy little wave. Next along were the two tankie husbands of Gina and Avril, both slim, fit looking young men in army fatigues standing a metre or so from Heidi's haughty looking mum swathed in real furs with her tiny-todgered mate Damian alongside who was in conversation with Ellie's tall, black rugby-playing archaeologist boyfriend. Romany had purposefully stood her granddad at the far end of the ground and who had now been joined by Louise George, in order, as she said running back to join Ginnie, 'he will see I get a try.'

It turned out to be a better idea than either of them had thought.

Did I say fifty spectators? Ginnie thought, more like a hundred and fifty with a separate coach load belonging to Supermarine and several others still coming in through the gates and then having to jump aside as Dixie boy roared up making the maximum noise on his Fireblade. She must have a word with Mandy, it was time her airhead of a boyfriend from the Sports Emporium was hurled somewhere violently by his Judo black-belt girlfriend. All the squad seemed to have friends and family there waving and gesticulating at their girl resolutely, some of whom she recognised from delivering and picking them up from practice.

I must calm down, thought Ginnie with her heart beating like a trip hammer. Stay cool and in the moment, too much aggression will only make me fuck up when the ball comes my way – as, according to Linsey – it would if she was unprepared for it. Should try a little *rapprochement* with myself otherwise it won't be Heidi in the sin bin but me, friendly or not. Then imagine how bloody stupid she'd look in front of *everyone* parked on the bully bench for ten precious minutes while the opposition spectators gave her two fingers and jeered at her.

For *everyone* on the side-lines, substitute Claude Dillon and who was standing out in the periphery of her vision like a brightly lit lighthouse on a dark day and becoming the only spectator to matter.

After a minute on the tackle bags supervised by Lindsey with her and Sherry hanging onto the two bags with Supermarine inked on them, the referee emerged from the changing room with two female line assistants.

'The pitch will be knee deep in the sisterhood' growled Heidi getting up from a particularly violent smash on the tackle bag that rocked Sherry backwards, 'with a veritable parliament of black whistle blowing owl's in charge of proceedings.'

'At least they're not crows' Rocky said getting to her feet from the next bag along.

Even though she had never heard the expression before Ginnie never doubted for a moment Heidi's word for the fact that the collective noun for owls was a parliament. Charms of finches and parliaments of owls, who ever thought of these things?

'What's the collective name for crows?' Ginnie asked Rocky when Heidi was out of earshot.

'A murder' replied the erudite pack leader with a lopsided grin.

'One minute to kick-off' bellowed the surprisingly strong voice of the young referee running towards the centre spot. On that Ginnie gestured to everyone to come to her for the huddle and took a deep breath in preparation to give the first motivational team talk of her life. When everyone was assembled in a circle with their arms around each other with their heads craned forward, except the two groundsmen who were gathering up the equipment, Ginnie cleared her throat.

'Right girls, the universal message that we are women and as such gentle giving creature's stops here and now. To be successful in this sport against other women, we must weaponize our skills and be hard and unrelenting in our physicality and totally committed to each other. If some great skank of an opposing girl...' she looked directly at Heidi and received a broad grin of friendly compliance ...'gives you an elbow in the kisser, reply in kind with twice as much force, when the ref isn't looking of course. The only difference between that player and you is that *she* will have a big bruise on her face and *you* will have the ball. So, hands in the middle Fannies, it's time to get bloody furious...'

'Way to go skipper' shouted Heidi slapping the top of the pyramid of hands and they all gave a cheer as they broke up to take their positions for Magical Mollies kick off.

Ginnie wasn't sure what her little speech had done for the team but it sure as hell had settled her down. As she took her position Lindsey, who had overheard Ginnies little team homily from the outside, gave her the thumbs up and a few voices in the crowd pretty much all the way around both side-lines were raised in a cheer as the referee blew for the start.

*

It was, Lindsey said afterwards, the perfect way to start a game of rugby. Magical Mollies nerveless drop kick from hand was high and landed three metres inside the Supermarine twenty-two metre line.

And underneath it with arms outstretched was the opposing scrum-half who'd confidently called that it was hers... before promptly letting it slide right through her open hands to the ground.

'Knock on, advantage to the Pinks' bellowed the referee as Ginnie, suddenly pumped to the eyeballs with adrenalin that she simply couldn't ignore and following up flat out, booted the ball forward whereupon it skidded untouched through the Supermarine defence and came to rest just over their try line in the corner. Before anyone could react a pink and black clad runner known as the Blue Streak shot past all the back-peddling Supermarine defence and fell on the ball before their full back had a chance to react. For a moment there was a stunned silence as Romany got up holding the ball with a big grin on her elfin face and waved at her granddad and Louise who were no more than fifteen metres away.

'Try' shouted the ref after a brief chat with her line assistant on that side and as the cheering started around the side-lines the entire team ran over to their rapid little traveller and engulfed her with hugs and high fives. Less than ten seconds it had taken the Fannies to score. Ginnie, remembering Lindsey's comment about the big team cheque books coming out for their lightning-fast winger, risked a look at Vera Godwin as she ran back to her position while Avril placed the kick on the tee just inside the side-line. The Supermarine Director was already waving her arms about while in deep conversation with her assistant and the coach of her second team.

With Avril's left-footed kick a near miss as it shaved the outside of the post, the score was 5 – 0 as Shannon, the Supermarine fly-half with the mass of piled high hair restarted with her drop kick from the centre spot. This time it was safely gathered in by Iona who flicked it outside to Gita. As the slim Anglo-Indian got up speed down the right wing with the ball tucked under her right arm, she was clattered into touch by the Supermarine flanker and led there prone for a while.

It was a brutal albeit borderline fair tackle for a supposed friendly around the Fannies winger's waist compounded by an overly rough leg drive after and well over the side-line that took Gita three metres beyond the roped off spectators' area. The ref let it go and called over the Fannies trainer and Lindsey sent Sherry over with a bottle of water and some soothing words. As Sherry was easing the shaken winger back to her feet Lindsey called Ginnie over. A look passed between Rocky and Heidi that said OK, we know where we stand now with this so-called friendly and what to do about it.

'It's no surprise after that start that they're double teaming on Romany and giving Gita the treatment,' Lindsey said quietly nodding towards where the speedy traveller was standing on her wing with two Supermarine defenders hovering close by. 'This means that there will be a big gap inside her so tell Mollie to favour the left side and you and Iona go that way with her on the next attack.'

Ginnie nodded and passed on the instruction to Magical and Tea -Tray as the revitalised Gita trotted back into position for the opposition line-out.

The Supermarine hooker threw the lineout ball to their lock, the solid looking grey blonde-haired girl who had been one of Heidi's nightclub opponents. It was caught neatly by the lock and passed back to their scrum half who this time held on to it before kicking it over all the forwards heads into the space in front of Gita and Iona. As the big, bustling short-haired lock charged through the Fannies forwards towards the ball she was elbowed heavily into touch by the revenge seeking Heidi who couldn't help but exact a little revenge for herself and Gita at the first opportunity.

'Unnecessary roughing' hollered the young referee holding her hand up for a penalty to the visitors.

'What am I supposed to do' the gangly Goth said running alongside the ref. 'Wash her feet in goats milk and carry her over our line kissing her arse in celestial homage?'

The spectators next to the play and those players on both sides who had heard the quip started laughing and even the referee smiled, but that didn't stop her awarding an extra ten metres to Supermarine for backchat. She might be young and inexperienced but this young lady was determined to make her mark as a disciplined official who wouldn't stand any nonsense. Ginnie placed a soothing hand on the shoulder of the fuming Heidi and walked back into position under their posts for the penalty kick alongside her.

'Just weaponizing my feminine elbows on the skanky one, skip' Heidi muttered.

Ginnie said nothing preferring to concentrate on the game.

Shannon, pinning her already unruly mob of dreads and stray strands back in place, coolly placed the kicking tee on the ground and with a free swing of the slightly used scarlet and orange Malice boot slotted the kick between the posts.

5 – 3.

Fifteen minutes of midfield toing's and froing's passed until the opportunity that the Fannies were waiting for came about. It came from the first scrum of the match on the left-hand side of the halfway line from a Supermarine put-in when the Fannies strong front row with Biggie Bagnall in the van reacted to a call from Rocky Cook and pushed the opposition pack back over their own ball. Picking it up from the base of the scrum, Sylvie, the replacement number eight threw it to Flipper Bryan and who, as if she'd been playing for years spun a beautiful long pass into Magical Mollies belly button on the right of centre. With two opposition players bearing down on her Magical fooled them both with a right feint and left sidestep before moving purposefully inside the Supermarine half. Drawing the next defender, she flicked the ball to the charging Ginnie just behind on her left who ran towards the waiting Romany before herself feinting a left pass to the speedy winger and instead swerving inside and through the gap left by the opposition centre who was acting as double cover with her own winger on Romany as coach Lindsey had noticed. Hardly believing her luck Ginnie was through and over the Supermarine twenty-two metre line unopposed. Seeing the fullback charging towards her from her right she again swerved inside her feeling her despairing fingers brush her sleeve, and was through and under the posts. Taking care to fall on the ball as they had practised time and again, Ginnie grounded it and was immediately awarded a try by the referee who had kept right up with play.

The Fannies and their supporters went wild and during the melee of hugs and high fives that followed from her team mates including a particularly strenuous hug from Heidi, Ginnie stole a glance at the side-lines where Aggy was jumping up and down with glee and Claude had his hand stationary in the air. Magical slotted the kick this time from just in front of the posts.

12 – 3.

'Brill try Skip,' Rocky Cook said as they prepared for the Supermarine kick off. 'One thing we'll need for the next game is a proper score board cos if we're gonna keep getting tries like this it will come in handy to see where we're at during the game.'

Ginnie tried hard not to smirk at the compliment and made a mental note to get a scoreboard made. Her dad was a carpenter by trade and could do that, couldn't he?

After longish period of error-strewn play with knock-on's, dropped passes and entering the ruck from the side instead of directly behind – standard mistakes from any rugby side let alone two new ones playing their first game, another long, mazy run from Ginnie broke the stalemate before passing outside to Iona who was only just prevented from exploiting the same gap her captain had made for her own try, before the ball was knocked from her hand by the opposing full back five metres from the line.

A couple of times Rocky was called upon with Biggie and Gina, to come to the aid of Magical as she was being chased down by the back-rowers of Supermarine, their experience of having played with Mollie or at least practised with her earlier in the season. They were very aware of how the younger Cook could turn a game with her genius side steps and feints.

Ginnie was everywhere. Cajoling, encouraging, giving her hand to grounded Fannie players to help them back to their feet and a threat whenever she had the ball in her own hands and was running at the opposition defence with Magical and Iona alongside.

Then, completely against the run of play, Supermarine scored a try.

It came from a long and somewhat despairing kick out of defence by Shannon and after a neat catch and kick forward by Avril; Ellie was penalised for being in front of her kicker and therefore off-side when she caught it and then ran past the lock. It wasn't a rule that most of the Fannies understood very well but, as Lindsey said later, the best way to din into the brain the many rules of this complicated game was to be pulled up for breaking one. The resulting line kick from Shannon took Supermarine to within five metres of the Fannies goal line for their line out, and the throw and catch by the short-haired powerful lock, obviously one of their star players, followed by her subsequent charge over the line shoved wholeheartedly by the other opposition forwards. It was a training ground try greeted with great relief and cheering by the Supermarine team and their travelling fans as they high-fived their way back into position leaving a muddy group of Fannie Howies slowly and painfully getting to their feet. With Shannon's trusty scarlet and orange Malice missing the kick from out wide the half-time whistle went with the score at 12 – 8 in the Fannies favour.

Where, Ginnie found herself thinking as she walked down to their posts for the break, had the first half gone? It was over in a trice.

Still, she had scored a good try based on the coach's clever observance...a captains well-taken effort with some evasive skill involved and had a couple of threatening runs and hadn't once been heavily brought down, knocked-on or dropped a ball.

It was a good feeling and she wanted more... especially if Claude was going to hold his hand in apparent admiration like that...or of course, he could have just been waving to someone else he knew on the other side of the pitch.

*

'Standout first half Ginnie' said Lindsey when they were sitting down under the posts with the team taking refreshing gulps of water from the ever-busy Sherry. 'We've got far more pace in the Petticoats than they have so that's where we'll win this game. The forwards are well matched but we must watch that big ash-blond lock. She's mobile, strong and has good hands. I want her closely marked so make sure that one of our flankers – J.J. or you Mandy -are always on her and remember she can't run if you have her around the legs. Gina, drop back a bit from the ruck if you can so when the ball does come back on our side you will have a bit of space to run at them with, and remember girls, they have double-teamed Romany so Ginnie, Mollie and Iona are having a field day running at their defence down the middle with their pace and swerve, so get the ball into Mollie and the skipper's hands and just watch the scoreboard roll. Heidi, Ellie, is everything alright, plenty of energy left?'

'We're just fine and having a wonderful time skank-hunting' Heidi said giving her fellow second row next to her a fist bump.

'Gita my love that knock you got right at the start was a heavy one and you've done well to get through that half. I'm bringing Jenny on in your place a little earlier than envisaged right away so you can rest. Also, I'm pulling you off Biggie, you've had a good half but fatigue is beginning to set in. Cassie, you'll take Biggies place at prop for the restart. The other subs will be coming on within ten or fifteen minutes. Mollie, Tanya, everything all right?'

Both girls gave her the thumbs up.

'Avril…?'

'I'd like a bit more of the ball but otherwise rolling along beautifully.'

'Yeah, me too,' said J.J. spitting a globule of South African spit into the turf leaving her mates wondering if she meant more ball or rolling along beautifully.

'Ginnie, have you anything to add?'

'Just this; Romany is being tied down by this double-teaming and although it's giving us other chances our little flyer having scored that try hasn't had a chance since. Perhaps we should swap wings between Romany and Jenny right from the off to confuse the markers and give Romany a bit more space.'

'That's a great idea – happy with that you two?'

Jenny, who was warming up with a few rapid press-ups nodded without pausing and Romany just grinned.

'Don't forget' said Ginnie to Romany as they trotted out to the far end of the pitch for the restart. 'We'll be kicking the other way this time so tell your granddad to go down the other end.'

'Bohica time Fannies' shouted Gina using her famous cry for the first time in the game as she charged into a ruck that had been set up by a long, sinuous glide from Ellie. This was after the Supermarine kick off stalemate had settled in for a few minutes in the centre of the pitch as the errors again began to take their toll until Rocky had fallen on the opposition knocked-on ball and Tanya had picked it up and passed it to the tall black lock for her first real run of the game.

'You heard the happy hooker' cried J.J. following Gina into the ruck with her strong presence and cry. Smuggled back legally from hand to hand the ball arrived in Cassie's hands for the first time and she had a little muscular trundle down the centre of the pitch for five metres before falling over. Flipping the follow-up ball from the ground to Magical, Tanya took a nasty clattering from the opposition flanker without the ball and the ref again blew up for unnecessary roughing.

'Dirty skanky bitch-focker' Heidi muttered to the flanker standing on her hand as she struggled to her feet. 'I'm reversing that penalty for abusive language' hollered the referee.

'Supermarine ball.'

As before the dreadlocked Shannon kicked the ball into touch around the Fannies five metre line. The last time they had scored from this position with a push-over try from the lineout from their big, muscular lock.

'On big A' their hooker called loudly lining up the throw and since the tall locks name was Amber, the Fannies forwards knew where the throw would once again be aimed..

'Get me as high as you can' Heidi hissed to Cassie standing just forward of the position of Amber. 'I'm gonna nick this from the hands of the twat kicker…'

With Cassie's superb strength behind and Rocky turn and strong lift in front of her, Heidi, her arms outstretched upwards to their limit, was hoisted around ten foot in the air and soured above the intended target. Grabbing the ball, she neatly turned it back to Flipper who was standing on her own line. From Flipper it went through the posts into Magical Mollie's hands who was at least two metres behind her own line. A feint and a quick jink and the clever fly-half left two charging Supermarine forwards face-planting the mud before passing to Ginnie outside her on her own twenty-two metre line. A fast-swerving run took Ginnie to the halfway line before she passed it inside to Iona who'd been tracking her run. Suddenly the changed winger Romany was hovering just behind and outside Iona as she moved inside the Supermarine half. Drawing her opposing centre into the tackle Iona passed it to Romany just before she was brought to the ground heavily. Sensing hesitancy from her two markers who had followed her to the opposite side but left a gap, and with forty metres of open space in front of her, Romany safely caught the pass and that was another nailed-on Fannies try. No-one was going to catch the flying Blue Streak who once again left her markers clutching at fresh air as she flew down her empty wing and arrowed in towards the middle and having crossed the line dotted the ball down behind the posts just as her granddad Tink and Louise arrived at that end.

The three of them hugged while the rest of the Fannies high-fived and whooped.

Lindsey said later that she had never seen a better end-to-end try executed by a women's side in her many days as a coach.

The small crowd went wild and a chant went up of 'Go Fannies, go!'

Ginnie didn't look at the spectators, she was too busy getting the badly shaken Iona to her feet and checking that she was alright to continue. When Magical again slotted the kick from in front of the post's the score was 19 – 8 to the home side.

Heidi was exuberant.

'The twat kicker has been well and truly twatted' she gloated to Ginnie as they took up their positions for the Supermarine restart.

'Just be careful, that referee has you in her sights after the last mouthful.'

'I know, the cherubic dark little angel is probably deeply, unreservedly in love with me and will want to rush me off to Bequia for a sumptuous beach wedding after the game.'

Ginnie just had to laugh as the ball once again came towards her from out of the dull but dry Saturday afternoon Wiltshire sky and she caught it easily and applied her own right Malice scarlet with orange diagonals boot to it with force and lofted it back down field and into touch on the halfway line.

Another penalty was awarded for unnecessary roughness as Judo Sawyer, who'd been having a quiet game thus far, slammed the Supermarine hooker to the ground using her 'going by' judo hip throw, which was fine until Heidi dropped onto the prone hooker with her bony knee slamming into her exposed ribs. As the referee called the penalty Heidi let out an exasperated 'Fock me ref I slipped…'

'Yellow card' shouted the young lady in black brandishing the ten minutes in the sin bin violation notice in Heidi's face. 'I've told you twice now about roughness and language so you can cool off in the bin.'

As Heidi trudged off muttering obscenities, she passed Ginnie who spoke quietly without looking at her.

'I suppose that means the Bequia beach weddings off now!'

'The magisterial black crow and I are temporary estranged' the simmering Goth said with just the hint of a grimace. 'When I come back on, I'm gonna piss in both her eyes so she can see clearly and then shit in her whistle to keep it quiet...'

As Heidi approached the edge of the pitch a small group of vociferous Supermarine female supporters began to boo her. The sarcastic finger they got was followed by a hostile lurch in their direction. Luckily Sherry got between them in time and dragged Heidi back to the halfway line to serve her penalty on the seat of shame before it became a red card.

On the touchline the haughty Mama Prager sunk even lower into her furs at the behaviour of her daughter while by her side he who would never look a Fannies team member in the eye without incurring the thought that his penis was of childlike proportions, was wearing a huge grin from ear to ear.

In the meantime, the Fannies were a forward short.

Lindsey took the opportunity to make another substitute by bringing on Kayla at Heidi's position of lock and removing the new wing of Jenny to the still shaky Iona's position of outside centre. The Tea Tray was visibly hobbling from the clattering she'd taken while helping to set up the last try and wouldn't be taking any further part in the game. The left wing was now empty with only the unused Stella on the bench with everyone except Heidi and the clot-spotted Billie Hayden now on the pitch.

'Warm up' Lindsey barked to Stella, 'you're on in five.'

'Where…what position\?' Stella asked getting to her feet.

'F. N. my dear, we'll just have to see what happens next' came the cool reply.

Sensing a chink in the Fannies armour Supermarine attacked with renewed gusto with their muscular short-haired lock – Heidi's night club 'twat kicker' to the fore.

A good catch of a high attacking ball from Shannon, whose hair by now was flying around her head like Methuselah's swirling snakes, was taken by 'Love-Bites' Gordon who also showed the presence of mind to call for the mark. Her resulting left-footed kick soured into the Supermarine half where it was dropped by the scrum half…not for the first time. Ginnie made a mental note to keep on bombarding the curly-haired little half-back who was obviously having a mare with catching the high ball. There was a confidence and surety about 'Love-Bites' play that was infectious and the others acted accordingly. Lindsey and Ginnie had noticed in training that the erratic bounce of the oval ball rarely fooled the army PTI and her sixth sense as to where it would go usually got it into her hands safely without mishap. Ginnie was also learning the same skill which was another plus in the Petticoats ranks. She was not up to Romany's extra rapid pace but she was comfortably up there with Iona now who had been a professional athlete and vied with her for the second fastest in the team when they did sprint tests. Lindsey's comment on her unexpected speed had been that, like Romany, she had natural cadence and balance. This ability was also earning her the right to be the captain and it was noticeable that after her try there was a new found confidence from them as a team in asking her positional and strategic questions. And when Rocky and J.J. did that with all their experience, it made her feel loved and wanted.

Scrum to the Fannies just inside their opponents half.

'Take whichever wing you want' she muttered to Romany and having seen her go back to her natural left side closely followed by her two markers, signalled Magical and Jenny to go to the right. Gina hooked the ball cleanly down channel one and it shot out the back to be snaffled by Flipper. She flicked it to Magical who kicked a sweet grubber into space for Ginnie to chase on the opposition twenty-two. Putting all her trust in a left bounce she swerved that way and there it was, sitting up perfectly for her to run onto and slide over the line in the corner for her second try. Tanya 'Flipper' Bryan celebrated this score with a complete airborne three-sixty and her watching twins and husband clapped their clever mum in glee.

Ginnie looked towards Lindsey who was just shaking her head in wonder. It took a force of will but she didn't look in Claude's direction.

With 'Love-Bites' missing the kick from out by the right-hand touch the score was 24 – 8.

Stella came on in place of Romany who was due a rest and immediately caught a long spin pass from Magical Mollie and had a good gallop down the wing before being shoved into touch ten metres short of the Supermarine line. Romany got a big hug from Lindsey before running around the pitch to get another from her granddad Tink and Louise George.

That last score, even though the speedy threat of Romany had been removed, seemed to sap the resolve of the Supermarine side that now needed three scores to win. Their coach did her best to inject some new life into the side and substituted five players including the entire front row, and as Heidi galloped back on after serving her ten minutes in the bin the score was still the same.

'Bend over, Heidi is coming again' the reinvigorated lock shouted her own version of Bohica rushing into a ruck after Supermarine won their own line-out ball before clearing their lines with a good kick from Shannon. And even when Mollie, unusually, dropped a simple pass from Ginnie, the mood remained upbeat as Rocky regained it. No more points were added by either team and then it was all over as the referee blew up for full time. A clear and decisive victory for the Fantail Furies...

Or to give them the name they would always be known as from this moment on, the Furious Fannies.

'The euphoria of winning' crowed Heidi as they waited on the touchline for the beaten Supermarine players, 'is laced with pure dopamine and will drag us to many greater victories...'

The handshakes were conducted by broad smiles and firm grasps from the Fannies against desultory finger twitches from Supermarine. Heidi and Amber scowled at each other and kept their hands apart, unfinished business was behind their neutral facial expressions and both knew that barring injuries they would be facing each other again in the following two weeks in the return match at Supermarine. Vera Godwin, their Ladies Director of Rugby made a point of congratulating Lindsey and then Ginnie on her own performance and the team play and confirmed the return match time at the Supermarine complex at South Marston. It would be, she said pointedly, an altogether different side that the Fannies took on there.

She turned out to be correct but not in the manner she expected.

Lindsey's post-match summing up in the changing room afterwards had been muted but succinct. Everyone had contributed to the victory but certain girls had been outstanding. Ginnie, for one had been a revelation with her two magnificent tries and excellent all-round play, Rocky and the other front row girls had been solid and her younger sister Mollie was, well, simply magical. Romany had also contributed two beautiful tries that only she could have scored. There *were* however, manifest problems to be addressed with discipline…she didn't look at Heidi but everyone knew who she meant, and the error count – to be expected in a brand-new team playing their first game – was far too high. But all in all, they should congratulate themselves on a job well done and if that was their thing, feel free to have a glass or two that evening because they'd all earned it.

And in truth, from the moment the ref blew to start the game Ginnie never gave Shannon's scarlet and orange Malice boots another thought and as for Claude, he was long gone when she emerged from the changing room.

Which was a pity because a few words of encouragement from him would have meant a great deal.

Chapter Fifteen

Saturday night after the game when Ginnie got home and when, eventually, her mobile stopped ringing with congratulations – first Aggy with enthusiastic comments about Ginnies play and captaining of the team with no comment about her father's Claude's enjoyment or otherwise, then Robert, her brother adding his gentle praise, followed by Malorie imploring her to 'come out and celebrate the great victory with the girls tonight.' Ginnie finally poured herself a large glass of Merlot and sank gratefully into her bath. Every muscle ached and she had a bruise forming on her thigh where she had caught a Supermarine boot in a ruck – *better than a Doc Marten's in the twat* – she muttered a la Heidi rubbing the bruised area. But, truth be known, she had hardly noticed the bang and it didn't stop her from scoring her second try afterwards and she hadn't stopped playing or needed any attention. So much for adrenaline eh.

After a long soak with twice topping up the suds with more hot water, she upended the Merlot again and took the two thirds empty bottle to bed and slowly finished the final glass while she checked her emails. It was Sunday tomorrow and a much-deserved free day, her washed hair could wait, she'd wet it in the morning and blow-dry some sort of shape into it. Her bedside clock said ten –thirty when she finally gave in and slept the sleep of the innocent.

Luxuriating in a lay-in on the Sunday morning with her aches beginning to diminish, her mobile started ringing again. It was her mother. Robert her brother and his wife Emily were on their way to church but had dropped in on their way and given her and Ginnies dad a run down on the game.

'You never told me you were playing rugby and the captain of the team. Your father was quite impressed when Robert told him how you scored two tries... whatever they are.'

After listening for a few minutes and gently turning down lunch with a small white lie that she was 'going down the club to sort a few things out,' Ginnie got up and stretched and then showered. After a light late breakfast, she carefully washed her shirt, shorts and socks and hung them on the small mobile put-up airing frame to dry. Then she cleaned her boots and went down the supermarket. As she was fighting her conscience by the wine racks over two or four bottles... again...she was just about to place two bottles in her basket when there was a light tap on her shoulder and she turned to see Iona standing there with a full trolley of provisions.

The former professional ice slider known as Tea Tray and who'd had a bloody nose towards the end of the game yesterday and was replaced, gave Ginnie a big, lemon-scented hug and then said her nose was just a bit sore but fine and that she had a nice juicy secret to impart. They paid and placed their shopping in their cars and went back into the supermarket café for coffee, cake, and gossip.

Sipping her coffee and taking a small bite from her Danish pastry Ginnie waited as Iona, the same as Aggy when she had something to impart, smiled and took her time. The power of us women knowing something,

Ginnie thought, turns us all into grinning mutes who hang on to the salacious facts until the last moment.

'Well?' she said in exasperation as Iona continued to munch her muffin contentedly.

'Okay,' she said finally, 'here's a question for you. If you had to guess what Heidi Prager's boy-friend – the one who drives her around in a Morgan sportscar, does for a living, what would it be?'

Ginnie didn't need long.

'He's a vicious and muscular tattooed cage fighter.'

'Try again.'

'Shaven headed nightclub bouncer?'

'Nope, try softening it a little.'

'A male ballet dancer who doubles up as a postman in his spare time but that's my last try.'

Iona giggled.

'As if, no his name is Dexter Keegan Stirling and he's thirty-six and a Don at Balliol College Oxford where he teaches degrees in P.P.E...'

Ginnie looked at her for a long moment with her coffee cup halfway to her mouth while she tried to figure this out before giving in.

'What is P.P.E?

'Philosophy Politics and Economics; I had to look that up as well. It's what they call the degree that runs Britain because of all the politician's that have taken it there.'

'And this Stirling is Heidi's boyfriend?'Ginnie gaped.

'Mad about her evidently and close your mouth, you look like a fish.'

She snapped her mouth shut. It wasn't the first time that had been said about her when surprised, some people, one particular man lately, was quite taken with her mouth when it was open.

'Well bugger me sideways and call me early,' Ginnie breathed out using a favourite curse of her Saturday nightclub friend Malorie with the boob job – the most libertine of the four and usually said after two a.m. and any number of vodka shots and with a strange man in tow in awe of her boobs.

Iona looked around and then leaned forward expectantly.

'They met through an online dating agency that specialises in matching up clever university types with, get this, *sophisticated like-minded partners...*'

'My flabber continues to be gasted.' Ginnie shook her head in wonder at the information. 'Not that Heidi isn't clever, she surely is and has provided me with some of the most hilarious quips I have ever heard, but this brain-box sounds way out of her league, wouldn't you say?'

Iona smiled in a secretive 'there's more' and then said, 'Maybe he is but there's more and well, I haven't got to the good bit yet...'

At this Ginnie took a good bite of her Danish pastry and chewed for a while as Iona toyed with her silence for the second time. Hooked and wanting the 'good bit' like an alcoholic craves the first drink of the day; Ginnie had no choice but to wait it out.

'It turns out that Dex as Heidi calls him, was married before to an ex-student. The marriage only lasted four years before a very acrimonious divorce, and when I say acrimonious, I mean open season for mudslinging warfare as she went for him online with everything she had.'

Ginnie faked a yawn, so far so mundane. Then Iona delivered her bombshell.

'Including the fact that his penis was simply enormous and much too big for her to accommodate without pain...'

The involuntary start of surprise that Ginnie gave caused her to knock over her half-filled coffee cup and a couple of valuable minutes went by as the lady behind the counter came out and cleaned up the mess with a cloth while Ginnie wiped down her damp jeans with a tissue. It at least gave her time to compose herself after the shock of Iona's last wonder of a statement.

'How do you know all this?' she asked when order had been restored.

'After the game yesterday Heidi asked me if I'd give her a lift home. Her mother and the mini-dicked companion had purposefully roared off without her because Mama dear was ashamed of the fact her daughter had been sent off. Heidi lives in Wroughton which is on my way so I said hop in. It was a bit tight in my little Fiat Uno with her long legs but she squeezed them in. Before we got to her mama's place – a wonderful looking large old barn conversion down a private lane with lots of land – she suggested a drink and we stopped at the White Hart. And there we sat for an hour as we did what girls do best which was to talk about our messy love lives while Heidi necked three pints of draught Guinness without a drop touching the sides and I had two sparkling mineral waters because I was driving.'

'And the overlarge member...?

Iona leaned forward again.

'By the time Heidi had finished the third pint she had lost any pretensions and opened out about him, not that she had many to start with. Turns out that the reason Dex's wife sued him for divorce was just that. His perforator was just too bloody big for her and...get this, she was granted said divorce on the basis that every time they made love, she was in great pain because of it...'

'Silly bitch didn't know when she was well off,' muttered Ginnie.

Iona giggled before resuming.

'All this was reported online and of course Dexy boy with his elephantine member was besieged by women from every angle after that, such that the poor man never had a moment's peace...'

'Yeah, I bet he didn't, my heart bleeds for the poor sod.'

'Having told me all this in the pub Heidi gave me the website address that reported the divorce and I, of course, looked it up as soon as I got home. Sure, enough everything she'd told me was there in black and white and the poor man had almost had a nervous breakdown afterwards because of the notoriety. Balliol, his college and at which before this he was a bit of a star teacher... in more ways than one I guess, then gave him a year's sabbatical during which time he travelled all round South America before coming back and resuming his post and by which time the fuss had died down. Six months later and around the time we were getting ready for our first training session, the two of them met through an online dating agency. Do you remember telling me around then that Heidi was a different looking girl at that first training session to the metal-faced Goth you'd interviewed, softer and altogether more feminine? Well, she'd met Dex by then and was probably beginning to enjoy the humungous ride, as it were…'

Iona stopped, giggled again at the wonder of it all and then looked at Ginnie.

'Talking about meeting Dexy boy, you know what this means?'

'Go on' Ginnie said having thought about it and failing to come up with an answer.

Iona giggled again before continuing. 'When Heidi introduces him to us at the club or somewhere, we'll both have to control our eyeline and not *immediately* look down at where his BSD lives…'

'BSD…' Ginnie said then the penny dropped and they both said it at the same time.

'BIG SWINGING DICK!'

They didn't stop giggling for a full five minutes.

As they were walking out to the car park Ginnie stopped and turned to Iona.

'*That's* why Heidi called Damian, her mother's gay companion, mini-dick. It makes more sense now; the poor little gay bugger never really stood a chance in comparison against her new boyfriends alleged monster.'

'Dexy boy, he of the enormous blanket cobra, is allegedly coming to the return match against Supermarine in two weeks' time,' replied Iona. 'If he stands alongside Damian on the touch-line it will be a case of…'she thought for a few moments, 'the great big steam train and the…'

'Hornby Dublo dinky model railway thingy…? Ginnie offered climbing into her car trying to keep a straight face before they both burst into laughter again.

*

Monday morning was manic in the office. It was Ginnies first full day as the Manager of Office Services and she moved into her own office at the far end of the open plan section. It was the same office that Aggy had briefly occupied but was now empty as the Management Trainee had moved on to Finance upstairs and was now starting a two-week course in London.

As she carried her few books and odds and ends into her new office Stan the Wink and a Pint Mackay arrived with an assistant. He gave her a big hug and congratulated her on playing a great game on Saturday.

'My son Martin and I thoroughly enjoyed it,' he said motioning to the assistant who was fastening a 'Manager' sign to the outside of the door.

'I always knew you make it,' Stan said pointing to the sign. 'That's why I left you that meeting table and chairs outside in the main office. Do you want a new set?' He nodded at the incumbent furniture.

'No these are perfectly fine, thank you Stan, and I owe you a pint. Trouble is I never see you in a pub.'

He gave her an extra big wink and another hug.

When Stan had left his son hovered around for a bit before hesitantly asking Ginnie if he could 'take her out for a drink or something.'

'It's the 'or something' that worries me Martin but no thanks, I'm already in a relationship.' She said it gently because Martin couldn't have been a day older than nineteen and it had obviously taken some courage for him to ask her.

Am I in a relationship? She thought when the disappointed young man had gone and she was trying the desk and the new large black leather chair on for size. Can you call it that if you haven't had a shag or even a proper kiss yet? She shouldn't use words like that anymore now she's a manager, especially if she becomes the regular squeeze of the Chief Executive. What was that word – consummated – that was it, and they hadn't *consummated* the relationship or, in Heidi-speak, *moistened* one another. One thing was for certain, with Aggy away and the nisi divorce deadline less than a week away now, he would want lunch today. She should be sure to tell him that she was becoming a popular girl whose star was in the ascendency what with scoring two tries and leading the girls to victory and now settled into her own office domain. On Wednesday she would start interviewing in here with one of the H.R. Officers. They had told her that the campaign in the local and national press for an extra twelve to fifteen Office Services Assistants had produced over eighty replies, twenty-two of which were being booked in for interviews. That was about as many as she had interviewed for the rugby team just a few short weeks ago. The candidates included men and women and wouldn't be such an oddball bunch of misfits and sex maniacs as that rugby lot...would they?

Sure, enough at twelve o'clock on the dot her mobile bleeped with a single word message. She answered his 'Lunch' with an 'O. K.' and then scampered out to the ladies to touch up her face and add some lip gloss. This would be their third lunch and the relationship and him becoming officially single matters were surely coming to a head.

He was waiting for her in the pub car park leaning against the Toyota door. As she pulled up alongside, he opened her car door and handed her out. Reaching back in to get her shoulder bag she closed the door and was about to turn and follow him into the pub when he leaned over and kissed her neck. As she straightened and turned his lips brushed hers. They were soft and lingered a few moments longer than a casual car park greeting should.

'I' he breathed into her face as she got a faint scent of Dior L'Homme, an aftershave that she recognised from a previous man who she couldn not place, 'have been waiting for you…forever it seems.'

'Well, I'm here now shall we go inside?' She said flippantly slightly worried that he seemed to have thrown his previous caution to the wind. He hadn't moved and was still standing there drinking her in.

He shook his head as if waking up and followed her in through the door.

'Don't you lock your car door?' He said moving to what had become their table in the back section.

'Nah, if someone wants to nick my old jalopy, they'd be doing me a favour. I badly need a new one and the insurance money would help.'

She didn't mention that now with her salary increase she could afford one.

He brought their drinks over with the menu, Diet Coke for her and a sparkling mineral water with a slice of lemon floating in the bubbles for him. He nodded at the daily specials chalked on a board.

'Hungary?'

'Ravenous.'

'A couple of medium-rare rib-eye steak sandwiches?'

'Hmm, that would be good.'

Having ordered he congratulated her on the victory against Supermarine and the part she played in it.

'And you scored two brilliant tries. You never told me you were that good.'

'To tell you the truth I surprised myself with the pair of them. Coach Lindsey said they were opportunistic and based on instinct…'

'And the return game is when?'

'A week on Saturday at the Supermarine sports complex at South Marston. Are you coming to that one as well?'

'Unfortunately, no, I'm in Singapore for most of that week and won't be back until the Sunday night. Does that mean you have this coming Saturday off?'

'Yes, the entire weekend is all mine…' Ginnie had a feeling where this was going because the next Saturday was the day his decree nisi was finalised.

'You know what day Saturday is?' He raised his eyebrows with the question.

'April Fool's Day,' she said with mock innocence.

'So, how about this for an idea,' he said taking a bite of his sandwich and chewing ruminatively. 'Not only is it the day I become a completely free man but I am also moving into my new apartment. Do you fancy coming along to have a look at the place and giving me a hand with my clothes and stuff…?

'Do you mean you can't take them off on your own?' Ginnie said with a giggle.

'Definitely not,' he said smiling.

He went on to tell her that his new 'apartment' was set in seven acres of prime Thames-side pasture and had been an old boat house. He had bought it seven years ago in an endeavour to save his marriage thinking perhaps the addition of a small river cruiser for gentle trips along the mighty river would help. Although it was only a couple of miles from their existing manor house, Frances had only visited the place once and decided she didn't like it. As for a small cruiser that received equally short shift and was never purchased. So, when they had finally decided to call their marriage off over a year ago and it had been decided that Frances would stay in the manor house, he'd had plans drawn up for a complete renovation on the boathouse to prepare it for his new bachelor existence.

'The builders are due to finish it today. I dropped in there on my way in this morning and they and the architects have done a brilliant job, particularly with a huge picture window which overlooks the river in both directions. I've got a specialist cleaning company coming in on Wednesday to deep clean the place and the few bits and pieces of furniture I'm bringing from the manor will arrive on Friday.'

She almost asked if that meant the bed but held her peace reminding herself not to be too much of a tart. He gave her a card with the new address on it and she noticed that it was called simply 'The Boathouse' Thames Towpath Lane, Lechlade and the postcode and did not have a telephone number. Still, she had his mobile if needed.

Before they parted and he gave her another and slightly longer brush of his lips at her car door, he murmured that Saturday couldn't come soon enough for him and he would be conscious of her presence in the office beneath him throughout the week.

'Get there whenever you like on Saturday' he said climbing into his Toyota. 'I'll be waiting.'

Chapter Sixteen

The week flew by. Before rugby training on Tuesday night, a physically low-key affair as there were still some stiff and sore muscles left over from the game so Lindsey took it easy by walking through some new moves. This suited Ginnie because her period had come on right on time on the previous Saturday night after the game and although relatively mild and since it usually lasted six days would be over by the following Friday and in time for her date at Claude's place on Saturday. Whoopee, a clear license to shag if it turned out that way and she didn't get hurt in the Supermarine rematch. She wasn't religious but someone up there was looking after her lately and if this series of luck continued, she might even have to attend church to thank someone and or light a candle.

On her way to training, she dropped into a late-night car exhaust, brake, and battery centre to have a new battery fitted. She didn't want to get in her notoriously badly starting car on Saturday morning primed for the big day in Lechlade only find the little sod wouldn't go. The heavily tattooed, grubby-nailed young man who fitted the battery while she waited leered at her and was about to offer a chat-up line when she fore-stalled him with a raised hand and a curt 'Peppery' put-down. 'Forget it.' Wrong time of the month mate, and I don't fancy you anyway...'

He grunted and went back to fitting the new battery.

Wednesday and Thursday she was interviewing for much of both days in her new office with a lovely black guy from H.R. called Raymond who knew all the pensions/holiday entitlements/sick pay, salary scales and so on, leaving her to concentrate on asking the pertinent questions about the candidate's ability to do the job, and on Thursday night Ginnie sat out training and just listened because she was still on the clot slot. It was altogether more intense because Lindsey wanted to concentrate the last three sessions before the game on certain weaknesses and strengths, she'd observed in the Supermarine line-up and style of play. A further day of interviews on Friday after which six job offers and eight thanks-but-no-thanks letters were signed by Ginnie under the heading of Departmental Manager – a new title she had looked at for some time with pride before signing each one and put in the post. This was followed by a twenty-minute interview update meeting with Steve Harrington, her direct boss, and Wessex Marketing Director. And then suddenly it was Friday night and time to think about the following morning.

Which she did by pouring her first glass of Merlot of the week and then having a quiet session with *Mud, Maul Mascara,* the autobiography of Catherine Spencer the former England ladies captain and her present from Claude. She quietly fingered the inscription on the flyleaf – *From C with love.*

It started with a book, she muttered to herself taking a pull at the Merlot, and tomorrow...?

Tomorrow. Tomorrow, tomorrow we will see what we will see.

After another one of her fitful over-thinking nights where she finally got off to sleep around four a.m.

These restless nights were becoming the norm when she had a big day ahead. She awoke at ten and although there was no rush felt behind the clock for some reason. Getting into her car at eleven-thirty which started first press getting a grateful kiss on the steering wheel, she drove to a local florist's and bought a beautiful bunch of budding white lilies bedecked with blue Irises and sprays of green ferns. A hundred and twenty quid down on battery and bouquet and I haven't even got there yet, she muttered to herself driving too fast towards Lechlade. As she turned down a private road sign-posted Towpath Lane she took a deep breath.

The first thing she saw was the gleaming grey and chrome Bentley looking very much at home alongside a large oak framed barnlike structure. As she got out of the car and leaned back in to get the bouquet from the front passenger seat, the plain but beautifully aged old oak front door opened and Claude emerged in a pair of faded cut down jeans and a soft red cashmere jumper with a broad smile on his face. For a man who must have greeted hundreds of dignitaries, bankers, politicians, and captains of industry over the years, his smile and strong hug of welcome was one of obvious relief. Perhaps he had doubted her arrival, she thought handing him the bouquet, either that or she was expected earlier. Never mind, that small cloud of doubt would do him good and she was here now.

With his right arm around her waist and the bouquet in his left he led the way into the building through the front door and up four glass steps...

And into what were quite simply the most stunning building Ginnie had ever been in and all she could do was stand there transfixed with her mouth open.

'Close your mouth, you know what it does to me' he grinned. 'Like it?'

It was like walking into a cathedral. One huge vaulted space with a high latticed oak ceiling and massive uprights and beams divided up into oak framed zones. At the far end was what he had called at lunch a glass viewing panel overlooking the Thames both ways. Some 'viewing' panel, it was the size of a wide-angle cinema screen and covered the entire end wall with a glass floating stairway attached to the side wall going up to a separate framed section at the top of the panel for what was probably a bedroom.

He pushed her forward gently and then pointed downwards.

The entire floor was glass with thin oaken level frames and swirling a metre beneath her feet was the water of the old boathouse. He pressed a remote switch and the dark water suddenly lit up underneath her feet making her start backwards.

'It's alright' he said gently pulling her back by the elbow. 'This floor will stand ten tons without breaking which means the roof could collapse and it would still be there.'

Ginnie probed forward cautiously with her leather boot-clad right foot making him laugh.

'It takes a leap of faith to trust it but look' he handed her the bouquet and ran and jumped up and down on the glass in the middle of the vast open floor making fish dart around underneath in the clear water.

'So' he said waving his arms around to encompass the huge room. 'The brief to my architects who are Fitzpatrick Huntington, the same firm who handled over a hundred redesigns of our High Street retail outlets over the last fifteen years, was one enormous room, with zones, of light and space and uncluttered minimalism.' He pointed down at the door they had just come in by.

'No doors other than the front and rear entrance and exits which are obligatory fire escapes, no walls, corridors, or ceilings with each area blending seamlessly into the next. Under this glass floor' he said jumping up and down again to reassure her that it was safe sending fishes again darting here and there 'flows a diverted tributary from the bank on the edge of my land downstream to link under our feet with the old boat house channel and back into the river out the front. Those fish are real wild Thames varieties and only an hour or so ago a rather large silvery fish, a chub…I think it was, lazily swam right under my feet. The builders, one of whom was a course fisherman, said sometimes he couldn't work because he was so mesmerised watching what swam by, especially pike, a predatory species that hide under here and wait to pounce on the smaller fry.'

What, like you are gonna pounce on me, Ginnie thought.

Still not quite trusting the floor she walked slowly out to the middle where he stood. Towards one side of the front viewing panel was a semi-circle of soft orange suede leather sofas with sharp corners and thin legs. It seemed a long way away. He led her across the glass floor to the panel and they stood and looked left and then right down the double length of the start of Great Britain's most famous river. There were several boats pottering along both ways although the season had not really started and ducks and geese preened themselves on his front lawn bank.

'That way' he said pointing off towards where Lechlade's equally famous old humpbacked stone bridge could be seen in the distance and where Aggy had fallen in the water when the two girls were trying to get out of the rowing boat, 'is where the river begins with a series of streams at a place called Thames Head at Kemble. There's a station at Kemble and from where I often catch the train to Paddington if I need to be in London, saves going in to the office and catching the train from Swindon station. That way' he pointed downstream, 'is where the Manor House is, a distance of some two and a half miles so Frances and Aggy are some distance away although my daughter has gone up to London for the weekend to meet her boyfriend's parents and then attend the course she is taking on Monday.'

Frances and Aggy, especially Aggy, she would have to talk to him about her if the 'relationship' got fully under way. She had a feeling that her friend and daddy's little girl wouldn't like it very much at all if her friend started shagging her father...

If...? Who was she kidding?

Dotted around the glass floor were several brightly coloured rugs which, he said, he'd bought to give the place a little warmth and colour. Then he waved towards a couple of enormous and extremely bright modern paintings on the walls each side of the sofas.

'Had those done especially for the space, the artist is a friend of mine.'

He was chatting away to give her time to take in what had obviously been a bit of a shock to her. His 'apartment' was an architectural glossy magazine showpiece. He took back the bouquet and walked towards the back of the building beyond the door through which they had entered.

'The kitchen, in case you were wondering, is back this way. There's nothing much to see as all the storage and appliances are hidden.'

And there it was, a zoned part of the huge open plan layout at the back and flooded in natural light from a series of grey skylight window frames with pale blue glass set in the slanting roof. With ultra-thin steel legs, the glass seated high stools didn't look strong enough to take the weight of a human being arranged around an island, the whole of the kitchen area was beautifully fitted out in grey marble and granite. This time the floor wasn't glass but a matching but slightly lighter shade of blue slate.

What was on display along the entire back of the kitchen area was two massive wine racks, white bottles of varying chateau on the left were obviously in a wired-in cooler and a variety of reds on the right in plain oak racks. There must have been a couple of hundred bottles.

'Behind those racks' he said pointing. 'Is a utility area and the only other door leading to a four-car garage and a four-acre water meadow that I have had planted with all the local species of wild flowers.'

Ginnie walked around the gleaming island touching here and there until she came to the only appliance on view, a hissing chromium coffee machine.

'I've had that out and bubbling away for a while in anticipation of your coming. Would you like a cup?'

She nodded still not quite ready to say anything.

He put the flowers in a blue glass art jug with the jagged shape of a lightning bolt and half filled it with water and placed it in the middle of the island and then made them two cups of coffee in twee little fine porcelain cups whose sides were transparent.

'Come on, let's go through to the viewing window, I've got something else to show you.'

When they were settled on the sharp soft suede leather orange semi-circle of sofas with their coffees, he picked up a remote from a side pocket and pressed a button. Three metres in front of them a large flat television screen eased down from above and stopped at head height. It was on with muted sound. Sending the television back up he then pointed the remote at the huge glass viewing panel.

'This' he said with obvious relish, 'is one of my special little boys toys.'

He nodded at the panel and before her very eyes it turned opaque and completely shut off the two-way view but kept the light bright. 'Privacy' he said softly, 'is very important to me and I don't want every Tom, Dick, or Harry gawping in through that window from their rowing boat or fishing peg. There's also the security to consider when I'm not here. This place is riddled with cameras and sensors and direct links to the local police station.'

She sipped her coffee and shook her head hoping that *when* and *if* they got down to it the local plod wouldn't be watching them.

'I have never seen anything like it' she said at last. 'Everything in here is just perfect and wonderful and you could fit my entire apartment into that kitchen area alone.'

'Do you like it?'

'It's simply beautiful and modern and looks like something out of one of those posh magazines in... Bequia or somewhere.' She remembered Heidi's quip about her joke beach wedding there to the young female referee.

'After living in the Manor for all those years, I didn't want any old-fashioned carpets, dark floorboards, two-foot-thick walls, multiple rooms, passages and corridors, brown cupboards and bookcases, skirting boards, mullions, decorated cornices and brown furniture with heavy brass fittings and chintzy furnishings. I wanted minimalism with quality, light everywhere and no dark corners or walls with plenty of space to spare. And because Fitzpatrick Huntington is essentially a firm of London retail architects, they were experts at working with strong glass so the design came naturally to them. Planning took a while, especially the glass floor and diverting the river but we got there in the end.'

'Did you bring anything with you from the Manor?'

'Only my clothes and a few personal effects. Mind you, I have too much of everything, at least twenty suits and double that number of shirts. It's all hanging in the dressing room up top. I brought it all over this morning with three trips in the Bentley.'

'Dressing room...?' She said.

'Follow me.' He stood up.

She looked at him warily.

'Is this an excuse to get me into your bedroom?'

'Of course,' he smiled and held out his hand. 'As at midnight I became a free man and want to cash in on that freedom with you as soon as possible.' He twitched the fingers of his proffered hand at her.

And of course, she stood and took it.

'This,' he said as they carefully negotiated the glass steps upwards that came directly from the wall without any support and looked as if they were floating, 'is the stairway to heaven for me with you here.'

It was a bit corny but she didn't say anything in response. The poor man had obviously been starved of non-family female company for a long time.

The bright and pure rounded copper bath was another revelation, as was the black marble wet room with matt black power adjustable sprays at all angles. His dressing room was open to the huge bedroom and consisted of row after row of quality suits and shirts and slacks and jeans all neatly hung. And then there was the bed, a double king-sized with black silk sheets and at least six black-cased pillows. Black silk, she thought; the enemy of semen stains and impossible to iron. I'm thinking like a woman who does her own washing and ironing, not that she had ever washed or ironed such beautiful material or slept in such surroundings before; it was just a practical female observational thing and anyway, Claude Dillon had probably never washed or ironed a sheet in his pampered life.

Nothing, Ginnie noticed up here, had a woman's touch about it. The bed, for instance, would have had any number of soft cushions in softer colours spread around it and a make-up chair, mirror, and table.

'That's a pity' he said softly looking at her as she looked around. 'Nothing up here seems to surprise you.'

'Oh, how do you know that?' she said knowing full well what the answer was and fully prepared to respond.

'Because those lovely red lips are not wide open in surprise.'

Then they were and his were pressed gently against them and his tongue was sliding purposefully into her eager mouth.

The first time they made love was no time for athletics or sexual patience but the simple expedient of a quick and urgent need. With the spread fingers of her right hand over his tight bum she pulled his hardness into her as he climbed on top and held him there as he pumped away for a dozen unstoppable thrusts before, with her gently sucking his tongue in her mouth, he emptied himself into her with muffled cries of release.

He never thought or was far too occupied to ask her if it was alright to do so. There's thirty years of the married pill for you, Ginnie thought soothing his trembling nipples with her lips. She said a silent prayer of thanks to herself for keeping her own pill going in the face of no reason to do so other than a Saturday night maybe with her mates. The pill was a takers charter that has since rendered old Maxie boy the bakers apprentice and his floury condoms redundant.

Having rested a short while they began to explore each other with him expressing a boyish delight at her erect nipples and firm breasts and what he referred to as a perfect body. In turn she nibbled playfully at his growing tumescence trying hard not to make comparisons that might...or might not have included her conversation with Iona about a certain Dexy boy and his BSD. Twenty minutes later she was sitting on him rocking her way gently to the first and possibly the most satisfying orgasm she had ever had.

They stayed there all the afternoon until early evening. Making love, nibbling, tonguing...*moistening*... and dozing and then doing it all over again until hunger drove them into the wet room for a joint shower prior to going down the road for a meal which then had to wait as they had another long, gentle fuck until, finally at around nine o'clock, they climbed hastily into some clothes and the Bentley for a couple of steaks down the road at a charming little pub well known to Claude called the Trout Inn.

Then back to the decidedly stained black silk sheets for some more moistening and then a deep and delicious sleep.

Where Ginnie kept dreaming about a glass floor that was made of water like the surface of a swimming pool and she sank down into it whenever she tried to walk across it to a huge picture window overlooking a river.

When she awoke with the sleeping area – she had been told not to call it a room, there were no rooms anywhere in this building – was bathed in light from the top of the morning viewing window, Claude was looking at her from a distance all of three inches.

'I've been watching you sleep for at least an hour,' he said quietly, 'a most wonderful and erotic sight.'

She reached for him under the black silk covering and wasn't surprised to find him ready again.

'Just fuck me' she said sleepily getting on her knees, 'from behind.'

The next time she woke up it was lunchtime and he was showered and in a battered old dressing gown and holding out a fine porcelain cup of coffee for her.

'You'll have to get some decent sized mugs. These thimbles don't hold enough coffee to kick start a girl's system.' She said draining the porcelain cup in one gulp.

'You shall have them tomorrow if not before but you'll have to be here to use them.'

She just smiled at him.

'The sun's shining so a gentle walk along the river before lunch somewhere and then...' He said.

'Ummm...only if you kiss me for ten minutes first,' she said.

He laughed. 'You must remember I'm an old man in my mid-fifties and must pace myself.'

'Nonsense, you're a stud who hasn't had any sex for three years so there's some making up to be done.'

He'd told her that last night. No wonder the poor man hadn't been able to hold it in for any more than a couple of minutes the first time, mind you, he'd made up for it since.

Before she left him on the Sunday night to go back to what would seem to her to be a miniature apartment after the cavernous and wonderful space of his boathouse, he professed to be in love with her. 'I am aware,' he'd said in an even voice holding her very tight after their umpteenth session of love-making that weekend before she left, 'that there is no fool like an old fool and that I am twenty – nine years older than you. However, I want you to know that I am in love with you and have been ever since you came into my office with your rugby team project. In my business life I have always treated honesty with a primacy because it follows you around until all your peers accept your word unreservedly. It is the same here and my love for you is genuine and heartfelt. I am not asking you to feel the same about me but to just give me a chance to prove my feelings. I am also conscious of the fact that I am your employer and that you are a friend of my daughter, both of which could play out badly in the current climate. I will not monopolise your free time at the expense of your other life but accept happily whatever time I can get with you…so there,' he sighed. 'Now you have it all.'

A 'primacy' another unusual but understood word she had never heard before, a fitting word in this context. She could see where Aggy got it from.

It was however, a beautiful speech and Ginnie was too emotional to reply.

Gently running her tongue around his hairy belly button buried in the small tummy where he carried an extra couple of pounds that they had joked about several times over the weekend but that didn't inhibit him in the slightest, Ginnie thought to herself that those seemingly genuine and heartfelt words were the nicest a man had ever said to her. Sure, she had had the occasional declarations of love before, usually driven by an excess of alcohol or as an inducement to getting her knickers off, but never anything delivered by someone with Claude's power, stature, and obvious truthfulness, besides him being totally sober and having had her all ends up for the last thirty-six hours. And she had been surprised by his vigour in their love making. For a man in his mid-fifties his staying power was amazing or, maybe it owed something to his three years of sexual abstinence. Either way the signs were good for their sexual well-being.

'Let's take our time with each other and see where we end up' she said softly, 'but there is one problem that you mentioned that *will* need to be addressed as soon as possible…'

'Aggy' he said.

'Yep, when are you going to Singapore?'

'Thursday for eight days, I will tell her tomorrow or Tuesday over lunch. There is also one other thing…'

'Oh?'

'Madeleine Moody has been my personal secretary for fourteen years and nothing escapes her attention. Although I have said nothing to her about us, she has a sixth sense and I wouldn't be surprised if she hasn't had an educated guess just by the way I react when I'm seeing you that there's something going on between us.'

'Okay' Ginnie said slowly not seeing anything too onerous about that. His grey-haired gate-keeper was only doing her job by protecting him after all.

Wasn't she?

After a long sloppy kiss by the front door, he led her to the car and opened the door.

'Can we meet out here on Wednesday evening around seven-thirty to eight, I will want, nay *need* to see you before I go to Singapore on Thursday?'

'Okay' she said. 'Just make sure that the big picture window is blanked out.'

*

When Ginnie got home on the Sunday night after she had a good long soak in her very small and functional bath with the shower attached to the taps by rubber hose and not a hint of black marble anywhere, she put on her old but comfortable jim jams, poured herself a large Merlot and sat up in bed in her Marks and Sparks green cotton sheets and had a think.

What had just happened? Had she *really,* just spent the entire weekend attached by the hips, lips, and caressing hands to the hard perforator of the CEO of the company she worked for, a wealthy Bentley-driving owner of a fabulous Thames-side boathouse who was newly single *and had declared his love for her?*

And I, she said quietly to herself, the captain of the Furious Fannies, have the bruises and sore fanny to vouch for all of it.

Chapter Seventeen

Monday and Tuesday flew by as she interviewed another eight internal candidates with Raymond. The Tuesday night training session was full on with Heidi and J.J. sitting it out on the slot bench – the 'clot' having been dropped because everyone knew what it meant and both were vital for the match on Saturday and would be available but in turn, Avril Gordon and Rocky Cook were a doubt.

'Don't worry about it with me' growled the pack leader. 'I've played with it before and it wasn't a problem.'

Nevertheless, Lindsey worked Cassie in the tight head position just in case and used Sheila Bates as a full back just in case 'Love-Bites' was also incapacitated.

Rocky had also brought along an old friend and former hooker with Supermarine. Alfreda 'Alfie' Cushing had been out of the game for two years, the first twelve months recovering from Glandular Fever and then, just as she was getting back into the swing, she was involved in a very nasty car accident in which her husband who was driving their car was killed. Her face still bore the marks of her impact with the screen and the subsequent plastic surgery and although everything was in place and individually sound, it somehow didn't seem to quite knit together giving her a lopsided, blurred, and mismatched look. Alfie was thirty-one and had been through two years of trauma and grief and a chance meeting in the Great Western Hospital where Rocky worked and Alfie was attending a routine visit, led to them talking about the Fannies.

'I'm a few pounds overweight but been keeping fit with a lot of running lately' she told Ginnie 'I used to enjoy my rugby at Supermarine so when Rocky said why not come along, I jumped at the chance.'

'You are very welcome' said Ginnie giving her a genuine smile and a hug, followed by Lindsey saying that she also might get a few minutes on the pitch on Saturday.

'Now the Bohica wonder girl has a bit of competition' said Heidi giving the tattooed Gina a big grin, which, of course, meant that someone had to explain to Alfie what the acronym stood for.

'Just what I need' said Alfie with a chuckle after it had been explained to her. 'A bunch of irreverent tarts who don't give a damn.'

Back to more interviews with Raymond in the office on Wednesday with Ginnie conscious that the lunch meeting between Claude and Aggy had taken place in the two days previous and tonight she would see how it had gone.

One look at Claude's face when he met her as she pulled up at the boat house that evening was enough for her to fear the worst.

'She stormed out of the pub when I told her'he said as they sat down on the orange soft suede sofa. 'Took me ten minutes to get her to sit in my car and hear me out. We had tears and a screaming fit and no matter how hard I told her that the relationship was all my doing and that you were an innocent party to all of it, she still wouldn't accept it...'

'So, I'm the scheming hussy who has bamboozled her father with her witchy wiles.' Ginnie said quietly. 'I feared as much.'

He turned her face towards him.

'It makes no difference. I can't stop her feeling that way and if she can't see reason I won't even try. The important thing for me is that *our* relationship isn't affected by *her* reaction.'

He talked to her softly for a long time and was convinced that his daughter would come round eventually when she saw just how much he loved Ginnie. Nothing was going to stop him from loving her and being with her. It was a marital absolute and she kept away from it. Finally, he pressed the button that blanked out the window and they made love on the circular sofa. He was very tender, very caring and took an inordinate amount of time to bring her to what she thought of later as the screaming pinicle orgasm of her life. Perhaps that was what it took to get to this nirvana, first lose a friend and then your mind to her expertly probing father.

When she finally fell into her apartment it was two o'clock in the morning and she barely had time to set her alarm for six thirty before she was asleep.

Stifling yawns she sat through two more interviews with Raymond on the Thursday morning, thankfully the final one in the afternoon was a no-show.

Training that night was another hard session.

'What works in rugby once' said Lindsey loudly standing in the middle of the squad under the floodlights, 'either works again and again or leads to other situations that cannot be covered because the opposition are too busy trying to cover the first move. I will explain.

Against Supermarine Romany, our little blue streak here blazes down the wing in the opening move of the game and scores a try. The opposition are suddenly aware that we have a blindingly fast winger about whom something must be done, so they double team her. And what did that do? It freed up space in the middle of their defence for our midfield trio of Mollie, Iona, and Ginnie to rip them to shred's. If they *hadn't* doubled up on Romany, *she* would have continued to exploit the space on the wing with her speed. So now they have a big problem to solve for the next game on Saturday. They *have* to cover Romany *and* our very fast and tricky backs otherwise the same will happen again, so how do they do that?'

'Drop their flankers back as extra cover down the middle and keep the double on Romany? Rocky offered.

'Good' said Lindsey 'but remember what I said at the start. What works in rugby once either works again and again or leads to other move's that cannot be covered. Dropping their flankers back as cover for Mollie, Iona and Ginnie opens space around the ruck and maul area for *our* back row so J.J, Judo and Billie at six, seven and eight will have acres of space to exploit and bound together can charge towards their depleted line and then redistribute or go all the way because they'll be back-peddling. If Supermarine *doesn't* withdraw their flankers as extra cover we'll just carry on tearing them up with the existing pace of our...'

'Petticoats' shrieked Romany with a big toothy grin that made everyone laugh.

It was coaches talk, most of which Ginnie understood but she was already beginning to put her own words together for her pre-match chat. It had worked the last time so why not again?

They also decided to meet at the club at twelve-thirty on Saturday and with Sherry at the wheel of the mini-bus drive out to Supermarine at South Marston together. Their opponents had arrived here all together and although it was a mere twenty-minute journey it obviously made for team togetherness for the Fannies to do the same.

'For a perfect arrival we could have soft plucked lutes to greet us with the billowing smoke of sacrificial vestal virgins blowing magisterial essence over the pitch...' Heidi drawled.

'Where on earth' said Flipper Bryan with a wide grin, 'are you going to get any virgins from two adult female rugby squads in this day and age?'

'Well,' said Rocky 'there's our little Blue Streak here...'

All eyes turned to Romany who just squirmed with embarrassment under their gaze.

'Don't forget me' said Gita fiercely and rather proudly from the edge of the circle. 'I have a traditional Indian mother who would shave my head and throw me out if I ever strayed before marriage.'

Even Heidi was lost for words momentarily as the team broke out into spontaneous clapping and cheering, virginity was obviously a subject that did not include any of them other than Gita and Romany, although some of the other singles probably didn't want to advertise the fact. Iona looked across at Ginnie and gave her a broad wink which the captain rather hoped was a reference to their conversation about Heidi's bull-hung boyfriend rather than something she had found out about her own recent sexual activity with Claude.

Heidi recovered later to refer to the pair of virgin wingers as the 'petticoats with a cherry on top.'

On the Friday morning in the office after vacillating backwards and forward over the decision to send or not, Ginnie finally sent a simple email to Aggy on her mobile.

Can we meet and talk?

Within what seemed like seconds she received the barbed reply.

No! Never!

The exclamation marks said it all. Aggy hated her and that was the end of their friendship and, she surmised, her former friends association with the rugby team. As for how Aggy and Claude would now get on, it was anyone's guess but according to him she would see reason…eventually.

Later that morning having had a meeting with Steve Harrington to report on the progress and further acceptances received from the interviews, she was getting ready to go down to the canteen to get a sandwich and bring it back to her office when her internal phone rang.

'Hi Ginnie, its Madeleine Moody…'

'Madeleine Moody has been my personal secretary for fourteen years and nothing escapes her attention. Although I have said nothing to her about us, she has a sixth sense and I wouldn't be surprised if she hasn't had an educated guess just by the way I react when I'm seeing you.'

Claude's words came back to her as she greeted Madeleine.

'Are you free for lunch today? I thought we could have a sandwich sent up here and have a chat…'

'Okay Madeleine, I'll be there in twenty minutes.'

'Fine, I'll get a selection up here and put the coffee machine on. See you shortly.'

No canteen visits for the Queen Bee and Claude's gatekeeper and her guests, thought Ginnie giving her face a quick once over in the ladies, on the top floor the sandwiches come to you.

This thought Ginnie pressing the button for the lift and deciding to remain neutral until Madeleine revealed what this was all about, should be very interesting. She would use a phrase she had learned during her college course. When you are uncertain about anything adopt the path of stoic resistance. In other words, don't give *any* fucking thing away.

Madeleine gave her a hug, another first, and waved her into the seat alongside hers behind her huge desk.

'Coffee…?'

'White with no sugar…'

'I hear you won your first rugby game.'

'Yeah; the first friendly home game against Supermarine almost two weeks ago now, we have the away game against them tomorrow.'

'Ready?'

'Sure am, and looking forward to it.'

'After the first victory, Claude' she said giving Ginnie a small plate and gesturing towards the large plate of mixed sandwiches on her desk, 'was very much looking forward to the return tomorrow, then Singapore reared its ugly head again…'

Didn't take her long to mention the prime reason she wanted me here, Ginnie thought giving her a small that's how it goes shrug and then adding.

'He goes there quite often?'

'This is his sixth visit in four months.'

'Crikey, what's he doing going there that often for?'

'I can't say anything because it's a strictly confidential business deal and potentially very big…'

Suit yourself, Ginnie thought. He's in love with me and will tell me if I ask him, we don't have any secrets about anything.

Madeleine leaned forward and smiled disarmingly.

'Cards on the table Ginnie, I wanted to talk to you today because I'm pretty sure that you and Claude are an item, as they say in all the posh magazines, and I think it's a bloody good idea…'

Ginnie blinked in surprise, both at the outright statement and the soft swear word. Madeleine didn't appear to be a lady who swore at any time, ever.

She opened her mouth to stammer out some sort of denial and then Madeleine held up her hand to let her continue.

'Let me tell you how I know and to put your mind at rest, it's nothing Claude has said, he wouldn't do that. It's just that after fourteen years of working closely with him as this company has grown from a small enterprise to the second largest building society mutual in the U.K, I have come to know the man very well. For instance, I even know the moment, or moments he fell in love with you when you first came in here to present your rugby project to him. After you left, he was like a cat on a hot tin roof, prowling around and muttering to himself. Ever since then when he's getting ready to meet you for lunch – and yes, I always know when because he's like a boy in a toy shop jumping around the office glancing at his watch every couple of minutes and giving himself a sly squirt of aftershave before leaving…'

She paused.

'You said it was a bloody good idea?' Ginnie repeated her words.

'Yes, I did and I meant it. Frances, his former wife, has treated him appallingly and pretty much ignored his very existence for years, no matter how hard he tried to please her. And this is a man Ginnie, who has got to the top in this business through hard work, brains, and a rare honesty in all his dealings, including with her. It's a bloody good idea because at last he's got himself a woman to love and that woman is you, my girl.'

Ginnie took a small bite of a segment of tuna and mayo and chewed thoughtfully, or she hoped it looked thoughtful; the truth was she was blown away by Madeleine's words and her mind was reeling. What was all this about? The nosey P.A. was acting like Claude's mother or a close relation of the family; someone put forward to ensure this upstart woman was fully brought up to date with the situation and put in her place… or is that too harsh for *her* blatant honesty. Inwardly, Ginnie was beginning to bridle at her intrusion. Or was there another explanation? Claude himself perhaps; somehow using Madeleine to check Ginnie out in some way? Nah, that was paranoid, take a deep breath and remain neutral, she told herself.

'Now' Madeleine continued, 'you can tell me to mind my own business but there was one thing I wanted to warn you about, trouble on the horizon, if you wish…'

Ginnie raised her eyebrows.

'Agnes,' Madeleine said, 'Daddies little girl...she's been spoiled by Claude all her life and she won't take your relationship lying down. You will, if you like, be replacing her in his affections.'

Ginnie almost breathed a visible sigh of relief. She had already met that one head-on with the exclamation marked email reply and was pleased that Madeleine, for once, was behind the actuality.

'Oh?'Ginnie said remaining non-committal but having to concentrate fully to remain so in the face of this unexpected intrusion.

'Oh yes, mark my words, that girl is capable of anything to keep uppermost in her father's affections.'

You can tell me to mind my own business...but mark my words. The staple introductions of the middle-aged gossip. This woman was just another top floor Minnie James with better access.

Madeleine smiled confidentially and leaned forward. 'More coffee...?'

She topped up Ginnies cup.

'Have you heard from him yet? 'Madeleine asked.

'No, I thought he only left yesterday.'

'He did but I've already had a couple of emailed instructions as has Lance Ferriby's P.A. This is their fourth visit to Singapore together in the last few months...'

Madeleine couldn't help the smirk that said he contacts me all the time yet you hear nothing, a fact I just had to let you know.

Lance Ferriby was the Finance Director, a spare, bespectacled bald guy of around Claude's age and who had obviously gone to Singapore with him...again. Not that Ginnie knew, or cared about this fact but she nodded in feigned interest.

They talked a little shop about Ginnies new job and how she was settling in and then, delighted and not a little proud of the fact that she had given nothing away, Ginnie said her thanks for the light lunch and escaped back down to her own office. This woman would have to be watched very carefully. It wasn't Aggy that Ginnie should worry about replacing in Claude's affections, but this interfering old busy-body.

Friday night was a decent two glasses of Merlot followed by a long bath and an early...ish night and try not to think about that audacious cow Madeleine Moody poking her snout in where it did not belong. Tomorrow was the big day of the return match and she wanted to be ready and clear- sighted for it. Just before she dropped off to sleep around eleven her mobile pinged with a text message.

It was from Claude.

'Good luck in the game tomorrow my darling. I will be thinking of you. All my love, Claude xxx.

Stuff that in your pipe and smoke it Madeleine nosey-parker Moody, Ginnie muttered to herself cuddling up to her mobile before dropping off, *you* only take down his dictation and remove his used coffee cup, *I* take down his underpants and remove his... She giggled as sleep and whatever weird dreams would accompany it slowly arrived.

Chapter Eighteen

When Ginnie woke up at about seven-thirty it wasn't the game that occupied her mazy thoughts or Claude but still the venal behaviour of Madeleine Moody. In her secret heart Ginnie wanted nothing to do with the woman but because of her position as Claude's long-time confident and P.A. that would be difficult. Better to maintain the neutrality and say nothing of consequence about her to Claude. 'Inane chunter' Aggy had once called this method of talking but saying nothing, it chimed perfectly with Ginnies own 'adopt the course of stoic resistance.' So be it, inane chunter and stoic resistance would be her default mode whenever that nosey old bitch was within earshot. If you didn't say fuck-all of irrelevance, fuck-all of irrelevance could come of it.

After her bath her mobile pinged with a message from Love-Bites Gordon that got her back into game mode. She was still on the slot and wouldn't be able to play today but would come along to support the girls. A bit of shopping in Sainsbury's with a bag of the usual suspects and then she ironed her pink and black shirt, shorts, and socks – socks? Who irons rugby socks? Well, today I do. Then she drove out to their home ground to get on the mini-bus to Super marine with the team.

'I'll have to be careful if we get pulled over by the police' said Sherry Moyes swinging down from the mini-bus driver's seat in the Wessex home ground car park and opening the boot lid for the girls to load their kit. 'Same as when I'm working during the week driving the lorry. My HGV driving license is still in my old name as a man with the corresponding short-haired picture,' he shook his shoulder length light brown wig. 'I'll have to whip this off and give me face a quick scrub to get rid of the slap if I'm pulled over…'

'You'll be alright' said Heidi, 'if its male uniforms just give them both a sloppy wet kiss with plenty of tongue and they'll let you go.'

'Same if they are female' said the proudly married sapphic Rocky Cook who had declared herself fit and raring to go on arrival and so Sheila Bates, who Lindsey had been practising with in the car park would be standing in at full-back.

'Morning girls' said Ginnie getting out of her car which again had started first pull at the point that Ginnie had decided was its second most important time.

'Here's the warrior princess' grinned Heidi, 'ready to whip the girl's into shape then skipper?'

'Whips' said Flipper Bryan joining them 'is the very last thing I need.'

'Why's that' drawled Heidi obviously in top form, 'the old man gave you a few lashes last night then to remind you who is in charge?'

'I should be so lucky' Flipper replied dropping her bag in the open boot of the mini-bus.

The girls were gathering prior to leaving, there was excitement in the air at the approaching game and the banter was spicy and, as usual with this sassy bunch, sexually charged.

There was a roar from the gate as Dixie smoked the back tyre of the Fireblade through the gate with Judo clinging to his back, only to be outdone by an even throatier exhaust roar as the tall guy who had dropped Heidi off and was, presumably, the Oxford Don boyfriend with the huge pork bayonet, gunned his stationary British Racing Green Morgan open topped sports car in reply.

'He has' muttered Iona who had come up behind Ginnie and whispered for her ears only 'the swinging dick motor to match the...swinging dick monster.'

'Come and say hello to a couple of the girls Dexter' Heidi shouted at him being out of earshot of Iona's remark, and the tall and smiling Oxford Don unlimbered himself from the Morgan and ambled over with a big grin on his face.

'This is Ginnie, capitano and supremo' Heidi said waving at Ginnie.

With Iona standing behind her and carefully watching her every move, Ginnie steeled herself not to look down at the approaching man's groin as she shook his outstretched hand. Having said hello to a few of the others, when he got to Iona it was Ginnies turn to watch *her* eyeline and once again the former winter Olympic athlete's eyes behaved impeccably.

So, there it was, both girls managed to ignore the obvious and didn't give the other the chance to gloat.

'See you there Dex' Heidi bawled at him as she swung into the mini-bus and her boyfriend settled himself back behind the wheel of the Morgan and gunned the motor again by way of reply.

Iona, who had sat next to Ginnie, leaned across her and muttered out of the corner of her mouth.

'Takes more than a BSD for us Fannies to take our eye off the ball, eh...?'

'Especially when there's an important game to be played' Ginnie replied with a smile.

With a few exceptions and surprise additions when they got there, the same people who had dropped them off regularly for training and turned up at the previous game would also be following them to South Marston for this confrontation.

'Come on girls' Sherry shouted at Kayla and Cassie, the last two and who were dawdling along the car-park towards them. 'Time we were away.'

'Anybody would think' said Cassie in her Welsh lilt climbing the step into the vehicle 'that it was England versus Wales at the Millennium Stadium in the Six Nations decider...'

'It more important than that' smiled Lindsey chucking a couple of tackle bags to those in the back seat and handing a net of balls to Ginnie because the boot was crammed full.

'All aboard the Joy charabang Fannies where you will join a veritable surfiet of other excitable, damp sublime gashes all raring to go...all except one that is... eh Sherry?'

The irrepressable Heidi humour nailed them all to their seats on board the mini-bus.

Adjusting her wig in the rear-view mirror Sherry started the engine and replied loudly that it was only a matter of time...and money, before she too had one.

Twenty minutes later they all climbed out of the mini-bus at the Supermarine sports complex in South Marston, an area that Ginnie knew well having been born and raised less than a mile away in Stratton and where her mother and father still lived, and had started her first job at the mighty Honda works whose grounds and test tracks abutted those of the Supermarine sports complex and whose name had come from the famous wartime aircraft called the Spitfire Supermarine that was built there by the Vickers Company.

Ginnie and Lindsey were greeted warmly by Vera Godwin at the steps of the mini-bus who also gave rhe two Cook sisters a hug and then led them into the changing rooms.

The changing room was charged with banter led by the irrepressable Heidi and the warm up seemed to go well with Lindsey barking out the moves and commands. With Rocky calling the jumpers, Gina was hitting Heidi and Ellie two out of every three times and the weather was dry with little or no wind. Romany the Blue Streak or 'our little luminous child of speed' as was Heidi's latest reference to the rapid little runner, seemed in particularly quick form. Ginnie, Mollie, and Iona also seemed very fluid finding each other on every dummy run and pass. A quick glance by Ginnie at the Supermarine girls practising down the far end confirmed that they had the same side with their captain Shannon with the robust short-haired blond forward Amber – Heidi's former night-club opponent – particularly loud with their positional cries. Shannon, Ginnie noticed, had discarded the scarlet Malice boot's for a pair of luminous green ones, perhaps she had been disappointed with the way they had worked during the first game or the competition offered by Ginnies pair had put her off. Ginnie patted her own scarlet with orange diagonals and the quote of 'Malice aforethought' came into her mind from something or somewhere in the past. There they were, shiny, snug, and ready for action. Apart from anything else they were the only pair she had. Ginnie also cast her eye around the few spectators that had already arrived and was stunned to see her mother, father and Robert waving back at her. Well, it was only about a mile to get here from home so they must have walked. And there, also waving at her, were her *four* faithful friends from the old Saturday clubbing nights, including this time the soon to be married Bella. Down the far end stood the ever-present Tink Cutler alongside Louise George and the other cluster of three hurrying over from the car park were Love-Bites Gordon and the two army husbands. A quick scan around the ground failed to locate Heidi's mama or her dinky-dicked companion. Seeing her doughty daughter sent off for ten minutes the last time was obviously shame enough for the haughty woman. A quick glance also failed to locate Stan the Wink and a Pint Mackay on the side-lines which gave Ginnie a slight feeling of disappointment because she liked the portly little fixer of all things necessary in the office. Perhaps her turning down a date with his youngish son had something to do with it? As for Emily, Robert told her when they had a quick chat before Ginnie got the players in a circle that his eight months pregnant wife was feeling 'a little lumpy' so had stayed at home. As she was talking to Robert her mother began to fiddle with her shirt which she wore outside her shorts, trying to tuck it into her shorts as if she was a little girl going to playschool, while her father maintained a 'wait and bloody see' brooding silence that said he was there under sufferance and she had better make it worth his while.

Pulling her shirt out of her shorts because that was how she liked it, Ginnie joined the squad circle just as the three officials that Vera had booked for the game, trotted out onto the pitch.

'All men,' Heidi drawled as they went by. 'Might get some proper magisterial decisions this time and I can stay on the pitch...'

'Sloppy wet kisses with plenty of tongue should swing it, eh Heidi, like the policemen.' Rocky shouted.

'Just play your natural game' Ginnie said to her tall lock 'and keep that hole under your beautifully sculpted hooter firmly shut and your elbows in...'

'Beautifully sculpted...' Heidi spluttered. 'Where on earth did you get shit like that from skip?'

'Michelangelo's David' Ginnie said flippantly remembering a picture from art class at school and the only lesson she had paid attention to because it had such a dainty little cluster in the todger area. Once again, she quickly wished that she hadn't responded down this somewhat learned path as Heidi's eyes lit up.

'There are three David's' came the louche reply, 'all have rather ugly big hooters and one, the best one in Florence which I *have also* seen, has had its cluster miniturised, a tiny little flaccid rosebud of a thing in the midst of all that rippling marble muscle...'

Giggles from all round from those in hearing distance; it was impossible to get Heidi away from a funny remark. Just then and right on queue Dex roared into the car park in his Morgan and Ginnie ignored the knowing look she again got from the fixated Iona from across the squad circle.

Ginnies talk this time was short and sweet. Stick to the basics, remember the special training sessions and moves they'd practised leading up to this game and don't give any ground or quarter to that bunch of skanks down the other end…'

The 'skamks' got a thumbs up from Heidi.

As they took up their positions for the Supermarine kick-off – Ginnie had lost the toss to the now scrum cap wearing Shannon to keep her hair in place and who'd decided to start – Heidi muttered to her. 'I'm the one with the foul mouth around here. You're supposed to be all honourable, steadfast, and fair and well-meaning to the opposition.'

'Bollocks' said Ginnie with a big grin purposefully rolling the vowels with a bit of broad Wiltshire.

Then the fussy-looking little black-clad ref blew his whistle to start.

When he blew it for half-time the Fannies were ahead by 19 – 0 and the first half had been something of a rout. Yes, Supermarine had again doubled-up on Romany but no, they didn't withdraw their flankers to stop the speedy and tricky centres of Mollie, Iona, and Ginnie from carving through the empty spaces of the midfield with total impunity. Again, it was Ginnie who scored the first try, a beautiful outside run and then a cut back inside the despairing lunge of the full back to dot the ball down under the posts. Mollie converted with nonchalant ease and it was 7 – 0 after ten minutes. Then it was Gita's turn to score her first try for the team after another mazy run from Mollie followed by a series of clever passes between Ginnie and Iona gave Gita a simple run in on the outside. Mollie missed this kick, 12 – 0 after twenty minutes. With five minutes to go to half time came the best try of all. Sheila Bates, who'd had a quiet and mainly inactive debut at full-back, caught a kick on her own twenty-two and set of across the pitch at a surprising pace. A perfect little pop pass in a practised scissors move with Flipper saw the bendy scrum half flick it inside to Iona on the halfway line, who switched against the grain to pop another perfect pass up to Ginnie coming back the other way. The gaps were yawning and the practised moves were meshing perfectly with Supermarine players sprawled all over the pitch as Ginnie sprinted down the right-hand side before feinting a pass to Romany and stepping inside off her left foot to run unopposed to the line and again dot down under the post. Another simple kick saw the score at 19 – 0. Risking a quick glance at her parents and brother as she trotted to the opposite end for the half time break, she was surprised to see her morose father clapping his hands and throwing a 'that's my girl' grin up and down the side line. Perhaps he was proud of his daughter for the very first time in her life.

'Best half of rugby any girls I have coached have *ever* played' Lindsey said as Sherry handed round the water bottles. 'You can't play better than that and as for you, Ginnie, a standout half of sheer brilliance. Rocky, you and the pack are winning everything and as for the other petticoats, simply stunning. The opposition just don't know which way to turn...'

The girls looked around at one another with the broad grins of a plan well-executed.

'Unfortunately, it's a job only half done so you now need to do it all over again because one thing Supermarine will do now is scrap and fight for every ball to get back into the game. There are no instructions for the second half other than keep doing what you are already doing brilliantly.'

And they did.

It wasn't the ultra-fast Blue Streak Romany that panicked the opposition now, it was Ginnie. Every time she got the ball in her hands the Supermarine players tried to gang up on her and rush at her leaving ever bigger gaps for Mollie and Iona to surged into and exploit. Iona got the next try with the conversion missed by Mollie, then, to great cheers and much backslapping from her teammates, Heidi took a line-out ball on the opposition twenty-two metre line and with Ellie, Rocky, Judo and J.J. mauling like lions behind her wrestled her way over the line for her first Fannies try. This time Mollie made the conversion and the score moved to 31 – 0.

Romany then got a ball just inside her own half and put the after-burners on leaving her two close attendants for dead. Unfortunately, the eagle-eyed line assistant saw her left foot just clip the side line before she dotted the ball down and the try was disallowed.

With all the subs on and playing as well as those they'd replaced and Ginnie exhorting the Fannies to keep their foot on the gas, the popular pack leader Rocky got the next one by forcing her way over the line with three defenders hanging onto her, followed by a last-minute and third try for Ginnie herself when she rounded a tired and dispirited defence to again place the ball down under the posts. Final score 45 – 0, a complete and utter rout.

The overwhelmed and weary Supermarine players were gracious in defeat and shook hands with many a 'well played' comment and Shannon, the opposing captain with her dread-locked hair now released from the scrum cap and back in her Medusa mode muttering to Ginnie that she was a 'star in the making and could go a long way in this game.'

In the showers afterwards everyone was jubilant with naked women pinching, splashing, and dousing each other with water and gel bubbles.

'Soapy fannies everywhere' drawled Heidi staggering out of the showers and grabbing her towel, 'and not a decent male perforator in sight.'

Again, Iona gave Ginnie a big open wink as if to say to Heidi *it's alright for you babe, you have the elephantine BSD of Dexy boy waiting.'*

Outside Lindsey drew Ginnie to one side.

'I've just realised something that may become important to us as we progress' the coach said quietly to her captain. 'Heidi does not just *play* in these games, doesn't even have to touch the ball but her menacing physical and sassy verbal's has the habit of turning every ruck, maul. line-out and scrummage into a battleground and that disconcerts the opposition. They're too busy watching her glowering presence to concentrate on their own moves...'

'Not to mention her ability to raise the team with her funny cracks' Ginnie replied with a wide grin.

'Oh, and Vera would like a word with you and me when you're ready' she added as her captain put on her soft brown leather jacket.

'What does she want?'

'She didn't say but I expect it's something to do with next season.'

Vera was waiting for them both outside and suggested they take a walk around the pitch were they could talk privately.

When the three of them got to the other side Vera turned to Ginnie.

'Have you any plans for next season?'

'Not yet, no, I thought we would try and get into one of the ladies leagues in the South West.'

'That was our intension as well,' Vera replied. 'And to that end I've had a telephone conversation with the Co-ordinator of South West 2, one of the National Challenge Leagues our first team had started in some eight years ago. The Co-ordinators name is Marcia Webb and I asked her weeks ago and before I spoke to you for the first time and when we first knew that a second fifteen was a possibility – what the situation was as regards getting our seconds into her league. Her answer was encouraging in that she wanted to expand the league by at least one more side and to let her know if we wanted that spot...'

'One more spot only?' Lindsey asked.

'That was what she said then. Now, these leagues are put together as you know Lindsey, to develop the ladies game and talent spot the best players. After the dismal showing of my seconds – especially today when we were worse than rubbish – I have decided along with the coach that we are simply not good enough to enter *any* league with our second fifteen next season...' she stopped and then looked Ginnie in the eye and then at Lindsey. 'But your team, are not only good enough for South West 2 but could easily win it and then get promoted...'

Ginnie still didn't say anything but her heart was beating very hard and she was short of breath through excitement.

'If that interests you what say I ring Marcia tonight and if that place is still available for next season put in a good word for the Fannies…?'

Ginnie nodded.

'What teams are in South West 2 now?' Lindsey asked.

'Let me see,' Vera said screwing up her brow in thought. 'Reading Bellfield Road Ladies are winning it at this moment with one or two games left to play, a side you would still know well I expect Lindsey, although they have dropped out of the Berkshire and Hampshire Division One since you were with them. …'

Lindsey gave a 'what did you expect without me' shrug as Vera continued.

'Second are Guildford Gazelles, third Newbury RFC, fourth Cullompton Ladies and the mid-table to bottom positions are between Portsmouth Valkyries, Plymouth Albion, Teddington Antlers and Ellingham and Ringwood Ladies…'

Seeing Ginnie still a little overwhelmed to speak, Vera waved her hands about to encompass the greater rugby playing world.

'It's a lot of travelling, especially Cullompton and Plymouth which require an overnight stay the night before or a very early start, but that's the penalty for playing in any of these Challenge leagues. You'll also need your own transport or some decent funding for hotels or wherever you overnight. Marcia will also need to inspect your ground and changing facilities but you will sail through that with your well laid out sports complex. Would you like me to ring her on your behalf…?

'Thank you, Vera' said Ginnie finding her voice at last, 'that would be bloody wonderful.'

'A word of warning that the two of you may well have already discussed' Vera said stopping and turning back at the far end. 'You have the makings of a standout team and in your short time together have developed the essential blend of pace, ability, and good strategic sense. As Lindsey here knows, prowling the side-lines of South West 2 games will be the scouts for the big Tyrrells League Premiership clubs on the lookout for new talent. They'll make unmatchable promises to get your best players and you only need to lose two or three key players before the rot sets in and the team goes downhill very quickly. This has happened to us and probably to you at Bellfield Road, Lindsey?'

Lindsey nodded, 'Yeah, two or three times. They will dangle all sorts of inducements like playing for England and getting a full-time paid playing contract and so on to get the players they want.'

Vera looked straight at Ginnie. 'The first target will be you as the captain and standout player. You might not have been playing for very long but you are a natural game changer if ever I've seen one and the beating heart of the team. And bear this in mind, Emily Scarratt who plays for Loughborough and is the current England Centre and about to be nominated as world player of the year, will be thirty-one soon which gives her another two or three years at most and although you don't take conversion kick like she does, you are a natural replacement with your fast and positive running game and motivating captaincy, so that's a carrot that will be dangled under *your* nose…'

Ginnie had read all about Emily in her Catherine Spencer *Mud, Maul, Mascara,* rugby autobiography and had watched her play for England on the television, but never would she have seen herself as a replacement for the England star, not even good enough to clean her boots.

When Lindsey and Ginnie climbed aboard the mini-bus there was a chorus of banter because the team had watched the three ladies walking around the pitch perimeter talking.

'Bin offered a transfer fee then to join the Supermarine outfit and lick 'em into shape' was one of the milder one's from the Welsh accent of Cassie Betts.

Ginnie held her hand up and the chorus subsided.

'I might have some good news to tell you about next season at training on Tuesday night. Now all of you have a few well-earned serious one's tonight because you have all earned it.'

'Wot's a serious one Heid,' Romany thin little voice said to Heidi, her guiding light and team hero, 'is that this sex stuff yer always on about?'

'Could be babe' replied Heidi making a sign of zipping her lips before just having to comment. 'But until the skipper tells us my lips are sealed tighter than a misers fist?'

That night when Ginnie took a well-deserved glass of Merlot to bed with her and the Catherine Spencer biography, it wasn't the game she fell asleep thinking about, nor Claude or Madeleine Moody, but the comments made by Very Godwin as they walked around the pitch after the game earlier.

You are a natural game changer if ever I've seen one and the beating heart of the team.

Maybe, just maybe I can really play this game…

Chapter Nineteen

Ginnie was a bit stiff when she awoke on Sunday morning but a long hot bath soon soothed the muscles with the inner woman then satisfied by muesli and toast. At ten-thirty she drove back over towards Supermarine to see her mum and dad with half a mind to see what sort of mood the old boy was in and if a good one, ask him to make a mobile scoreboard as per Rockys suggestion. She didn't want to get ahead of herself but *if* they were to play in South West 2, they'd need one and her dad being a fully trained and very good carpenter was, if the mood was right, just the man for the job.

Not only was he in the mood but leapt out from behind his Sunday tabloid and rushed across the room to give her a big hug.

Bloody hell! Ginnie thought, he hasn't given me a hug since.... since...since never. Then it was her mum's turn for an elongated cuddle and ten cheek kisses. Who knew that all it took for a family love-in around here was to score a couple of tries on the rugby pitch? After that the old boy was a pushover for the scoreboard and even drew up a sketch with several excellent ideas as to what was needed on it and promised to have it ready in plenty of time for the start of next season.

'And since' he said with a bit of a smirk, 'I'll be there to watch every home game without fail, and some of the away matches as well if mum wants to go, I'll even operate the bloody thing for you.'

'I don't think' her mother said quietly 'I've ever been so excited in my life when you scored that first try and to think that was the first rugby game I've ever seen and dad had to explain what was happening to me.'

Ginnie drove away after an hour suffused in a righteous glow of familial pride. Where had they all been for the last ten years when she had got her first job at Honda, then paid for and passed her driving test at the second try followed by her HNC diploma– also paid for by herself – and then the subsequent job and *first* promotion at Wessex Mutual – all of which she reported to them to a general receptive air of yawning indifference? Not a hug or a kiss in sight for those great life-changing moments. Not even mentioned by these two parents although her lovely brother always said well-done for every achievement. Best not to mention the fact that her CEO and an obviously highly successful and rich man was in love with her, or the fact that she was now a departmental manager at Wessex. I don't want to overwhelm them with too much good news all at once and besides, it seems that the only turn-on as far as she was concerned for them was of a sporting nature. It was also wise not to mention her happiness with Claude, her bubbles in matters of the heart have a subsequent habit of getting pricked so bin that for the time being along with the marital absolute...

And then it just got better as her door rang at two-thirty in the afternoon and when she opened it who was stood there looking suitably tired and travel weary with his flight number bedecked suitcase by his side, but Claude.

'I managed to get on an earlier flight out of Singapore that got me into Heathrow three hours ago,' he said quietly reaching for her.

He said he'd have to leave her bed by midnight to go back to the boathouse for some rest and a change of clothes in preparation for another day of important meetings at the office starting in the morning.

'But you weren't supposed to be back in the office until Tuesday'

'I know' he said speaking into her open lips after they had caught up in the only way they knew how with a quick and frenzied fuck. 'But matters have moved on rapidly after these meetings over there and Lance and I needed to come back for an urgent board meeting that I have called on my mobile for tomorrow.'

He hadn't told her that Lance was accompanying him to Singapore but Madeleine Moody had as a way of proving her superior knowledge over his movements. She decided not to mention her light lunch with the meddling old bat.

'And there was I thinking you'd come back early to see me,' Ginnie pouted.

'That was my real reason' he said lifting her over him and slowly letting her down on his semi-erect perforator. 'But don't tell my board members that.'

The travel weariness seemed to wear off very quickly with their love-making until he fell fast asleep wrapped around her. Ginnie let him sleep and setting her mobile for a five-a.m. call to give him time to get to the boathouse for a shower and change of clothes and back, joined him.

Ginnie was also busy on the Monday morning. Six of her new staff had started and she took them around the department and introduced them to the assistants who would be mentoring them. At lunchtime she had a call on her mobile from Vera Godwin who said she had spoken to Marcia Webb, the South West 2 Co-ordinator yesterday and had tried to ring Ginnie to pass on the message a couple of times in the afternoon.

'I'm sorry Vera, I was out all the afternoon and didn't get back until after one in the morning and haven't had time to pick up my messages yet today...'

She had heard her mobile ping a couple of times while her and Claude were *moistening* one another and could hardly tell Vera that, could she. Sorry babe, I was shagging my boss from mid-afternoon until midnight and then was too exhausted to pick up my mobile.

She also had a fleeting thought while talking to Vera about what her nosey neighbours had thought about having a gleaming Bentley parked in the empty slot next to her battered old jalopy.

Vera said it was all good news and she was to ring Marcia this evening to discuss the relevant facility inspection details and that the co-ordinator also had a potential warm-up game for the Fannies this coming weekend.

'That's brilliant, who against?'

'You'll have to ask Marcia tonight' Vera said going all secretive on her. 'But I think you – and Lindsey – will like it. Let me know how you get on...bye.'

Ginnie smiled at this, she had a pretty good idea who it might be against just by the evasiveness and mention of Lindsey in Vera's answer.

Two minutes later there was a ping from her mobile and Marcia Webb's address in Salisbury and her email, landline and mobile number came through.

At seven thirty and with a glass of her favourite French red poison in her hand and her Spotify top twenty on softly in the background she dialled Marcia's mobile and introduced herself.

'Vera Godwin gave you and your side a tremendous plug,' Marcia said by reply. 'Forty-five nil on Saturday, wasn't it?'

'Yeah, we were on top form and Supermarine had an off day.'

Marcia laughed. 'I'll say, Vera has decided on the back of it to keep them out of South West 2 for another year at least.'

'So,' Ginnie replied crossing her fingers. 'And does that gives us a chance to take the slot?'

'Definitely, providing your ground and facilities measure up and Vera says they're good as well.'

'Yeah, it's that bundle of tenner's I keep slipping her,' Ginnie giggled.

'I have a proposition for you' Marcia said ignoring the quip. 'There is a team who have already won South West 2 with a game to spare and will be promoted for next season. Their last game of the season was due next Saturday away against Ellingham and Ringwood Ladies. Ellingham had to cancel due to a flu bug that's decimated their squad and the league winners would like to play this last game before wrapping up for the off season. Would you like to play this side in place of Ellingham?'

'Who are these secretive league winners?' Ginnie asked pretty much knowing the answer.

'Reading Bellfield Road Ladies.' Marcia replied.

Lindsey's old side and who had summarily dismissed her as coach after eight years in the job and then been demoted. Now they were on top again and due to go back up next season.

'A good side and we'd love the opportunity to play them.' Ginnie said giving nothing away although Marcia must know about Lindsey's dismissal. 'Home or away…?'

'Well, they were scheduled to play Ellingham away down at Ringwood and because I can kill two birds with one stone by seeing your side play *and* go through the obligatory facility check and meet you at the same time, what say we arrange it for your place next Saturday?'

'That' said Ginnie looking upwards to where the great god of rugby was still looking after her sat on his puffy white oblong shaped cloud, 'would be brilliant.'

'By the way, is the official name of your team the Furious Fannies?'

Ginnie giggled. 'That's one of our nicknames, among others. Officially we're called the Fantail Furies…'

Marcia was good enough to chuckle before replying.

'Okay, I'll set it up now with their coach Sylvan Greening. I know he'll be pleased and they won't have to travel so far as Swindon is a bit closer than Ringwood to Reading. Have you got any RFU sanctioned officials you can use? It's only a friendly but I like to keep things as clean and rules conscious as possible.'

Ginnie grimaced. 'Not yet but I think Vera can help me out with some.'

'Okay, arrange that with her and email me your pitch post code and any other contact details and I'll pass them on to Sylvan.

Sylvan, thought Ginnie ringing off. What an unusual name for a rugby bloke. Having pinged Marcia, the contact details she rang Vera to thank her and who said she'd happily arrange the officials. Later she rang back with the details.

'The only trouble is I couldn't get the same three women who did our first game and put your big lock in the sin bin for ten minutes. This time it will be an experienced male referee called Harry Wainwright although the line officials will be women.'

'That's fine' replied Ginnie. 'As for Heidi it served her right for answering back' she added feeling slightly disloyal to Heidi.

'How will Lindsey feel about playing against her old side…?' Vera asked.

'I don't know, I haven't told her yet, that will be my next call…'

'Good luck with that and the game. It should be a cracker and If can get away I might even come and watch the fireworks myself.'

Lindsey took the news coolly but Ginnie knew that when she put the phone down the coach would probably do an air punching war dance with glee at this early opportunity for revenge.

'And by the way' Lindsey said before ringing off, 'I got a full-time warehouse job today and start next Monday…in Swindon.'

'Congratulations' Ginnie said thinking about pressing the end button before muttering. 'Just don't fuck it all up by kicking Sylvan Greening in the bollocks on Saturday …'

'If only…' Lindsey sighed ending the call.

Training on Tuesday night was brutal. Lindsey worked them mercilessly on all their drills and it wasn't until they were sitting in the changing room trying to get the energy together to take off their kit and shower that Ginnie told them why.

'The good news girls' she said scrapping a mud clod from the bottom of her left boot and, as was now standard, throwing it at Iona on the other bench 'is that not only do we have a home game on Saturday – our last until next season – but it's against the league winners who will then be promoted out of the league that we're joining, so it's a one-off chance to show the clever bitches what we can do.'

Cheering all round with Cassie doing her now familiar muscular body builders pose.

'And then next season' Ginnie held her hands up for silence, 'we have been accepted into the same league – South West 2 – that these winners are vacating.'

Longer and louder cheering with a couple of whoops and a dozen high-fives thrown in.

'Who *is* the game against on Saturday then?' Iona said returning the clod with interest when the noise had died down.

Ginnie looked at Lindsey standing by the door. She wasn't sure if the team knew about her dismissal from their next opponents.

'We're playing Reading Bellfield Road Ladies. The game will be here and refereed by an experienced male official with RFU assistants running the lines.'

With Rocky, Mollie and J.J. leaping to their feet and slapping Lindsey on the back, the changing room erupted with very loud and raucous cheering.

They knew alright.

'So that's why you ran us into the bloody ground tonight eh coach?' This question came from Flipper Bryan.

Lindsey grinned sheepishly. 'Can't have you letting me down for this game, in truth it was their current coach, a slimy prick called Sylvan Greening and who used to be *my* assistant, who got me thrown out, so there's a lot riding on this game for me personally.'

'Fock me' Heidi drawled and everyone waited for something witty befitting the occasion to descend upon them from the glib lips of the Goth, 'even Shakespeare's Henry the Fifth at Agincourt didn't have this motivation. If ever this little ol' team of novice viragos and punch-drunk has-beens needed some incentive to *fill up the wall with our English dead,* and for us to fight tooth and claw for every metre and scrap of possession, this, my team of fallen and still rising angels, is surely it.'

Ginnie cheered along with the rest of them thinking that would have made a brill speech from her just before the kick-off...if she'd have known that quote from Shakespeare about Agincourt.

Unforetunately, her and the almighty bard were complete strangers.

*

Wednesday in the office was again very busy with three more new starters to absorb into the department Ginnie was half expecting a one-word ping about lunch at their usual place but it didn't come and then, just as she was tidying her desk up prior to going home for a quiet night at ten minutes after five, there was a ping with a short message.

What say I bring a Chinese or Indian takeaway and a bottle of wine around to your place on my way home?

Fine, make it Chinese.

So much, she thought having sent the reply, for my quiet night in.

At eight o'clock he turned up. She knew he was coming because she had been waiting by the window as the evening began to darken waiting for the Bentley's dazzling lights to turn up. Then he came in the white Toyota which was far better because her neighbours wouldn't take any notice of that. It kinda belonged in the car park whereas the Bently was conspicuous and memorable and was totally out of place.

'I noticed the other day' he said coming up for air having had a long, lingering kiss just inside her front door at which he couldn't use his hands because they held a bottle of wine in one and the takeaway bag in the other., 'that you like a glass of Merlot.'

Ginnie took the bag and bottle from him into the kitchen and looked at the label. 'My Merlot is about six quid a bottle, this looks far more expensive.'

'You're worth it' he said coming up behind her and wrapping his arms around her waist.

'We'd better eat this while it's still hot' she said taking the boxes out of the bag, 'otherwise we'll never get to it…'

'Crispy duck' he said letting go, 'where's your corkscrew?'

She opened a drawer and eventually found it and handed it to him. 'My bottles are usually screw-top so it doesn't get much use.'

In the event they got through half the meal and a glass of wine each on her little kitchen table before he couldn't wait any longer.

'Watching you eat is torture' he said reaching for her prior to them leaving a trail of clothes on the floor between the kitchen and her bedroom – a scene so beloved of romcom film makers everywhere, Ginnie thought looking back at the debris as he quickly drew down her freshly talcum-powdered panties and added them as the last item to the trail. Within seconds he was buried in her up to the hilt and her legs were around his waist while she gently sucked his tongue into her mouth.

When they hadn't seen each other for a few days their love-making was beginning to take on a pattern. Teenage-like and unable to hold back for the first one he would ejaculate within a couple of minutes and then, after a short rest, took a long time to gently bring her to a shattering orgasm the second time. After that they just nibbled, tongued, and stroked their way to whatever happened afterwards before falling asleep. It was during one of these sessions that he asked her what her favourite swear word was.

'Bollocks' she said without hesitation lifting her head from his.'When I'm on my own of course…'

'That's not the one you use just as you're about to… explode…'

'What do I say?'

'Fuck me…very loudly over and over.'

'Oh well…and so you did.'

'I love it, turn's me on, makes me want you even more.'

'What's yours?'

'I don't have one now although as a young man I swore all the time, but being a CEO constantly in meetings with people, directors, business people and employees, I was forced to make a determined effort not to use epithets at all…'

'Is that a posh word for swearing?'

'Yeah, but I might start to rewind the clock back when we're making love, it seems somehow a more fitting way of celebrating the…er…the grand finale.'

'Go for it, babe, now might be a good time to start.'

He only got as far as an elongated groan.

'Needs some practise' she said. 'Let me show you…'

Vaguely aware that he left her sometime in the early hours, Ginnie finally awoke in a bit of a panic at seven-thirty having failed to set her alarm. Although it was an hour later than she normally got up, a quick throwing of her scattered clothes into the wash basket followed by a shower and out the door for work by eight-fifteen got her back roughly on schedule. She would try and get away from the office on time tonight to go home and collect her gear for training tonight. It was the last training session of the season before the final and Lindsey's revenge game against Reading Bellfield Road Ladies on Saturday.

Mid-morning, she got another ping on her mobile whilst issuing some instructions to Simon Courtney, the young man who had taken her supervisors job and was now jointly one of two who reported to her all the time. When he'd gone, she opened the phone to a line of smiley emoji's followed by a message from her brother to 'Aunty Ginnie.' 'It's a girl! Emily gave birth to a healthy and beautiful seven-pound baby at two a.m.

both doing well – call me later I'm catching up on some sleep! Love Robert.

Seems like we both didn't get much sleep last night she thought, although we were making babies, not producing them.

The slot that night at training was not good news. Gita was on it having just come on, Ellie looked a close thing and wouldn't really know until Saturday morning and Iona – a vital cog in the speedy back row alongside Ginnie – was also touch and go. Nevertheless, training was again intense with Lindsey concentrating on some of the known strengths of their opponents and how to nullify them.

'They have a very fast and tricky fullback and captain called Samantha Arthur. I trained Sammie right from her entry into lady's rugby five or six years ago and I understand she'd still there and performing right up to the same standard. I looked up their record for this season last night and Sammie can't be touched with twenty-four tries in eight games – that's an average of four per game and she has already nailed down the golden boot handed out by the league for the most tries scored in a season. She will attack from deep wherever a gap appears and has a mazy style of running that's difficult to counter – not unlike Ginnies. She's not as fast as Romany but fast enough and added to a good sidestep and early swerve off her left or right foot and superbly balanced can take some stopping. They will try and get the ball to her with space out wide and just let her go. Rumour also has it that she is being considered for the national squad although she now in her thirties and may be getting too old for that. Our best way of countering Sammie is to drop both our wingers back as soon as she gets the ball and hope to slow her down or at least get in a tackle before she gets away. Romany, I want you to watch her like a hawk and as soon as she breaks clear – with or without the ball in her hands – run her down.'

In view of what happened during the game, afterwards the squad were beginning to think that Lindsey had a chrystal ball.

There was a lot more stuff like that with at least eight others in the side well-known to Lindsey from her time with them.

'This male coach with the precious name...' Heidi drawled. 'Is there anything we should know or could do about him, some sort of special abuse to wind him up?'

'Yeah, but he's not proper precious cos he's married with two kids. Anyway, a good kick in the gonads when no-one's looking would be good,' grinned Lindsey.

'Wot's gonads Heid?' cried Romany looking around for her heroine and getting everyone laughing.

'It's Jewish my little lightning streak, a foreign language that I don't speak but bollock's ring's a certain familiar bell...'

Romany again opened her mouth but was forestalled from asking what *they* were by Heidi's raised hands.

Must be something to do with sausages again she surmised to herself.

Friday late-morning and Ginnie was having a cup of coffee in her office after a busy couple of hours when there was a tap on the door and Jenny Hynes, Wessex Computer Technician and member of the rugby squad poked her head around the door.

'Hi Jen, c'mon in and take a seat.'

'So, this is where you spend your day cooking up flash motivational pre-match speeches to make to the team. Eh?'

'I leave most of that to Heidi; she's the expert, coffee?' Ginnie gestured to the coffee pot sitting in its own percolator, another perk of management.

'Great, black no sugar, like my men...' Jenny sat down and looked around. 'Nice office you got here...'

'I've only been in here for two and a half weeks and still feeling my way around.' Ginnie placed a China cup of black coffee on her desk coaster in front of her.

'Knowing I work in the same place as you and because you shot off last night from training before we could mention it and the fact that time is tight, the girls asked me to put a couple of ideas to you today...'

Ginnie lifted what she hoped was a managerial eyebrow.

'Saturday is our final game and as things stand the last we will see of each other until we resume training for next season sometime in late July or early August. And the consensus is that none of us want to wait that long so it was suggested that we continue training each week, not Tuesdays *and* Thursdays – one night per week will do. It means that the team can continue to bond and keep our fitness and training moves ticking over...'

Ginnie nodded. 'A great idea; Tuesday would probably be better for me but either will do, any preference's shown by the girls?'

'Yeah, Tuesday won hands down.' Jenny took a pull at her coffee cup. 'Good coffee, better than that rubbish we get from the machine in the Technical Services Office.'

'Columbian – I buy it myself and bring it in, Okay, Tuesdays it is, you said a couple of ideas?'

Jenny grinned. 'They also want an end of season party, a big old excuse to get the glad rags on and get pissed. The general idea being that we've never had a few glasses of something serious together as a group and it's high time we did...'

Ginnie joined in with her infectious grin. 'Where and when?'

'No idea where, somewhere local I suppose but that's up to you, but the Saturday following the Reading game was suggested...'

'Great,' Ginnie said, 'leave it to me. We've got a fair bit of money left in the kitty, certainly enough to put on a bit of a shindig anyway...'

They chatted for a couple of minutes about general rugby matters while Jenny finished her coffee then left. A couple of minutes thinking time later Ginnie called Ellie on her mobile and left a message to call her. Five minutes later Ellie rang back.

'What sort of function rooms do you have at the hotel?' Ginnie asked her.

'A big one for three hundred guests plus, used for wedding receptions and big company Christmas parties, and two smaller rooms, one holds a hundred at a push and the other about fifty.'

Ginnie told her about the idea for the squad party and the date knowing that Ellie had missed training the night before because of the slot and wouldn't have heard about it from the girls. She agreed to check out the fifty- and one-hundred-person rooms for availability and prices on the date and get back to her. Five minutes later she did just that. 'The one-hundred-person room is available on that date and I can even come up with a D.J. and combined vegetarian and meat-based buffet for £425 for the night. I've seen the buffets for these do's and they're not bad. That price, includes my staff discount of £75. There will be a bar at which people can buy their own drinks or, if you're feeling flush you can put an amount behind it for them to just use up until it's all gone...'

'Do you mind going to a party there, after all; you do work there so it's not so much fun for you?'

'Parties are people not places and I wouldn't miss a squad do with our lot for anything.'

'Book it for me with the D.J. and buffet and I'll get back to you about the bar. Will they want payment up front?'

'Nah, they know all about the rugby squad cos I keep on telling them about us and besides, you're already an account customer from the interview rooms you hired. Pay them afterwards...'

Ginnie rang Jenny on the internal phone and told her it was done and she would print out some invites for everyone and give them out after the game on Saturday to let them know the venue and the date.

'You move as fast off the pitch as you do on it' Jenny said by way of a compliment.

I rather like that comment Ginnie thought putting the phone down.

That evening on her way home Ginnie dropped into the Great Western Hospital Maternity Suite to see her new baby niece. When she eventually found the right place in the vast hospital complex, Robert was there sitting by Emily's bedside holding the new arrival with a beam of pure pride on his face.

'Say hello to Violet Lily' he said lifting the bundle in his arms up to Ginnie. 'Aunty Ginnie is here and will make you into a star rugby player when you're a big girl.'

Ginnie made all the appropriate remarks about how beautiful Violet Lily was and left after half an hour. As she walked into her apartment her mobile rang. It was Claude.

'Do you have a current passport?' he said after greeting her with 'how's my lovely girl today?'

'I'm fine and I've just been up the hospital to see my newly born niece, another lovely little heart-breaker to be called Violet Lily born to my brother and his wife yesterday. And yes, I do have a current passport, why do you ask, are we going somewhere nice?'

'Maybe, next question, have you any holiday time from the office due?'

'I get three weeks and haven't taken any so far this year.'

'You get *four* weeks now you're a manager, I believe. Can you take the week off starting a week on Monday and we'll leave the day before on the Sunday for seven days?'

'Providing I get through tomorrow's game without breaking my leg or something and Steve Harrington lets me go for the week at such short notice, yes. Oh, and one other thing, I've arranged an end of season party for the squad and their partners on the Saturday night which will be the day before we leave. If we're going anywhere the next day, I'll have to keep off the booze otherwise I'll have a sore head.'

'I've already checked with Steve and he's happy about it and thinks you deserve a break so no problem there. As for the party, can *I* come as your partner? That way I'll be there to keep you upright and we can leave from my place on the Sunday morning and drive straight to the airport. As for the potential broken leg, I'll simply just have to carry you everywhere.'

That's why he's a big boss, Ginnie thought; he figures things out before asking the questions.

'There is only one small problem' she said. 'The party will be attended by a few people from Wessex as well as the squad and if we're together...?'

'Tongues will wag' he interrupted her. 'But I intend to come and watch the match against Reading tomorrow as well so they can start to wag then when I give you a big hug and a kiss afterwards. Its time you and I went public anyway, don't you think?'

'Fine by me' Ginnie replied. 'Can you tell me where we might be going for the week?'

'Not yet, it's a surprise and besides, I haven't booked it yet because I needed to make sure you were alright with it. If you're up for it after the game tomorrow, why don't we have a quiet meal somewhere and then stay over at my place. And I'll tell you where we're going then? Perhaps we could do the same on the following Saturday after the party so you'll need to bring your suitcase with you and we can drive up to Heathrow from the boat house the following morning...'

'Sounds good to me' Ginnie said, 'should I pack for good weather or snow and ice.?'

'Sunshine and skimpy evening wear, even if we don't go anywhere and stay at home...'

After they had finished Ginnie had a rummage around for her passport which she hadn't used for a couple of years when she'd spent a week in the Canaries with another short-term boyfriend who proved a complete performance disappointment and been binned as soon as they got back. She was relieved to see that the passport still had a few years to go and she didn't look like a gargoyle on the photo either.

So, she said to herself eyeing up the Merlot but giving it a miss because of the game the next day, matters are moving forward and he's happy to go public at the match and squad do. That will sure raise a few eyebrows, especially when it gets back to the office... and the nosey cow that controls his working life. As for Iona, her eyebrows will go through the roof as well now that Ginnie had her very own MSD to play with...

'MSD...A Medium Swinger being a more fitting description of Claude's more than adequate stats and a decidedly more comfortable fit than the reputed BSD of one Dextor Keegan Stirling, Heidi's beau..'

Chapter Twenty

'Victory is an insatiable nympho bitch that requires wins all the time in order to satisfy the craving, so we must keep giving her the fix…and don't forget' Heidi drawled pulling a pink and black ringed sock up her long right limb to the knee 'the euphoria of winning is laced' she put her right boot on and in sync with her words tightened the lace 'with pure dopamine and will drive us on to even greater victories…'

Heidi finished her quotes and boots then leaned back in the changing room, pulled up her shorts and grinned around at the squad as they prepared for the home game against Reading Bellfield Road Ladies.

What a beautiful yet raunchy way of putting it, thought Ginnie not for the first time with the lock's clever quotes. I wish I'd have thought of that, it would have made another great captain's quote in the pre-game huddle.

'So far we've played two, won two' replied Flipper Bryan, 'soon to be three and three.'

Cassie stood up completely naked and to cries of 'give us some muscle sass Cass' strutted to the middle and took up her body builders pose with bulging muscles everywhere. Everybody then broke up as Romany leapt to her feet also naked stood beside her with her skinny arms and legs and in the same pose. They were, in shape, just about as far apart as two women could get without an ounce of fat between them.

'Victory is an unstoppable nympho stick insect streaking down the wing' J.J. shouted referring to Romany's lack of muscle and Heidi's quip.

'Can you have a virgin nympho...?' cried another voice that sounded like Gina 'the happy hooker' McKinnon.

'Sausages' shrieked Romany holding her pose alongside the still posing Cassie and contributing to the furore with the only contribution she knew.

'Seen more meat on a butcher's apron' Rocky Cook said pointing at the skinny flyer.

'Careful Romany, mind Cassie don't eat you for a snack,' rumbled Biggie Bagnall.

And on it went as the Fannies got in the mood for battle.

Sherry came in. 'The opposition have arrived' she said, 'and brought three buses full of supporters with them...'

'Blimey' said the naked heavily tattood Gina pulling on a pink and black hooped sock, 'who're we playing, the Red fucking Roses of England?'

'Bring 'em on' said Heidi.

To everyone's glee the elegant Ellie had survived the clot and was fit to play and Sheila Bates would be replacing Gita who hadn't survived it. The other replacements had all been promised the last fifteen minutes or more depending upon injuries.

Before the warm up Ginnie was introduced by Vera Godwin to Marcia Webb, the co-ordinator of South West 2 and the league that the Fannies would be joining next season. Marcia had driven up from her home in Salisbury to conduct the necessary facility inspection. Vera then left the two of them to have a look around which only took ten minutes as Marcia could already see the outside facilities and was very happy with the changing rooms and showers and various dryers and machinery which, she said, paraphrasing Lindsey, were among the best she had seen in the league.

When the Fannies trotted out for the warm up the jeering crowd supporting Reading occupied one entire side of the pitch and were the biggest crowd the Fannies had played in front of. The Reading team hadn't emerged yet but their supporters contented themselves with catcall's, jeers, and whistles when they saw Lindsey, their former and replaced coach walk out of the changing rooms with a look of grim determination on her face, then burst into loud cheering when the Reading team finally raced out onto the pitch with practised zigzags and lots of helicopter arm spinning. Five of them then ran over to the opposite side-line from their supporters and coach and approached the spot where Lindsey had taken up station and shook her hand, including their number fifteen and captain and star player Sammie Arthur about whom they had been warned.

The stern-looking black clad referee then ran onto the pitch with his pair of female assistants with each of them sported the appropriate RFU badge on their carefully pressed black breast. As he passed Heidi the Goth lock smiled sweetly at him but received no acknowledgement back. Heidi opened her mouth to say something but was blocked by Ginnie who said 'Shut it, Heidi, lets at least start the game with a clean sheet.'

'I was about to wish him a happy and peaceful game,' Heidi grinned.

'Yeah, sure you were.' Ginnie replied spinning a rugby ball at her.

Although there was rain in the air it had held off thus far as Sammie and Ginnie ran to the centre spot to toss for kick off and ends. Sammie's smile and handshake were genuine enough and Ginnie allowed herself a small grimace in return as the referee tossed the coin. Ginnie won with 'heads' and said they would stay where they were and take the kick off. Back in the team huddle Ginnie spoke firmly but briefly and tried to keep the emotion out of it.

'Fannies, it's time to get furious again. You all know who we're playing for today and why, so hands in the middle and let's make sure everyone else around this ground hears it as well, so let's hear it for our special coach...for...Lindsey!'

As the loudly shouted word rang around the ground as the object of it standing with her lips compressed in the thin line of total vengeance allowed a single tear to slide down her tightly clenched cheek. Her girls knew that there was more in this game for her than any other she had coached.

Heidi put her arm around her second-row partner Ellie and shouted loud enough for most of her own team to hear.

'Come my big warrior mate, we have the smelly burrow coverts of the skanky Reading sisterhood to kick firmly back up the M.4.'

Then the ref blew for the off and Magical Mollie lofted her drop kick high into the grey Wiltshire air and led by the jerky gallop of Heidi alongside the smooth glide of Ellie the Fannies Howies charged downfield after it.

For the first ten minutes nothing much happened with the Fannies emotional energy evenly matched by the Reading discipline and good handling keeping the game in midfield. Then the Reading fly-half received a back pass on her own twenty-two metre line and without looking kicked a cross-field spiral at no more than head height to her left...and straight into the running hands of Sammie Arthur the star try-scoring full-back who rounded Sheila Bates, Gita's replacement easily as she caught it and set off unopposed towards the Fannie try line some sixty metres away. It was a training ground move that they had exploited many times before and had contributed to any number of tries to Arthur's twenty-four of the season so far. With Romany a long way from the person she was supposed to mark tightly and most of the Fannies stuck in midfield and only Love-Bites Gordon to beat, Sammie feinted left and stood her up with an in-and-out right swerve leaving the army PTI on the ground. The way was clear now to the Fannies line...or so Sammie thought until racing across on a diagonal from her wing the Blue Streak that was Romany, finally waking up to what she was supposed to do when following Linsey's instructions to the letter with her tell-tale forward crawl swimming stroke of a gallop, began to eat into Sammies lead. Five metres out Sammie glanced to the side and sensed that she might be caught and swerved back to the left to gain a little more ground. Then, as she had done twenty-four times that season, the Reading captain prepared to launch herself into dive and slam the ball down in the corner. Somehow it never happened because the flying traveller hit her in mid-air in a crunching collision and they both tumbled into touch before Sammie could get the ball down.

The Fannies supporters on the side-lines erupted, the Reading fans stifled the cheer they were getting ready to roar with the try and as Ginnie and Iona helped Romany to her feet the Reading coach Sylvan Greening raced across to his player and captain who hadn't moved from where she had landed five metres outside the side-line and well over the rope.

Lindsey arrived on the scene and put her arm around the now standing and muddy faced Romany.

'If you play this game for another twenty years you will never make a better try-saving tackle than that' the coach said to her little speedster and star winger.

'Fair tackle, pink line-out ball on the five-metre line' the ref bellowed.

It was five minutes before the Reading coach and his replacements managed to help the clearly dazed and injured Sammie off the pitch. In the meantime, Lindsey had gathered the Fannies around her and, after everyone had congratulated the tough little traveller Romany on her great tackle, were listening carefully to the early instructions.

'There's the usual hole down the middle if we can get through and around their forwards we will be playing to one of our great strengths. Its looks as if Sammie, their star fullback is finished for this game after Romany's great tackle so tie up their forwards with mauls and then get the ball to Mollie, Ginnie, and Iona to rip through the middle with their trickery and pace…'

As the Bellfield Road captain was eventually helped slowly from the pitch and a replacement got ready, the Fannies squad quietly passed the ball around to stay warm. For the first time it gave Ginnie a chance to look around on their side of the pitch to see who was there supporting them. Then the ref. blew to restart the game with a Fannies line out on their own five-metre line.

Soaring above everyone else the elegant Ellie took the ball cleanly and her fellow Howies latched onto her as she landed and they began to move steadily down the pitch until, along with the Reading forwards who had been trying to stop the moving maul, the whole group of them collapsed in an untidy melee of bodies on the pitch. As the players from both sides began to get to their feet, a stocky Reading player began to shout at Harry Wainwright.

'Ref...'Ref... That bitch bit my fucking nipple hard in that maul and it bloody-well hurt!'

The opposition prop ran after the referee tugging at her shirt over her right breast complaining loudly. Wainwright, who had just called a scrum for the Fannies because of the collapsed maul, suppressed a smile and looked over at his line assistant, Hilary Farrisha and who was nearer to the alleged incident and raised his eyebrows by way of an enquiry. Receiving a shrug of indifference from her he motioned for the teams to carry on with the scrum with the put-in to be taken by the pink and black clad Fannies scrum half.

'If I could I'd take me bloody shirt off and show you the teeth marks' the aggrieved Bellfield prop shouted at him again. Wainwright held his hand up to stop the scrum forming and walked to the where the indignant prop was standing with one hand on her hip and the other massaging the painful nipple outside her blue and white striped shirt.

'You' he said pointing at her, 'will get on with the game or spend the next ten minutes in the bin… understand?'

In his six years officiating in the South Western rugby union leagues, Harry Wainwright thought he'd heard it all but never a complaint that someone had been bitten in the nipple, but since this was his first game in charge of two female team's he supposed it would give rise to a plethora of other new complaints involving the female anatomy. That anatomy may be different and the voices pitched higher but the language of rugby conflict– the growled curses all over the pitch – was still the same. Regardless of gender the rules were also the same and he was determined to referee it the same as he did with male teams.

As the aggrieved and still muttering and massaging Reading prop moved reluctantly to her position in the scrum and glared at Heidi Prager, the Fannies lock and who she obviously held responsible for the alleged nipple bite. Heidi smiled sweetly at her then blew her a kiss before speaking in her posh low voice.

'I'd rather 'have sexual congress with a dead dung beetle than bite that flabby focking deflated balloon bag you call a nipple, ya fat-arsed skank.'

Heidi's low voice was just loud enough for the bitten and aggrieved prop to hear but not the referee. For those close by on the Fannies side who also heard, it was a typical remark from their funny and antagonising destroyer designed to wind-up the recipient. It worked beautifully. Before her team mates could stop her the now seething and grossly insulted prop jumped at Heidi swinging a meaty fist at her head. Luckily for the Fannies lock the bunched fist sailed harmlessly over her shoulder and before she could reload the prop was swamped by her own players and pulled away.

Inwardly Harry Wainwright smiled to himself. He might have been expecting something different, a little more ladylike circumspection perhaps or certainly less violence, but ladies' rugby was the same as their male counterparts, retaliatory actions for alleged indiscretions, pride in the shirt and occasional punches like this more usually known, and appropriately here, as 'handbags.' He reached inside his pocket and pulled out a card.

'Unnecessary roughness' he said loudly brandishing the yellow card at the avenging Reading prop and pointing to the touch line 'ten minutes in the bin and the next one will be red... away you go.'

As the aggrieved prop slouched off muttering threats of what she was going to do to Heidi's head when she came back on, ten metres behind the Fannie's reformed scrum, Ginnie Joy, their standout captain and inside-centre player, turned to Iona Pierce, her outside-centre.

'Welcome to League Two of the South Western Division' she said with a broad grin.

'There will be a lot more of this stuff next season and I for one just can't wait.'

'As long as its Heidi doing the biting neither can I' replied the former attractive professional athlete named after a Scottish island.

Ginnie smiled and again took the time to scan the side-lines where the Fannies own fans were standing.

All the usual suspects from the previous friendly were in attendance including her mother and father and Robert – Emily had brought the baby home this morning and was getting help from her mother at home with the little girl and who had moved in for a few days so Robert could get out for the game. Next came Heidi's haughty Mama and Damian, he of the supposedly tiny todger standing next to – paradoxically – the now notoriously well-hung Balliol tutor Dexter, then Flippers husband and the three-year-old twins in identical denim rompers, Stan the Pint and a Wink Mackay with his son, the two army husbands of Gina and Avril with Ellie's tall black archeologist boyfriend, and, standing on his own down by the corner flag Allan Dix, now with his arm in plaster having fallen off his Fireblade the day before and when, luckily, he didn't have Mandy 'Judo' Sawyer on the pillion seat. For the first time the two of them had arrived at thie meeting for the mini-bus at their home car park earlier quietly in a taxi. Next to Dix, Vera Godwin, the Supermarine Director had been able to come and was standing with Marcia Webb, the South West 2 co-ordinator. Down the far end stood Louise George and Tink Cutler, placed there by Romany as was now usual in the hope of seeing her score another try – although if they had seen her great tackle, they would know it was as good as a try if not better. On the halfway line Lindsey and Sherry stood with the Fannies replacements. Ginnies Saturday night clubbing foursome had not come for this game and, disappointingly as far as she could see, neither had her lover Claude…

Her lover and becoming the most important person in her life and who, above all, she wanted to show just how well she could play this game…again.

Having scanned the home crowd twice Ginnie was about to give up when Ellie, the tall second row nudged her and nodded towards the now quiet away crowd touchline and said

'Isn't that Aggy?'

And there she was clinging on to her father's arm standing in the middle of the Reading supporters where Ginnie hadn't thought to look. Reason, as Claude had said later about his headstrong daughter, had prevailed and she was here. Both the Dillon's presence gave Ginnie a warm glow of satisfaction and seeing her looking Claude nodded and smiled and then looked down at his daughter who also had a shy grin on her face.

Then the ref blew up for the restart and they were off again although now Reading was without their captain and star player who was sitting on a chair with a blanket around her holding an icepack to her shoulder, and the Fannies were still on a high after the try-saving tackle by Romany.

Where on earth, thought Ginnie, did they get ice from? There wasn't a machine or fridge in the dressing rooms so they must have brought it with them in a cold box. Another thing she might have to think about next season. The only medication Lindsey carried around in her shoulder bag was an aerosol of that magic freezing spray coaches tend to slather on all knocks, a bag of cotton wool, a roll of sticking plaster and some bandages. Sherry carried a water rack full of bottles and that was the total of the Fannies medical or revival equipment.

Ellie won the restart lineout again cleanly by plucking Gina's throw out of the air and feeding it back to

Flipper on her own line who passed it sideways to Mollie who, in turn, kicked a good spiral into touch ten metres inside the Fannies half. Reading knocked on from their throw in and the next scrum of the game was called with a Fannies put-in just inside their own half.

'A screecher' Flipper called to her forwards loudly as they went down for the scrum and then shouted the same to her half-backs as she prepared to put the ball in. It was a bold call and an unlikely move they had only played around with during training. Still, it had been called by Flipper, the one player who had to make it happen and now they would see if it worked. Flipper put the ball in to Gina's feet and hanging from her two strong props of Rocky and Biggie the hooker got a good clean heel of the ball back down channel one which was held in the back of the stable scrum by Billie Hayden for a couple of valuable seconds. This was a vital albeit short delay to give Flipper time to get around behind her. Picking up the ball Flipper stepped back a metre and then dummied a pass to Magical Mollie who was moving parallel to her ready to receive it. With the scrum still intact from both sides Flipper, with the ball tucked under her right arm then pulled off the 'screecher' move which meant she had to run straight back at the scrum positions and jump up onto Billies broad back, dap down her left foot down on it to get balance, hop to Gina's back landing on her right foot, another hop to the opposition second rows back on her left foot followed by the final hop over the head of their still crouched flankers and, remaining frozen in her scrum position their number eight and then to the ground. It worked perfectly and with the three-step balanced hop she had run over the middle backs of the entire sixteen woman scrummage, seventeen if you counted the opposition scrum half frozen to the spot by the scrum tunnel by the sheer audacity of the move. As Flipper landed, she stumbled, not an unexpected outcome given the dexterity with which she had performed the unusual move. Just before she hit the ground, she managed to get the ball away to Ginnie who was charging up around the scrum in anticipation and was now slightly behind but alongside her in expectation of receiving the pass if she could pull it off. Scooping up the ball from her ankles before it hit the ground Ginnie got into motion. She was only just inside the opposition half and there was still a great deal to do. Swerving early into towards the centre Ginnie rounded her opposite number and then drawing the next defender got a call from Iona and passed it inside to her. Iona set off towards the wing where Romany was waiting and having drew the final defender out of position the outside centre passed it to the speedy traveller who tucked it under her arm and went arcing around under the posts to dot it down.

Reading's only hope now was that the experienced referee would disallow it and they all looked at him in anticipation of the try being refused for some infringement or other...

'Try' he bellowed raising his hand under the post and shaking his head as if to say that he wouldn't dare disallow such a wonderful and unusual try.

The 'screecher' named inevitably by Heidi and which had never worked once in training, had worked perfectly here when it really counted.

Nothing, Lindsey later said, had ever been seen like it in a professional game let alone by a ladies team who had not yet played a game in any lower league in anger. J.J. said that she had seen a film of a similar attempt by a men's team in a South African international some years ago but it hadn't worked because the scrum half had fallen off the top of the scrum and dropped the ball.

The home fans went wild. Flipper did a pair of 360's, one each for her twins who giggled and jumped around with glee, and Lindsey did a jig around her part of the pitch as Romany ran to and hugged her granddad Tink. The opposition just stood with their hands on hips looking at their feet stunned by the move and the fact it had been given. Some of the three buses of travelling supporters grudgingly clapped the mighty effort by Flipper and nodded their acceptance of a unique and beautifully executed move. As Mollie lined up the kick Ginnie looked over to where Claude and Aggy stood. He had both his hands in the air and his daughter a hand over her mouth in utter disbelief.

Mollie slotted the kick comfortably and the score was 7 – 0.

Flipper called the 'screecher' three more times loudly during the first half at subsequent scrum's just to see the panic on the opposition faces as they charged around all over the place uncertain where to stand to defend against it. She was only winding them up and knew the chances of it working twice in one game were non-existent, especially as it had never worked in training but that wouldn't stop her cheekily winding the opposition up by calling it.

An offside penalty against Gina gave Reading a three-pointer kick ten minutes later and the score moved to 7 – 3.

Then Iona got deliberately punched in the face by the Reading hooker and for the second time in two and a half games had to leave the pitch with a bad nosebleed. That it was a deliberate and vicious attempt to slow down the Fannies speedy backs there was no doubt because Iona, Ginnie, Mollie, and Romany were beginning to boss the game and cut through the Reading defensive lines with impunity and were only stopped from scoring two more tries by last gasp desperate tackles including an ankle tap on Iona when she was two metres from the try line. Then the bulky and rather ugly hooker from Reading and obviously one of their enforcer's, fell on Iona when she was down followed by two of her forward team mates over them acting as cover. The punch was hidden from the ref by these flopping forwards who were only penalised for falling on the ball. Meanwhile Iona was left spread-eagled on the ground with blood pouring from her nose when the marauding Reading forwards had got to their feet. The punch also owed some payback for Heidi's hidden nipple bite as well as the fact that the Fannies speedy petticoats were threatening to boss the game.

As Lindsey and Sherry tended to the dazed and bleeding Iona, Heidi and Rocky went after the Reading hooker and had to be pulled away from her by Biggie and Ellie. The ref, who said he hadn't seen anything untoward about the brutal punch on the defenceless Iona then reversed the penalty and gave it to Reading, adding insult to injury by placing his hand in the pocket where the red and yellow cards were kept as Heidi and Rocky protested. Luckily, Wainwright didn't get the threatened cards out and let the two Fannies forwards off with a caution. Ginnie spoke quietly to the angry Goth lock and calmed her down, losing her at this stage would be a bad move.

'We will get our own back on that vicious hooker' the skipper said 'but it had better not be you or that ref will have *you* off as well. Leave it to the rest of us this time, okay?'

With the Fannies camped on their own line defending desperately the whistle went for half time leaving them still in front by 7 – 3.

At the half-time huddle Ginnie and Lindsey had a quiet word with J.J. and Judo, the Fannies two highly mobile flankers and who were without doubt two of the most accomplished scrappers in the team. They didn't have the exquisite verbal delivery of Heidi nor the overt aggression of the lock and strength of Rocky and Biggie, but could be relied upon to go about their mission with patience and stealth.

Two minutes after the restart Ginnie again scored one of her now exceptional tries when collecting a popped pass in a reverse move with Flipper and Mollie on the half-way line, she arrowed through a gap straight down the middle. As the replacement full back and one of the Reading wingers converged on her from two sides, she kicked a short lob over their heads and then ran through the middle of them and collected the ball without it touching the ground. With twenty metres still to go Ginnie swerved towards the left wing to avoid the converging wingers and dived over the line for the try in the corner. The ref immediately raised his hand again and blew for the try causing Ginnies team mates to high-five her and the home crowd leapt about in glee.

As Mollie lined up the difficult kick from way out on the touch-line, Ginnie stole a glance at where he-who-mattered-most was standing with his daughter, and caught him with both hands in the air again, this time with his thumbs up amid the gleam of ownership. Mollie managed to get the kick over the bar and through the posts and the score moved to 14 – 3.

With the game drifting away from them the Reading players began to lose heart for the battle giving Mandy Judo Sawyer and J.J. the chance they had been waiting for as the ugly prop who had viciously punched Iona fell on a loose ball. Immediately the two Fannies flankers dropped on her with Mandy first holding her down while J.J. spread-eagled her stance over them both and reached in to collect the ball. Mandy held both her hands up high out of the ruck to show she had legally let go of her grounded opponent beneath her while her team mate grabbed the ball. Suddenly there was a loud crack followed by a scream of pain from the grounded Reading hooker and Wainwright blew up to halt the game. Once again, the Reading coach and his assistant rushed onto the pitch and attended to the downed player as they protested to the official.

'It was a fair tackle and she was not held in by the Fantails player' Wainwright said loudly awarding a scrum to the Fannies. It would, however, be some time before they could take the scrum as the crack that had reverberated around the ground was the broken arm of the Reading hooker. As she was eventually helped off the pitch by coach Greening with the broken arm hanging uselessly down by her side, Heidi nodded at Mandy's boyfriend down at the other end of the pitch with his own arm in plaster and spoke quietly to her.

'Nice one, Judo. Are you sure your boyfriend broke his arm falling off his motor bike?'

A somewhat rueful Mandy answered with a muttered fact that deliberately breaking an opponent's limb with a leg grip and twist on the floor was a flagrant disregard of the gentle rules of judoka combat – let alone rugby union – and as a black belt she should have known better.

'Fock that, Mandy,' hissed Heidi. 'That ugly skank deserved it, her punch has probably broken Iona's nose. Break a few more arms and legs and make the fockers really pay…'

Luckily the ref was not a party to either of these girls' words as he was earnestly repeating his decision to the Reading coach on the side-lines that because Mandy had both hands in the air the tackle was legal and the injury accidental.

With two of their key players off with injuries and feelings running high, not to mention being stoked up by their irate coach and three busloads of fans exhortations and the fact that they were 14 – 3 down to a team of newbie no-where's, the thin tissue of respectability snapped for the Reading players and they began to openly seek revenge instead of concentrating on the basics of the game.

Sheila Bates, who had replaced Gita on the wing and had been showing a fair turn of speed in training, was then taken out by a high tackle resulting in a red card for Reading and forcing Lindsey to make an early replacement to replace the injured winger. After further pushing and shoving from the two sets of forwards the referee called together the two captains, Ginnie for the Fannies and the assistant captain for Bellfield Road who had taken over the armband when Sammy Arthur had gone off in the early part of the game. Pointing out that it was a friendly and as such should be played in the spirit of that title, Wainwright emphasised that if the Reading side did not settle down and play the game within that spirit and the rules, he wouldn't hesitate to abandon it in favour of the Swindon side.

It was a warning too late; the final red card had brought with it an aggrieved equivalent colour red mist over the Reading players eyes and although beaten were still egged on by their animated coach and crowd. Greening was also feeling the pressure of playing against the coach he had learned under and replaced and who was now bossing him with a team of newbies.The promoted visiting side were being taught a rugby lesson by a bunch of considered novices and now lost all shape, temperament and character and the Reading side continued to go after each Fannie player with the ball as if to commit GBH. With Ginnie running around issuing calming words the Fannies, including Heidi and the flinty-eyed Rocky, their two most battle conscious and fiery forwards, held their cool magnificently. With Lindsey then bringing on all her remaining replacements of Sylvie Greatorex, Alfie Cushing, Jenny Hynes and Cassie Betts, the fresh bodies gave the Fannies further impetus and another Ginnie opportunity try following a muscular but fair tackle on the Reading open-side flanker from the bristling and muscular Cassie. This time, catching the ball after the crunching tackle from the Welsh former body builder the try owed everything to Ginnies pace and early swerving skill as she exploited the many defensive gaps now appearing in the Reading defence and sealed the game with another beauty under the posts. Goaded beyond their inability to respond correctly after Mollie slotted the kick, the demolished and demoralised Reading team completely lost their cool and began to lash out everywhere. The ref finally had enough after a flagrant haymaker punch aimed at Ellie's beautiful head that fortunately she managed to duck under. Brandishing another red card at the Reading forward who had tried to remove Ellie's head, the ref then called off the game in favour of the Fannies. The three-bus and formerly boisterous crowd from Reading were silent as their demoralised, shamed team hung their heads and trudged off, while the outnumbered supporters of the Fannies cheered to the rafters as their team skipped and high-fived their way to the changing rooms.

'Give us another screecher Flipper' came the shout from one section and Tanya duly obliged with a double 360 causing her twins to both fall on the ground as they tried to imitate their clever little gymnastic mum.

It was, said Lindsey later in the changing room, a comprehensive victory for both brilliantly played rugby and wonderful discipline. Flipper's standout try – the mighty 'Screecher' – was the score of the season, nay, all seasons of lady's rugby that she had ever seen, and Ginnie's skill and two tries again were game-breakers. And as for little Romany their talisman and mascot, she was simply unstoppable and had tackled like a demon as well.

Nobody mentioned Judo's malign but beautifully executed tackle and even Iona, whose nose was fortunately not broken although she still had cotton wool stuck up each nostril and a loose tooth, and Sheila with her sore red-rimmed neck from the high tackle, grinned and cheered with the rest of them.

'It's a much easier game' drawled Heidi from her position sprawled on the changing room benches 'when our brilliant petticoats hitch up their frilly hems and perform miracles like Flipper and the Skipper today.'

Flipper and the Skipper. Three games in and the rhyming monikers were already set.

'Here here,' said Ellie. 'And little Flip pulls off the Screecher at the first time of asking…'

'Yeah, don't I know it' said Billie Hayden ruefully rubbing her shoulder. 'When we practised the move in training Flipper had trainers on. Now I've got her stud marks in my back to prove that she pulled it off.'

'You and me both' said Gina, the other stepped-upon srummager in the wonder move, ruefully rubbing her trodden-on tattoos.

'You'll both get over the stud marks and be left with the wonderful memories of a game when the black crow of judicial hegemony put on her hanging hat and completely focked the opposition villains. And don't forget' Heidi continued 'some people would pay a lot of money to have Flipper run over their bare backs with studs on. Add in a good horsewhipping around the bare buttocks and it would be an erotic heaven…'

Everyone laughed except Romany who didn't understand what her heroine was talking about and no-one asked what hegemony meant but Ginnie made a mental note to look it up when she had the chance.

Heidi looked at the perplexed Romany who was still thinking about what her heroine had said.

'Don't ask my little streaker, this time just don't ask…'

Lindsey took it up.

'The dynamics of rugby whether played by men or women will always depend upon the ability to maintain your cool in the most difficult circumstances. Cool and fair play in the face of adversity will get referee's on your side as we saw here today and once the ref is onside the game gets easier. Suffice it to say that I have never been so proud of a team I've coached in my life; it was a magnificent and highly disciplined performance.'

'And don't forget' Ginnie shouted when the cheering subsided handing round the leaflets she had printed in the office, 'We have training on Tuesday only from next week and then have a big party to go to next Saturday with our best frocks on and partners and with free food *and*...a free anything you like to drink bar!'

It was a full five minutes before it was quiet enough again to hear Romany's aside to her heroine Heidi.

'Does tha mean I can get pissed wif you Heid?'

'It certainly does my little blue streaker but don't use that wee-wee word to your granddad Tink. Just say you're going to a party to get as happy as an inebriated newt...'

Chapter Twenty-one

'Did you have any idea what brilliance you were getting when you were interviewing the team a mere eight weeks or so ago?'

Ginnie was naked and led with her head on Claude's chest in his enormous black satin sheeted bed at the boathouse. They had eaten another Chinese take-away he had picked up on the way back after the game, made delirious love as soon as they got in the door before falling back into bed. It was now almost midnight and they were just lolling on each other stroking and caressing whatever part they could reach.

'I knew that there were some good former rugby players in there like Rocky Cook, the pack leader, and her sister Mollie at fly-half. Both had played for Supermarine, and J.J, the open-side flanker had played to a high level in the South African women's league, but other than that it was selection by instinct and, dare I say it, apparent fitness, size, and body shape. The other great slice of luck was in getting Lindsey Chene as coach. Her experience, strategy calls and wise council have been a godsend and without which we would not have done so well.'

'What was your motivation to start the team anyway?'

'As I said to one of the girls during the interviews, Iona, I think. I wanted to make a category difference to my rather mundane life, do something completely different but with my own contribution and control.'

'You've certainly achieved that' he said before kissing her neck.

'So far' she said, 'but there's a long way to go and next season in South West Two will be a big test. The teams in that range from Plymouth to Portsmouth so there will also be travelling and occasional overnight stays to factor in.'

'And you' he said stroking her hair. 'I've watched two games so far and in both you were magnificent and the one I didn't see because I was in Singapore and which was the away game at Supermarine, Stan Mackay told me you were again simply outstanding.'

'Spying on me through your facilities manager eh,'

'Not at all, I was talking to Stan and his son at half-time today and he said that you were a revelation and a natural if ever he'd seen one. The standout player of the team so far. .his words.'

Ginnie kept quiet. It was lovely to hear such praise, especially from such a lovely man as Stan the Pint and a Wink Man Mackay and who had been such a help and supporter of her and the team.

'The other thing we were discussing was this strange but miraculous phenomenon whereby you've got together a diverse group of women and in a few short weeks got them playing so well as to be raising eyebrows all over the local game. Seemingly, by default you have discovered the perfect blend of skills, speed, and commitment such that here's almost an invincibility about the team now every time you take to the field for a match. If you keep this rate of improvement up there's no telling where the Fannies can go in the seasons to come. I overheard one of the Reading fans today saying to his mate that *you* are a cert for an England Red Roses spot next year if ever he's seen one...'

Ginnie had heard this once before from one of her team mates and chose to keep away from it. Like her burgeoning relationship with Claude, it was too early, too ecstatic and too much to hope for.

Recipes for disaster if ever she had seen them.

'Winning those first three matches were a dream but that will also present us with problems next season because Lindsey is convinced the bigger clubs will come a-calling waving their cheque books.'

He nodded at her answer as Ginnie changed the subject.

'And Aggy, she was pleased with our performance today?'

'Delighted, she said she would give you a call on Monday in the office to apologise for being so unreasonable a bitch about us and can't wait to get back in the squad for next season. The performance today really turned her on and she wants to become a part of it again...'

'What made her change her mind?'

He smiled. 'Several thing's really. First, Frances, my ex-wife, turned up at home with a new man in tow, he's an old friend of ours from our university days who has been hovering around on the side-lines for years waiting for us to break up so he could make his move...'

'Did you know about him?'

'Oh yes, Frances, he and I were all close friend's way back then and he's always carried a torch for her. They've probably slept together a few times when I've been away on business recently but hey ho, I'm pleased for them. Seeing her mother with another man was another reality jolt for Aggy, then there was her own romance with Alistair, the A & E doctor. He came to see me here last week and asked if I minded that they got married in a year's time or so. Quite sweet and old fashioned really…'

'And you said over my dead body…'

He chuckled and kissed the top of her head. 'Not at all, I was pleased for them both and he seems like a good sort. Anyway, she would have still gone ahead and married him if I had said no so it was, like you and I, pointless to go against it. Love can't be denied. Anyway, all these new relationships going along swimmingly brought Aggy to her senses and made her realise that what you and I have is just as special as the others so after Alistair had told her I was fine with their potential marriage, she came to see me all contrite and said it was time she stopped acting like a silly child. Besides which she also misses the friendship and relationship you and her had. Coming along with me to the match today and seeing how well you all played together also made her realise just how much she misses the game as well.'

'So, that only leaves the one outstanding question and to which you promised me an answer tonight…?'

'Where, he said getting out of bed and padding naked across the floor to his changing room area where his jacket hung, 'are we going on holiday next Sunday the day after the party?'

He came back with a large brown envelope and quickly moved it out of her range as she snatched at it.

He nodded at her overnight bag and dirty rugby kit standing over by the top of the floating glass stairway. 'Are you getting your mind around what to pack for warm weather?' he waved the envelope at her again and this time let her grab it.

'I'm planning, as you said, skimpy dresses and bikinis only. I have also asked Steve Harrington for a due day this Wednesday to go shopping.'

Due days were a Wessex recruiting aid whereby each employee got a free paid day off every four months provided they hadn't taken any time off in that period. These three extra free days a year didn't affect their statuary holidays and worked very well as an inducement for when recruiting staff as Ginnie had found out recently with her interviews.

She didn't tell him that she had planned to spend a great deal of money this coming Wednesday in a visit to Bicester, the outlet village of note and a mere forty-five-minute drive away where all the couture fashions would be available at low prices. She had in mind something stylish from Vivienne Westwood in the shape of two new dresses and another bikini, not to mention a couple of pairs of sandals, a pair of heeled sling-backs and four new pairs of very sexy knickers with matching bra's. Her friend Malorie always said that new knickers and a bra were a statutory must when going away with someone for the first time because that was all he would want to see anyway and then, once they were off, quickly forgotten until the next showing. And she still had another week to go yet, plenty of time to get even more nice things, if of course, the destination in this brown envelope was one that required it.

She took out the airline tickets which were in a red, white, and blue British Airways first class folder.

'It was' he said quietly, 'you that suggested it to me...'

'Me!' she said not remembering ever saying anything even remotely connected to holidaying to him.

'The words you used when I first brought you here to the boat house and you looked around and said, and here I quote, "it's simply beautiful and modern and looks like something out of one of those posh magazines in….?"

She looked at him and then down at the beautiful tickets in her hand as the penny dropped.

'Bequia' she said.

And there it was. Two tickets in her and Claude's name for a First class return B.A flight out of Heathrow to Barbados with a connecting flight from Barbados to Bequia with Bequia Air. Underneath was the hotel booking for a week in the garden suite at the Five Star Beach Hotel on Bequia Island.

Thank you, Heidi, Ginnie thought and from whom she had pinched the Bequia quote when the Goth lock was jokingly referring to where she was going to marry the young female referee before they had fallen out over her yellow card. Then Ginnie had a sudden panicky thought that she would be *on the slot* when they were away, a thought which was immediately forgotten as she realised, she would come on the Sunday they got back so that was fine. They could shag with delirious impunity in the golden glow of the Caribbean all night and every day until then. Speaking of which, she thought looking at him, this gorgeous and perfect man deserves a reward.

'Come here' she said carefully placing the tickets on the floor beside the bed and reaching for him...

When she got home on the Sunday at teatime after most of the night and day in bed in lubricious moistening with her lover, she was game weary and shagged out. A long hot bath saw her in bed by eight-thirty followed by ten straight hours of deep and dreamless sleep that not even the recent occupancy of the glass floor of the boathouse and the wonderful holiday to come could disturb.

On the Monday Ginnie and Aggy had met for lunch in the office canteen as they used to and had had a good hug and then chattering reunion to seal their *rapprochement*. They had slipped right back to where they left off with a good old gossip and there was lots of it to catch up on. Ginnie brought Aggy up to date with Heidi's exceedingly well-hung boyfriend and other bits of squad tittle tattle that she had missed and in turn Aggy had told Ginnie all about Alistair, her boyfriend and soon to become fiancé' and the nervous visit she had made to meet his parents in London. Aggy would be bringing Alistair to the party on Saturday and wanted to accompany Ginnie to Bicester on Wednesday.

'I need a couple of decent party frocks as well and could do with a good old girl's day out spending money.'

They hadn't discussed Bequia with Ginnie merely mentioning that her and Claude were 'going away for a few days somewhere hot.'

Ginnie had also thought to bring up her meeting with the interfering Madeleine Moody but decided against it. She hadn't even mentioned it to Claude yet and doubted if she would.

Then she didn't have to.

'Have you had the third degree from daddy's gate-keeper yet, meaning has Madeleine Moody got her claws into you?'

Regarding the question Ginnie decided to be deliberately obtuse. 'Nope.'

'You will soon, believe me in the shape of an invite up to the top floor when Daddy is away to be told things about him that only she knows. It used to drive mummy mad when she came into the office, it was as if only Madeleine knew this stuff and she had to prove it by demonstrating her all-knowing to his nearest and dearest. We even had a nick-name for her…'

'Go on…'

Aggy looked around to make sure no one was within hearing distance.

'It was the Poisoned Dwarf…'

Ginnie giggled appropriately.

'Why would she do that?'

'We used to think it was some sort of mother complex, a way of demonstrating that *she* was privy to stuff about Daddy's business life that no one else was. Mummy used to say that annoying as this was it was easily avoidable and was better than him having a dolly bird as a P.A. waggling her boobs under his nose and batting her eyelashes at him all day…'

'Like me, you mean?' Ginnie grinned.

'Yeah, just like you but in fairness to your good self he has never looked at another female until you came along. He came right out and told me that your relationship is the real thing alright and was another very good reason for me to see sense.'

Ginnie was delighted to hear that Aggy and her mum Frances not only shared her thoughts on the nosey old cow Madeleine but had long ago coined their own very apt private nickname for her. Added to which, taking a day off for the boss's daughter to go shopping was no problem at any time although in fairness to Aggy she didn't abuse the privilege and Ginnie would be delighted to have her along. Adding to this was the extra warm feeling and further declaration by Claude to Aggy that their relationship was the real thing.

And besides which, being driven to Bicester in her new BMW would make it an altogether better shopping experience, albeit a rather fast and slightly mad passenger experience because Aggy's accident hadn't slowed her down one little bit.

They both stood up to go back to their offices.

'You do realise' Aggy said capriciously as they parted outside the canteen 'that if you and Daddy get married, you'll be my step-mother...'

Too stunned to reply all Ginnie could do was gape at her.

'The wicked step-mother' Aggy threw over her shoulders in a cackled pantomime of a voice and then giggled all the way down the corridor leaving a smiling and slightly perplexed Ginnie standing there thinking about the marital absolute that had just been mentioned...

*

There was a definite air of happiness and banter at the training session on the Tuesday night as if they had come through an entire season of victories to get through to this point. Much of this was due to the coming party on the Saturday and at which Claude had suggested that he would contribute twenty bottles of good champagne so that everyone could be greeted by a couple of glasses to get them in the mood and the occasion off to a good start. Ginnie didn't tell the girls about this so that it would come as a surprise. She did however, tell them that she would be putting a thousand pounds behind the bar and when that was gone, they would have to buy their own because the kitty would then be empty. Claude had also said that he would be topping the float back up to five big ones for when the new season started so they would have plenty of cash for their next run of games in South West Two.

'Everyone seems to be in a good mood tonight,' she said to Lindsey as the girls pinched each other's bums and generally indulged in some mud-throwing, groping and rude banter.

'That's because they've all found a second home here, or, in some cases a first home where they can bugger about with an oval shaped ball for a couple of hours with other like-minded members of the sisterhood without a care in the world *and* have a good laugh at the same time.' Lindsey replied.

'Thanks to Heidi,' Ginnie giggled as the tall Goth tweaked Ellie's left nipple and scooted away as the sinuous black beauty chased her with mock intent. Thanks also to the tall lock I'm also going first class to Bequia on Sunday she thought.

Lindsey chuckled. 'Yeah, where would we be without the wonderful Heidi. Oh, that reminds me, something occurred to me after the game on Saturday but you had already shot off before I could mention it? When Sammie Arthur, the Reading captain was taken off injured after that great try-saving tackle by Romany, the armband reverted to their vice-captain. We haven't appointed one yet but will need to before next season because the South West 2 rules demand that we have one in place before kick-off in case the captain is injured. D'you have anybody in mind as your number two?'

Ginnie thought for a few beats.

'Not Heidi, too combustible and ready to retaliate, but Rocky, I should think?'

'Agreed, she's a natural pack leader and has all the girls respect, but only if you go off for any reason. There isn't a captain in any of the leagues better than you, both tactically and your superb ability to score tries....'

Despite herself Ginnie found herself blushing.

'I'll tell Rocky later then' she said trotting out to where the other girls were now rolling around in a huge mock scrum screaming 'Bohica' and 'lash my back with the screecher, Flipper baby.'

On the Wednesday morning Aggy collected Ginnie from her flat and they sped off Bicester Outlet Village in her new BMW, courtesy of her insurance pay-out – plus an additional few thousand from the bank of mum and dad – from the write-off of her other car in the whiplash accident. As Ginnie knew, the accident hadn't slowed her down at all and they overtook everything.

With over 160 shops of luxury brands, boutiques, lifestyle, beauty and high-class home-wares advertised at up to 60% off, Bicester Village was a shopping girl's paradise. And because Ginnie hadn't told Aggy that she was going to Bequia with her father, and would be principally shopping for that venue preferring to let the myth perpetuate that she – as well as Aggy – were looking for dresses for the squad party on Saturday. How long that lasted would probably be until Ginnie started buying a couple of bikinis – no-one goes to rugby parties wearing a bikini thought Ginnie and Aggy was sure to ask where, although she wouldn't put it passed Heidi or Cassie to turn up wearing one.

After a forty-five-minute-high speed whirl of raised fingers and muttered curses from Aggy at slower vehicles, they locked the blue BMW in the huge Bicester Village car park and hurried into the long mall of shops already busy with bag-carrying shoppers. After the first hour and a half they stopped for coffee having purchased absolutely nothing.

'Nothing' said Ginnie sipping her Cappuccino with a chocolate star in the froth 'seems to take my fancy although I was almost tempted by those high-heeled sling backs at the last place. Trouble was you need to be able to walk and dance in them and after four hours in those I'd be crippled for life.'

'Yeah, they did look good on you though, they'd be okay for a dinner date if Daddy is taking you somewhere nice where you could sit down and don't have to totter about like a newly born giraffe...'

It was an open if unintended invitation to mention Bequia but Ginnie wasn't tempted. She did wonder if Claude had mentioned it to his daughter and she was waiting for Ginnie to say the name, but decided he had not. After vacillating Ginnie went back to the shoe boutique and bought the five-inch heeled sling backs.

Their next session was altogether more successful. Aggy bought a nice Stella McCartney dress for the party and in the same shop Ginnie, having tried on and debated in front of the mirror with her friend for ten minutes, finally bought a simple black short-skirted evening dress by Gucci.

'Ash blondes in simple black dresses' Aggy said as they walked out of the shop with their bags. 'All you'll need to complete the beautiful classic look is a good tan...'

It was too good a lead to ignore.

'Which I will hopefully be getting next week' Ginnie said blithely.

It took a few beats for the penny to drop.

'Going somewhere really nice to get one then?'

'Sure am' Ginnie said lapsing into their old trope of keeping the other guessing as long as possible.

Realising that she was back in the old supermarket queue behind the double trolley women who couldn't find her credit card, Aggy rolled her eyes and walked on before stopping and facing her friend.

'A long trip...?'

'Yep...'

Another few steps before Aggy just had to ask.

'You lucky little minx, just *where* is he taking you?'

'On Sunday we're going to the Caribbean for the week.'

'Lucky old you' Aggy muttered somewhat morosely.

Saying no more and realising that this was an awkward hurdle along the way that they're newly reformed friendship would have to get over to progress, Ginnie just looped her arm through Aggy's and they covered the next few shops in a mutually strained silence.

Then Aggy suddenly brightened up, grinned at her own attitude, and steered Ginnie towards a swimwear shop.

'You'll be requiring a sexy bikini or two then' she said opening the boutique door and pushing her in.

'I could do with one myself for the coming summer as well.'

Lots of girly giggling followed as they each tried on various patterns and types and with both size tens there was lots to choose from.

'I like this one 'Ginnie said emerging from the changing cubicle tucking her perfectly shaped but small breasts into a yellow polka-dot two-piece.

'Turn round' instructed Aggy. 'It also looks good from behind with just enough of your shapely bum hidden.'

They came out of the shop with two pairs each. After the bikinis it was the turn of the lingerie and Ginnie, again aware of the sexual awkwardness of the flimsy garments because she would be using them in the intimacy of her and Aggy's beloved father's bedroom, said there was nothing she fancied and besides, she had a whole drawer full of tights and underwear at home.

Another Victoria Beckham dress for Ginnie was bagged up followed by a cashmere jumper for Aggy and laden down with bags they called it a day and headed back to the car.

'Y'know' said Aggy accelerating away from the car park, 'for a potential witchy step-mother you're fun to shop with...'

'Ahhh, you just wait until you start staying out too late at night with that Alistair of yours, my girl, then you'll see just how witchy with your privileges I can be.' Ginnie put on the pantomime cackle Aggy had used when the term was first mentioned.

If only, Ginnie thought as Aggy gave the first of many a single finger on the way home to a slow to get away from the traffic lights white van as she zoomed around it.

The end of the week was hectic. On the Thursday Ginnie called in her two supervisors and told them she was taking the following week off and because they had a dozen new starters in the section arranged the different training schedules. Her text inviting everyone she could think of plus partners or friends to the squad party sent on the Monday, received a flood of eager acceptances – including some surprises – and gave her an ever-expanding list that finally totalled out at sixty-five. On the Friday she managed to get a last-minute appointment with her hairdresser for the Saturday morning for a trim and highlights touch-up, then Claude sent her a one-word text late on Friday morning saying 'lunch?' which, having accepted with her usual single word affirmative meant she had to rearrange her nails for the Saturday after the hair appointment. Saturday, she thought driving out to the Plough lunchtime to meet Claude, would be frantic what with hair, nails and then packing everything for the holiday *and* party *and* be at the boat house by around five to get ready to go...after, of course, they'd had a *moistening* session....

Claude was his usual cool and calm self as they sat down in the Plough but noticed that Ginnie was both late and a little flushed.

'Busy?'

'Frantic but all organised now, I think' Ginnie replied and then told him about her and Aggy's shopping day in Bicester omitting the step-mother references.

'I'm pleased that you two have got back together so quickly' he said after ordering a steak sandwich for them. 'It makes everyone's lives so much easier given the latest news…'

'Oh…?'

'Frances rang me on Wednesday; she is to remarry again to our mutual friend while you and I are away next week. He's moved into the manor and Frances, being an old-fashioned sort – as I suppose I am – wants to tie the knot to make their union legal. A quickie wedding has been arranged at a local registry office and then they're also away on honeymoon. I sent them flowers yesterday and my very best wishes and am very pleased for them both. Now everyone is happily moving forward again with their lives…'

'Do Frances and her new husband-to-be know about us?'

'She does. I told her on the telephone three weeks ago after we had first made love following the degree nisi and when I knew there was no turning back, for me at any rate. Even though Frances and I were divorced and both free, I thought it was for the best. As you know, I'm not one for romantic intrigues and prefer openness and honesty.'

Their steak sandwiches arrived giving Ginnie a chance to digest both the food and his news.

'How did Aggy take the news about her mother's wedding?'

'Surprisingly well although I haven't seen her this week but she called me last night to gauge my reaction and was equally happy about it. It seems all three of the Dillon's, Frances, Aggy and myself, have quickly found love…'

They finished off their sandwiches in silence giving Ginnie further thinking time. Matters were moving along at pace and needed thinking about... didn't they?

'Oh, before I forget' he said wiping his mouth with the paper napkin. 'I arranged with my vintner to deliver thirty bottles of good champagne to the hotel yesterday with the strict instructions that they put it in the cold cabinet right away because it will need two days to chill to the correct temperature. How many are coming to the party?'

'Sixty-five acceptances as at this morning,' replied Ginnie thinking that she also had a vintner for her six quid Merlot as well... if Sainsbury's counted as such.

'That should give them all a couple of glasses each to get the thing going. Will they have enough champagne flutes?'

'I expect so but I'll check with Ellie who works there.'

'Another thing. I took the liberty of inviting Madeleine Moody and her husband to the party on Saturday. I hope that's alright?'

'Fine by me' Ginnie said reminding herself to give the poison dwarf a wide berth where possible or at least to say nothing that could be interpreted wrongly.

'Her husband, Jim, has M.N.D. and is in a wheelchair and the poor woman has had a devil of a time with his illness over the last couple of years. He's going downhill fast and only has a few more months to live so I thought a night out would do them both a bit of good...'

'Poor man' Ginnie replied feeling guilty about her initial and previous thoughts about the nosey Madeleine.

When they parted outside Claude held her close and kissed her.

'What time you aiming to get to the boathouse tomorrow?' he asked as they parted.

'Five o'clock...ish'

'And the party starts?'

'Seven-thirty.'

'I'll order the taxi for seven. Should give us a little time for a...' He let the sentence tail off but Ginnie knew what he meant and had already anticipated it. He moved towards his white Toyota with a parting shot over his shoulder.

'I can't wait. A whole week of you all to myself in the Caribbean, don't forget your passport.'

Phew, Ginnie thought driving back to the office. Frances sure didn't let the grass grow under her feet as a single person, she could have waited a few more weeks for the sake of decency, and then, with Aggy and Alistair they could have had a triple wedding...

That's enough of that marital absolute stuff you silly cow, she admonished herself pulling into the office car park before ringing Ellie on her mobile to check that the hotel had enough champagne flutes and getting the answer of 'hundreds darling' from the sinuous black girl.

Chapter Twenty-two

Getting wiser to her man's preferences for a quickie when they hadn't seen each other for a short while, Ginnie didn't put her party make-up on or heels and dress apart from full gloss lipstick before arriving at the boat house at five fifteen. He took one look at her red, moist, and purposefully parted lips, new highlights and trimmed bob and grabbed her at the door and hustled her up the floating glass stairs and into the bedroom.

'I'll get your suitcase from the car later' he said before burying his eager tongue down her receptive throat. As she fell towards the black satin sheets, she kicked off her jeans and knickers and raised her legs up and locked them around his waist and still with her tee-shirt on, guided him into her and had a brief thought that after a busy day, the party and holiday mood had finally got going here.

Ten energetic pumping minutes later they lay panting in each other's arms spent and happy to be together. Finally, Ginnie wriggled out of the now damp tee shirt.

'I've just spent a fortune at the hairdressers and now look like a scarecrow' she whispered into his ear before gently running the tip of her moist tongue around the whorls. He just moaned into her shoulder by reply and then began to gently suck her erect nipples.

After a further ten minutes of sucking and nibbling and with all garments discarded, she sat on his semi-erect penis and gently squeezed him to another orgasm. Then, with the clock showing six-fifteen and with a taxi booked for seven, they roused themselves, took a leisurely power shower with the jets directed all over their bodies with their lips locked together and hands rubbing soapy gel all over each other before Claude, with a long sigh finally began to towel himself down and dress while Ginnie dried her hair. She chose a medium blue suit for Claude with an open necked navy silk shirt and dark brown loafers. Apart from a discrete but obviously expensive slim silver watch and small silver cufflinks he wasn't one for male jewellery, which pleased Ginnie. Men with big medallions around their necks and wrists laden with bracelets were a particular dislike of hers having had a couple of useless males who favoured them. A dab of Dior L'Homme after-shave completed Claude's preparations and he sat and watched her get ready with a grin of ownership playing about his lips.

Putting on her new high heeled sling backs Ginnie remembered to put her comfortable old black ballet pumps in her shoulder bag. The high stiletto heels were designed to tighten her calf muscles and give shape and length to her legs but dancing in them later at the party would soon cripple her for the coming week.

At five minutes to seven the taxi arrived just as she had finished her hair and wriggled into the black Gucci. Having added a pale blue pashmina to her bare shoulders and the high-heeled sling backs, with her make up and comfortable shoes in the shoulder bag, Ginnie was ready. She would put her slap on during the thirty-minute journey.

'I will have licked it all off again by the time we get there' Claude whispered handing her into the back seat of the taxi 'if I can keep my eyes open long enough...'

He yawned as an acted afterthought but resisted the urge to lick her and stayed awake until they arrived unruffled at the same time as a line of cabs disgorged some of the others.

*

'I have to say and against all my expectations, becoming a part of the Fannies has done Heidi an enormous amount of good, although after her yellow card in the first game I had my doubts...'

Jean Prager, Heidi's haughty mamma spoke in a carbon copy drawl of her daughters in a friendly, elbow touching way to Ginnie. Her friendliness was completely against the haughty demeanour she gave out at the early game. Mind you, she was on her third glass of bubbly and although it wasn't a beverage Ginnie thought she was any stranger to, Jean Prager's, along with other tongues, were being loosened all around them.

Jean's gay companion Damian, forever tarred with the mini-dick sobriquet from Heidi's unmerciful ribbing and another one of her special quips that Ginnie would never forget *gay as a huzzah's helmet plume* and now, for the first time in memory was minus his driving gloves, nodded earnestly from his position by her mammas side.

'In return' Ginnie replied taking a sip of her first glass, 'she is without doubt the funniest girl in the squad and has us all falling about all the time.'

'Yessss...' Jean said drawing out the affirmative, 'although her humour can be...how shall I say... somewhat cutting or even agricultural at times...' She looked at Damian pointedly after this forcing him to flush and look away, he knew to what she was referring.

Ginnies eyes were kept forcefully on his face.

'She has also' said Ginnie determined to stand by the girl that had made her laugh more times in the short time they'd known each other than anyone, 'turned into a very good rugby player.' She nodded across the room where Heidi stood next to her equally tall boyfriend and next to the diminutive Romany in her lovely green evening frock and who was, as usual, looking up at her heroine with adoring eyes. Standing firmly by his granddaughter's side clutching a champagne flute in his huge, gnarled paw was Romany's grandad Tink Cutler and who had been persuaded by Romany to come along 'just to keep an eye on her.'

'Ginnie' said a voice behind her that she immediately recognised. 'Can I introduce my sister Skye, her husband Michael and my...escort Dan.' Ginnie shook hands with the three of them then kissed Iona on both cheeks getting a larger than normal aroma of lemons.

'And this is?' Iona said looking at Claude who had been politely attentive on Ginnie in the half an hour they had been standing around and who, for a man born to mingle and smile at people he'd never met before, had quietly gone about the business of looking after his girl because it was her night.

'Claude' Ginnie said introducing her lover and standing back as he expertly shook hands with Iona and her equally attractive sister who was also a mother, together with her husband and Dan.

'Dan has his own gym' Iona said before upending and emptying her flute. 'I've been taking two classes a week there and Michael is a...?'

'Building Surveyor' he said responding to the questioning look from his sister-in-law. 'And the completely smitten servant of one of the two Scottish island named Pierce girls…'

Skye rolled her eyes. 'It's amazing what a couple of glasses of champagne will do to a husband's attitude,' she said following the eyeroll with a broad smile at Dan.

Right in cue a girl bearing a tray of full champagne flutes had miraculously appeared alongside Claude. It was a knack that Ginnie was to get to know well, his ability to seemingly without anything other than a small smile, raised eyebrow or purse of the lips was able to summon people to his every whim without any apparent effort.

Did people know he was a powerful CEO at the top of the second largest mutual in the country? Certainly, Jenny Hynes did because she also worked for Wessex and was also here but Ginnie had not mentioned it to anyone else. He didn't look any different to anyone else other than the excellent cut of his suit so it must be jungle telegraph Ginnie decided, waves of charismatic power simply rippled unseen from him through the ether.

Placing Ginnies, Sky's and Iona's empty flutes on the tray Claude them passed them full flutes leaving Dan and Michael to change their own.

'To the Fannie's' Claude said quietly and they all raised their flute's and took a swig.

'Can I steal her away for a moment of girl talk?' Iona said steering Ginnie away by the elbow.

She kinda knew what was coming.

'Beautiful frock and shoes' Iona said when they were a couple of yards away…'and as for that lovely man, you kept him quiet…'

'You're looking pretty good yourself' Ginnie said, 'and Claude's a recent...acquisition.'

'Rubbish' grinned Iona. 'He's your boss and a very rich man. She looked around the room, 'Some of the girls have been talking and have also noticed that your sugar daddy hasn't taken his eyes off you since arrival. Good on ya gal, nothing less than you deserve....'

'Have you met Alistair, Aggies boyfriend?' Ginnie said prompted by the sugar daddy bit to get away from what she now knew was already the gossip of the night and nodding to where Aggy and Alistair, and an elegant Ellie and her smoothly dressed archaeologist lover were laughing together across the room.

'Not yet but I will later. I hear Aggy's coming back to the squad soon and will be a rival for my or your place...'

'Not mine' Ginnie said sniffily and then grinned.

The shaven-headed D.J. and his purple-haired girlfriend – collectively called Jethro Allstyles, a reference to the fact that they carried all the different styles and types of music – and who had arrived late and spent the last thirty minutes feverishly hauling their stuff in and setting it up, finally got going with some background Adele numbers and someone said the buffet was now open. Guessing what would be coming soon Ginnie slipped her expensive sling backs into her shoulder bag and put on the old comfortable flat ballet shoes.

'You suddenly shrunk by four inches or so' Claude said.

'I want to be able to walk with you next week in you-know-where without pain and blisters and we'll be dancing soon...'

'Dancing…! Don't wear me out, I got to preserve my energy…'

'You'll be fine' she said standing on tiptoe to give him a peck on the lips that was seen by almost everyone in the room.

Ginnie and Claude sat with Madeleine Moody and her wheelchair bound husband Jim complementing a Wessex table and were joined for their buffet by Stan the Wink and a Pint Mackay and his son Martin. Stan and Claude were old friends with Claude head-hunting the Facilities Manager from Nationwide when Wessex was getting big enough and needed to employ the experienced Facilities man. Stan's son Martin, however, was in awe of his Chief Executive and sat quietly eating and watching while the others made a fuss of Jim, Madeleine's very ill husband around whose neck she placed a bib and fed and cajoled and wiped the drool from his chin and helped him to sip a glass of champagne like he was a child.

As they finished Magical Mollie Cook's boyfriend, Eric, a welder by trade and dressed in the complete Teddy Boy outfit of long black drape jacket glinting with silver threads and black velvet collar, white frilly shirt with a black slim bootlace tie, drainpipe trousers and two-inch thick blue crepe soled shoes known as brother creeper's, flicked his double dropped front curls into place over his forehead, brushed his fingers through thick dark sideboards and approached the D.J.

Two minutes later the D.J. announced that as per his logo he was cranking up the mood and volume by request with a medley of rock 'n roll standards and put on Good Golly Miss Mollie by Little Richard. Skittering out of their place on the sisters Cook table where they had been eating with Rocky and Linda, her social partner, and Vera Godwin and her husband George, the appropriately named Mollie, dressed to match Eric in a blue and white short gingham dress with her hair in a pony tail, skittered and bounced across the centre of the floor in a perfect jive rhythm. For pretty much the rest of the raucous number they gave an exhibition of jive-dancing that could have graced the Strictly final. As Little Richard gave way to Elvis and Blue Suede Shoes, Tanya 'Flipper' Bryan took to the floor with her husband Tim and they too spun straight into a perfect jive rhythm to accompany Mollie and Eric. As the rest of them increased the beat with clapping in time and cheering the pair of dancers were joined by Gina 'Bohica' McKinnon and her husband Dave together with Avril 'Love-Bites' Gordon and her husband Mike. The army girls and their tankie husbands also swung immediately into fast expert jiving with the others and the four couples spun, flung, bent, and skittered around the floor in perfect timing with the crowd cheering them on and clapping in time. By the time Elvis had given way to Gerry Lee Lewis and Great Balls of Fire, Heidi's boyfriend Dexter Keegan Stirling had taken to the floor with Jean Prager, his girlfriend's now tipsy mother, and although the standard of timing and innovative jive moves dropped slightly with them, the enthusiasm was cranked even higher as Dex and other couples began to get in the groove. Ginnie could feel Iona's eyes looking knowingly at her as Dexy boy swung into the jive but once again she kept her eyes firmly raised at head height. Snide glances with Iona at Dexy-boys BSD suddenly began to seem disloyal to Claude. Jimmy

Corbett, the head groundsman, and his pretty little blond wife Sally were next to hit the jiving groove and they too immediately hit the rhythm..

Who knew we had so many expert jive-dancers in the squad Ginnie thought as Claude caught her eye and raised his eyebrows towards the floor in an invitation to join them. Here comes a couple of tone-lowerer's thought Ginnie getting to her feet but no, Claude could jive as well and because he could drag her along with him and after a couple of missed spins they picked up and were surprisingly good because they had never danced anything together let alone a jive. As with most things Claude did, he was quietly effective and could really dance and didn't perform the expected and totally uncoordinated dad-dancing men of his age are tarnished with. He was a neat and in-time and knew all the moves without being overly demonstrative. Mind you, she thought getting his hand at the third spin, jiving belonged to his time as a young man and if anything, it was her who struggled to get her jive timing together while Claude moved expertly to grab her flailing hands until she started to spin correctly. By the time Roll-Over Beethoven by Chuck Berry hit the speakers the floor was heaving and the mood for the evening was set.

And still the free champagne kept coming.

After the rock 'n roll set everyone was puffing and gasping for breath and the D.J. slowed the tempo down. Ginnie danced a slow waltzy type thing with her brother Robert. He had brought Emily along but still being a little sore and not getting much sleep from the new-borne lusty-lunged Violet Lily, the new mum was taking it easy on the side-lines while Ginnie and Roberts mum

Elizabeth exercised her new right as a new grandma by proudly doing the baby-sitting with their dad at home.

With the tempo varying from dance to dance and the floor pretty much always full, the bar was then declared open for any drinks the guests required – or the thousand quid Ginnie had told them was the limit was spent – the evening really began to swing.

Having been somewhat out-danced by the expert rock 'n rollers, Dexter again took Jean Prager on the floor for an up-tempo exhibition ballroom number while Heidi took a turn around the floor with the smaller Damian. Jean Prager, reunited with her haughty look and with her neck arched back and to the side and with the lightest touch of the tips of the fingers of her left hand on Dex's shoulder, the pair whirled around the outside of the floor like a couple of predatory hawks in search of prey. Their double-time quick-step looked for all money as if it was out to gain the lap record until, after a couple of rapid circuits Dex came to a sudden and expert stop on the beat and bent his partner over the table occupied by Cassie Betts and her husband Les and the long blond-wigged Sherry Moyes and her companion, a shaven-headed fellow lorry driver called Ronnie. Besides Madeleine Moody and her wheelchair-bound husband Jim on the other side of the floor, they were the only six people not dancing. As the serious faced Dex bent his haughty partner over the table the hugely laughing Cassie placed an open hand on each side of her lips, opened her brown eyes wide and stuck her tongue out in what is commonly referred to in urban slang as a vagface. At that precise moment Emily Joy, the new mum and Ginnies sister-in-law was just coming back into the room having been for a pee. Since she was still sore from the birth and wasn't being overly active Ginnie had asked her to take a few photos on her mobile of the event and she chose this moment to snap the first one. Although Emily was far too well-behaved as a junior school teacher, she wouldn't know a vagface if it jumped up and hit her although her photo turned out to be a classic and one of the best of the evening because it seemed to capture on Cassies tongue-out face the joy and diversity of the evening. This photo was proudly exhibited along with others taken by Emily as the centre piece in a blown-up collage on the wall of the Fannies changing room for the whole of next season. Cassie's joyful vagface appealing to everyone – particularly those of a Sapphic persuasion – and was much aped and kiss-blown during their pre – and post – match preparations. Fortunately, for the innocent snapper Emily, she never saw the result on the changing room wall otherwise she would have been horrified. It also encouraged Sherry and Cassie to drag their somewhat reluctant partners on to the dance floor to shake something.

Everyone began to dance with everyone else with Ginnie in great demand although she tried to keep the slow numbers for Claude. Ellie's tall archaeologist boyfriend was next for Ginnie followed by a couple of dances with her other favourite Wessex man the portly Stan the Wink and a Pint Man Mackay and who, despite his near retirement age, could also hold his own in the modern shake-it-all about moves without joining the dad-dancing frenzy of an uncoordinated whirling dervish.

As Ginnie was dancing with Stan, Iona went sailing by hanging on to Dexter and couldn't resist giving her a look that said guess what's swinging around between us two. J.J. had turned up with a smallish cockney man with a short greyish crew-cut called Willie who worked on the buildings that she'd found somewhere, and despite the size difference the two of them obviously hit it off because they stayed together for pretty much every dance. Ginnie, taking a breather, took the opportunity to sit with her Saturday night friends who had all been supporters of the side and had turned up here with various partners. Malorie, her large enhanced cleavage to the fore stopping just short of exposing her nipples, was clinging on to a handsome dread-locked West Indian man called Develin, Bella was with her fiancé and made Ginnie promise to come to her hen night in three weeks' time at a venue in Bristol, while Sheila was with an old flame of Ginnies called Leo who had only lasted for a couple of dates and from memory and unusually for a Saturday night pick-up, she hadn't slept with and whose surname she had forgotten. Marie, the fourth and last member of the Saturday night crew and who had come without a partner, had been dancing with Gavin Morris, the other groundsman who was single and\ hovering on the edge of the group ready to move on her again when she stopped talking to Ginnie. Bella later told her in the toilet that her own D.J. booked for the evening of her wedding reception in five weeks' time, had messaged her that very morning to say he would be in prison having just been given six months for smashing someone over the head with a large bass speaker and would therefore be unable to DJ the evening

QUINTON RUMFORD

of her reception. She had been trying to replace him all day and arrived here in a panic having been unable to find a replacement. Fortunately, she had just been saved by the versatile Jethro Allstyles who would be free on the right of her wedding reception and glad to attend with all his varieties of music which would suit the differing age groups of the two families.

For the Saturday night girls and their escorts, the evening was young and they would be going on to a local night club afterwards until the early hours as usual, and this time Ginnie was glad not to be going on with them. Those errant days were over…she hoped.

While Ginnie was still talking to the girls Claude was getting his share of floor invites and took a turn with Heidi and then Ellie, both of who were taller than he was and then invited his P.A. Madeleine Moody out onto the floor.

'We have a liking for the taller girls then?' Ginnie said re-joining him for a close-up slow number.

He grinned at her and pulled her close so he could talk softly into her ear.

'You're right about Heidi, she is simply hilarious and love-bombed me as a great fan of yours. She said that wherever you go she will follow. If you open a half a pound-a-go cathouse down at the docks she will join you because it's sure to be – her words – a roaring focking success!'

'Cheeky minx' giggled Ginnie. 'I'm worth more than a fifty pee a fuck…fock…aren't I?'

'I'll have ten thousand quid's worth right away with you' he blew gently into her ear. 'That should keep you occupied for a while.'

It was all she could do not to turn her head and slide her tongue into his mouth and lasso his tongue and gently suck it the way he liked. 'Wait a short while, darling,' she whispered 'and you can have it all next week for as long as you want…for nothing'

Well okay, she thought, for the small fortune he'd spent on Bequia then.

Claude was an ever-present by her side except when someone else approached her for a dance and then he graciously stood aside. At one point Dexter was making a bee-line for her when he was just pipped to the request by Allan Dix the manager of the Sports Emporium, Fireblade owner and faller-off and boyfriend of Mandy Judo Sawyer, black belt and who still had his arm in plaster. Ginnie wasn't sorry Dexter was too late because she just knew if she took the floor with Heidi's boyfriend, she would have to endure Iona's knowing looks about what was bobbing about between them. It was such a joyous occasion and she didn't want to spoil it with unspoken looks or distractions about Dexter's supposedly enormous penis and Damian's opposing little Hornby Dublo dinky toy, when her entire being was concentrated upon her own very special man and their coming week together. She had looked up a posh penis word attitude last week after Iona had told her about it in the supermarket, and it was phallocentric. Her lovely Claude might not have the swinging beast of Dexter between his legs but what he did have perfectly fine by her, even if he was twenty-nine years older. If she was phallocentric about a trouser snake, she wanted it to be about Claude's…Besides, Claude and his love and fine treatment of her including his generous donation of the champagne to this party and their coming week together in Bequia, was capturing her heart and she didn't want to be disloyal to him with unscholarly *phallocentric* thoughts. That sort of crap was behind her and now she was falling in love with Claude and that feeling had been earned by his attentiveness, fine values and exquisite manners and honesty. Such impeccable attentiveness and obvious love from a powerful man was an aphrodisiac and bound to have an effect upon her and she didn't want it spoiled by thoughts of what swung or clung to the loins of other men. A creature of breeding, erudition, or high manners she would never be but she could demonstrate loyalty and love in her thoughts for a special man with the best of them.

As it was, she had to be careful not to get the flailing plaster-of-Paris arm across the kisser from the enthusiastic but completely uncoordinated Dixy boy and who, unlike the coordinated Stan the Wink and a Pint Man Mackay was doing his best to imitate a whirling, armour-armed dervish with a dad-dancing habit. You'd think with Mandy, skill at Judo and quiet, confident manner, she'd get something better than the idiot Dixey but there it was.

Ginnie danced, whirled, and talked animatedly to everyone, usually with Claude by her side.

Suddenly the D.J. was announcing the last number. There was a strict timing imposition of eleven-thirty on when he had to stop playing music so that the other hotel guests could get some sleep. Not that Heidi was in the mood to listen because after the final number when everyone except the wheelchair-bound Jim Moody and Tink Cutler had taken the floor and finished dancing the last number, the tall Goth emerged from her table with Dexter behind her holding her waist followed by Jean Prager holding his and Damian clinging on to hers. As Heidi led her small four-person crocodile out onto the floor others began to join on the back and the D.J. picked up the mood and announced that, as usual, he had the very and most old-fashioned accompaniment required at hand and put on a loud conga...

Da-da-da da-da da...DA! Heidi kicked out her right leg on the last beat and her partners behind followed suit.

Cassie Betts dragged her skinny husband Ron to the tail and grabbed hold of Damian's waist from behind.

Da-da-da da-da da...DA! Heidi again kicked out her left leg on the last beat followed by the others behind her as the crocodile moved down the side of the room. Lindsey Chene was next and jumped up and grabbed Ron Betts from behind and was immediately joined by Iona and Dan and her sister Skye and her husband Michael as the conga snake grew longer.

The nine of them did a turn at the end with Heidi adding waved hands to the ensemble as the moved in time down the middle in a straight line. In true copy-cat style the other hands joined hers in the air.

Da-da-da da-da da...DA!

The jive dancers of Mollie Cook and Eric, Tanya and her husband Tim and the army girls with their tankie husbands were next on the back of the growing snake where they added a few spins to the movement.

Da-da-da da-da da...DA!

The sinuous mover Elelendise and her boyfriend whose name Ginnie could never remember were next to join the lengthening line closely followed by J.J. and her diminutive but demonstrative cockney companion called Willie. To encompass the expanding line the D.J. turned the volume up a notch and the right and left feet began to shoot out in better time with Heidi's as the tempo and volume increased. Ginnie whispered in Claude's ear and he reacted to her suggestion by grabbing Madeleine Moody and pushing her to towards the last in line who was now Charlie Bagnall, Biggie's brother who was clinging on to the back of his sturdy sister.

Da-da-da da-da da…DA!

Ginnies Saturday night friends, Bella, Malorie, Sheila, Marie, and their companions were next with the line now stretching all the way down the room. Seeing her father clinging on to Madeleine Moody, Aggy appeared behind him taking Alistair along with her while Ginnie was encouraging others to join the ever-expanding conga that now snaked around the room.

The D.J. took the volume up another notch as the anxious eyes of the duty manager appeared at the door. With the increase in volume the conga line shouted louder.

DA-DA-DA DA-DA DA…DA!

In response to an aggressively shouted DA! From Heidi to his face the duty manager beat a hasty retreat.

Heidi's ever lengthening snake now took up two lengths of the dance floor. Every seven beats she shot out her left and then right foot after a further seven and was loosely followed by the shuffling, spinning and swaying line of feet behind her.

Sitting it out was becoming an impossibility as everyone made shapes and kicked or waved something in the air as they joined or were pulled onto the swaying, lengthening snake beat.

Kayla Taylor and her partner Sheila Winters, sitting with Jenny Hynes and her husband Paul, were cajoled by those passing to join on the back and they did so with Paul almost falling over a chair as he got up to join. Rocky Cook – who had been waiting patiently for her partner Linda to return from powdering her nose in the toilet – finally grabbed her on re-entry and they were joined on the back of the now three lengths of the room snake by Louise George, the Community Traveller's Liaison Officer responsible for getting Romany on the squad, and her quietly sitting Civil Service husband Dennis. There were very few left sitting and those were also being jollied out of their seats by Ginnie. She lifted Alfie Cushing to her feet and pushed her gently towards the snake end and then made a beeline towards Tink Cutler and Romany. Romany, receiving a waved invite from Heidi dashed to lead the entire snake at the front with guidance from her heroine behind her. Following his granddaughter Ginnie gave Tink a shove and managed to get the heavy traveller up on his feet for the first time and attached to the back of the line holding on to Alfie Cushing. As Heidi with Romany in front of her headed out the door and into the corridor that led to the reception area, Dexter leapt out of the snake line and nipped back inside the room where Ginnie was just getting on the end of the snake. With a blood curling whoop that would wake the dead he grabbed a hold of Jim Moody's wheelchair handles and gesturing to the D.J. to turn up the volume because the snake was heading out of the room, whipped the brake off the wheelchair, spun it around and shot down the corridor on the outside of the snake with Jim hanging on for all he was worth as they overtook a forest of waving feet and caught Heidi and Romany at the front as they began to make their swaying way across the reception area.

DA-DA-DA DA-DA DA...DA!

Led now by the madly waving and joyously drooling Jim Moody in his wheelchair enthusiastically pushed by Dexter, the snake reached the front door where an obliging returning guest held the door open.

As the back of the snake disappeared out the door a couple of guests were joined on the back by two members of staff. It wasn't raining and weaving in and out of the parked vehicles the snake made its way around the packed car park collecting a few miscellaneous taxi-drivers and home-goers on the way. By now they were shouting their own beat in time with Heidi because the music couldn't be heard out here.

DA-DA-DA DA-DA DA...DA!

Led now by Jim Moody with now a slack but loose gleam to his drooling lips as he was gleefully pushed along by Dexter, with Romany and then Heidi rocking along behind at the head of the near eighty-person snake, they headed back towards the front door. Madeleine Moody, having been surprised by seeing her infirm husband with a maniacal look of sheer joy on his face going the other way at the head of the column, broke off to skitter alongside him asking if he was alright and trying to wipe the drool away from his mouth with her hanky despite his waving arms to stop her.

'Madame' Dexter bellowed at the fussing wife, 'get back in line in the ranks otherwise you will be shot for insubordination...'

And with a look of utter surprise on her face she did.

'Which way, General?' Dexter shouted down at his charge.

'Aaagh' Jim Moody articulated again waving his floppy hands around like an airport guide parking a Jumbo Jet.

'Gotcha General, Westward it is,' Dexter bellowed down at his waving charge as he, Romany and Heidi picked up the rhythm and went in to the front door with their snake stretching out behind them as they again picked up the music from the DJ who had kept it going despite having no-one to play for.

DA-DA-DA DA-DA DA...DA!

'Onward my Congolese Army' shouted Dexter moving across the reception area, a cry taken up by Heidi and Romany and then echoing back down the streaming, swaying line....'

As the wheelchair-bound Jim Moody with a waving Dexter behind him followed by the now eighty-person snake approached the reception desk – a position tonight occupied by a very disapproving Maggie, the receptionist and colleague of Ellie who had told Ginnie during her squad interviews that she couldn't stand the game of rugby and preferred her pastimes simple and quiet like dog-walking and embroidery – she picked up the telephone to look busy. Like the Duty Manager, her boss for the night, she obviously didn't like the conga either and tried hard to ignore the many blandishments to join in as it wound its way passed her station.

Jim Moody waved his hands at the corridor and made a noise like a lovesick frog clearing its throat.

'Which way, General?' Dexter shouted down at his charge again.

'Aaagh' Jim Moody articulated again waving his floppy hands around like another but different airport guide parking a jet.

'Gotcha General,' Dexter bellowed down at his waving charge as he, Romany and Heidi picked up the rhythm and went forward with their snake stretching out through the outer door behind them.

'Onward Congolese' shouted Dexter, a cry taken up by Heidi and Romany and then echoing back down the streaming line....'

DA-DA-DA DA-DA DA...DA!

Finally, in four swaying and shouting lines and still holding the rhythm, the entire snake and another twenty miscellaneous folk it had gathered arrived back in the room where it had started with the DJ still, despite a severe warning from the night duty manager to turn it off, the valiant musical provider had kept going. The last through the door back into the event room where it had all started was Ginnie who had deferred to several guests and hotel staff including the night cleaning lady who had clung onto her as they approached the room breaking off to grab her bucket and mop before someone in authority – namely the irate duty manager, saw her and started shouting about her P45.

D.J. Jethro Allstyles gave one last loud blast of DA-DA-DA DA-DA DA...DA!

And then switched off the incessant beat and everyone erupted into a roar of joy and began to clap as the exhausted Heidi collapsed to the floor with Dexter alongside her.

Thanks to Heidi and Dexter it had been an exuberant and fitting finale. Jim Moody might be dying and not remember his conga journey for long but everyone else would and as his wife again began to dab at his drooling lip's he was one happy little wheelchair bound but terminal invalid.

*

After the wild trip around the hotel in the Conga and the many heartfelt hugs and kisses goodbye Ginnie and Claude finally settled in the back seat of their taxi and set off for the boathouse.

'Enjoy yourself?' the flushed Ginnie asked looking at him.

He kissed her tenderly before replying.

'I've had a wonderful time. It was the best party I have been to in living memory,' he replied with his lips against her cheek. 'And as for that conga at the end, I thought that went out with the arc.'

They were silent for a couple of miles before Ginnie spoke again.

'You know, the day I walked into your office and presented my ideas for a ladies rugby team sponsored by Wessex, someone, somewhere – a magician, mystic or sorcerer of some sort – waved a magic wand over my head…'

He hugged her. 'Ask your benevolent sorcerer what's going to happen next?'

'I have a pretty good idea what it will be.' She said squeezing his hand in hers.

'Oh...?

'Tomorrow you and I are going to an enchanted island for a magical week together.'

'And then...?'

'Then the Fannies will start training for next season and away we go again...'

'And then...?'

She turned to look at him as the headlights from a car coming the other way flashed light and then shadow across his face.

'Who can possibly say,' she whispered crossing her fingers tightly not wanting to tempt fate as the marital absolute again reared its head.

He places his lips close to her ear.

'I can my darling. For you I will buy an exquisite piece of this turning earth anywhere in the world and lay it at your dancing feet and live there with you for the rest of my life and watch you play your rugby. When you have the ball in your hands and running at the opposition, the rugby pitch becomes the cathedral of your soul and you are reborn...'

What a beautiful thing to say, she thought snuggling up under his protective arm.

The rugby pitch becomes the cathedral of my soul and I am reborn. It was the most beautiful expressions to and about her the like of which she had never heard in her life before, including those frantic words shouted into each other's open mouths at the height of passion. With this man and the team, I have everything I could ever want and I *am* reborn

The End

NOTE; *The Furious Fannies – Season One* – and book two in this series, has now been written and will be published third quarter of 2025, and the third book in the series *The Furious Fannies – Foreign Fields* will be ready mid 2026.

9 781836 153375